More demon fun from Kathy Love

Truth or Demon

What a Demon Wants

Demon Can't Help It

Devilishly Hot

Devilishly Sexy

Devilishly Wicked

Read more Angie Fox in

The Real Werewives of Vampire County

Don't miss Lexi George's Demon Hunting series

Demon Hunting in Dixie

Demon Hunting in the Deep South

Demon Hunting in a Dive Bar

Demon Hunting with a Dixie Deb

So I Married a Demon Slayer

Kathy Love
Angie Fox
Lexi George

ZEBRA BOOKS
KENSINGTON PUBLISHING CORP.
http://www.kensingtonbooks.com

ZEBRA BOOKS are published by

Kensington Publishing Corp.
119 West 40th Street
New York, NY 10018

All Kensington titles, imprints and distributed lines are available at special quantity discounts for bulk purchases for sales promotion, premiums, fund-raising, educational or institutional use.

Special book excerpts or customized printings can also be created to fit specific needs. For details, write or phone the office of the Kensington Sales Manager. Attn.: Sales Department. Kensington Publishing Corp., 119 West 40th Street, New York, NY 10018. Phone: 1-800-221-2647.

First Brava Books Trade Paperback Printing: September 2011
First Zebra Books Mass-Market Paperback Printing: September 2016
ISBN-13: 978-1-4201-2052-3
ISBN-10: 1-4201-2052-2

10 9 8 7 6 5 4 3 2 1

Printed in the United States of America

Contents

Hot!

**Kathy
Love**

Chapter One

"You *cannot* keep making your staff disappear."

Finola White smoothed back her stylish chignon, then looked away from the mirror toward her head editor.

Tristan's brows crowded together in a full grimace, his lips in a hard line—not a good look at all. The expression distracted from his polished grooming and designer suit.

One's looks should never be marred by unattractive emotions. Tristan needed to learn to school his features to show his feelings in a more appealing manner. Like she did.

His lack of control irritated her. Both with his features and with his words.

"You forget who you are," she said, her voice soft, melodious, but leaving no doubt what would happen if he didn't remember who was the boss. "You also forget this problem actually originated with you."

Tristan didn't speak. Wise boy.

She returned her attention to her own reflection. Yes, he should learn to be more like her. She was upset, but she didn't let that show on her face. She certainly wouldn't let some silly, *and nosy*, human employee, who worked in . . .

"Where did that wretched woman work again?"

Tristan released a slow breath before answering, "The mailroom."

Finola dropped her Guerlain KissKiss Gold and Diamond's lipstick onto her desk. She supposed at $62,000 a tube, she should be more careful with the cosmetic, but really? Tristan could be so wearing. He was actually upset about an employee from—*the mailroom*?

"You cannot be serious. You are getting worked up about this"—she shuddered—"human for what reason?"

She tilted her head, not bothering to hide her confusion. Although *she* could make confusion look quite endearing, so why would she hide it?

"This is the twelfth employee since February."

Finola couldn't manage to keep the frown from creasing her brow. Just briefly.

"Well, it's October now." Surely, that wasn't such a horrible track record.

"We're not in Hell, Finola," Tristan said, his voice beseeching. "Humans notice when other humans just disappear."

She considered that, then shrugged. "Fine."

She smoothed a smoky gray shadow over her lid. She didn't have time to argue with Tristan tonight. She had to get ready for her romantic dinner at Jean Georges with . . . now what was his name?

Oh well, that didn't matter. She knew he would be stunningly handsome and would photograph well beside her. Men were as important an accessory as jewelry and shoes.

And one must always consider what the paparazzi might catch.

A romantic dinner with *the* Finola White. That was a photo op no savvy member of the paparazzi would consider missing.

She couldn't let silly stress over an unimportant human taint her enjoyment of the evening—or affect her perfect smile.

She stood, smoothing down her formfitting Halston gown, in her signature color, white.

She reached for her white cashmere wrap and her Swarovski crystal-encrusted clutch. She paused in the doorway of her glass-walled office. "But you do understand why this one had to go?"

Tristan hesitated, then nodded.

She offered him a small, sympathetic smile that didn't quite reach her pale, pale gray eyes. She didn't feel sympathy, but she knew she wore it well. It gave her features an ethereal quality like some altruistic soul pleading for monies for starving children or something.

"This disappearance is your fault." No sympathy laced her voice.

"Yes." He nodded again, having the good sense to look contrite. After all, he was her right-hand man for a reason.

"Send a memo to the mailroom to hire a person to replace . . ." She fumbled to think of the human's name, then shrugged. She waved her clutch dismissively. "Have them hire someone new."

She started out the door, then paused again. "And tell them a male this time. An attractive one. My magazine is about beauty; I shouldn't have to look at ugly staff."

"Of course, Finola."

She strode through the maze of her inner offices toward the elevators, pleased her new Jimmy Choo sandals were exceedingly comfortable. Then she sighed about her head editor's concerns.

Tristan might be upset with her, but she was right. The human woman needed to go. The woman had not only seen that Tristan wasn't exactly human, but she'd had dreadful fashion sense too.

* * *

"He's the one?"

"Yes, I knew as soon as I saw him."

Charlie's gaze shifted back and forth between the two men, who peered at him like he was a creature from another universe. And even though Charlie wanted to shift—nervously, he wouldn't lie—in his chair, he resisted the urge. Instead he remained perfectly still, the metal of the folding chair cold against his rigid spine.

The chair was the only piece of furniture in the small room. A nondescript cube with gray-painted cinder block walls and a concrete floor. All that was missing was a bare lightbulb swinging overhead, and he'd believe he was in some interrogation chamber.

Okay, this was truly the weirdest job interview he'd ever experienced, and if he wasn't so desperate to work for *HOT!* magazine in any capacity, he'd walk out. But he couldn't. He'd tried every other way of breaking into the industry's most successful magazine. Now, he was willing to take this route. The mailroom. Far, far from where he wanted to work as a staff photographer for *HOT!*, but it was a foot in the door.

The man with the name Eugene emblazoned on his blue work smock moved away from the other one. Slowly he walked around Charlie, rubbing his chin and nodding. His blue eyes were intense as he studied Charlie.

Eerie eyes, Charlie realized. So blue, the color appeared almost fake. But he didn't seem like the type of guy to wear colored contacts. Maybe the lack of light from working in the basement made them all a little strange.

The guy disappeared behind him, and Charlie suppressed the cold shiver that snaked down his spine.

Yeah, this was weird. Very weird.

Finally the man reappeared and stopped in front of him. Then he nodded for the other man, the one innocuously named Dave, who'd been conducting the interview before it took this odd twist.

Both men stepped to the side, several feet away from Charlie. But not far enough that he couldn't make out a few of the things they were saying. Things like "Are you sure?" "Even if he is the one, would his looks pass?" and "What about the red hair?"

Would his looks pass? How good-looking did you need to be to work in a mailroom? Not that he considered himself ugly. He raised an eyebrow as he regarded the other two men. They were hardly hunks themselves. And his red hair . . . well, he'd heard about that his whole life, but it wasn't a valid reason not to hire him.

Charlie paused, frowning. What the hell was he doing? This was nuts. The one? Needing the right look? His red hair? Yeah, this wasn't a good idea.

He'd started to get up when the two men noticed and returned to stand in front of him.

Charlie told himself he wasn't feeling intimidated as he settled back down, waiting.

Eugene regarded him, narrowing his eyes as if he was trying to see something beyond Charlie's features, something deep inside.

Charlie shifted, deciding it was time to gracefully tell them maybe this job wasn't exactly what he'd anticipated.

Before Charlie could find the right words, Eugene's intense expression dissolved into a wide smile, revealing white teeth—almost perfect except for a slight gap between the front two. And just like that, the strange vibe in the room disappeared.

"Charlie Bowen, I think you could be perfect for the job. Just the guy we've been looking for." Eugene held out a hand to him.

Charlie blinked, a little dazed at how quickly the at-

mosphere had changed. But after a moment, he accepted
Eugene's handshake, noting that the man's grip was perfectly normal. No cold, clammy skin. No death grip. Just
a customary welcome.

"I will let Dave show you around," Eugene said, offering Charlie another warm smile. He nodded to Dave, his
blue eyes intense again, and for a moment, Charlie got
that feeling something was still not quite right here. As if
the two men were having some silent exchange. But then
Eugene was gone, opening the door to step out into the
bustling workroom beyond.

"Ready?" Dave asked.

Charlie wasn't sure, but he nodded. "Yes."

As soon as he stepped out into the busy mailroom, his
concerns faded. The room buzzed, people busily doing
their jobs like diligent bees in a hive. The most presti-
gious hive in all the New York fashion industry. Maybe
even the world.

This was a good thing. One step closer to his dream
job. Maybe he was going in through the back door, but he
wouldn't be the first to get creative to land the job of his
dreams.

Weird job interview or not, he was where he'd always
wanted to be—working for Finola White Enterprises, and
more specifically *HOT!* magazine. And soon, he would get
his portfolio in front of the queen bee herself. The powerful, notorious and insanely successful Finola White.

Once Ms. White saw Charlie's photographs, she would
realize she had her next star photographer right here under
her very nose.

Chapter Two

Charlie sighed as he bundled another group of mail, then dropped it onto the appropriate cart next to him. He repeated the process, then repeated it again.

The cart he was loading would go to the fifteenth floor. The main offices of *HOT!* magazine. A place that had become his version of the end of the rainbow. He could see the end, he knew the pot of gold was out there somewhere, but he couldn't seem to reach it.

The fact was he'd been working in the mailroom for a month now and all he saw was this workroom and this sorting station.

In his hand was a parcel labeled clearly with the great Finola White's name. He stared at that name in black, serif font, imagining what it would be like to work directly with her and her art department instead of here—he glanced around and couldn't contain the slight grimace that curled his lips—here, in strangeland.

He hadn't mistaken the oddness he'd felt when he'd been interviewed. Over the past few weeks, he'd realized the staff of the mailroom *was* strange. He couldn't place his finger on what was odd down here. It was just an intensity, a vibe in the air like the work went beyond mere mail delivery. Even though that was exactly what they did. Deliver mail.

He dropped another stack onto the cart. He knew that all too well.

And he didn't even get to deliver it. He just sorted the mail and processed the mail, and subsequently never left the mailroom. Not how he'd envisioned his plan.

When he'd come up with this scheme, he'd actually imagined that he'd at least be in the vicinity of Finola White—or members of her artistic and design staff. In the offices where he could slip his portfolio into the mail and thus in front of some important person who would be wowed by his work and hire him on the spot.

Genius in a blue mailroom smock.

But so far, he hadn't even seen any of those people. And he was losing hope. A month down here and he was starting to believe his brilliant plan was utterly stupid. He was closer to his dream job when he was doing wedding photography. And while brides, mothers of the brides and, well, anyone involved with weddings could be high-strung and demanding, they had nothing on this mailroom staff.

He looked around, watching his coworkers bustle around like they were doing some sort of clandestine service that was keeping the free world safe from imminent danger.

It's just mail, Charlie wanted to shout, but instead he took his frustration out on the rubber band he used to secure another bundle of missives.

He really shouldn't get mad at his fellow coworkers. It wasn't their fault that the closest he'd come to photographing high fashion was when he happened upon a *HOT!* photo shoot in Bryant Park, and stopped to snap a few pictures like some inquisitive tourist. Not quite what he'd imagined when he'd started here.

He looked up from his work to see two men watching him and whispering. Clearly about him. Another older woman at her computer watched him too.

Okay, even if he didn't have a plan and just wanted to work in a mailroom, this place would still strike him as strange. Everyone just exuded weirdness. Apparently it was a prerequisite for working here.

"And what does that say about me?" he muttered to himself.

Charlie sighed. He might as well be in the deepest, darkest circle of Hell rather than the lowest level of 66 West 46th Street in the heart of the garment district.

He looked around again. A woman who looked like a Russian fitness instructor circa 1960 was typing furiously on her computer as if she was inserting top secret data rather than logging in received packages. Another man, wearing a bow tie with his royal-blue work smock talked to Eugene, the mailroom manager, their heads tucked close together, again like they were sharing some cloak-and-dagger plot.

Let's face it, Charlie, old boy. Even if you did manage to get your portfolio in front of some bigwig, as soon as they discovered you worked in the mailroom, they'd probably cast your photos aside. No matter how good they were.

He should just quit.

"Charlie."

Charlie fought back a groan. Great, Innocuous Dave. Man, when he'd considered this guy average and dull, he'd been right on the mark, and that was what made him so awful. He was a boring, long-winded pain in the ass, following Charlie around like a shadow, watching Charlie's every move, repeating and repeating the importance of the mailroom and the way to perform even the simplest of tasks.

Pride in your work was one thing, but this went beyond that toward obsession. Creepy obsession.

"Charlie," Dave repeated, his voice clipped and emphatic. He stopped on the other side of Charlie's sorting area, his dark eyes serious, but also snapping with another emotion. Excitement? Anticipation? Worry? Charlie couldn't really tell.

Charlie waited, sure this was going to be another lengthy diatribe on the importance of mail sorting. He needed to quit. This place was sucking away his soul. And if he was wise, he'd do it before Dave started talking—otherwise he'd be stuck listening to something that made no sense and would likely go on for what felt like hours.

Charlie set down the envelopes on the metal sorting table and opened his mouth to do that very thing, but Dave spoke first.

"You are being promoted."

Charlie's mouth snapped closed; then he said, "Promoted?"

"Yes, you will now be delivering and collecting the mail for the fifteenth floor," David announced, leaning forward as he said the floor number, as if he was revealing a secret assignment.

His mission—should he choose to accept it.

Despite his thoughts just seconds earlier, Charlie found himself smiling. "Great."

Instead of looking pleased at Charlie's acceptance, David pursed his lips, regarding him critically. "You need to realize this is a significant advancement. A very important part of the mailroom's operation. You are expected to pay great attention while up there."

Charlie nodded, even though he found it hard to believe his new job was that significant. It was just pushing a cart around, handing out mail and picking up mail. But he *would* pay a lot of attention while up there. To who might really advance his career.

Charlie forced an earnest expression. "I will take it very seriously."

Dave still looked unimpressed. But he didn't say anything more, because Eugene had joined them.

Eugene was a bit less intense and strange than Dave, even with his eerie blue eyes and cryptic advice.

"I've been impressed with you, Charlie."

Charlie nodded, trying to look pleased by his boss's words.

"I've been watching you and I think Dave was right; you are going to be a great asset to our team. Just remember, you are our eyes and ears in this company. You have to be aware of what is happening around you and be ready to report back to us."

Charlie frowned. Okay, he *had* considered Eugene less odd—until now. What could they possibly expect him to report?

But he simply nodded. The sooner he got his portfolio out there, the better.

About half an hour later, Charlie had his cart loaded and he boarded the elevator. Elton, a small, elderly black man with a gravelly voice and gnarled hands, stood beside him.

"Now remember, your assignment will be to oversee the fifteenth floor," said Elton.

Assignment? Oversee? Why did Charlie get the feeling he was in some spy movie? A bad one at that.

He almost commented on that fact, but decided Elton wouldn't appreciate his sense of humor. Weirdness abounded in the mailroom. Senses of humor, not so much.

Instead he asked, "How long have you worked for Finola White Enterprises?"

Elton turned, regarding him with rheumy, but intelligent eyes. His voice was raspy and fervent, reminding Charlie of some zealous preacher. "We do not work for Finola White. We work for Eugene Edwards. Remember that."

Charlie couldn't quite suppress his amazed smile, but he wasn't going to argue with the elderly man and point out it was Finola White who signed their paychecks—not Eugene.

He shook his head slightly. Ah well, he should have known normal conversation with one of his coworkers was going to be a long shot anyway.

The elevator dinged, signaling they'd made it to the fifteenth floor. The stainless-steel door slid open, and Charlie wasn't pondering Elton's strange wording and odd loyalty any longer. Because he'd not only found the end of the rainbow, he'd made it over it. He truly understood how Dorothy had felt when she'd stepped out into Oz.

The *HOT!* lobby greeted him as though he had left a black-and-white world and stepped into Technicolor. Bright, beautiful colors and lines. A magical, exciting world even more incredible than he'd imagined.

The main greeting area was ultramodern and expensive. Glass and chrome and recessed lighting cast red light down the walls. Fiery, red velvet furniture with high backs and angular styling surrounded an asymmetrical, glass sofa table. Dramatic and fabulous cover shots from *HOT!* lined the walls. The place reflected the magazine's title. A sort of chic, trendy, sexy version of Dante's Inferno.

At the front desk, a stunningly gorgeous woman with a pageboy shag, in vogue because of Heidi Klum, talked on a sleek chrome-plated phone. Her voice was smooth and efficient. She only vaguely acknowledged Charlie and Elton as they stepped out of the elevator.

Charlie pushed the mail cart as Elton followed along, just a few steps behind. Charlie picked up the first bundle of letters, most of which he knew was junk mail, which was why it was being delegated to the receptionist. She could sort through the unimportant stuff.

Charlie placed the bundle on the edge of the large glass desk that reflected the red lighting so that it appeared to almost shimmer and move like a pool of molten lava.

Amazing.

The woman didn't register him right away, but finally she glanced at him and nodded. But Charlie found he couldn't move, or tear his gaze from her face. For just a moment, something about her features seemed to change like a disturbing, unattractive mask falling over—or away from—her beautiful features.

But then, as suddenly as he'd seen the strange transformation, it was gone. The woman was as lovely as he'd first thought.

Charlie quickly shoved the mail cart away from her desk.

"Everything all right?" Elton asked, regarding him closely with those hazy eyes of his.

Charlie nodded. "Yeah, fine."

It must have been the lighting playing tricks with his eyes. That was the only explanation.

They left the reception area, stepping through floor-to-ceiling, frosted glass double doors. The decor here was similar to the waiting area. More angles—both hard and soft. Red recessed lighting. Glass. Chrome. But unlike the quiet of the front office, this area was abuzz with people at work, creating the most popular fashion magazine in the industry. Artists, fashion consultants, designers, writers, editorial directors, assistants . . . and of course, photographers. They were all here.

Quickly, Charlie's weird vision was forgotten as he

became inspired by the creative vibe snapping in the air. Yes, this was exactly where he belonged. Working with these—

"Minions of Satan."

Charlie looked away from the bustling businesspeople to peer at the little man beside him.

"What?" Had Charlie heard the old man correctly?

Elton pursed his lips, disgust clear in his eyes, but then he tamped it down. "Nothing. Just don't like this place. Too . . . soulless."

Charlie regarded the old man for a moment, then couldn't resist smiling. "Well, it's not the mailroom, I grant you."

Yeah, there was a hotbed of warmth and emotion.

Elton's gaze held his, and for a moment Charlie had the strangest feeling of being pinned in place by that dark, hazy stare.

"You will find out your place, soon enough. Until then don't be charmed and seduced by what these people want you to see. In fact, you of all people should be able to see past that."

Charlie didn't have any idea what the old man was talking about. What did Elton know about what he could see and couldn't see? And what did he mean anyway?

He had no idea how to respond, so he refocused on the job at hand, deciding that was the best course of action. But again, he wondered if being crazy was a requirement for working in the mailroom, and if so, was he doomed to be nuts too?

Charlie pushed the cart along, delivering to one desk, one office, after another. And even with Elton following disdainfully behind, Charlie allowed himself to bask in the creativity around him.

Even though the atmosphere was so much more appealing than where he'd been working, he couldn't say that any of the *HOT!* employees were any warmer or kinder than the mailroom staff. In fact, Charlie could have been invisible. But the air of excitement and creativity made up for the cool atmosphere.

Finally Charlie came to the heart of *HOT!*—the inner sanctum. Finola White's offices. Charlie hated to reference *The Wizard of Oz* again, but he did feel like he was approaching the great and powerful Oz. He glanced at Elton, who lingered even farther behind him, his hazy gaze guarded, his stance rigid.

He was tempted to hum the tune of "If I Only Had a Brain," substituting the words, "If I only had a personality."

Then Charlie dismissed his coworker's behavior. Being on this floor was too incredible to focus on Elton.

Finola's wing—and that was really what it was—was huge. The walls were made of glass, giving this section of the offices a strange endless feeling, like a mind-boggling maze. A labyrinth, stylish and elaborate, that clearly separated the company's owner from the rest of her staff. He could see a large meeting room with a circular white table surrounded by high-back red velvet chairs that still managed to look minimalistic despite their oversized design and luxurious fabric.

Next to that was another office with more glass and shiny metal and beyond that, lost in a sea of glass walls and chrome, he caught flashes of what must be Ms. White's office. He could make out gleaming white—white furniture, wispy white drapes, white carpeting.

Finola was known for her affinity for white. It had become part of her image . . . to match her name and her fair, almost albino, coloring. All an image designed to make an impact.

But as he approached those glass rooms, it became clear he wasn't going to set foot in her private lair. Instead he was stopped by a woman seated behind a huge glass desk that matched the receptionist's desk back in the main lobby.

"You are not allowed back there. I'll take the mail," she said, standing as she spoke.

Charlie frowned, focusing on the woman, who was more than likely Ms. White's secretary or personal assistant. He blinked, his eyes not seeming to adjust—as if he'd been looking at the sun and now was trying to see details in the shadows.

She was not at all what Charlie would have imagined of Finola's personal assistant. Though dressed in clearly expensive clothes, she appeared mousy in her simple black turtleneck and pencil skirt. He blinked, realizing a strange, hazy halo of pale yellowish light seemed to outline her whole form. But when he focused on her again, it was gone.

Yeah, the lighting in here was really messing with his eyes.

But what dazed Charlie more than the optical illusions was the woman's warm tone as she spoke to Elton. "How are you today, Elton?"

"Not too bad, Annie. Not bad," he answered, his voice almost friendly.

"Your gout is better?"

"Oh, much better."

"That's good, Elton." Annie smiled, but then her expression grew serious. "Any word from Sheila?"

Elton shook his head, his near smile fading. "No. I'm afraid we're all thinking the worst."

Who was Sheila?

The woman, whose desk plaque read Annie Riddle, shook her head too, clearly distressed. "I just don't see how she could have disappeared without a trace."

Elton didn't respond, except to purse his lips, but Charlie got the impression he wanted to say more.

Who on earth were they talking about? Was it one of Elton's family members? It was clearly someone they both knew. Had this Sheila worked here?

But before Charlie could inquire, the glass double doors burst open, followed by two women, their voices raised in anger.

"I made you. And I can just as easily get rid . . . end your career."

"This isn't what I wanted! I never agreed to this!"

"Oh yes, you did. You wanted it more than your very soul."

Charlie gaped at the two women, first stunned by their sudden, raucous appearance, then stunned literally by who they were.

The woman telling the other that she could make and break her was Finola White. And he couldn't help but stare.

She was even more striking in real life than in the photos and television interviews he'd seen. Nearly six feet tall with long, blond hair that was so pale it was almost white. Her skin was so pale it looked almost translucent, as if made of perfectly constructed rice paper. No freckles or moles or even a hint of rosiness to her cheeks— nothing to mar the perfect alabaster. Her eyes were gray, the color of an overcast sky at midday. And her lips, the only vibrant color in her features, were ruby red, the exact color of the velvet of her furniture.

She looked almost . . . unreal . . . fantastical. Like a creature from a fairy tale.

"Do you hear me?" Her voice was unbelievably sexy and utterly cold at the same time.

Charlie's attention shifted from Finola to the person who was receiving her harsh diatribe.

Instantly he recognized that woman too. And while Finola amazed and wowed him, this woman made his whole body react, and hum to life.

Ava Wells, the most famous and sought-after model in the industry today. The absolute definition of super-model. Just as Finola was more striking in real life than in photos, Ava was also a surprise. She was as lovely as in her photographs, but much more accessible than he would have imagined.

As tall as Finola, Ava didn't have the icy beauty of her boss. Instead her skin shone like warm honey and her lush, dark hair glittered with hints of ginger and mahogany. Her lips were full and her eyes dark and soulful. She was hot, raw emotion, while Finola was cold, untouchable re-straint.

He had always considered Ava Wells stunning and amazingly photogenic, but he'd never considered her his type. Not until this moment. Very clearly his body thought otherwise. Every one of his nerve endings tingled with awareness of her.

The women glared at each other, but finally Ava broke their challenging stare, looking away.

"Yes, Finola," she said, all the anger fading from her voice as if Finola's ice had doused her fire.

"Good," Finola said, her lips twisting—smug and petulant at the same time. She then glanced at her assis-tant. "Do you plan to just stand there staring, or are you going to do some work?"

Annie scrambled to gather up a clipboard and pen. Then she hurried out from behind the desk. On her way past him, she snatched the stack of envelopes he still held, forgotten, in his hands. He noticed that she barely looked at him as she did so. Then she followed her clearly demanding boss back into the glass maze.

All three watched them leave as if too stunned by the events of the last few minutes to react.

After long seconds, Ava gathered herself and turned to leave. For the first time, she seemed to realize that Char-lie and Elton stood there.

Her dark eyes flicked over Elton first, then shifted to Charlie, and to his surprise, lingered.

Her cheeks grew rosy pink and her gaze dropped to the floor. She mumbled something that he could barely hear. An apology.

For what?

On long, shapely legs, she moved around them and disappeared back into the main offices of the fifteenth floor.

Charlie stood still, shocked by everything he'd seen in this little waiting area. But of all the things he'd seen and heard, it was the crushed look on Ava's face as she hurried away that stuck in his mind.

Of course, it had to be a little embarrassing to get a dressing down from *the* Ms. White in front of the lowly mailroom staff—but she *was* Ava Wells and they were—well, the lowly mailroom staff. Everyone knew Finola White's reputation of being very hard to please, so Ava hardly had reason to feel ashamed. Frustrated, irritated, riled maybe, but she'd clearly been humiliated. And Charlie had seen something else on her face . . . something deeper. A sort of hopelessness.

"Come on," Elton said from beside him. "I can't stomach all this depravity and ugliness."

As Charlie followed him back to the elevators, he considered Elton's word choices. He didn't understand what had been so depraved—he supposed the fashion industry itself could be seen that way. Especially by someone like Elton, who clearly did not appreciate this world.

But ugliness? He supposed he had seen some of that too. Finola had been very harsh with Ava, but that wasn't surprising, really. Everyone knew Finola had discovered Ava, at some restaurant the rumors said, and pulled her from obscurity to modeling stardom. Finola obviously thought Ava owed her.

As far as Charlie could see, that was the only ugliness

they'd witnessed on the fifteenth floor. This was a world based on beauty. Ugliness just didn't seem to fit.

But as they passed the front desk, he remembered how the receptionist's features had seemed to morph and distort.

It's just the lighting, he repeated to himself as he entered the elevator. This was a beautiful world and he wanted to be part of it.

Chapter Three

"Hey Charlie."

Charlie looked over his shoulder as he hung his work smock in his locker to see Innocuous Dave in the break room doorway.

"Eugene wants to see you before you go."

Charlie fought back an annoyed groan and nodded.

He grabbed his backpack and hoped this chat wouldn't be as long as one of Dave's. He was ready to head home and go through his portfolio to make sure, when the time was right, it was ready to be presented.

He walked to Eugene's office only to find that Elton was with him. Treading carefully, he moved closer to the door, interested in what Elton would say about Charlie's work today.

Charlie smiled to himself again as he remembered the older man's comments. He supposed the mailroom rivaled the *HOT!* staff for drama.

"He definitely saw things," Elton said. "A few times I was certain of it."

Charlie's smile faded to a frown. Were they talking about him?

"So he can do that job?"

"Yes, I think he can. I think he's more talented than Sheila was."

Eugene snorted. "That's a big statement."

"I know."

Charlie listened, still not sure they were talking about him. But who else? And they were mentioning this Sheila again.

"Charlie?" Eugene called, startling him. "Is that you?"

Charlie straightened, but stepped away from his spot just outside of Eugene's office door.

"Yeah." Charlie managed to keep his voice casual. "Dave said you wanted to talk to me."

"Yes, I need you to bring this up to the fifteenth floor before you leave for the day." Eugene held out a manila envelope.

Back to the fifteenth floor without Elton in tow—Charlie wasn't going to turn that down. His curiosity about what the two men were discussing, even working on his portfolio, could wait.

"Sure." Charlie accepted the missive without hesitation.

Oh yeah, he'd love to go back up to the fifteenth floor. Not to mention he might see Ava Wells again. A long shot, but it couldn't hurt to hope.

He hadn't been able to get her beautiful face out of his mind. Or the desperation in her eyes. She wouldn't still be around, he was sure. But going up and looking around couldn't hurt.

Once on the elevator, Charlie glanced at the envelope. It was handwritten with only the name of the recipient and the office number.

Carrie Hall, Room 1520.

Charlie knew exactly who Carrie Hall was. The head of *HOT!*'s art department and his second choice to sneak his portfolio to. After Finola, of course.

But then again, after meeting—okay, *seeing* the great Finola White today—maybe he should go with Ms. Hall. She hadn't been in her office earlier when he'd dropped off her mail, but there was no way she could be any more intimidating than Ms. White.

He looked down at the envelope again. He wondered who had sent it, and why via the mailroom. He didn't know for sure, but he imagined that all intercompany correspondence was handled by secretaries and assistants.

The elevator shuddered to a stop, and he stepped back into the amazing splendor of *HOT!* A different receptionist sat at the lobby desk. She was not as gorgeous as the first, more a pretty girl-next-door type, and unlike the daytime receptionist, she acknowledged him.

"Sorry, we are closed for the day."

Charlie glanced down at himself, realizing he no longer wore his awful, royal-blue, mailroom smock. Nor did he have his ID.

Crap.

So instead he held up the manila envelope. "I'm from the mailroom. I'm supposed to deliver this to Carrie Hall."

The receptionist frowned, and for a moment, she was clearly unsure what to do. Maybe she was new. He watched her as she debated, squinting slightly as the same kind of hazy, yellow aura appeared around her as he'd seen around Finola's assistant. He narrowed his eyes more; it *had* to be some strange effect of the lighting in the lobby areas. It was the only thing that made sense.

Then Elton's voice echoed in his head. *He definitely saw things.*

Had he been talking about this strange optical hallucination? But how would Elton even know what he'd seen? Charlie hadn't mentioned anything. He hadn't even commented on the lighting.

Just then, the phone rang, startling both him and the new receptionist.

After a few moments and several "yeses" and "of courses," she hung up the phone.

"That was Ms. Hall. She is expecting you. Please go on back." The receptionist tilted her head toward the door.

Charlie didn't hesitate, figuring he'd better take the entrance while it was offered. But as he stepped through the frosted glass double doors, he wondered how Ms. Hall had known he was there.

Then he chuckled to himself. She'd obviously known he was on his way up because either she'd requested the materials in the envelope or Eugene had contacted her to tell her Charlie was coming.

Yeah, time to cool it with the crazy suspicions. He was reading way too much into everything, making even the simplest happenings seem somehow a weird conspiracy. Too much time down in the underworld of the mailroom, obviously.

He made his way through the red hallways to Ms. Hall's office and knocked.

"Come in."

Charlie carefully turned the doorknob and poked his head inside the office. Ms. Hall leaned over a light table, peering through a magnifying loupe at several sheets of negatives spread out in front of her.

"Ms. Hall, I'm here with an envelope for you."

She stood immediately, the loupe forgotten in her hand. Instead of reaching for the envelope, or showing any interest in it whatsoever, she studied him from behind a pair of stylish dark-rimmed glasses.

In fact, she regarded him for such a long time, he actually shifted from one foot to the other, feeling like a misbehaving schoolboy called to the principal's office. Of course, how he'd misbehaved was a mystery to him. He was again reminded of the conversation he'd overheard between Eugene and Elton.

Finally, Carrie offered him a slight smile, as if somehow he'd passed the same criteria for approval that he had with Eugene.

"Thanks, Charlie," she said, accepting the eight-by-ten manila envelope. "It is Charlie, right?"

"Yes."

She nodded, her thick auburn curls bouncing around her pixyish face. Intelligence crackled in her eyes and Charlie got the feeling not much slipped past her. Which was why, of course, she was the art director. Attention to detail.

Charlie nodded his good-bye, then headed back through the desks and cubicles toward the main lobby. Many employees were still working even though it was well past the time he'd normally leave for the day. But of course the people up here worked to meet deadlines, not to punch a time clock. And the magazine had to be ready and perfect, no matter how long the hours.

An employee carrying several bolts of fabric samples staggered past him. Dark purplish circles stood out under the man's eyes, and his complexion was sallow, as if he hadn't seen the sun or felt fresh air in weeks. And again Charlie got the impression of a yellow halo around him, but he ignored it.

Maybe he should look into getting his eyes checked.

Just then a tall, lithe figure with a mane of rich mahogany hair appeared in his peripheral vision, as if to prove to him that his eyesight was just fine. The person turned a corner to disappear down an adjoining hallway.

Ava. There was no missing her lovely form and graceful walk.

Charlie didn't even consider whether he should follow

or not; he simply moved in that direction as if she was the moon, mysterious and beautiful, drawing him to her like an ocean tide.

As he turned the corner, he was surprised to find a set of utilitarian gray doors that looked almost startlingly stark and colorless when compared to the flash of the rest of the office.

Would she really go down here?

He placed a hand on one of the doors, trepidation giving him pause. Not because he didn't feel that he should be following Ava, which would be a sane reason, but because he felt almost as if when he went through those doors he would see something forbidden.

Shaking his head, he laughed slightly. When had he become so cloak-and-dagger himself? What could he possibly discover beyond these unmarked, gray doors? A stunningly gorgeous supermodel?

Save me now.

He pushed open one metal door and stepped into a hallway. He glanced behind him as the door clicked shut, the sound echoing down the glaringly white hallway with its harsh, fluorescent lighting.

This was the janitorial section of the office, he realized as he walked farther into the austere corridor. More gray doors dotted the walls, some with signs revealing a trash room or janitor's closet. Others were unmarked.

What on earth would Ava Wells be doing back here?

For a moment, Charlie even questioned whether she had really come down here. The hallway was empty. Silent. Where would she have gone?

He glanced over his shoulder, debating leaving. But instead he wandered farther down the hallway, realizing a freight elevator was at the very end. Maybe she'd taken the elevator for some reason. But whatever her reason, she was gone now.

He turned around, heading back to the offices, when he heard a noise. A noise somewhere between a moan and a whimper. He paused. The hallway had fallen silent again. So silent he wondered if he'd just imagined the odd noise. He waited a moment longer, then decided he must have.

Great, first his eyesight. Now his hearing.

He took one step, and heard the noise again. This time closer. He looked around, realizing whatever the strange noise was, it was emanating from the gray door marked with a sign, George Ramirez, head janitor.

Charlie moved over to the door, leaning forward to listen. Inside, he heard something that sounded almost like . . . crinkling plastic? Then that desperate whimpering moan.

Without further thought, he grabbed the knob and shoved the door open. He gaped as he discovered exactly where Ava Wells was.

She sat on the bare concrete floor, her already short skirt hiked even higher to reveal more of her beautiful, supple thighs. Scattered all around her was the evidence of her pleasure, and on her fingers were smears of something white and creamy.

Neither spoke; they just stared at each other.

Chapter Four

Ava stared at the man standing inside the doorway, his hand still on the knob, his hazel eyes wide with . . . well, it had to be disgust, right?

She looked down at her sprawled, unladylike pose, the sticky white cream on her fingers. What else could he think?

She straightened up, tugging at her tiny Marc Jacobs skirt with her clean hand, wishing the silk had more give. As she moved, wrappers fell to the floor around her, the clear cellophane splotched with more thick cream.

Oh God. Her cheeks burned with shame. What she'd been doing was revolting, mortifying, wicked in the most hedonistic way. This man had to be appalled.

She looked up from the evidence of vice, expecting him to make a face of utter aversion and leave her there, sitting amid her sticky mess and mortification.

But instead his eyes flicked from her flushed face to the hand coated in her guilty pleasure.

He surprised her further by stepping fully into the room, and releasing the knob. The door slammed closed behind him.

He regarded her a moment longer, then came over to crouch next to her. His gaze left her to focus on the box next to her left knee.

"May I?" he asked, his voice, rich and deep, not quite matching his boyish good looks.

She nodded, unable to speak. She still couldn't believe she'd been caught, caught right in the middle of the act. And instead of leaving in disgust, he was going to join her.

He reached into the box, pulling out one of her favorite indulgences. The plastic crackled under his touch as he opened the package.

She watched in dazed confusion as he remained sitting on his heels and took a bite.

"Devil Dogs are my favorite too," he said after swallowing the bite of snack cake. He smiled with obvious enjoyment, the curve of his mouth lopsided, appealing like an adorably naughty boy sneaking a forbidden treat.

Sneaking a forbidden treat. That was what she'd been doing, but she was pretty sure she didn't look adorable. She looked . . . well, pathetic.

She glanced down at the last bite of cake held forgotten in her hand. She stared at the chocolate and cream for a moment, trying to think of something to say. This wasn't how she wanted this cute guy, with the kind eyes to see her, hiding in a janitor's closet scarfing down snack cakes. The stereotype of a binge-eating supermodel.

Of course she wasn't really a supermodel. But she certainly couldn't tell him that.

"Pretty tough day, huh?"

Ava met his gaze, surprised at his comment. How did he know? She studied him for a moment, realizing she'd seen him before. He'd been outside Finola's office today. He'd seen the fight.

Her cheeks flushed hotter.

"Yes," she managed.

He nodded, his hazel eyes sympathetic. She stared at those eyes, light brown flecked with deep green. She was surprised as she felt tingles of awareness skip through her body.

"Can I help?" he asked. She really did like his voice; it was deep and rich and nice, like strong coffee sweetened with dark chocolate. Smooth, sweet.

Her gaze roamed his face, realizing he was more than cute, really quite handsome. Oh, how she wished he could help. But she simply shook her head.

He studied her for a moment, then to her surprise, reached forward and ran his thumb along her lower lip. She remained still under his brief touch, even though her body rioted with sensations she didn't understand.

"Cream-filling," he said, and she blinked, trying to understand what he was talking about. Then he held up his hand and she saw a smudge of frosting on his thumb. To her utter amazement, he lifted the pad of his thumb to his mouth and sucked the confection off.

Her belly—and lower—constricted at the sight and she found herself squeezing her thighs together to alleviate the sensation. It didn't work.

The man popped the remainder of his own Devil Dog into his mouth, then licked his fingers again when he was done, heightening the unfamiliar tightness in her belly and between her thighs.

"Well, you can't stay here," he said. "The floor is cold and hard. It's going to ruin your skirt."

Ava couldn't care less about her skirt, but he was right. She couldn't hide in the janitorial wing indefinitely. She couldn't hide at all.

She found she admired the length of his legs, and the hint of powerful muscles in his thighs as he rose. Then she realized he was holding out his hand, offering to help her up.

She hesitated, then slipped her hand into his, immediately aware of his strong, slightly work-roughened palm and long, tapered fingers curling around hers.

He pulled her up, then dropped his hold to bend over and clean up her mess. Seven empty wrappers. He had to be thinking something about that. But when he straightened, she couldn't distinguish any judgment on his attractive features.

He wadded up the mess and tossed it into a gray trash can in the corner of the office. He placed the almost-empty box of Devil Dogs on the janitor's metal desk.

"Thank you," she said, offering him a tentative, self-conscious smile.

He smiled back and again she was intrigued by how charming his lopsided grin was.

He opened the door for her, and waited as she peeked out, not seeming surprised by her surreptitious behavior. She supposed he knew binge-eating snack cakes wasn't an acceptable activity for a model. And she hoped he understood she couldn't be caught, especially by Finola White herself. She also hoped he wouldn't mention this to anyone else. She'd been in the gossip rags for much less. But overeating would particularly enrage Finola. That was *not* how her boss wanted her top model labeled.

Finola owned her, and there would be a huge price to pay for defying her. Far beyond just being replaced as the face of *HOT!* magazine. Beyond being fired outright. She would gladly accept either or both punishments. In fact, she would happily go back to the days when she'd been simple Addy Wellmeyer, but that wasn't going to happen. That girl was long gone—signed away, along with her immortal soul.

She stepped out into the hallway, which was blessedly empty, not that she expected anyone of importance to be in this area.

So who was this man? And why had he come down here? Maybe he was of importance. He had been waiting outside Finola's office today.

She peeked at him, taking in his clothing. A simple white button down and black pants. Basic black oxfords, scuffed, not very dressy. He looked like a waiter, but that didn't make any sense here.

She had a feeling he did work here though. In fact, she was sure of that, but where?

She studied his handsome face, a friendly face, a sincere face. From her experience, that wasn't the norm in this environment.

For a moment, her chest tightened with apprehension. It was impossible to know whom to trust here. What if he was one of *them*? What if he was in the hallway spying for Finola? One of her lackeys.

"Why don't we take the freight elevator?" he said, startling her when she realized he'd caught her looking at him.

He gestured to the metal elevator doors at the end of the hallway.

She considered him for a second, then nodded. She had no idea why, but she trusted this man. Maybe it was the kindness in his hazel eyes. Maybe that kindness was a ruse, but right now, she needed to believe there was still someone in the world, at least in her world, who was exactly what he seemed.

She followed him, trying not to look at him again. The door finally dinged and slid open. Again like a total gentleman, he waited for her to enter.

Neither spoke as he hit one of the buttons, and the elevator started downward. For a brief moment, Ava realized she had no idea where this elevator went or where she was going. But before she could be too concerned, the door opened into another back hallway.

"Uh, I wonder where we are."

Ava looked at him, then around. "I—I don't know."

"Well, I guess we'll find out." He pointed to an unmarked door on their left. He strode over and pushed it open, just a bit, looking out. Then he glanced back at her, a smile making his face go from handsome to beautiful.

"We can go out this way."

She nodded, again finding it strange how readily she just accepted whatever he said. He pushed open the door, and Ava stepped into a large workroom with different stations set up here and there.

"Welcome to my glamorous world."

This time as she looked at him, recognition hit. She remembered now. He had been standing with a mail cart. He'd been delivering mail when Finola had been yelling at her.

She glanced around, curious. The place was relatively quiet now, only a few mailroom employees milling around, none of whom hid their surprise as she followed—she supposed she should have asked her conspirator's name—through the large work area.

"I just have to get some things from my locker. Then I will walk you out."

She nodded, leaning against the wall outside the little employees' break room. As she waited, a few more people watched her, some trying to be subtle with their curiosity, others a little more blatant. Ava shifted, feeling awkward.

"Okay, all set."

Ava knew her relief was clear on her face as she turned to her "new friend." He smiled, something almost sympathetic in his eyes as if he saw and understood her discomfort.

He gestured for her to head down another hallway. He fell into step beside her. She noticed, from the corner of her eye, that he'd donned a lightweight jacket and had a backpack slung over his shoulder. He looked like an average guy leaving work. A normal guy. Her heart pounded painfully in her chest and an almost crippling longing made it hard for her to breathe.

"Here we are," he said, the heavy metal door scraping loudly as he shoved it open. Cool evening air greeted her, and she pulled in a deep breath, trying to push away these strange feelings pulling at her.

She knew it was false freedom, but she loved the moments when she stepped out of the *HOT!* building. She could pretend she was just normal. Well, sometimes.

Normal like him.

"Do you need me to hail you a cab or anything?"

She shook her head.

He waited for a moment, as if he expected her to say something, then he nodded. "Okay. Well, be careful."

Just another moment's hesitation, then he turned to head down the sidewalk. A sudden, almost panicked feeling tightened her chest, making her breathing shallow.

She couldn't just let this man walk away. Something intense and deep told her she had to hang on to him, even for just a moment.

"Wait!"

He spun back to face her, his eyebrows cocked in surprise and question.

"Would you like to go get a drink with me?"

Chapter Five

Charlie blinked. Had Ava Wells just asked him to go get a drink? He had to have heard wrong, but he was damned if he was going to ruin his fantasy and ask her to repeat herself.

"I— Yes, sure I would love to get a drink with you."

She smiled, confirming he must have heard her correctly. Her expression was lovely, although he noticed a strain around her mouth. A tightness that made the curve of her lips appear almost brittle.

She joined him, starting down the sidewalk. He fell into step beside her.

After a moment, Ava glanced at him. "Do you know a bar we can go to?"

Charlie couldn't stop the smile that curled his lips. She'd asked him out, but didn't have a bar in mind. She shot him a sidelong glance when he didn't answer, and he realized her eyes looked different in person than they did in photos. They were wider now, rather than almond-shaped and sultry. And at this moment, she looked almost innocent, like a wide-eyed babe rather than an exotic, sexy supermodel. Not that she wasn't still stunningly beautiful. More so, if you asked him.

"I know a place on 8th Street, but I'm sure it's not your usual type of hangout. It's just kind of a local dive bar."

Her chin bobbed up and down even before he finished. "That sounds perfect."

She can't possibly think this is perfect, he thought as they stepped into the narrow, dim bar. The old, uneven wood floor shifted slightly under their feet, and they could probably hear it creaking if Patsy Cline wasn't crooning from an ancient jukebox in the corner.

Charlie came to Dino's maybe once a week—more lately—since the bar was just a block from his apartment. Joey, Dino's son and the bar's nighttime bartender, nodded to him as Charlie ushered Ava toward the back where there were more private booths. He suspected Ava wouldn't want to be recognized here. And while Charlie wasn't sure whether Joey knew he had a celebrity in his bar, the appreciation in his dark eyes definitely said he noticed her all right.

As they sat down, Ava confirmed his decision about going with privacy. She pulled a hair band out of her small shoulder bag and caught up her thick mahogany hair, tugging it back into a ponytail. Hardly a whopping disguise, but the casual hairstyle did enhance the softer, younger quality he'd noticed as they were walking.

He frowned, again struck that her face seemed altogether different than in her photos. Her cheeks seemed fuller, not as if she'd gained weight, but as if she had a healthy, feminine softness that wasn't normally caught in her photos. Her shots always flaunted angular cheekbones and a cut jawline. Both of which were her signature style.

Of course, he certainly knew better than anyone the tricks of the photography world. Makeup, lighting, lense effects, airbrushing.

But sitting across the table, Ava looked almost like a totally different person from the famed supermodel. Not that Charlie found that a bad thing. The Ava sitting across the crummy table from him was real. Not some image on a magazine page. He found her gorgeous.

Joey joined them, tearing Charlie away from his speculations. The bartender placed two laminated, single-page menus in front of them.

"The usual?" he asked Charlie. Charlie nodded and thanked him. "And for you, lovely lady?"

Ava didn't react to Joey's easy compliment—no smile, no batting her eyes. Instead she looked at Charlie as if that was easier somehow.

"A double shot of whiskey. Straight up."

Charlie supposed he shouldn't be shocked by her drink request, since he didn't know her, but he was. Even more surprised than by the binge-eating episode.

Joey gave a low whistle. "I like a woman who doesn't mess around."

Again Ava didn't acknowledge the bartender. She continued to stare at Charlie. After Joey walked away, she dropped her gaze, picking up one of the worn, smudged menus.

What was going on here? Charlie had figured the binge-eating thing was just a reaction to her fight with Finola. He still did. But there was something more happening— he could sense it. He'd sensed it back at Finola's office when he'd seen the sadness in her eyes.

"Would you like to talk about it?" he finally asked, deciding maybe that was his best bet. Sitting here speculating about what was wrong was pointless.

Ava's head shot up, staring at him with those wide, far too innocent eyes. Something flashed through them, hesitation, mistrust, maybe fear. He wasn't sure.

Joey returned, placing her whiskey in front of her and a lager in front of him.

As soon as the bartender left, Ava picked up her glass and took a deep swig; then her lovely face crumpled as she smothered a gag with the back of her hand. She shuddered, setting the glass down a little too hard. Tears glittered in her eyes.

Charlie smiled sympathetically. Well, he'd been right. "Not your usual drink, huh?"

She shook her head. "No." She shuddered again, but to his surprise lifted the liquor back to her full, rosy lips. This time she took a smaller sip and managed to keep most of the disgust off her face.

He sipped his own beer, fascinated by watching her, wondering how he'd got here. What was going on with this woman? And why was she hanging out with him?

Once her glass was empty, he tried again. "Is the whiskey helping?"

She considered the question for a moment, her nose wrinkled like a small child debating a difficult problem, then shook her head. "Not really."

He couldn't contain his smile. Ava Wells was much more guileless than he would have ever imagined. Her image was exotic, worldly, sexy—never the beautiful ingénue. He wondered why—he would absolutely love to photograph her this way.

"Well, if the whiskey isn't working, maybe talking will. Are you upset because of your fight with Finola?"

She stared at him, and he couldn't quite decide if she

was surprised by his directness or not. Her dark brown eyes roamed his face.

Finally she tilted her head and asked, "Where are you from?"

Charlie frowned. Well, that wasn't what he'd expected her to say, but he supposed it was good that she was talking at all.

"I'm from a small town in Ohio."

Her eyes lit up. "I'm from Kansas."

She said that as if they were from the same state, the same town even. But maybe just both being from the Midwest was enough. Was she homesick? Was that it? Maybe she wanted a break from modeling, and she wanted to go home. That might explain Finola's irritation with her. Maybe.

She picked up her glass, seeming to forget she'd already drained it, then she set it back down.

"But Toto, I don't think we're in Kansas anymore," she muttered under her breath at the empty highball glass.

Charlie raised an eyebrow at her words, surprised at the echo of his own recent references to *The Wizard of Oz*. But she wasn't excited about the world of Oz like he was. She was clearly tired. Maybe even a little jaded, making it interesting that he couldn't see anything but youthful innocence on her features.

Charlie sighed, feeling a little helpless. Maybe she'd just had a rough day and needed an escape from her exciting supermodel life.

He looked around the run-down bar; he could certainly offer her that.

He picked up his own menu, his fingers sticking to a smear of half-dried ketchup along the edge. At least he hoped that's what it was.

"Why don't we order something?" he suggested, waving his menu slightly, offering her a smile.

She shook her head, then nodded. "Actually that sounds good."

They stared at their menus, both silent.

"See anything you want?" Charlie asked, finding their silence heavy, uncomfortable.

Ava didn't look up, but instead answered his question with one of her own. "Is your family still in Ohio?"

She was good at that, he realized. Answering his questions with an unrelated question of her own.

"Yes."

"Do you have siblings?"

"Yes, two older sisters."

She smiled then, a wistful little curl of her full lips. "The baby *and* only boy? I bet you got bossed around."

He grinned back, liking that smile. "Just a little."

Her smile deepened as she looked back at her menu. "I think I will get the meat loaf. Have you had it? Is it any good?"

Charlie had eaten here more times than he was willing to admit. But the prices were decent and he didn't have to eat alone—well, not exactly alone.

"Nice choice. It's pretty good. Homemade."

She glanced up at him, her smile stunning. A strange skittering sensation danced through his chest.

He looked back to his menu, surprised by the odd feeling.

"Is your family still in Kansas?" he asked.

He glanced up when after a moment, she hadn't answered.

She continued to look down at her own menu. Charlie couldn't see her eyes, but her lovely smile was gone.

Finally she nodded, just a tiny bob of her head. "My mother is there—she's the only family I have."

Charlie wanted to ask more, but he could tell by her

closed expression she didn't want to expound on the topic. Like she didn't want to talk about Finola White. Tonight, she wanted to forget for a while. He could try to help her with that.

"My middle sister used to make me dress up as a girl," he said suddenly, not even aware he was going to share that embarrassing little tidbit until it was already out of his mouth.

Ava's brows drew together, then to his pleasure, she laughed.

"A girl? But she already had an older sister."

"Well, she wanted all sisters. So I attended many a tea party in her old dresses."

A sweet, infectious giggle escaped Ava's full, ruby lips. "Do you still don a dress now and then?"

Charlie widened his eyes, feigning a look of offense. Then he managed an equally believable sheepish smile. "Okay, only when I'm going to a very special tea party."

Ava laughed again. The sound thrilled him as much as if he'd made the winning catch at a big game. Or flown to the moon. Or made a sad supermodel forget her problems just for a few moments.

Joey returned to take their orders. Charlie ordered the same meal as Ava, and Charlie was glad to see that she asked for a soft drink rather than another stiff one. Maybe she didn't feel quite so much like she needed to drown her sorrows now.

Ava took the last bite of her meat loaf, allowing herself to enjoy the home-cooked meal, even though it definitely wasn't on her model's diet.

She also watched the man across from her, just letting herself enjoy him too. He was funny and sweet and handsome, but not in the fake, perfected way of most of the men who filled her world. Men with features and physiques she'd found so attractive when she'd been a young girl flipping through fashion magazines and celebrity rags in her tiny bedroom in Kansas. Oh, how she'd coveted that world, those perfect people. What a silly, stupid girl she'd been.

Because right now, she couldn't imagine finding anything more appealing than slightly shaggy auburn hair, a lean build and a goofy—and wonderfully adorable—grin.

He reached for his beer, and Ava noticed how long and strong his fingers looked against the glass. How nicely muscled his forearms were with his plain white shirtsleeves rolled back. How perfectly shaped his lips were, not too full, not too thin. Kissable lips.

She blinked at that thought, then decided that she could hardly be shocked her thoughts had gone in that direction. She'd been aware of him all night. Aroused by him, if she was being honest.

He was really quite gorgeous in a way she wished she'd appreciated before she found herself in the terrible world she now inhabited. A world of faked perfection. Where no one was real, or genuine, or kind.

But would he be sitting across from her now if she was still average, old Addy Wellmeyer? She shoved that thought aside. She was Ava Wells now—and for once she was going to enjoy the benefits of giving up everything to become this person. The world believed a woman like Ava Wells got everything she wanted. Oh, if they knew the truth.

But tonight . . . tonight, she was going to get what she wanted.

He was just taking a sip of his beer as she asked, "So you said you live near here, huh? Can we go back to your place?"

His eyes widened mid-swallow as if he was going to choke on the golden liquid. But he managed to lower his glass and school his features into a semblance of calm. The only other sign of his surprise was the slightly too loud clatter of his mug hitting the table.

"Umm, yeah. Sure. Of course we can."

Chapter Six

"Well, this is it."

Charlie watched as Ava wandered around his small living room. A tiny room that was practically eaten up by a worn sofa and an even shabbier recliner. He winced as her fingers traced a crack in the ancient vinyl along the arm of it.

"My father had a chair just like this." Her voice sounded wistful, distant. "He loved that chair."

Charlie felt slightly better that she wasn't disgusted by his motley assortment of furnishings.

The vinyl creaked under her weight as she sat down on the recliner. She had that distant look he'd seen at the bar. She was sad again, struggling with something, and Charlie didn't know how to chase her sorrow away. Not for good anyway.

All he could do was be a good host and listen if she decided to talk.

"Can I get you a drink?"

She looked up, her dark eyes refocusing on him.

"Um, sure." Her voice sounded a little sheepish, not

the same as the confident woman in the bar who had asked to come over here.

"I think I have some beer, a bottle of wine, although I don't know how good it is. Soda and milk."

"A little wine would be good."

He nodded and rushed away to his tiny galley-style kitchen. He hated to admit it, but he was rattled. Ava Wells in his apartment. Yeah, he needed a drink too.

He rummaged around in one of the drawers until he found the corkscrew. Reaching for the wine, he made a face. It was white and should have been served cold. Oh well. It was probably going to taste so awful she wouldn't even notice it was room temperature.

He pulled down two wineglasses, plastic ones he'd nicked from a New Year's Eve party last year. Pulling another face, he filled one glass and downed it.

Yep, terrible.

He refilled the glass as well as the second one.

Glasses in hand, he headed the few feet back into the living room. When he entered the room, Ava was no longer in the recliner. Instead she stood in front of one of his photos that he had framed on his wall. A moody black-and-white of a bride in her gown, no veil, lost in her thoughts. Thoughts that were clear on her face—hesitation, doubt, fear. Second thoughts.

Needless to say, that shot didn't make it into the wedding portfolio.

"This picture is amazing."

Charlie opened his mouth to tell her he'd taken it, but something stopped him. Maybe a concern that if he told her he was a photographer, she would think he wanted to use her. He wasn't quite sure what stopped him, but he simply held out the wine.

"Here you go."

Ava glanced away from the photo and took the glass.

She sipped the golden liquid, not seeming to notice the unpleasant taste. Her attention returned to the picture.

"She looks so uncertain, yet I bet she went through with the wedding anyway. Because she thought it was what she should want."

Charlie took a swallow of his wine rather than tell her that the bride had, in fact, gone through with it. He was far more interested in why Ava Wells seemed to understand all too well that sort of resignation to fate.

She took another long sip of her drink, then turned back to Charlie.

"Are you going to show me the rest of your place?"

His eyes widened as he realized exactly what she meant, then nodded. "Sure."

Man, she sure had a way of shocking the hell out of him.

He turned, glancing back to see if she was following.

"This is the bathroom," he said, flipping on the light to show her the tiny room that managed to hold a pedestal sink, a toilet and a stall shower—just barely.

"Very cute."

Charlie smiled at her, appreciating her generous way of saying "too small."

"And . . ." He snapped on the light, which illuminated his bedroom, another crowded space that contained his dresser and queen-sized bed. He was pleased to see he'd actually made his bed this morning. Sheer luck, that.

Ava slipped past him, reaching out to test the firmness of his mattress. "This is nice."

Charlie laughed.

"Hardly, but it's affordable and clean," he said, choosing to misunderstand her meaning and act as if she was referring to the apartment rather than the bed. "And I don't plan to stay here forever."

"Planning for bigger and better?"

He smiled. "Of course."

She nodded. "Sometimes we should just enjoy what we have. Bigger and better isn't always best."

Again Charlie wondered what had her so unhappy, so dissatisfied, but he remained quiet.

She wandered farther into the room, setting her plastic glass on the nightstand, a nicked, dark wood affair that he'd picked up at Goodwill.

Then she turned and walked back to him. Just inches away, she stopped.

"What's your name?"

Charlie froze, his eyes wide. Had he really not told her his name? Since he knew hers he supposed he'd just felt she must know his. Silly of him.

"It's Charlie. Charlie Bowen."

She smiled. "Charlie. I like that." She reached out and touched his jawline. Then she leaned forward and pressed her lips to his.

Ava hadn't dated as much as most people would think a supermodel had. But she wasn't exactly an innocent either, and still she wasn't prepared for how her body reacted to Charlie's kiss.

She realized she'd managed to startle him again when she first touched her lips to his. He froze against her gentle touch, but only for a fraction of a second, then his hands came up to either side of her head, those long fingers of his tangling in her long, wavy hair. After that, control was all his as his lips moved over hers with strong sureness.

He angled his head, and hers, and the kiss deepened. His tongue brushed against the seam of her lips, silently, teasingly asking her to open for him.

She did, without hesitation. She wanted to taste him, to feel him. And it was better, more powerful than she could have imagined: hot little flicks of his tongue like small licks of fire sizzling throughout her body; a low burn that was quickly escalating to an inferno.

She whimpered, surprised and excited by her instant, violent need for him. But Charlie seemed to mistake the sound for distress, because he immediately pulled back, stepping away until he backed into the dresser. His gaze roamed her face, concern clear in his golden-green eyes.

"Ava—" He ran a hand through his hair, making the dark auburn locks more adorably disheveled. He shook his head as if to clear his thoughts.

He laughed, but this time the rich timbre fell flat. "I can't believe I'm saying this, but I don't think we should do this. You are clearly upset about something tonight. And I don't want you regretting anything."

She stared at him, feeling a slight sting of rejection, but also realizing that real concern clouded his hazel eyes.

"Ava, I really don't mean to—"

She raised her hand to stop him. "I appreciate your kindness. I guess—I guess I have had a rough day, and that is affecting my thinking."

Charlie made a pained face, and she wanted to tell him that his kiss was affecting her thinking too, but decided she might seem desperate. And Ava Wells wasn't desperate.

Addy Wellmeyer was desperate though. And Addy did not want to be alone. Addy wanted this man.

She wandered over to the nightstand to finish off her glass of vinegary wine. Not that she really noticed the flavor. Or cared. She just wanted the mellow feeling the alcohol would eventually give her.

"Could I have some more?"

"Of course." Charlie appeared almost relieved by her request. He came forward and took her plastic glass. Their fingers touched briefly and her body was right back to burning intensely for him. It was amazing, and a little disturbing.

"I'll—um—get that for you," he said, and it was heartening to see that the mere touch had affected him too.

He took the few steps to leave the room, then paused in the doorway, glancing at her over his shoulder as if he wanted to say something more. But instead he just nodded and disappeared out of the room.

Once he was gone, Ava collapsed onto the edge of the bed. What was she doing? How was this going to help her situation in the least? Well, it wasn't; that was the answer. But she really didn't care. She liked being around this man. Charlie—she even liked his name—made her feel like the person she'd once been. She didn't want that feeling to stop. But of course, it would have to eventually.

Finola White would never agree to her star supermodel dating a lowly mailroom clerk. If he even wanted to date her. Finola owned her, lock, stock and barrel. And Finola chose who she dated. Finola chose everything.

She considered getting up from the bed, but instead found herself sliding back against Charlie's soft pillows. She curled onto her side and allowed herself for a moment to imagine what it would be like to date a man like Charlie. To share this comfy bed in this cozy little room.

Now she wondered why she'd had such big dreams, and had done the unthinkable to attain them. Now she just wanted to go back to simple dreams, a home, a family, a person who loved her for herself, and happiness.

Too bad those dreams were now as unobtainable as she'd once believed the jet-set lifestyle, wealth and fame of being a professional model was.

But just for a moment, she was going to close her eyes and pretend she had the simple dream. Simple happiness with a good man at her side.

Charlie finished pouring a glass of wine for Ava, then braced his hands on the counter and closed his eyes. What was going on here? Ava Wells was in his apartment . . . in his bedroom, apparently willing to have sex with him and he'd turned her down. What the hell was wrong with him?

But he knew the answer. He'd been honest when he'd called a halt to their kiss—and what might have followed. He didn't want her regretting anything she did tonight.

He groaned, wishing just for a moment, he could be a selfish jerk.

But he couldn't. He was doing the right thing, and he could certainly control his libido—as uncomfortable as it might be.

He pulled in a deep breath, then opened his eyes. This was a woman who had something very real bothering her, and she needed a sympathetic friend more than a one-night stand.

Which really sucked, but he was a gentleman—unfortunately.

He braced himself, because his body wasn't feeling nearly as gentlemanly as his mind. He forced a calm expression and headed back into his tiny living room, sure that Ava would be out of there by now. But she wasn't.

He frowned, then turned toward the bathroom. The door was open and the light out. That meant she still remained in the bedroom.

He wanted to groan again. He had to be honest—he didn't know how much temptation he could take.

He moved slowly, reluctant to be back in his closet-sized bedroom with a woman he was more attracted to than any woman he could recall. Ever. He took one more deep breath, then entered the room.

Ava lay on her side, cuddled down among his pillows like some rich golden jewel against his plain gray bedding. Her dark hair was spread around her peaceful face. Her long legs curled up into an almost fetal position, her hands pressed palms together by her cheek like the perfect image of a small, sleeping child.

Again he was struck by how breathtakingly lovely she was, but not in that glamorous, couture way that most of the world saw her. She looked angelic and sweet. He wanted to kiss her, but he maintained control.

"Ava," he said softly.

He was greeted by a small sigh, then a long even breath. She was out cold.

He considered waking her and seeing her home, but she looked too serene, more serene than he'd seen her since meeting her outside of Finola White's office. And he got the feeling she needed her rest.

Quietly, he left the room to put the wine in the kitchen, then returned to stand in his bedroom doorway, watching her for a moment.

Ava Wells in his bed.

He smiled, shaking his head. He could never have predicted how this day would play out when he'd forced himself out of bed at the grating beeping of his alarm clock this morning.

Without much contemplation, he walked over to the desk wedged in beside his sofa and grabbed his Canon EOS, the black digital camera's weight nice and natural in his hand. He hadn't taken many pictures since starting his mailroom odyssey, and he missed the feeling of his camera.

He then went back to his bedroom and inched toward

the bed. Cringing slightly at the sound of the shutter, he took a picture of Ava. She didn't rouse, so he took another and another.

Maybe he was driven to photograph her among his pillows as proof that Ava Wells had been in his place, in his bed. But once he started shooting, he was overcome by the need to capture the way she looked right this minute, the need to capture her easy, natural beauty.

She was stunning.

He snapped at least twenty or thirty photos of her.

Finally he set the camera aside. Studying her from every angle as she slept made him long for similar peace. She looked so wonderfully tranquil and calm.

He contemplated the lumpy Goodwill couch that sagged horribly in the middle, then glanced back to his bed. Ava hadn't moved from her curled position and she certainly didn't take up much room on the mattress.

He could grab extra blankets, one for her and one for himself and they could both share the bed without even coming in contact with each other. And he would, of course, sleep in his clothes, he justified to himself.

He fished two blankets from his closet and carefully tucked one around her sleeping form. He switched off the light, but left the living room lamp on, in case Ava woke up and was disoriented.

Then with slow, even movements so as not to bump the bed any more than necessary, he slid around the side against the wall—not an easy feat given the lack of space in the small room. The mattress dipped as he finally eased down onto it, but Ava didn't stir. He stretched out beside her, heedful not to touch her, both for her sake and his own.

As he lay stiffly beside her in the shadowy light, he realized he'd been very right not to allow their embrace to continue and escalate. After all, if she could fall asleep so quickly, she surely was not feeling the kind of arousal he'd been experiencing—and still was.

Sighing, he turned on his side too, following the line of her body with his own, but not touching. Parallel spooning, if there was such a thing.

He lay that way for a long time, his mind whirling with the events of the day, and eventually, though he would have thought it impossible, he fell asleep.

Chapter Seven

Ava woke slowly, blinking her eyes, trying to gain focus in the dim light. She stretched, wondering what time she'd gone to bed. There was a faint light illuminating her bedroom, but she didn't think it was sunlight.

She rolled onto her back and stretched, feeling lazy and ready to doze off again. And she would if time allowed. She turned toward her nightstand to check her alarm clock, but instead of being greeted by the red glow of digital numbers, her gaze fell onto a shadowy shape close beside her.

She rose up, her heart pounding almost sickeningly in her chest. Who was that?

She looked around her room, realizing right away this wasn't her expensive Upper East Side loft. Where the hell was she?

She started to fling her legs over the side of the bed, wanting to get out of this strange place, when her memory returned. She glanced back to the form sleeping beside her.

Charlie. An odd sense of relief weakened her tightened muscles. Odd because she didn't really know this man, yet she was more than relieved to see him; she was happy. She remained still, allowing her eyes to adjust to the light until she could make out each feature of his handsome face.

Without thinking about why, she found herself settling down beside him again, facing him, studying those lovely features.

When awake, he was very good-looking, but asleep, his features were impossibly perfect. Like a sculptor's rendering of a young and beautiful poet or artist. A sensitive face. His dark lashes fanned out against his cheeks, almost delicate. His lips, parted slightly, were a study in masculine beauty. His jawline was cut and strong. She could make out the shadow of beard appearing on his chin and cheeks.

She'd seen more beautiful men than she could possibly count. Models with perfect bodies and flawless faces, but not one of them had appealed to her as this man did.

Her fingers, which had been curled tightly into the pillow as if to stop her from touching him, flexed and before she thought better of it, she gently caressed his jawline, the bristle of facial hair tickling her fingertips. Her body reacted instantly. She wondered how that coarse hair would feel against her lips, brushing over her soft skin.

She shifted a little closer, his scent enveloping her. A faint mixture of soap and maybe laundry detergent and something warm and musky. Her skin tingled and her nipples tightened and puckered against her lace bra.

What was it about this man? She should just sneak out now while he slept and pretend this night had never happened. But she couldn't seem to get her wayward body to obey her mind.

Instead she continued to lie beside him, her fingers lightly exploring his features. God, she wanted him so badly. So very, very badly.

Her fingers moved from his jaw to trace his lips, fasci-

nated by them. The fullness of the bottom lip. The slight
bow of the top one. And the amazing memory of how his
mouth had felt moving against hers. Soft yet strong.
Greedy yet generous. She closed her eyes, replaying their
kiss as her fingers played over his mouth.

When she finally opened them, she realized his eyes
were open too. Her fingers stilled, but she didn't snatch
them away as she thought she would have. Instead she
began to stroke him more, his lips, his chin, his jaw. Her
eyes locked with his.

He didn't stop her caresses. Instead he remained perfectly still, watching her with those lovely hazel eyes. As
if caught in a trance, she rose up, leaning over him. Only
then did he move, shifting over onto his back.

Ava studied him a moment longer, her fingers resting
on his lips, then slowly she replaced her fingers with her
mouth.

It had to be a dream. That had been Charlie's first
thought when he opened his eyes to find Ava in his bed,
her whispering caress brushing over his face. He'd even
hesitated to stir, sure that somehow any movement would
make her vanish like a wonderful, sensual dream.

But now with her lips pressed to his, he knew she was
truly there and very real. And in his slightly dazed, sleepy
state, he wasn't sure he had the strength to stop what he'd
somehow managed to deny himself earlier.

In fact rather than pushing her away, one of his hands
came up to knot in her hair, while his other curled around
her back, pulling her tighter against him.

She made a small noise low in her throat, and even that
didn't have the effect it had had earlier. No warning bell
this time. The soft whimper only fueled the need bub-
bling up inside him like a flood rising wildly over an already weakened dam.

Then in one deft movement, he shifted so he was the one leaning over her, pressing her back into the mattress. Their kiss deepened as he took control, unable to rein in his desire for her. And her hands tangling in his hair and stroking down his shoulders and back were as frenzied as he felt.

But by some sheer miracle he did manage to pull away, searching her face for any signs of apprehension. Regret.

Nothing but desire was reflected back at him from her beautiful, hooded eyes. Her lips parted, deep pink and damp from their kiss. She reached up and touched his cheek, her fingers trembling.

Did she shake with need? Or was she uncertain?

He caught those delicate fingers and held them against the side of his face, stroking his thumb over the soft skin of her hand.

"Are you sure?" he asked, his voice raspy with longing and sleep.

She nodded, even before he finished his sentence. "I want you, Charlie."

Four words had never had a more powerful effect on him. He didn't need to hear any more. His own need was far too strong to be halted again. The dam was broken.

He returned his mouth to hers, teasing her soft, full lips, tasting her, nipping her. Her tongue brushed against his in return, more longing welling up inside him.

A low moan vibrated in her chest as he pressed kisses down the side of her neck and across her collarbone. His mouth traveled down the valley between her breasts, hindered only by the neckline of her sweater.

He stopped long enough to reach for the hem and push it up. Ava helped him, pulling the garment off over her head and tossing it to the floor.

She fell back against his pillows, her skin looking golden and flawless against the black of her demi bra. Even in the dim light, Charlie could see the dusky pink of her nipples through the fragile lace.

He lowered his head and licked one of those rosy peaks through the material. She whimpered, writhing under him. He sucked in deeper, loving her reaction, the feel of that tight little nipple straining to be farther into his mouth. He nudged the bra out of the way to taste her bare, beaded flesh.

He continued to torture first one nipple, then the other as his hand stroked down the outside of her thighs. Her tiny skirt had ridden up in her sleep.

He sat back, needing to see what she looked like. Her skirt was nearly up to her waist and underneath she wore just a wisp of lace panties. She bent a leg, the pose so wanton and sexy, his cock hardened almost painfully against his pants. Then his gaze moved from the triangle of cloth between her thighs to her face. Despite the sensual invitation of her position, her expression was a little uncertain. Her dark eyes watched him, wide, unsure, clearly trying to read his reaction.

If he didn't know better, he'd have said she was afraid he might reject her. Her expression was almost that of a sweet innocent making love for the first time.

"You are so lovely," he said, realizing that he was probably saying the same thing men always told her. But the words were true.

She smiled at him, but he could see her worries didn't seem to be assuaged. Her eyes were still huge, her smile not quite banishing the doubts there.

He struggled to find words to explain how amazing he found her, but then decided maybe the better bet was simply to show her with his body.

He gently parted her legs and situated himself between them. Then, starting at her feet, he ran his hands up over her instep, curving his fingers around her delicate ankles, up the long, shapely length of her calves. To her knees, which caused her to wiggle. He paused there, grinning evilly as he toyed with them again and again, loving her ticklishness. But her breathy giggles and squirming stopped as soon as he moved on to stroke her beautiful thighs, the skin smooth and soft under his palms. Then she began to wriggle again, but not because it tickled.

She gasped as his exploration stopped right at the top of her thighs, his thumbs very close to the wisp of lace covering the lovely mound of her sex.

"You have such beautiful legs," he murmured, sliding his hands back down to her knees, only to slip slowly back up them again. His thumbs were even closer to her sex now. This time the tips of his thumbs fingered the lace of her panties.

She still watched him, but he noticed the anxiety that had darkened her eyes was now clouded with lust. She released a shuddering breath, then bit her bottom lip.

His cock pulsed at the sight. Did she have any idea how sexy she was? She must, but for some reason, Charlie wasn't certain of that.

He shifted again, sliding down the mattress, and though Ava didn't make a sound, Charlie could feel her frustration as his hands left her thighs.

But he didn't leave her disappointed for long. With his mouth he repeated the same path his hands had taken, focusing first on her left leg—kissing the top of her foot, her calf, nibbling at her knee until she wiggled and fought back giggles. Then up her thigh, where he pressed hot, open-mouthed kisses over her baby soft skin. His tongue licked and teased, previewing what he intended to do between her thighs.

Again, he stopped just at the edge of her panties. The musky scent of her arousal teased his nose, making it hard for him to stay focused on his slow, erotic torture.

God, he wanted to taste her. He could also feel the heat emanating from her and he wanted her hot, moist excitement on his tongue.

But he forced himself to repeat his erotic trip up her right leg, and by the time he reached the apex of her thighs this time, they were both panting with desperate need.

"Charlie—" Her pretty voice was raw with desire. Desire for him. "Please. Please."

He smiled against her inner thigh, then very carefully, as if he was unwrapping a fragile piece of crystal, he pushed the lace aside. Her labia glistened pink and wet in the dim light. He fought back his own groan.

He ran his tongue up the center of her sex, her arousal salty and sweet and delicious.

Ava gasped, her hand knotting in his hair, her hips pivoting upward silently, urging him for more.

He obeyed, this time parting her labia with his thumbs so he could focus on her tight little clitoris. And as he flicked and swirled and sucked, Ava writhed against his mouth. Small whimpers and moans spurred him on, until she strained tight against him, her muscles taut and her breath catching as an orgasm gripped her.

But Charlie didn't stop. He continued, his tongue pressed to the sensitive nub, but this time he also inserted a finger inside her, stunned at how hot and very, very tight she was.

Startlingly tight.

"Oh God, that feels good," she gasped, her breath coming in shallow pants as she wriggled herself more firmly against his lips and deeper onto his finger.

Soon she was making sexy little moans that drove him dangerously close to the edge, without his even being inside her.

After her second orgasm shook her limbs and stole her breath, Charlie moved away to peel off his own clothes.

Then he tugged off her panties, not even bothering with the skirt. Desperate to be inside her, he positioned himself over her.

Ava looped her arms around his neck and pulled him down to kiss him. He lost himself in her passionate kiss and the sensation of her hands stroking down his back, fingers digging into the skin and sinew of his shoulders.

"I want you deep inside me," she whispered against his ear, her words breathy, desperate, almost pleading.

He growled low in his throat. He wanted nothing more than to be buried inside her gorgeous body.

Her hand curled around his hardened length, angling him against the opening of her sex. He groaned as she positioned him, then lifted her hips so the tip of his erection entered her tightness.

So tight. So hot. And so damned wet.

He couldn't stop himself; he couldn't go slowly. He had to be inside her. Deep inside her. He thrust, filling her.

She arched, crying out, her hands clamping down on his buttocks, keeping him lodged all the way inside her. She pulsed and squeezed, her internal muscles nearly making him climax right then and there.

But he gritted his teeth and managed to maintain control. How, he honestly didn't know. She felt so damned good. And she looked so damned beautiful underneath him, her dark hair tangled wildly around her face. Her cheeks flushed, her eyes hooded. The picture of ecstasy, but again like some artless ingénue who was completely unaware of her own sex appeal. No falseness, no pretense. Just giving in to her own desire. That alone was enough to make him come.

He kissed her, his lips hungry and possessive over hers. She truly drove him mad. He couldn't remember any woman ever arousing him so intensely, so frenetically.

He continued to ravage her mouth, her own lips devouring him back, as he slowly began to piston his hips. Moving in and out of her in a deliberate, steady motion, totally at odds with the wildness of their kiss.

But soon their lovemaking took on the same frantic need of their kiss, as if they were caught in a flash flood of their own lust. Charlie thrust deep into her, and she tugged and pulled at him, her nails biting his skin, urging him to take her even harder.

Yet somehow he kept his own release at bay until Ava cried out, her body stiffening under his, her vagina pulsating, her breath coming in broken, fragmented gasps.

He shouted out, following her into mindless, wondrous oblivion.

Careful not to crush her, he collapsed half on her, half beside her, his arm and legs still draped over her warm, flushed body.

He studied her profile as she lay there, her breathing slowly evening out, a slight curve to her full lips. She was so different from what he would have imagined.

She turned her head and smiled at him, the gesture so sweet, so utterly adorable, his heart constricted painfully in his chest.

Still recovering from wild sex, he told himself to explain the sensation, even though he knew he was lying. But if he was smart, he would continue to lie to himself. Otherwise it would be far too easy to feel far too much.

Yes, she might look like a lovely, down-to-earth, girl-next-door curled up beside him right now, but she was a world-famous supermodel—and the supermodel didn't end up with the mailroom guy.

But you aren't a mailroom guy, he reminded himself. Not really. And Ava just might date a photographer. That was if he could actually get his career going.

"That was wonderful," she said, her voice low and soft and as sweet as her expression.

Charlie smiled back at her. "Yes, it was. Much more than wonderful. Amazing. Stupendous."

She giggled, although the action was cut off by a yawn. She blinked, her dark eyes growing heavy. She even managed to make exhaustion look delightful. Of course he was part of why she was exhausted—and that was a big turn-on.

He ignored his cock, which stirred against his thigh. She was too tired for another round. In truth, he was too, but apparently some parts of his anatomy didn't quite get that.

She cuddled up against him, her skin smooth and warm, and soon he was dozing off too. His last thought was that he'd just had the most amazing day of his whole life.

Chapter Eight

"Charlie, I need to talk to you."

Charlie struggled to keep his expression blank as he turned to see Eugene in his office doorway. Not the greeting he'd like on a good day. And so far, this had not been a good day.

But somehow he mustered up the control to simply nod and follow his boss into his small square office.

Eugene gestured to the metal folding chair on the opposite side of his desk. The one where Elton had been sitting yesterday evening. Had that been only yesterday? It felt like a lifetime ago now.

Eugene took a seat in his squeaky computer chair.

Charlie sat down, praying this wouldn't take long. He didn't think he could handle any speeches about the importance of the mailroom that ultimately made no sense whatsoever.

"So you were down here last night with Ava Wells."

Charlie met his boss's gaze, managing to keep his expression blank, even though he was actually stunned by Eugene's comment.

"Yes," Charlie answered, wondering why it mattered.

He also hoped Eugene didn't question him about why she'd been down in the mailroom with him. He wouldn't tell Eugene he'd been sneaking the woman out of the building so she wouldn't get busted for binge eating snack cakes. That was a fact Ava wouldn't want anyone to know and Charlie planned to respect her wishes.

"Why?"

Charlie gritted his teeth. Of course, he would ask.

"She . . . she's doing a series of fashion ads where a mailroom is the setting—and, um, she wanted to see a real mailroom."

Yeah, that was a believable story. Not.

Eugene studied him for a moment with those unnaturally blue eyes of his; then he nodded. "Well, that was nice of you."

Charlie nodded too, deciding that saying nothing more would be the best way to get out of here.

He was wrong.

"But we cannot have random people down here. We would not be welcome to attend a board meeting in Ms. White's office, and the same goes for our mailroom."

Charlie frowned slightly, trying to decide how that analogy made any sense. The two were not in the least bit comparable, but he supposed it shouldn't surprise him. More of this crazy "the mailroom is so important" rhetoric.

As if reading Charlie's mind, Eugene added, "I believe I have mentioned that the mailroom does a very important job and—"

Charlie pulled in a deep breath, then rose. He really couldn't handle this talk yet again—not this morning.

"I get it, Eugene. No more models in the mailroom."

Which Charlie was pretty sure wasn't going to be a problem if this morning was any indication.

"I'll get to our very important work now," he added, unable to keep the sarcasm out of his tone.

He started to leave the office, but Eugene's low, stern voice stopped him.

"You don't even begin to understand what goes on down here."

Charlie turned back to the strange man with his eerie eyes. "We sort mail. We deliver mail. It's pretty simple, Eugene."

Eugene regarded him, his expression unreadable. Those eyes of his looking even more eerie than before. Finally when Charlie would have just walked out, he spoke.

"We do far more than that, and when I know you are ready, I will explain that to you. But you are going to have to believe me when I say we are far more than just a mailroom. And I cannot have unapproved—" he hesitated as if struggling with the right word—"individuals down here."

Charlie frowned at the man, wanting to continue this disagreement. To tell him he was being ridiculous and grandiose and frankly a little delusional, but he caught himself. He was frustrated and itching to take it out on someone. But getting fired now wasn't going to help his problems.

So instead Charlie nodded. "I understand."

"No," Eugene said, his voice not just stern but now almost ominous. "But you will understand."

Charlie nodded again and left the office.

He had no idea what Eugene was talking about, and honestly he didn't care. Not when he was still trying to process the events of earlier this morning. Or rather the *event*.

He'd woken up, and Ava had been gone. No waking him to say good-bye, no note, no nothing. She'd just vanished as if she'd never been there at all.

And it didn't take a rocket scientist to figure out why. Despite their amazing sex, which he was confident had been as amazing for her as it had been for him, she wasn't going to trade in her model or actor or rock star boy-friends for a lowly mailroom clerk.

He opened his locker and stared at his mailroom smock, the royal-blue badge of how far from Ava Wells's world he was. The ugly coat that might as well be a serf's rags in comparison to her royal finery.

He sighed, pulling out the coat. As he shrugged into the dreaded garment, he made up his mind that he had to make a move soon. He needed to get his portfolio in front of someone.

You are a photographer and Ava will date a photographer.

He'd get his portfolio ready tonight and put it in front of either Finola White or Carrie Hall by tomorrow. He shut his locker with a determined slam, but then he hesitated. No one would probably even look at his work. They certainly wouldn't take him seriously. He couldn't rush this. He'd just started delivering mail to the fifteenth floor. Soon he would become familiar with some of the *HOT!* team and then they would be more willing to look at his work. It was the best plan.

He just didn't want Ava to forget about him. If she was even interested, period.

Ava stared at herself in the large mirror as the stylist yanked and pulled her hair, teasing it into a style quite reminiscent of what her hair had looked like when she'd woken up in Charlie's bed that morning.

Ava closed her eyes, her head jerking with every tug of the comb, but she didn't imagine the tugs being caused by the plastic teeth of a comb. Instead she remembered Charlie's fingers tangled in her hair, his mouth on hers, his erection filling her, making her feel more complete than she had in . . . forever.

Every moment with him had made her feel more alive

than she had in years. And the last image of him, asleep, stretched on his stomach, his body bare, his skin golden, would stay with her forever. Even now, amid the bustle of models getting ready for the shoot, her body reacted to that final image.

Final image.

Leaving this morning was the hardest thing she'd ever done, but she knew she had to go. And she had to go without saying good-bye. If she woke him and saw his crooked, adorable smile, those beautiful, golden-green eyes filled with kindness and warmth and desire, she never could walk away.

And she had to walk away. Any contact with her put him in danger. He wasn't a small rebellion like gorging herself on Devil Dogs or Ho Hos. Yes, he'd been a forbidden treat, but not one she could repeat.

Finola wouldn't allow it and Ava was frightened of how she would put a stop to the relationship. Finola had done horrible, awful things in the past. Ava knew she would do so again without hesitation.

As if thinking about her made her appear, Ava heard Finola's voice coming in her direction, insulting each model and stylist as she made her way toward Ava.

"Gino, that makeup is atrocious. She's modeling high fashion, not straddling a motorcycle for a calendar."

"Oh dear, dear God, please tell me she's not wearing that dress. It makes her look like a poorly made float in some hometown parade."

"Bette, it's hair. Style it, don't turn it into a nest for returning swallows."

Ava didn't have to open her eyes to know Finola had reached her. But after a slow breath through her nose, she did open them.

Finola stood beside her chair, with Tristan, her toady, right behind her. They both regarded Ava in the mirror. Ava stared back, trying not to flinch as she met Finola's pale gray eyes—eyes that saw everything. But Ava remained stoic, keeping all emotion off her face. That ability was perhaps the one advantage her years in front of the camera had given her. She could control her expressions.

In her head she repeated that Finola couldn't know anything.

She doesn't know. She doesn't know. She can't know.

Yet her little chant didn't convince her. Finola White wasn't just a controlling, powerful boss. She managed to know everything, whether you were good or bad, naughty or nice, sleeping with a mailroom clerk. She was like an evil Santa Claus, but instead of elves working for her, she had minions from Hell.

Ava's gaze flicked to Tristan. And Tristan was not to be trusted any more than Finola.

Ava returned her look to her boss, feeling herself start to panic, guilt wracking her. How could she drag a wonderful, nice guy like Charlie Bowen into her awful world? Even for a night.

"It's good to see you are back into work mode, Ava."

Ava blinked. Finola never gave compliments, unless it was to herself.

"The hair is perfect," she said to Fritz, Ava's stylist. Fritz beamed, brushing his own styled, shag cut away from his face.

"And the makeup is exactly how I imagined this layout looking. Mussed. Sexy. Sultry."

Finola turned back to study Ava in the mirror, those almost inhuman—well, they were inhuman actually—eyes roaming over Ava.

"Yes," Finola said with a smile, and Ava's muscles loosened as relief filled her. "I'm pleased."

Then Finola continued, those pale eyes locked with Ava's again. "You look just like you've crawled right out of bed after a delicious night of pleasure with your lover."

Ava's breath hitched, and she prayed she'd caught her reaction before her evil boss saw any signs of surprise.

Then, to her own amazement, she managed a smile too. "Well, clearly Fritz is a magician. God knows I can't recall what it's like to look like that."

She laughed and Fritz joined her.

Finola smiled too, but Ava couldn't decipher whether her boss really believed her comment. Tristan's expression didn't change, but then the beautiful demon never sported any expression other than elegant ennui.

But to her relief, Finola and Tristan left to go inspect the photo set. And to her dismay, she knew she could never see Charlie again.

Chapter Nine

"I need you to take this up to Ms. Hall."

Charlie looked up from tidying his workstation to see Eugene holding out a manila envelope. Since that first day, nearly two weeks ago, Charlie had gone up to Carrie Hall's office at least six more times to deliver similar envelopes. Envelopes always without any return address and only with Carrie's name and office number handwritten on the outside.

And they were always delivered when the *HOT!* offices were officially closed for the evening.

Charlie accepted the parcel.

"What is this anyway?" Charlie asked just as Eugene would have walked away.

His boss paused, but didn't look back. "I don't know. Just a letter that needs to be delivered, I suppose."

Charlie frowned as Eugene disappeared back into his office. Eugene had been cool toward Charlie since their brief confrontation, if you could even really call it that, the morning Charlie had woken up to find Ava gone. Charlie hated to admit it, but he rather missed Eugene's strange little pep talks. Even Innocuous Dave had been more standoffish. Charlie couldn't say he missed his lengthy lectures, however.

Charlie flipped the envelope over and over in his hands, wondering what could be inside it.

We are far more than just a mailroom.

Charlie had thought about that comment many times over the past couple weeks. He still had no idea what Eugene meant, but he did find himself watching his coworkers more closely, both in the mailroom and in the *HOT!* offices.

And he always kept an eye out for Ava. But aside from thinking he saw her back in Finola's glass office one time, he hadn't caught a glimpse of her.

Charlie grabbed his coat and then headed for the elevator. As usual, Ashley, the night receptionist, manned *HOT!*'s lobby when he stepped out on the fifteenth floor.

"Hi, Ashley. Just bringing Carrie another package."

Ashley smiled, and Charlie told himself he didn't see the yellow aura that still appeared around the young receptionist every once in a while. In fact, Charlie told himself he didn't see a lot of things up on the fifteenth floor. But over his couple weeks working up there, his vision problems seemed to be getting more pronounced.

He'd written most of the strange visual effects off to lack of sleep, which he'd struggled with since his one night with Ava. Or working long hours—he found being in the mailroom was actually preferable to kicking around his tiny apartment. And certainly the lighting and his overactive imagination weren't helping. Hell, maybe he really did need to look into getting glasses. Anything was better than acknowledging that he was seeing very odd things up on the fifteenth floor.

This evening, when he reached Ms. Hall's office, the door was ajar as if she was expecting him, and she sat behind her desk typing furiously on her laptop.

"Hello, Charlie." She greeted him without pausing her work.

"Hello."

He set the envelope on the edge of her desk and turned to leave, not wanting to interrupt her work.

"Don't go," Carrie said, still typing. "I want to talk to you. And could you close my door?"

Charlie frowned, confused by what she could possibly want to speak to him about, but did as she asked, then returned to her desk. Carrie was always friendly and made small talk when she wasn't busy, but she'd never requested anything like this.

She continued to type for a few more seconds. Finally she hit enter, then closed her computer.

She looked up at him and smiled. "So tell me, Charlie, are you happy delivering mail all day?"

Charlie shook his head, unsure how to answer. "Um, I'm not totally unhappy." Sort of true, he guessed.

She laughed. "That's diplomatic. Diplomacy will certainly help you up here."

Charlie wasn't sure what to say.

"Eugene says you have a talent."

"Really?" Again he couldn't hide his confusion.

"Yes. He says you have a pretty amazing ability that could be very useful to this magazine."

He shook his head. "I'm not sure what he'd be referring to."

"He says you have a good eye."

Charlie frowned. Had Eugene gone into his locker and seen his portfolio? Charlie had the black binder in there, waiting for the right moment to show it to Carrie. He had decided Carrie was his best bet, since in his weeks of working the fifteenth floor, he hadn't even met Finola. He never even saw her, except when she whisked through the offices, barking orders or shouting demands.

But Eugene must have seen his photos; it was the only thing that made sense. Charlie thought he should probably feel angry that his boss had looked at his private stuff, but since Eugene had clearly been impressed by what he'd seen and recommended him to Carrie, he could hardly take offense.

"I—I have wanted to show you my portfolio for a while, but I didn't know how you would react."

Carrie's brows drew together over her glasses. "I would like to see your work. Yes."

"I could get it now."

She shook her head, then tapped the envelope he'd just placed on her desk. "I need to deal with this first. But tomorrow. Come up after work. I'd love to see what you have."

"Okay," Charlie said, feeling more excited than he had in weeks. Maybe his situation was finally changing.

"Just out of curiosity," she said, "do you have any pictures you've taken while working here? Of employees or other people affiliated with *HOT!*?"

"Um—" Charlie paused, not sure if he should admit that he did. "I have taken a few pictures. Mostly of a photo shoot I saw in Bryant Park a month or so ago."

"I'd like to see those too."

Charlie nodded, wondering why. They were hardly his best work, but he'd show her whatever she wanted. Then for a moment, he wondered if he was actually going to be in trouble for shooting those pictures. Maybe it was considered some breach of the magazine's privacy policy or something.

But Carrie didn't look upset. She simply looked like a smart businesswoman interested in seeing his work. Better not borrow trouble.

"Okay," he told her, grinning. "I'll have my work ready for you tomorrow."

"Very good." Carrie then reached for the envelope, pulling out a letter cutter to open it. Clearly she was done with him.

His mind whirling with this exciting news, he stepped out of Carrie's office and straight into someone, a woman from the whirl of skirt and flash of hair, nearly bowling her over in his rush to leave and get to work on his pictures.

His hands automatically shot out to steady the person.

"I'm so sor . . ." The words dwindled to a halt as soon as he saw whom he'd run into, whose arms he held.

Ava stood directly in front of him, her expression as shocked as his. She looked amazing in an evening gown in golds and browns that accented her warm skin tone and dark eyes. Her long hair bounced, full and wavy, around her bare shoulders.

Then once the surprise wore off, Charlie noticed she looked tired. Her golden skin was not radiant with its usual healthy glow and her dark eyes were shadowed with purple circles as if she hadn't been sleeping at all. But even with those noticeable flaws, she still was the most beautiful woman he'd ever seen.

"Ava. How are you?"

For just a moment, her eyes seemed to eat him up, moving over him with blatant, intense hunger, but then she glanced away over his shoulder and her face, so alive with emotion, simply shut down.

"I'm fine. No harm done." She shrugged off his hands and stepped away from him.

Charlie frowned, confused by her reaction until he saw she was no longer paying attention to him, but to Finola White, who sauntered toward them dressed in a slinky white gown, followed by a severely stylish man in an expensively cut suit.

* * *

Ava prayed Charlie would be so insulted by her cool behavior he would leave before Finola reached them, but he remained rooted to his spot.

"Ava, my dear," Finola purred, or at least Ava was sure her boss thought it was a purr. To Ava it was like nails on a chalkboard. Her already tense muscles stiffened more as she watched Finola's attention land on Charlie. "Who is your friend?"

Before Ava could deny even knowing him, Charlie spoke. "Hello, Ms. White. I'm Charlie Bowen. I'm just one of your lowly mailroom staff."

Finola smiled at that. She liked to be reminded that she was surrounded by peons.

"Ah, you must be new then."

Charlie nodded, offering her that adorably quirky smile of his. "Yes, I'm fairly new."

"But you've had enough time to meet my Ava, I see."

Charlie glanced at Ava, and she wasn't surprised that his pleasure at seeing her was gone, replaced with a look of cool indifference. His dismissal hurt, even though she'd done the very same thing to him, and she knew it was the safest reaction for both of them.

"We've met."

Finola nodded, her pale gaze still moving between the two of them.

"Well, I don't want to keep you," he said, bowing just slightly in Finola's direction. Then he nodded toward Ava.

"I'm sorry again," he said, his voice polite, but just for the briefest moment, Ava saw a flash of hurt in his hazel eyes. Then he headed toward the main lobby. Ava forced herself to not watch him go.

"Well, he's a good-looking man," Finola said, having no such qualms about watching him leave. "I see the mailroom took my advice to hire more attractive people."

"So it would seem," Tristan said. "And more industrious too. It seems quite late for mailroom staff to still be working."

Apparently that point didn't interest Finola, because she turned her attention back to Ava. "Shall we go? We are expected at dinner already."

Ava nodded, relieved that Finola hadn't sensed anything between Ava and Charlie. Relieved and heartbroken all at once. She knew she'd done the right thing by snubbing him, but it had been so hard. She'd wanted nothing more than to throw herself into his arms and hold him close. She'd thought of him nonstop for the past two weeks and seeing him was as wonderful as it was painful.

She wanted nothing more than to see him again.

Rejected. That was the only word to describe how Ava had reacted to him, at least in front of Finola. She had barely acknowledged him. But Charlie knew what he'd seen on her face when their eyes had first met. He'd seen happiness and pain in her gaze, but she'd managed to suppress both emotions, quite efficiently.

And all because Finola would not approve? No, she probably wouldn't, and Charlie had already heard for himself that Finola felt as if she owned Ava. So the cold shoulder had been for Finola's benefit, he was sure.

But that would change once Carrie hired him as a staff photographer. Then he'd be in a position to date Ava, and what could Finola really have to say about that?

Of course, this was all assuming his analysis of the situation and Ava's reactions was correct. Maybe he hadn't read her right, and she wasn't interested in him at all.

He unlocked his apartment and went straight to his camera. All he knew for certain was he needed to do first things first, and that meant getting his pictures printed and ready to show Carrie tomorrow night.

That had to be his first priority even though he wanted

nothing more than to find Ava and discover exactly what she was thinking. He popped the media card out of his camera and headed right back out the door. Fortunately he knew a good photo lab that could get him his prints by tomorrow morning.

He'd get this job, and then he'd get his woman.

Chapter Ten

Charlie knew he could count on his buddy at the photo lab: Lou assured him the prints would be ready by noon tomorrow and would be perfect. Part one of his plan was in place.

Now he had to believe that his work would speak for itself and secure him the job working with Carrie. And once he was working for *HOT!* magazine proper, he'd be that much closer to convincing Ava to date him seriously.

As he approached his apartment building, he slowed his steps, realizing someone sat huddled on the stoop.

Probably a vagrant. But after a few more steps, Charlie could feel his skin prickle with awareness, even though he still couldn't clearly see who it was. The person straightened as if sensing him too.

"Ava?" he called, sure he must be imagining her. Then the streetlight caught some of the golden glimmer of her evening gown and he could see the mahogany highlights in her hair.

He hastened his pace, hurrying to her. She held her bare arms around herself in an ineffectual attempt to stave off the chill lacing the spring air.

Charlie immediately pulled her against him.

"What are you doing here?" After the weeks of silence and her dismissal earlier tonight, she was the last person he'd expect to find waiting at his doorstep.

She looked up at him, and the raw emotions he knew he'd seen on her face earlier were back. Her eyes were filled with a myriad of emotions. Concern, sadness, fear, desire.

But right this moment, with her finally in his arms again, he could only focus on the desire. That one emotion gave him hope the others could be soothed away.

Without letting her respond to his question, he kissed her. He had to. He had to taste her, feel her heat and response, to know that he wasn't alone in his desperate need.

She whimpered, the sound despairing and desirous all at once. They kissed with devastated yearning for minutes, hours, Charlie didn't know, but when they finally parted, there was no denying their need for each other any longer.

Even as Ava shook her head and said, "I shouldn't have come."

"Why?" Charlie just couldn't understand what could be so awful that it warranted their staying apart when they were both clearly suffering.

"You just don't understand how dangerous this could be." She looked around her as if she suddenly realized they were still out on the street.

No, he didn't understand, but he knew he wouldn't be able to truly talk with her until they were in his apartment. And she was freezing. He kept his arm around her as he ushered her up the stairs.

Once they reached his apartment and they were in the privacy of his living room, he pulled her back against him. Again he kissed her senseless. But then he forced himself to stop. He needed to understand what was really keeping her away from him.

"What is so dangerous, Ava?"

Ava, her cheeks flushed from her reaction to him and her full lips puffy from their kisses, crossed her arms over her chest, this time not from the cold. This time in a stance of protection. She really was scared. He could see it in her eyes. In the tenseness of her body.

"I just shouldn't have come here," she finally said, then she met his gaze, her dark eyes pleading. "But after seeing you today, I couldn't leave things like that. I had to let you know I care about you. And I had to be with you one last time."

Charlie didn't comment, but he'd be damned if this was going to be the last time he saw her. Instead he smiled, reaching for her hands.

"Are you worried because Finola wouldn't approve of her star model dating a mailroom clerk?"

Ava laughed, the sound humorless, weak, nothing like her infectious giggles. "She'd do far more than disapprove."

He frowned. Was Finola so controlling that she would destroy Ava's career rather than see her with a man she didn't think appropriate?

"Well, that doesn't matter now," he told her, offering her an excited smile.

"What do you mean?" Ava didn't appear pleased by his enthusiasm. If anything, she looked more worried.

"Finola won't be able to disapprove of me long, because Carrie Hall wants to see my photographs."

She shook her head, her brow wrinkled with confusion. "Your photographs?"

"I'm a photographer. I only took a job in the mailroom at Finola White Enterprises to get my foot in the door and my work in front of someone who could hire me as a staff photographer. And now that is about to happen. I'm meeting with her tomorrow evening."

"No!"

Charlie frowned, stunned by her emphatic rejection of the idea.

"But this is perfect," he said, confused by her stricken expression. "I'll get the career I've dreamed about and Finola won't object to one of her models dating one of her photographers. It's kind of a perfect solution, if you ask me."

Ava stared at him, trying to control the panic welling up inside her, making it hard for her to breathe. Charlie couldn't do this, he couldn't lose his soul to Finola White too.

"Charlie, there is no such thing as perfect. And if there were, you certainly wouldn't find it working for Finola. I know that all too well. You have to believe me, you don't want to work at *HOT!*"

Charlie smiled, humoring her. He obviously thought she was being overdramatic, hysterical.

"You are worth it to me. I would walk through the fires of Hell to have a chance to be with you." He touched her face, his long fingers stroking her cheek.

For a moment, she closed her eyes and allowed herself to savor his touch, nuzzling against him.

Then she said, "But would you sell your soul to the devil?"

"Without hesitation."

That terrified her.

Charlie moved the hand stroking Ava's cheek to the back of her head, pulling her close to him. She didn't resist, rubbing her cheek against his chest.

"I'm so glad you came," he told her, deciding they weren't going to get anywhere discussing his plans further. "I've thought about you constantly."

"Me too," she murmured, not lifting her head from his chest. "I can't get you out of my mind."

Happiness filled him. "I'm glad I wasn't alone in this agony."

She smiled then, peeking up at him, looking so sweet and adorable. "Misery loves company, huh?"

He shook his head. "Not as much as pleasure does."

Without warning, he swung her up in his arms, amazed that despite her height, she weighed virtually nothing. She released a surprised squeak, but then settled trustingly against his chest and arms, her own arms looped around his neck.

This time, he wasn't as lucky as the first. His bed was a jumble of comforter and sheets. But he didn't care and somehow he didn't think Ava did either. After all, the bed was going to look far worse by the time they were done.

He eased her down onto the bed, then straightened to admire her. The gorgeous silk gown with its warm colors and fine detailing should have looked out of place, silly even, against the muddle of his simple, utilitarian bedding, but somehow it was perfect.

Ava looked like she was posing for one of her fashion campaigns, glamorous beauty amid the everyday. His body reacted, desire curling down through his belly, centering on the part of him that grew rock hard at the sight of her. At the idea that he could have someone so amazing in his plain little world.

She smiled at him, the gesture tremulous and lovely, and again he was stunned she could be so sexy, yet so innocent as well. The combination was powerful, heady—like the lure of a particularly mouthwatering scent or the captivating melody of a beautiful song. He was so drawn to her. To every part of her. Her beauty. Her sweetness. Her

emotions. Her laughter. Her thoughts. Everything about her
aroused him to the point that it was almost painful.

As if reading his mind, she moved her gaze down his
body to the center of his aching need. Her gaze was like a
physical touch, but only a brush, a tease. He needed more
than that.

He peeled off his jacket, tossing it onto his bureau. Then
he quickly undid the buttons of his shirt and shrugged it
off.

Ava rose from the bed then, coming to him, pressing
her hands to his bare chest. Slowly she ran them over
him, downward across his nipples, over his ribs, down his
stomach to the waistband of his pants.

Her delicate fingers paused there, toying with the button at the top of his waistband. She smiled at him, the
gesture sweet and very naughty at the same time.

He groaned. "Planning to torture me, huh?"

She leaned forward and lightly bit one of his nipples.
He gasped, fiery sensation shooting from the spot where
her teeth connected with skin, straight to his loins. His
cock leapt, pulsing. Hard, needy.

She smiled, the curl of her lips erotic torture against
his heated skin.

"I seem to recall you making me suffer a little before
giving me what I wanted," she murmured.

"Yes, I did," he said, unrepentant.

She laughed, the sound sending hot shivers down his
spine. "Well, now it's my turn."

She kissed him then, a sweet lingering kiss, but after a
few moments, her lips left his to press to his collarbone,
his chest, to each of his nipples. She teased the hard tiny
peaks with her teeth and tongue for a few moments, then
continued downward.

Soon she knelt before him, her hands on his hips, her
mouth tracing a hot, moist path over his stomach, her

tongue dipping into his navel, before her lips stopped at the top of his waistband.

He could feel her warm breath brushing the fine hair around and below his navel. Her fingers curling into his hips, gripping him with her own longing, her own desire.

She released him, moving to the button of his pants, then the zipper. His cock jumped under the slight brush of her fingers as she worked. She smiled and his cock leapt again, reacting to every part of her. Just like it always did. Just like he knew it always would.

Carefully she eased his pants down. Charlie fidgeted for a moment, toeing off his shoes, then she removed the pants from around his ankles. Her fingers returned to his boxers, now working them down his body. The waistband snagged just for a second on his erection, causing them both to laugh, but as soon as he stood before her naked, her laughter died away, replaced by unbridled yearning.

Almost reverently she brushed a finger down the length of him, teasing the sensitive underside of his cock. She did it again, seemingly bemused by his reaction to even her most feathery touch.

Then he watched, entranced as she lowered her head and mimicked the caress of her finger with the tip of her tongue. He groaned, his hand coming out to tangle in her hair, as his own head fell back and his eyes closed. She could practically bring him to his knees with a single fleeting lick.

But he didn't have time to ponder her power, because he was soon overwhelmed. Her hand moved to hold him, her fingers curling around his girth, her other hand testing the weight and texture of his testicles. That alone was pure bliss, then her hot little mouth came down to surround him. Lick him, suckle him, swirl around the sensitive head in whirls of delicious torture.

She continued to pleasure him with her hands, with her

wicked mouth, until he was right on the precipice of release. He didn't want to come that way. Not when he could be buried deep inside her, a part of her body in the most primal way a man could be a part of a woman. Nothing else would do.

He caught her under the arms, easing her up to her feet.

She smiled at him, her lips glistening. "You didn't like that?"

"Oh, you know full well I loved it."

Her expression took on that innocence again, the vixen of moments before vanishing. "Did you really?"

He laughed, amazed she could have any doubts. He kissed her, tasting hints of himself mixed with her own flavor. Possessiveness filled him, pulling him taut with the need to claim her, make her his.

He found the zipper at the back of her dress, pulling it down. Then he helped her glide the fluttery fabric down the subtle curve of her body until she could step out of it. She stood before him in just a strapless bra the golden color of her skin and a matching set of panties. And her very high, strappy, gold heels.

"I'm going to remember this look forever," he whispered.

She smiled, but Charlie could see a hint of sorrow in her eyes. He kissed her, not allowing her sad thoughts to take hold.

Then he eased her back toward the bed until he had her lowered underneath him. They kissed for a long time, basking in the wonderful sensations of skin against skin, but eventually that wasn't enough. He pushed off her panties, her own impatient fingers helping him. Then he was touching the very core of her. His finger dipping inside her tight wetness, his thumb rubbing her clitoris in rough little circles until it pulsed and quivered under him, until she cried out with delight again and again.

Only then did he slide inside her, stretching her, making her take every inch of him. He made love to her, long and hard, making sure that she was aware of nothing but him and the friction of where they were joined. Finally, after her voice was hoarse from her cries and her body shook, drained by the strength of her orgasms, only then did he allow himself to come, his own orgasm so powerful his muscles seized with the power of it, only to turn to trembling jelly as exhaustion overcame him.

But before they both drifted off into satisfied sleep, he pulled her tight against him, his arm anchored around her narrow waist.

"Please don't just leave this time."

She shook her head, brushing a lock of hair from his cheek. "I won't. I promise."

Chapter Eleven

"So you are going to stay here, right?"

Ava nodded at Charlie, even though she knew she shouldn't stay. She just couldn't bring herself to leave the haven of Charlie's small apartment. She felt safe here, which was an illusion of course, but she wasn't willing to give up the fantasy. Not quite yet.

"I would call in sick, but I can't today." He didn't add why he couldn't, but they both knew he wasn't about to miss his appointment with Carrie Hall. And they also both knew he wasn't going to be talked out of it, so there wasn't much of a point in even mentioning it.

During the early morning hours after they'd just made slow gentle love to each other, Ava considered telling him the truth. Several times it was on the tip of her tongue to simply say, "Finola White is a demon. And going to work for *HOT!* is not like making a pact with the devil. It *is* making a pact with the devil."

But in the end, she kept silent. Charlie wouldn't believe her. In fact, he would probably just think she was mad. After all, wouldn't she, if she didn't know the truth firsthand?

So all Ava could do was hope the interview didn't go well. Not that she had much expectation of that either. Now that she realized all the photos hanging on Charlie's walls were taken by him, she knew he was incredibly talented. And with Finola's wicked help, he could become the most renowned photographer in the world.

But at what cost?

"Okay, I'll be home a little late. But don't leave. Maybe we can even go out and celebrate." Again he didn't say what they'd be celebrating.

She nodded. "I will be here."

Charlie gave her a lingering kiss so sweet and lovely, her eyes misted.

When he pulled away and saw her tears, he frowned. "Please be happy. This is a good thing."

She nodded, even though she knew better.

After he left, she curled up on his bed, wondering if she should follow, but she really didn't believe she could stop him. No one could have stopped her.

Charlie still didn't understand what had Ava so upset. Okay, so Finola White was a control freak; he could deal with that. This was the perfect solution to their problems, at least as far as he could see.

A bell jingled on the door of the photo lab as he entered to pick up his prints.

"Hey, Charlie," his friend Lou called to him from behind the counter, but his greeting didn't sound as chipper as it normally did. Right away, worry filled him.

"Hi. Are the prints ready?"

His friend nodded. "They are, but I've got to tell you, some of them turned out pretty strange. There's some crazy light flare in several of them, and I can't figure out what it's from. I checked your media card, and the flare isn't there when I view them on the computer. But when I print them, it appears. And I know it's not the processing, because I redid them a couple times."

Charlie frowned. "That doesn't make sense."

"No, it doesn't. But on the upside, the pictures you took at Bryant Park turned out very cool. That was one crazy and creepy photo shoot."

Charlie nodded, but he wasn't sure what his friend was referring to exactly. The Bryant Park shoot was just models dressed in different rainwear. And though they did create a pretty cool sprinkler system for the rain shots, it wasn't as amazing as Lou made it sound. And creepy? He didn't get that comment at all.

Since Charlie was running late for work, he didn't look at the pictures, figuring he'd get them sorted out and see what was usable during his lunch break. In fact, when he got to work, he was on the go nonstop. He didn't even have time to locate and thank Eugene for putting in a good word for him with Carrie. He'd actually wanted to ask why he had, since Eugene had clearly been irritated with him over the past couple weeks.

Charlie grinned to himself at lunchtime as he headed to his locker to grab the pictures and finally sit down and look them over. This was probably Eugene's way of getting rid of him since Charlie clearly didn't take his mailroom duties seriously enough.

Charlie's smile faded as he opened his locker and saw that the bag with his prints was not leaning against the inside wall of the locker where he'd left it.

He pulled out his jacket, his backpack. It wasn't somehow stuck in his coat. And he hadn't placed it in his backpack. He even opened the lockers on either side of his own. The prints weren't there. They were simply gone.

He looked at his watch. He didn't have enough time to take the media card back to Lou and have him print more.

What the hell was he going to do? And where could

the prints have gone? He knew exactly where he'd placed them, so someone must have taken them. But why?

The rest of the day went by rather quickly. Charlie still didn't see Eugene, who might have taken the photos. After all, he'd clearly had no qualms about going into Charlie's locker to look at his portfolio.

But his portfolio was still there. Why take what was for the most part nothing more than snapshots?

Unless someone wasn't happy about his taking pictures of *HOT!* staff. Maybe he'd been right to be worried about that yesterday.

Oh well. He was going to have to hope Carrie would be impressed with the rest of his portfolio.

At about half past six, Charlie boarded the elevator, his nerves getting the better of him. What if this didn't work out? He'd dreamed of a photography job like this forever. And now he had his relationship with Ava riding on his success too. He found it hard to believe Finola would make her life difficult if they were both working for her.

He managed a smile for Ashley, who didn't comment on the fact he didn't have an envelope with him tonight. Once he reached Carrie's door, he stopped, willing himself to calm down. He could only do what he could do.

He knocked and Carrie immediately answered.

"We've been waiting."

We? Charlie entered the office to see Eugene standing by Carrie's desk. What was he doing here? But then Charlie decided maybe it made sense since the man had recommended him. Yeah, maybe that made sense, but Charlie wasn't convinced. Nor did it make sense that Carrie locked her office door. But Charlie remained calm, walking farther into the room. Then he noticed his prints spread out all over Carrie's light table.

"Where did you find these?" He walked over to the table, looking at the photos he hadn't even seen yet. Lou had been right, the ones of Ava, which Charlie hadn't been sure he was going to share, had strange yellow light flares appearing all around her sleeping form.

Just like the yellow auras he'd seen around several of the employees up here. Then his attention moved to the Bryant Park photos. He leaned closer, not sure what he was actually seeing.

Then he quickly backed away. Many of the models looked the way the daytime receptionist looked. Like their beautiful model faces had morphed to reveal hideous distorted features.

"You've seen all the things you captured here before, haven't you?" Carrie said, coming to stand beside him. She picked up several of the pictures, studying them closely.

"No—I—where did you get these?" Charlie demanded again. "What do you want?"

Carrie smiled at him, her expression the same as always, affable, intelligent. Eugene looked the same too.

"You have a talent, Charlie. One we really need."

"What talent is that?"

Carrie held up one of the pictures of Ava. "Did you see that when you shot this picture?"

Charlie shook his head.

"Do you ever just see things like this without the aid of your camera?" Carrie asked.

Charlie hesitated. "I have. But only here on this floor."

"Well, that certainly makes sense," Eugene said, and Carrie nodded.

"What the hell is going on?" Charlie demanded.

"I'm about to tell you something you aren't going to believe. Or at least, you will have trouble believing it, but I want you to keep an open mind, because we need your help." Carrie's voice was calm and very reasonable.

He waited for her to continue.

"*HOT!* magazine—all of Finola White Enterprises—is run by demons." She spoke in a hushed tone, so hushed he had to move closer to her to hear, and even then he was certain he couldn't have heard her correctly.

"Demons?"

Carrie nodded, her lips pursed into a grim line.

"Demons in the figurative sense, right?" Charlie said.

"No," Eugene said, his voice very serious. "In the very literal, very dangerous sense."

Charlie's gaze flicked back and forth between the two of them. They were crazy, certifiably so. They had to be. Demons. Demons?

"We need you, because you can see them. You can also see the humans who have sold their souls. They are the ones with the yellow light around them."

Humans who sold their souls.

Charlie started to open his mouth to tell them they were utterly insane, but Ava's comment suddenly echoed in his head. The comment about selling his soul. Did Ava believe this nonsense too?

If she did, she didn't want him to be a part of it. She'd practically begged him to not pursue this. Yet she had said similar things.

"I know this is very hard to believe," Eugene said.

"Just a tad," Charlie said wryly.

"We are trying to stop them. Demons are running the whole fashion industry, and it's only a matter of time before they spread to other industries," Carrie said, her tone just as serious as Eugene's.

"And you"—he turned to Carrie, "and you and the mailroom"—he said to Eugene—"are the ones designated to stop this takeover."

Both nodded and then, to his surprise, pulled out government ID badges. Carrie had hers tucked into the inside of the waistband of her trousers, while Eugene had his in an inside pocket of his jacket.

Charlie scanned the badges closely, seeing both of them were listed as belonging to a branch of the NSA.

"That's great," Charlie said. "But how would I know if they are real or not? My fake driver's license looked legit too and I was only sixteen."

"You are right," Carrie agreed. "But what would be the point of this, if they aren't real? You know what you've seen with your very own eyes. These pictures are just more proof."

Eugene nodded. "What would be in this for us?"

Charlie couldn't think of a thing. And if the mailroom was a cover for a government operation, that certainly explained the intensity of the place.

"So who are the demons?" he asked, amazed he was even entertaining their story.

"Finola for certain. She is, of course, the head demon."

"Of course," Charlie said, still not sure what to make of all this.

"And Tristan is very likely one. He's definitely her right-hand man," Carrie said. "But that is why we need you. You have a gift. You can see them. And you can see the humans who—"

"Sold their souls," he finished for her. "I got it."

He considered what they were telling him. "Was I hired because of this?"

Eugene nodded. "Yes."

"But how did you know I had this ability?" Charlie asked.

"You can see demons and those bonded to the demons; I can see special abilities in humans," Eugene explained.

"So everyone in the mailroom has special abilities?"

Eugene shook his head. "No, some are straightforward military, installed here in case things get violent. Others are computer experts, hackers. Actually very few have any psychic abilities, if you will."

This was amazing. Just . . . amazing.

Charlie walked over to the pictures, picking up one of beautiful Ava sleeping. "So Ava has sold her soul?"

"Yes," Carrie said.

"To be a supermodel?"

"Yes, that would be my guess."

Charlie put the picture down. "If I help you, will you get her soul back for her?"

"That's our plan," Eugene said, his voice not as confident as Charlie would have liked. Funny, his uncertainty actually made the story somehow more believable.

"I should be up front with you. I'm pretty sure I'm falling in love with Ava Wells," Charlie told them.

"All the more reason to help us," Carrie said with an encouraging smile.

They kind of had him there, didn't they?

"Okay," he said with a sigh, still not believing he was buying into any of this. "Explain to me what my job will be."

Ava stopped pacing as soon as she heard Charlie's key in the lock. She flung herself at him as soon as he stepped inside the living room.

He caught her, holding her close, his surprised chuckle music to her ears.

"You are okay," she said, kissing his cheek, his lips. He returned the kiss, before smiling down at her.

"I'm fine."

"What took you so long? I was starting to get worried."

"Well, it took a while for them to explain what my job would be," he said slowly.

Ava frowned, confused. She couldn't imagine it would be that hard to explain what a staff photographer's duties were.

"It seems there's a lot involved when capturing demons."

Ava didn't react for a moment, then repeated, "Capturing demons?"

He nodded, then pulled out a picture and handed it to her. "And saving the humans who sold their souls for their dreams."

Ava looked at the picture, realizing it was of her, sleeping in Charlie's bed. That first night they were together. All around her sleeping form was a yellow light, a halo.

"Is this how you see me?" she asked.

"Sometimes. I see auras around those who have sold their souls. With the demons I see the real features that they keep hidden behind the masks of human faces."

She watched him for a moment. "You seem to be taking this pretty well."

He considered her, then nodded. "Well, it is true, isn't it?"

Ava nodded. "Yes, it is."

"Then we need to get your soul back, and apparently I can help do that. So I have no choice but to accept the assignment."

She smiled at him, leaning in to press her lips tenderly against his. She lingered for a moment, then pulled back to regard him, her eyes filled with unshed tears.

He started to speak, to comfort her, she was sure, but she pressed her fingers lightly to his lips to stop him. She needed to explain how she'd ended up in this situation. She wanted him to understand how she'd gotten mixed up with Finola White.

"I honestly didn't understand what I was doing," she said and he didn't need to ask what she referred to; he knew. "I grew up with just my mother. My father left us when I was less than a year old, so I don't remember him. And my mother had no help from her family; she really struggled to keep us going. She wasn't a bad mother; she took care of me and made sure I had what I needed, but I always knew she resented being stuck with a child. She'd dreamed of being a model or an actress herself. And having me, well, she saw that as holding her back.

"So at a very young age I started to imagine what it would be like if I could be a model or actress, so my mother would be proud of me and not regret having me. I would fulfill her dreams and make her realize she'd done the right thing to have me."

Charlie took her hand, running his thumb soothingly over her skin.

She continued, "Right out of high school, I came here to try and get a modeling contract. Maybe some acting roles. But I quickly realized I wasn't going to cut it. Not in a city like this. Then by sheer chance, or at least I thought it was chance, I met Finola at a play where I was ushering—that was the closest I ever came to the stage. She must have sensed some sort of desperation in me, because she told me I was stunning. That she could see me in front of the camera. That I could be the next Cindy Crawford."

"And what girl doesn't want to hear that," Charlie said, offering her an understanding smile.

She forced a tremulous smile back, still ashamed she'd so willingly sold her soul. Even though she knew Charlie understood.

"So I signed on the dotted line, giving her myself and as it turned out, my soul. And she did make me a star."

"But—" Charlie prompted when she fell quiet for a moment.

"But," she sighed. "That didn't actually give me what I wanted. I made it big, buying my mother a beautiful new house, a new car. Trying to give her everything she imagined she would have in her youthful dreams, but none of that mattered. She's still distant, still resentful, because now not only did I ruin her dreams, I stole them."

Charlie pulled her into his arms, hugging her tight, holding her with the tenderness and caring she'd always wanted from her mother.

"I'm sure she is proud of you," he said, his hands stroking her hair and her back. "I'm sure she just doesn't know how to show you after being reserved for so many years."

Ava nodded, realizing that while her mother's detachment still hurt, she wasn't going to let it ruin the one true, real happiness she'd ever found. She was going to make sure Charlie knew exactly how she felt about him. She wouldn't hold back the way her mother had.

But she also had to be realistic.

"I don't want you in any danger, so how are we going to make this work?"

Charlie frowned, clearly not following her shift in topic.

"How are we going to be together?" She smiled, her eyes shining with the growing love she felt for him. "Because I do want us to be together. Very, very much."

He laughed, the sound rich and joyful. "I want us to be together too. And Carrie assures me that she can persuade Finola we are the next super couple. Top model and hot, new rising photographer. Maybe we'll even get a nickname like Avlie or something."

Ava laughed. "Or Charva. Well if you put a trendy enough spin on it, Finola will go for anything. She's a demon who loves her celebrity."

"Maybe that will be her downfall."

Ava sighed, suddenly feeling that she might just have a shot at a happy future after all.

"You didn't answer me though," she said, leaning

back to look up at the man she was very quickly falling in love with.

"What didn't I answer?"

"I asked if that woman in your pictures was how you see me. Not the light, the woman."

"You mean, *you*," he said with one of his crooked smiles. "Yes, that's exactly how I see you."

Ava's heart swelled in her chest, overcome by joy. "You see Addy Wellmeyer. You see the real me."

"Ah," he said as if things suddenly made sense to him. "Well, you, Addy Wellmeyer, are the most beautiful woman I've ever seen."

"You are the most amazing man I've ever met."

He smiled. "Nah, I'm just a guy with a good eye."

What Slays
in Vegas

Angie
Fox

The events of this novella take place a year after the events in *The Dangerous Book for Demon Slayers*.

Chapter One

Shiloh rushed down a long hallway at the back of The Seven Deadly Sins Casino and cringed as she pushed through the human-repelling energy shield.

Zap!

The static electric shock zinged her down to her toes. Half the time it frizzed out her hair. She so didn't need that tonight.

She was late.

She was starving.

She was about to be ambushed by a loopy bear of a hellhound. A smile tickled the corners of her lips. "Hey, Rufus."

The hound's red eyes brimmed with excitement as he danced in place, waiting. Rufus might be a well-trained guard, but he was still a puppy at heart.

As soon as she came within striking distance of the Video Surveillance room, Rufus shoved his head against her hip and buried his wet nose in her hand.

"Attention hound," Shiloh said, scrubbing him on his coal-black head. She didn't really have the time, but she had a soft spot for the beast. Shiloh had always wanted a hellhound.

Maybe someday—if she ever got a life of her own.

Rufus whined and followed her with adoring eyes as she turned the corner toward the She-Demons assignment desk.

A middle-aged fairy hovered behind a workstation that had seen better days. His bowl of candied Mag Mell Mushrooms sat within easy reach. A bribe. Shiloh should know. She'd given them to the jerk last night—anything to get a better post than the one she had.

"You're late." The fairy glared at her over his Elton John–style reading glasses.

"I know." Traffic on the Las Vegas Strip was hell this time of night. And Shiloh refused to live at the resort and casino, like the rest of the succubi. For one thing, she liked to think she had some life apart from her devil of a boss. For another, well, it's not like the rest of the demons accepted her anyway.

Shiloh planted her hands on his desk. "Please tell me you've got something good for me, Jeebers."

She'd been stuck in Gluttony for the past week and if she had to finger-feed one more pork chop to those over-grown louts, she'd scream.

Oh for the days of the Romans. At least most of them had wanted grapes.

The fairy wrinkled his nose. "That's Mr. Jeebers to you," he said, sounding like a munchkin. He adjusted his glasses and ran a tiny finger down the screen of his laptop. "Succubus 14 . . . I have your assignment right here. Entertainment Room Three. Sloth."

Gah. "You have to be kidding. I've been off Lust for a month. I'm starving!"

The fairy began filing paperwork. "You're only a half-breed. You can make it longer than the regular girls."

"You don't understand. I need to eat too." She fed off

lust. The boss didn't allow takeout. She had to eat here at the casino and only during her shifts. How was she supposed to make it a week in Sloth?

All she did there was lie around and massage men's temples while they snoozed. She needed sex. Now. Or she was going to flip over one of the sloths and have her way with him.

"Mr. Jeebers. Give me a break. Please."

He stopped filing for a moment and gave her a long-suffering look.

"I'll buy you a six-pack of the good stuff."

"A case," he countered.

"Fine," she said, although she wondered what a case of Fitz's Root Beer would run her. It didn't matter. She was desperate.

Jeebers selected a large red file. "Hmm . . ." he said, removing a work order, "we only have one left. And we're not done checking him out."

"I'll take it." Shiloh snatched the eight-by-ten glossy photo from the fairy's hand.

"Damien," she said, noting the striking man in the picture. It was a security photo, taken near the gambling tables downstairs. It appeared this man liked to play poker for stacks of cash. How very human. Although the alternative—playing for lost souls—made her stomach curl. She didn't like to think about those tables, even if she'd never had a soul of her own. It was just creepy.

She shook off the feeling. A demon like her couldn't change the way things were done. She just needed a decent meal. And from the looks of him, Damien would be a five-course feast.

He was ruggedly built, with broad shoulders and great taste in suits. The one he wore fit him like a dream. He had a well-defined face, sharp around the edges with dark hair that was deliciously unkempt.

She tried to picture him in leather. Mmm . . . yes. He

could be a bad boy. Then she pictured his hard body wearing nothing at all.

Even better.

She ran a French-tipped fingernail down the photo. Still, something bothered her. He had a certain air about him that appeared wholesome, maybe even angelic. "Damien—" She chewed on her generous lower lip, trying to locate the source of her niggling doubt. "Just Damien? No last name?"

The fairy shook his head as he reached for the photo. "Lies don't stick to the page."

She held it out of the fairy's reach. "Tell me something I don't know." She slapped the photograph down on the desk. "I'll take him."

Jeebers snatched it up. "He requested a full succubus."

"He's not going to know the difference." Not the way she was keyed up.

Jeebers looked like he was about to protest.

"A demon is a demon," Shiloh said quickly. "Besides, don't you want that sweet, fizzy Fitz's Root Beer? I'm the only one who can get it for you." Thank Hades she had a friend in St. Louis, where they made the stuff—a human friend who had more than fairy money to spend.

Jeebers looked torn.

"You haven't had Fitz's Root Beer in how long?"

"Two years," he answered pitifully.

"That's too long to wait," Shiloh coaxed.

"Do *not* tell anyone," Jeebers snapped, his tiny fingers pounding her change of assignment into his computer.

"Nobody." She threw up a hand. Succubus's honor.

"Napthulo will have my wings."

"Napthulo isn't going to know anything."

She didn't want to screw up her relationship with the boss, either. Napthulo was the all-powerful demon lord of Las Vegas, not to mention the only one in the last millennium who'd offered her a steady job. There was a lot of prejudice against half-breeds.

"Be upstairs in ten minutes sharp," the fairy said, snatching up the photo and stuffing the entire work order into another file.

"Are you kidding? I'll be there in five," Shiloh said, resisting the urge to kiss the fairy on his knobby little head.

She dashed for the changing rooms. It took everything she had not to rush up to the Lust room in jeans and a T-shirt.

Fawzi the ifrit stood guard outside the She-Demons dressing room. His copper skin gleamed. Gold cuffs on his wrists bound him to the casino and their master, and long, spiraling horns cropped up above each ear. He'd been Shiloh's bodyguard for the past four centuries and it drove him crazy that he couldn't follow her home.

"You look happy," he said, his voice low and rocky even as she reached up and planted a quick kiss on a bulge of muscles between his elbow and his shoulder.

"Lust," she sang, dancing past him.

"Perfect," he grinned, showing a set of ultra-white teeth. "You've been a bear this month."

Shiloh banged through the door, knowing he'd follow her.

She shoved her way past a clothes rack displaying everything from gowns to sequined panties. "No more Gluttony. No more Greed."

"Now I can protect you from more than day traders and mountains of shrimp cocktail, yes?"

"Oh yes."

"Wear the gold." Fawzi tossed a shimmering gown toward Shiloh as she ducked behind the dressing screen.

"Las Vegas Barbie. How original."

"It's your lucky color."

True. Although she'd had her luck tonight talking Jee-bers into giving her this assignment. Anything else was gravy.

Shiloh slipped into her favorite pair of gold spike heels. She kept all her shoes back here, where no one fiddled with them. She could have hidden a whole marching band behind the screen. None of the other girls bothered with modesty as they dressed.

She zipped the dress up the side, under the swell of her breasts.

Perfect.

Shiloh brushed past the ifrit to make a quick check of her makeup in the battered mirror behind her dressing table.

He wrinkled his nose. "Do I smell barbeque sauce?"

"Probably." Fawzi had the heightened senses of his genie ancestors. At least that's what she told herself. Friggin' Gluttony room. Two mineral baths and she still felt like she'd been slathered in KC Masterpiece.

To be safe, Shiloh dabbed Chanel No. 5 on her pulse points.

Sure, she had natural allure. She was half-succubus, and pleasure demons positively oozed sex. But her other half was human, so she also had to count on Chanel, MAC, Lancôme and that little trick where she dabbed Preparation H under her eyes after a particularly grueling night.

"Hold this." She handed her purse to Fawzi while she shoved her street clothes into her locker. The ancient ifrit pinched her lime-green bag between two fingers as if she'd asked him to tote around a dead possum.

As if she was asking much.

She took the bag from wussy boy, shoved it on top of her clothes, and spun the combination lock. "All set." She slipped her arm around his and let his soupy warm power wash over her as he shifted them up to the sixty-ninth floor.

Lust.

At last.

They reappeared in an ornate hallway dripping with Jazz-era charm. Gleaming sconces cast a warm light over hunter-green walls and plush red carpeting. Carved wood doors lined the hall.

An echo of cinnamon incense hung in the air.

"You ready?" Fawzi asked.

"Overdue," she said, disengaging herself from his arm.

Fawzi shrank into a wisp of yellow smoke. He hovered near her ear. "As I am sworn to protect—"

"So you will be at my side." Yeah, yeah. Whoever thought it was a good idea to repeat the blood oath every night had been smoking the hookah too hard. Fawzi would stay by her side until she had the human under her thrall. After that? Well, neither one of them really wanted him watching.

Shiloh touched her hand to the bronze handle of the Lust room. She straightened her shoulders, shook out her hair, and put on her most delicious smile.

Come and get me, boy.

The room smelled of cinnamon and sex. The crimson-veiled sconces on gold walls gave the room a warm glow. Heavy curtains blanketed the windows. At least a half dozen men and women lounged on suede couches, amid tables laden with candles and discarded clothes. Her fellow succubi had started without her. That's okay. She could catch up.

The mysterious Damien sat stone-faced on an over-sized chair apart from the rest.

Yow. He was even better-looking in person.

He was dressed down for the evening, in seductively snug blue jeans and a silk club shirt, yet he still looked like a million bucks. It was the way he held himself, she decided, like he belonged there.

She sauntered toward him. Joe Cool, this one. She'd warm him up.

He studied her, his sharp features betraying nothing.

"I'm Shiloh. I hope you haven't been waiting long." She draped herself on his lap, running her fingers through the chocolate-brown curls at the nape of his neck. "And if you have, I'm worth it."

He smelled divine, like fresh grass and sunshine.

Then he did something strange. He looked her in the eyes. It surprised and delighted her. Most men were too busy looking at her other assets. But Damien simply watched her.

She smiled, feeling quite beautiful as she drew her fingers over his strong jaw. Shiloh admired his lovely hazel eyes as she let her fingers snake past his collarbone, down his chest. "What do you want to do, Damien?"

He caught her wrist. "Talk."

Her mouth curved. "I think I'm insulted." She rubbed herself against him.

His desire was evident. He didn't need to hold back.

She wanted this as much as he did. Probably more.

Shiloh straddled his lap, trailing kisses along the salty skin of his neck. Her nipples tightened; the pleasure rose up from her very core as she rubbed herself against him.

She felt herself grow wet, needy. Hades, she was desperate. She didn't even know how desperate until—

"Stop." His absence struck her like a blow as he lifted her away by the shoulders.

"What?" She blinked, pushing the hair out of her eyes.

A muscle in his jaw twitched as he glanced behind her, at the couples scattered through the orgy room. "Let's go somewhere private," he said, almost to himself.

"My pleasure," she said automatically, relieved that it was merely a change of location. She wouldn't—couldn't—stop now.

Her dress rubbed painfully over her swollen breasts as

she slipped a hand into his. His grip was warm and firm as she led him to her favorite room in the back.

The purple silk pillows and gold trim reminded her of the pleasure houses in the Far East. Sandalwood incense burned in the small gold tin at the door. Tiny white lights glittered over the ceiling like stars.

"Lie with me," she said, tumbling down onto the pillows with him.

He reached inside his jeans. But instead of taking them off, he withdrew a small bottle of shimmering blue liquid. "Drink this," he said, his voice husky.

"What is it?" She asked, helping him along with the buttons of his Levi's 501 jeans.

He caught her wrist. "It's my own private cocktail."

Fawzi hovered near her ear. She'd almost forgotten about him. "I don't like it," the ifrit growled.

"Oh yeah?" Well, if she could get Damien to stop talking, she was all for it.

Besides, it wasn't like she couldn't handle it. She could drink gasoline, for sin's sake. It gave her quite a buzz, but then again, Amoco Unleaded tasted better than tequila.

Cheaper too.

No. The wisp of yellow smoke hovered between Shiloh and Damien. *I do not like this.*

And I need to get laid.

She caressed the tiny bottle.

Damien reached for the buttons on his jeans, seeking to undo her work. "Is there a problem?"

She covered his hand with hers. "None," she said.

I wish you to leave, Fawzi.

The ifrit dissolved away.

She'd pay for that later. But now? "I'll drink."

The corner of his mouth tipped up in response.

"Kiss me first," she purred.

He cupped a hand under her chin, effectively stopping her sultry advance. "Drink."

Shiloh smiled. She liked a man who knew what he wanted. "You win." Her breasts tightened with anticipation as she made quick work of the buttons on his shirt.

"What are you doing?" he asked, moving to stop her.

She caught his wrist with her hand. "I'm drinking it my way."

He hesitated a moment, then relaxed. "Good." She pushed the shirt the rest of the way off. His chest was smooth and firm.

His eyes darkened as she tipped the bottle and made a pool of blue liquor right above his belly button. His breathing quickened as she drizzled it up over his chest and toward his heart. She stopped right above his left nipple.

Shiloh felt her own pulse speed up. "Delicious."

She eased the top of his boxers lower on his hips and touched her tongue to the groove of skin at his hip bone. He groaned as she licked her way upward, teasing him until she found the cocktail she'd poured.

Her tongue tingled. Mmm . . . it tasted like Sweetarts. She lapped up every drop. And then she went back for more.

He watched her as she took his nipple between her teeth and bit down. He gasped.

She smiled. It was like he'd never been touched before.

"How do you feel?" he croaked, breathing like a man half-possessed.

"I could ask you the same question."

He met her halfway for a searing kiss. He wrapped his arms around her and hauled her against his chest. Heat poured through her as her thirsty body responded. She moaned, eager for more.

She pushed. He pulled. They shared a brief, hot moment of passion before he shoved her away again.

Hells bells.

He wore a steely expression, as if he were fighting it.

Why? He'd come to her for pleasure.

She raised herself up on her knees and slipped the gold straps from her shoulders, baring herself from the waist up.

His eyes blazed.

She could feel his desire like a physical presence. His lust rose up, feeding her own.

Yes.

He surged for her, wrapping his arms around her once again. His warmth felt glorious against her bare skin as she sat in his lap and kissed him over and over again. Her core pressed against the hard length of him, grinding, pushing until they were both shuddering with need.

Oh yes. She needed lust.

He tore his mouth away. "Hold it," he said, breathing hard. He blocked her with his hand as if she was about to strike him instead of kiss him again. "Now it's time for you to tell me about your boss."

What on earth gave him that idea? "No."

"Listen." He unwound himself and stood facing her, his jeans open, his boxers low on his hips.

"Ah, but see . . ." She slipped off her panties and stood naked in front of him. "I am not a very good listener."

Damien clearly couldn't take his eyes off her. So why was he backed against the wall?

She grasped his pants and his boxers and dropped to her knees. Before he could make any more silly requests, she had the full length of him in her mouth.

He tasted delicious, like nothing she'd ever had before. The lust flowed through her, feeding her. She felt glorious, alive.

He gasped as she worked him.

His lust soared and so did hers. She fed off his desire and her own. She craved him. Needed him. Wanted to please him like no other.

Her power surged and slapped against his.

His?

He had power.

Amazing. Oh what a bonus. He wasn't human. He was different. The same, yet gifted. Special.

Delicious.

She slid her tongue down the full length of him.

"Shiloh," he groaned.

What was he? She had to have another taste. And another. And—

He seemed almost desperate now as he bucked against her. He was saying something else. She didn't listen. She didn't care. The only thing she needed was to taste him.

He drove his hands through her hair. "You don't understand." Each word came out as a short, desperate attempt at speech. "I can't."

They rolled down onto the pillow-strewn floor. Had he seen his erection? "Oh, I think you can."

He cupped her breasts, running his thumbs over her nipples. An amazed expression crossed his face as she practically purred. "I don't—" he began.

They lay side by side, cocooned in silk. "Then why did you come here?"

They were both slick and hard, out of breath.

He shook his head slightly, as if he couldn't quite understand how he'd gotten there. "It's impossible for me to—"

"What?" she asked, cocking a leg over his hip and slipping him inside of her.

His expression—pure ecstasy mixed with shock— might have made her smile. If she hadn't been so turned on. Because at that moment, he flipped her over, grabbed her hips and drove into her.

His power rose up again, slapping against hers as he took her hard.

Yes. She shoved back against him, giving as fiercely as she got, reveling in the pleasure as he gave her the strength and the energy and the surge of pure heat she'd craved for as long as she could remember.

Instinct ruled as they exploded into a frenzy of caresses, licks, kisses and pounding need. There was no drawing back this time. No control. She basked in the wild passion, the utter possession.

Opening her senses, she drank in every bit of him, naked and sweaty under the twinkling white lights. She gloried in his moans, his wild abandon. Her body arched under his as they both shuddered and reached the final climax.

Chapter Two

Sunlight stung her eyeballs even though she hadn't opened them. Shiloh covered her eyes with her arm and groaned. She felt dizzy, weak. Her head throbbed with the worst hangover since that three-day wine binge through Sodom, Gomorrah and Zebiom.

And she hadn't even had any alcohol last night.

She stretched, sore from last night's activities with Damien. At least one thing had gone right. Damien had been exactly what she needed.

In fact, he was amazing.

So why'd she feel like hell?

She blinked against the bright morning, wishing she could lie in bed for the rest of eternity. Maybe she'd just close her light-blocking shades and go back to bed.

She didn't even remember making it home last night.

In fact, she didn't remember anything after that blinding orgasm. Strange. That had never happened to her before.

A flutter of a grin crossed her lips. If she was going to remember one thing, let it be her night in the Lust room.

She groaned into a sitting position and threw one leg

onto the floor, stopping short when her toes came in contact with carpet. Her bedroom had hardwood floors. Shiloh's eyes flew open and she gasped as she saw a nicked wooden end table. A white ceramic lamp. Beige curtains. She was in a hotel room.

Out the window, she could see the roller coaster at the New York-New York hotel. Oh thank Hades. She flopped back against the pillow. She was in Vegas. Okay. She placed a hand on her chest. She was a few blocks from home. No need to panic.

Breathe.

Although something on her left hand didn't feel right. It was like a heavy weight on her finger. She glanced down to the hand on her chest and shrieked. There, on her left ring finger, was a gold band with a diamond on it the size of Switzerland.

She stared at it like she'd never seen one before. In all fairness, she hadn't. At least not on her hand.

From her right came a bellowing snore. She scrambled off the bed and stood staring down at Damien, tousled and wickedly naked.

What the hell happened last night?

She didn't remember a thing.

She rubbed her temples. *Think, think, think.*

Okay. She went to work, bribed the fairy, practically mauled Damien. That part had been a lot of fun. She'd felt her power flow out of her in an amazing orgasm and then . . . nothing.

Just a cheap hotel room, a hot man and a diamond ring.

She yanked at the gold band. It was big enough to slip off easily, but it refused to budge. The obnoxious diamond clung as if it were welded onto her.

It glinted in the morning sun, mocking her.

She couldn't be married. Succubi didn't get married. Ever.

Her eyes stung and she rubbed at them. Even if she wanted to get married, she couldn't marry a client from the Lust floor. It didn't matter that he was the best sex she'd had in a thousand years.

And how dare Damien sleep at a time like this?

"Get up!" She crawled across the bed and yanked him onto his back. Her heart stuttered when she saw that he wore a gold band on his left finger too. Oh Hades. She'd been afraid of that. "Wake up. This is an emergency!"

He threw his arms up over his eyes. "What's the . . . ?"

"Damien"—she yanked his arms down—"what did you do to me?"

He gazed at her with bleary eyes, confusion tumbling across his features. "What are you doing here?" he asked, his voice gravelly and a bit too indignant for her taste.

She smacked him with her pillow. "That's what I want to know."

He sat up faster than she expected. She could see he was still woozy. "Don't touch me," he warned.

"You sure didn't mind it last night," she shot back, pleased when a flush crept up his neck. Bull's-eye. "Now fess up. What did you do to me?"

With the grace of a cat, he was out of bed. He strode toward a shiny silver suitcase on a luggage stand, displaying his frustratingly perfect butt.

He yanked the case open, his eyes on her the whole time. "I didn't do anything to you." He reached inside with one hand and grabbed hold of something she couldn't see.

Frankly, she didn't care. "You made me pass out. Want me to show you what happened next?" Maybe he had some memory of it. She shoved her obnoxiously ringed hand at him. "You married me."

He blinked twice and slowly removed his hand from whatever was in the case. "I couldn't."

She planted a hand on her hip. "Check your hand, sweetie."

He lifted it out of the case and went white as he stared at the gold ring on his finger. "I can't be married," he said to his hand.

She had to smile. Briefly.

Oh, who was she kidding? This was a mess.

Shiloh swept toward the window, wanting to get as far away from him as she could. This was too much. It had to be a mistake. Getting married meant giving her power away. Seducing only one man for the rest of her life. She couldn't do that. She had a job. A career. Her boss was going to kill her.

She stumbled over an empty champagne bottle as she scanned the room, trying to make sense of what had happened the night before. A gigantic pink teddy bear with an "I ♥ Vegas" button sat next to a half-empty room service tray and what appeared to be her wadded-up dress.

He slammed his suitcase closed. "What did you do to me last night?"

She turned to find him glaring at her, menace in his eyes.

"You were the one with the fancy shot, you jerk. You drugged me." Which proved he was a fool because drugs didn't work on her.

"You were the one who drank it," he said, yanking a pair of jeans from the closet.

Did she ever. She watched him pull on a pair of worn Levi's and remembered just how she'd drunk the cocktail off of him. She felt a delicious tightening between her legs. "Fess up. What was in it?"

He sighed and drew a hand through his hair. "I suppose it doesn't hurt to tell you now." He placed his hands on his hips, which only made his abs look better, damn him. "I gave you truth serum. It was *supposed* to make you cooperate." His jaw flexed. "Instead, you seduced me."

"That's my job!"

"You made me pass out," he accused.

"Me too. I don't remember anything after our scream-ing orgasm."

He looked like he could grind marbles with his teeth. "Don't say that word."

"*Orgasm?*" she asked, watching him flinch. "What are you? A prude?" She felt something slippery below her foot. "Oh," she gasped as she realized she was stepping on a photograph of her and Damien posing with a minis-ter.

She snatched it off the floor.

There she was, radiant in her gold dress, smiling like it was her wedding day. She had both arms wrapped around Damien, who had a hand on her hip and a rose in his teeth. They stood under a trellis with a red-and-gold sign that read The Hitching Post Wedding Chapel.

"Yeek." She tossed it back on the floor.

He'd found photos too. Stomach tumbling, she hurried over to where he was sitting on the edge of the bed, flip-ping through a stack of pictures. She gasped at the proof of their post-wedding limo ride. Shiloh and Damien kiss-ing underneath the Las Vegas sign. Shiloh and Damien pretending to be tigers outside the MGM Grand. Shiloh and Damien inside the limo, kissing like the ship was about to go down, while long-haired, painfully skinny members of a rock band cheered and toasted them with bottles of Captain Morgan. He squinted and studied the last picture closer. "Who are these people?"

"How should I know?" They were all mortals. She could count the mortals she knew on one hand.

He turned to the next photo of them making a toast while standing fully clothed in the pool at Caesars Palace. Unbelievable.

She shook her head. "You're sure guzzling that cham-pagne."

He turned to her, frustration written across his face. "I don't like champagne."

Sweet Hades. Shiloh stalked toward the window. "We have to fix this."

She felt like a caged tiger. She couldn't get married. She needed to crave all men. If she had truly given herself to this Damien, then she'd only crave him. Her magic would be gone.

It was too awful to contemplate.

She had to test it.

"Shiloh," he began.

"Hold up." She craned her neck, hands on the window in search of a man, any man close enough for her to test her powers. Maybe the marriage didn't take. She was obviously out of her mind when it happened. She might still have her powers.

She spotted a man in a harness washing the windows on the side of the closest building. Bull's-eye.

Please work.

And please let that man be buckled in tight.

She reached deep down inside and summoned her powers. She felt the desire build in her core and the lust radiate from her. She writhed her hips, reveling in it before she shot it out toward the man and hit him with a lust bullet he'd never forget.

It left her panting, needing.

He kept washing the windows.

She gave a small gasp.

No!

She tried again, winding her power until she was almost ready to jump out the window and take him herself. She channeled the desire until she was wet with it. Then she threw it all at him.

Nada.

Shiloh whimpered, resting her head on the glass. The

man kept washing windows as if he hadn't just been seduced by the woman who'd brought Julius Caesar to his knees.

Her magic was gone. She was tied to this Damien. How was she going to be able to go to work tonight? She could get fired, banished. She'd be a laughingstock. Only the second succubus in the history of she-demons to get married.

The first succubus wedding had touched off the Great Slaying of 2009. Shiloh had been the sole survivor, and only because she was a half-breed.

She'd helped Napthulo come back, build his business from the ground up. And now she was about to screw things up again.

She leaned back against the window, panting with unspent lust.

Damien stood on the other side of the bed, a mirror of her desire. Damn it. She hadn't even been aiming at him.

"Stop it," he said, his voice hoarse. He stood rigid, as if the mere act of moving would cause him to leap across the room and take her.

She wouldn't mind if he did.

Yes, she would. *Get a hold of yourself.* She had to stop this. "We need to get an annulment," she said. Legally and spiritually. "Now."

This had to end. And then she'd burn the pictures, shred the dress and forget she had ever met Damien.

Damien was slowly going insane. There was no other explanation. He could hardly take his eyes off Shiloh, and not because he was trying to decide how to take her out. He wanted her. He craved her seductive pout and her silky skin and the way she laughed right before she . . .

Oh God. Get a grip.

Yeah right. He wanted nothing more than to walk across the room and take Shiloh against the window. Hard. At the same time, his body felt like he'd been hit by a garbage truck.

He focused on his aching head in an attempt to take his mind off his growing hard-on. It had to be her succubus charms. Only he was immune to succubi. That's why he'd gotten this assignment. Besides, Shiloh wasn't turning on the charm. She wasn't playacting anymore. She was mad and scared and frustrated and hot as hell. Damn.

Damien couldn't believe he was attracted to the she-demon.

Again.

He was a demon slayer. He needed to slay. Good thing his twin was off axing demons in Detroit or he'd have had a field day with this.

"Today," he said, backing away as if she were the most dangerous creature on the planet. To him, she was. "We'll get an annulment today."

He knew a priest. Well, an exorcist. The only problem would be convincing Father Riley not to banish Shiloh on the spot.

To think he'd had a switch star in his hand, ready to kill her this morning, until he learned they were bonded. Marriage meant a meshing of powers. Lord help him.

"After the annulment, we never breathe a word of this." She swallowed hard, still backed against the window, gloriously naked, the morning light gleaming through her blond hair like a halo. She knew what he wanted.

Heaven, she wanted it too. That thought nearly sent him over the edge.

He tossed her the slinky gold dress, which clung to every curve, barely covered anything and would probably make things worse. "Will you please put some clothes on?"

He scrubbed a hand over his face. He was a demon slayer, for God's sake, a holy warrior. He'd lived a righteous life, avoided temptation. His body was his temple. For thirty-five years, he hadn't even allowed himself to have sex. Until last night.

This was so screwed up.

She was watching him. He knew that look. It had come right before she'd jumped him and made him lose his mind.

He was supposed to break into Napthulo's casino. He was supposed to drug a succubus into giving him the password to the demon's inner sanctum. He was supposed to slay Napthulo to blow the whole operation sky high.

Instead, he had sex, got married and made tiger faces outside the MGM Grand.

"Get dressed." He might not make it if he had to tell her again.

Damien fished his cell phone out of the pocket of his jeans, groaning at the erection that made it even more difficult.

"Accept the universe," he grumbled under his breath, clinging to the second Truth of the Demon Slayers as if his life depended on it.

Father Riley answered on the first ring and agreed to be at their room in a half an hour. Damien would explain everything when the priest arrived. Hopefully by that time, he'd be able to understand it himself.

"Father Riley?" Shiloh squeaked, her dress half over her head. "The exorcist? I can't see him." The dress slid the rest of the way over her body. "Not that I have anything to hide," she added quickly.

They might as well get this out in the open. He shoved the phone into his back pocket. "I know you're a demon."

She had the nerve to look offended. "I'm not a demon."

Shiloh certainly wasn't what he'd expected. In their natural state, succubi were plastic creatures, almost like department-store mannequins. They'd touch a man and mold themselves to fit his every desire.

This one had barreled into the room, hot and blond, even though he preferred brunettes. Then she'd stayed in her human form all night from the looks of the photographs. This morning too. She didn't talk like a she-demon. Or act like one.

She didn't even smell like sulfur. "You are a succubus, right?" he asked. His demon slayer instincts registered her as a threat, but that didn't necessarily mean she was a demon.

Shiloh chewed at her lip.

Oh no. No wonder the serum hadn't worked. "Tell me what you are and I can better protect you."

She gripped her gold dress, ready to lift it and run. "Or kill me easier."

"I can call Father Riley up here to tell us." It was a bluff, pure and simple. The good father couldn't see into her heart any more than Damien could. But it worked.

She swallowed hard. "I'm a half-breed."

He could have cursed. But he didn't. "I asked for a full succubus." His powers, his truth serum, only worked on full-blooded she-demons.

She pushed a lock of blond hair away from her eyes. "They were all busy, okay?" she snapped. "Besides, I didn't see you complaining last night."

He had to end this. "Fine. We're going to go downstairs and see Father Riley." They'd get their annulment and then . . . He didn't know what. One step at a time.

She didn't look convinced.

"Father Riley won't send you back to hell," Damien explained. At least not in public.

She didn't appear too comforted. "Back to hell? I've never even been to hell." That was surprising. He'd assumed all demons were from hell. "Besides"—she crossed her hands over her chest—"You don't know Father Riley."

Damien had a pretty decent idea. The good father had been trying to exorcise the demons that had emerged since the Vegas Cleansing of 2009. But it didn't make sense to banish this one. At least not right now. "Father Riley won't kill you. I won't let him."

"Who are you?" she asked slowly.

If she only knew.

He stood in front of the door, blocking her only way out. "I'm the best thing you've got going right now."

She cringed. "And I thought this morning couldn't get any worse."

That actually offended him. There were a lot of women over the years who would have probably been glad to marry him. If he'd allowed himself to date.

Now that he'd actually made love for the first time, she was afraid he was going to send her to hell. "Listen, sweetheart. If I was going to slay you, I would have done it last night."

Her mouth gaped open. "I married a demon slayer?"

He actually enjoyed that. It wasn't easy to pull one over on a demon. Or a half-demon, as she happened to be.

Her emerald-green eyes were round with surprise. "I had *sex* with a demon slayer?"

He gave her a piercing look. "I'm not even supposed to have sex."

He'd had more important things to do—like this job. He'd shut down the demon portal into Las Vegas. Considering what had happened the last time demons got out of control here, that was a good thing.

She shook her head, her thoughts a million miles away. "I married a holy warrior. My boss is going to kill me."

"Join the club." He'd never live it down.

"No, I mean really kill me." She sat down on the bed. "At first I thought I could just lose my job. Or be mocked for the next six thousand years." She looked up at him. "But Napthulo will slaughter me for this."

He believed her. Her boss was as bad as they came.

"Stay away from Napthulo," he told her. No good could come of her confessing her sins to scum like that.

Besides, Damien was too close to nabbing the demon lord of Las Vegas. He didn't need her to blow his cover.

"We'll get an annulment." Damien sat down next to her. Still, he was careful to place himself between Shiloh and the door. "You can call in sick to work for a few days," he told her.

"A few days?" she asked, her eyes pleading.

"I'm close to taking the whole place down. You don't want to be there anyway."

Why was he protecting her? He'd always had a soft spot for damsels in distress but this was ridiculous.

"You'll be under guard, of course. I can't have you warning them." He just needed to get through to a full-blooded succubus. "You are one of the only half-breeds working for the boss, aren't you?"

He couldn't imagine Napthulo surrounding himself with lesser demons.

"I'm the only one," she said, her voice small.

"Good." He hoped she was telling the truth.

She rumpled her dress between her fingers. "You used me," she said. If he didn't know better, he'd think she was hurt. The truth was, they'd both taken things from each other.

"You seduced me," he reminded her.

She looked up at him then, unshed tears in her eyes. "That's totally different. You knew what you were getting."

He most certainly did not. He was a standout among slayers, known for his power to resist succubi. Now that he knew what had gone wrong, he was going back in.

Napthulo had made a fatal error. According to spies on the inside, he'd opened up the Vault of Power. It was the very portal that had brought him into this world—and the one that could send him back to hell for good.

"Have you been in Napthulo's Vault?" he asked her.

The question surprised her. "No. Of course not. It's completely off-limits."

Maybe so, but the demon was greedy. He was placing the final touches on his latest project, The Fire Storm, a mega hotel that some slayers believed could transport souls directly to hell. Damien wasn't sure if he believed the hype or not, but whenever a demon opened a portal, it never turned out well.

He needed access. He needed to bring one of Napthulo's demons under his control. And if not this one . . .

Damien stopped.

Why not this one?

Shiloh studied him carefully. "Why are you looking at me like that?"

She was smart. She was on the inside. He knew he could work with her and he certainly had something on her.

"You want an annulment, sweetheart?"

"Of course. That's what we've been talking about."

"I'll give you an annulment, as soon as you help me take down your boss."

Panic flashed across her features. "Oh no."

It was perfect. He didn't need to depend on a serum. He had his own personal demon, one that had to be loyal or face the consequences. "You said yourself Napthulo is going to kill you."

Her breath came in short pants. "Only if he finds out about you," she protested.

"He will," Damien promised. Let her know what it felt like to do good.

Her eyes widened in horror. "Don't say that."

Damien couldn't help grinning. This could work out better than he'd hoped.

He closed his hand over her cold, shaking one. "Work with me, Shiloh." He hadn't chosen this any more than she had. But maybe, just maybe, he could ax Napthulo and at the same time, show this half-demon the light. "I may just be the best thing that ever happened to you."

Chapter Three

Shiloh still couldn't believe what she was hearing. "You want me to betray the demon king of Las Vegas?" She stared down at Damien, who was sitting smug and comfortable on the bed.

Napthulo was feared and revered by demons everywhere. He was one of the original fallen angels. He commanded thirty-six legions in hell. He'd blasted Pompeii on a dare.

And right now, he liked Shiloh. She was his special pet, the quirky little half-demon who had helped him back into his glory.

She chewed at her lip. The one he could ignore and starve because she wasn't as good as the others. The one he wouldn't miss, now that he had his Vegas business up and running.

Her stomach knotted at the thought. Shiloh stood, her toes grinding yet another wedding picture into the carpet. The blasted things were everywhere.

She couldn't stop a demon slayer on her own. Damien was going to try to take down The Seven Deadly Sins Casino and frankly, she didn't want to be anywhere close when it happened. She'd been nearly roasted alive the last time a slayer came to town. The Great Destroyer had taken out every succubus in North America.

Shiloh had barely escaped because she was a half-breed. But it had given her a sunburn she'd never forget. Now this slayer wanted her help to blow everything up again.

Damien leaned forward, elbows on his knees. "You said yourself he's going to kill you."

She glared back at him. The slayer was one to talk. "You could kill me."

In fact, the first thing he'd done this morning was reach into that silver suitcase with the strange symbols carved all over it.

It hit her like a bat out of hell. "You were going to kill me this morning."

"Slay you," he corrected.

Oh, this was just too awful to contemplate. "Kill me."

He gave a small, satisfied smile. "But I didn't."

Well, didn't he deserve a medal? "Glad you managed to hold yourself back," she said, scanning the room for a weapon that might fend off a demon slayer. Everything was bolted down. As if a cheap lamp would stop a switch star.

He was following her now, amused.

She grabbed the obnoxious pink teddy bear. She wanted to toss it at his head. But the jerk would only laugh harder. Instead she wrapped her hands around the grinning bear's neck and squeezed.

These demon slayers thought they were so high and mighty. Yes, some demons were out of control. She could admit that. And the succubi at The Seven Deadly Sins Casino were as plastic and heartless as they came. But this guy was ready to damn her before he even knew her—after he'd slept with her and stolen her powers. She gave the love bear's head an extra twist.

Damien placed a hand on her shoulder. "Take me to Napthulo's portal." It wasn't a request. It was a demand, from a man who was used to getting what he wanted.

She shoved the bear against his chest. "Why should I?" She was sick of being treated like everyone's puppet. "You know what? Smite me. Go ahead. I dare you."

The demon slayer stood there, not quite sure what to do with the stuffed bear. "Shiloh, I don't want to smite you."

Fat lot of nerve he had. "Oh, so you'll marry me, but you won't smite me."

"Damn it, Shiloh." He tossed the bear on top of a thoroughly ravaged room service tray. "I know you're not mixed up in this and I don't want to see you hurt."

"Too late for that," she groused.

"I just need to reach Napthulo's portal."

Now that took the cake. "How am I supposed to know where to find Napthulo's portal?" He'd bound himself to her, wouldn't let her go and now he was asking the impossible.

"It's in his bedroom," Damien said.

"Oh." Imagine that. "I know how to get in there."

"I figured as much," he said, digging his fingers through his hair.

For once, she kept her mouth shut. It was true. Only succubi were allowed in to please Napthulo in his private chambers. Although it usually meant every succubus but Shiloh.

The demon had hired her to get the business going again. He still bore a grudge against half-breeds. But she could enter, just like the others.

Of course he didn't expect her to be leading a demon slayer into his lair. Curses. She'd finally carved a tiny piece of freedom for herself and now this demon slayer was going to blow it all to hell.

She crossed her arms over her chest. She didn't owe

Damien anything after last night. She didn't owe her life to Napthulo either, even if he thought he owned her. "And why on earth is Napthulo keeping the portal in his bedchamber?"

Damien gave her an arched look. "Demons are arrogant."

True. "And it's not like any of the girls would bother it." Succubi lived to please.

Besides, a portal had brought every one of the girls, save Shiloh, out of hell and to Vegas. Why would anyone want to destroy one?

Anyone besides Shiloh.

Her stomach flip-flopped.

She needed time to think, decide. Someone was going down and she needed to be on the winning side. The demon slayer was cocky. Smart, too. She had no doubt he was powerful. But Napthulo hadn't survived since the dawn of time by being stupid.

If only the demon slayer would leave her alone. Her mouth went dry as Damien trailed his fingers down her arm. Heat and raw energy radiated from his fingers. Was it a caress? Or a warning?

His hazel eyes bit into her. "Napthulo is going down, Shiloh. Do you really want to cling to him?"

Shiloh groaned. "It's not that simple." Not for someone who was bound, like her.

She turned toward the window, to the rising sun over The Strip. The demon slayer actually seemed concerned whether or not she'd be hurt by the fall of Napthulo. It was strange. The demon certainly wouldn't spare a thought for her.

Yet there was more at stake than just her life. She might not mind seeing the demon go down, but she had friends inside that casino and she refused to hurt the few creatures who'd dared to care about her.

"Work with me," he insisted.

She whirled to face him. "Why? Have you decided to kill me after all? Mr. Kill Things First and Ask Questions Later?"

He threw up his hands. "I'm a demon slayer. What do you want me to do?"

"For your information, there are other creatures in that casino that have done nothing to you." There was Fawzi, who only wanted to protect her. Rufus, the sweetest hellhound who ever lived. Neither one of them would know what to do in hell, or wherever Damien sent them. "You're talking like you have a right to just slay whoever you want."

He actually seemed surprised at that. Arrogant jerk. He stood so damned tall and resolute.

It wasn't right and it wasn't fair and—

"It's happening, Shiloh," he said, as if daring the very demons of hell to stop him. "Whether you want it to or not."

"Has anyone ever told you you're an asshole?"

"No," he said, as if the very idea shocked him.

Hades have mercy. She rubbed her eyes, trying to think.

It wasn't that she had problems with the idea of betraying the mighty Napthulo. Shiloh was half-demon after all. Evil deeds came with the territory.

If anything, the other demons would be impressed.

And if news made it as high as Satan, the devil himself wouldn't mind. He admired treachery.

Maybe she could work out a compromise. "Okay, Saint Damien."

He scowled. "Don't blaspheme."

She ignored him. "If you're going to try to take out Napthulo . . ." She couldn't stop it. She could only survive it. "If I help you, you have to get me and a few of my friends out. Unharmed." Napthulo and the plastic demons could find another way out of hell as long as Fawzi and Rufus were safe.

He leaned a shoulder against the wall by the window. "I can't rescue demonic minions, Shiloh." He didn't even pretend to consider it. Which ticked her off.

"You say that as if you didn't sleep with a demonic minion. Hmmm . . . last night."

Desire crept over her as she remembered the way she'd backed him against the wall and taken him in her mouth. He sure hadn't minded her then.

"Shiloh," he warned.

Her body flushed and she let out a little moan as the desire washed over her. She needed a touch of comfort right now, some nice healthy lust.

He looked stricken.

In fact, she could go for a morning snack. Most of the time, she could go longer, but whatever had bound their powers seemed to have intensified her ardor. In fact, she was as hungry as if she'd gone days and days without.

His gaze dropped to her chest. She felt it like a touch. Her nipples tightened almost to the point of pain as she strolled toward him, hips swaying. He watched her like a starving man.

She brushed her breasts against his chest. "Let go." She ran her tongue along his collarbone, his throat, that sensitive spot behind his ear.

"Shiloh. We can't." His voice was hoarse now, uncertain.

She rubbed against the length of him. He was hard as a rock. "Oh, I think you're ready. And I'm certainly ready."

"No," he said, breathing hard, eyes on the ceiling. "We can't do that again. Ever."

But he didn't push her away.

"Say it," she whispered in his ear.

"What?" he croaked.

"Say the word." She ran her fingers down his chest, down to where his jeans were slung low on his hips. "Sex."

She teased him, her touch lingering where his jeans met flesh.

He licked his lips. For the first time, she saw his carefully crafted wall crack. "I don't need to say it. You know what I mean."

Amazing that this man, who had so much to give, held himself back so fiercely. "You're too uptight to say it."

He looked her in the eye, struggling in a way she'd never understand. "Which is why it can't happen again. Ever."

Wrong answer. "You should have thought of that before you let yourself get bonded to me. I need sex from you, Damien." She dropped to her knees in front of him, flipping open his top button, then another. And another. "I can't feed off anyone else."

"Feed?" He said it like the idea revolted him. "Get up." He pushed off the wall, buttoning his jeans, stalking toward the other side of the room.

Shiloh dropped her hands to the floor, aching with unspent lust. She had to be the only succubus who had such a hard time getting sex.

Damien paced by the door, still hard as a rock. Why was he being so difficult?

"You're going to stop the seduction right now," he ordered. "We have work to do."

If she didn't get the demon slayer back into bed—soon—she was going to explode.

He continued on as if she wasn't about to throw herself at him again. She would if she thought she could get away with it.

Damien pulled on a T-shirt. Then he selected a gray sweater out of the closet. He finished with a leather jacket.

"Fine." She slowly rose to her feet, so turned on it hurt to move. She'd never had a partnership. She wondered what it would be like to be an equal. "I'll help you on one condition."

"Shiloh," he warned.

"Let me get my friends out. Fawzi is an ifrit that Napthulo won in a card game with Nostradamus."

Damien raised a brow.

"Fawzi is harmless, a captive." Like her. "And Rufus is a sweet little hellhound." She stood her ground as he scrubbed a hand over his chin, frowning.

He paused, shoulders stiff. "Agreed," he finally said. "Partner with me and no harm will come to your friends."

Her stomach tingled with the weight of what she was willing to promise. She also felt a surge of power. It was a heady feeling to decide her own destiny, even though she'd just leapt headlong out of her predictable world.

She rested a hand on her hip. "Well, demon slayer. It looks like we have a deal."

He laughed at that. "Yes, I suppose we do." He studied her, the mirth fading from his eyes. "I'm not a man who compromises easily."

And she was one who had always compromised too much. "I like a challenge," she teased. It felt new, exciting, to take a stand at last.

He gave an exaggerated groan. "Of all the gin joints, in all the towns, in all the world, you had to walk into mine."

"Yes, well, it's not yours yet." There was a mega demon to be dealt with first.

"True," he said, switching to business mode. He moved over to the silver suitcase, snapping the clasps closed. "We missed our window of opportunity last night, but I have my contacts trailing the demon. As soon as there's another chance, we'll jump on it."

She braced herself. "Napthulo is incredibly smart. We'll have to move fast."

The sight of Damien next to the suitcase reminded her of a time not too long ago when he'd stood in that same spot, gloriously naked. Hades. He looked almost as good with his clothes on. Almost.

Shiloh trailed her fingers down her gold dress. "I think it would help if we had sex."

Damien about choked. "No."

"Fine." She pouted. "We'll do it your way."

She'd lead a demon slayer into the inner sanctum. She'd take down her boss. She'd find a way to save her friends. And come hell or high water, she'd find a way to free Damien too.

Chapter Four

He should have just slayed her and saved his sanity. Instead he'd nearly taken her. Again.

Damien leaned his head against the back wall of the slowest-moving elevator in Vegas.

"Do you want to wear my coat?" he asked.

She fiddled with the gold chain around her neck. "I'm already dressed."

It didn't count. Her gold dress clung to every curve. He remembered what those curves had felt like under him last night. And above him. And . . . he felt himself grow hard. Damnation.

The door dinged open in the lobby. "Come on," he said as he launched himself off the wall. "We'll get you a ride home," he added, trying not to cringe.

So this was it. Damien, who had slayed countless minions of the devil was about to send a demon home in a taxi.

Heaven help him, it almost felt like a victory.

She tilted her head. "Do you realize that when you run your hand through your hair like that, it makes it stick up on end? You look like Matthew McConaughey."

He led her through the lobby of the hotel. "I have no idea who that is," he said, trying to focus on the clanging slot machines, the milling tourists, anything but her.

When they reached the cab stand outside, he relented. "I'll call you when it's time to go back in. In the mean-time—" he stared at her from her pink painted toes to her mane of unruly blond waves. She was a walking wet dream. "Act casual. Tempt the masses."

She cocked her head. "You think that's what I do?"

Truthfully, he had no idea. He fought back a wave of jealousy. She'd gotten under his skin easy enough.

He dug through his wallet for cab fare, cursing himself for his weakness. He didn't want her seducing anyone else. He wanted her attention.

This was so screwed up.

At long last, he tucked her into an aquamarine Gossamer Cab and watched her drive away.

Shiloh did not look back.

It shouldn't have bothered him, he told himself. She had her head on straight, at least for the moment.

He made his way to the elevator bank.

Damien was still stewing as he shoved his card into the door slot of his hotel room. He just had to work with this woman until he could take down her boss. Then he'd let her go.

Damien frowned as the hotel room door clicked closed behind him. He surveyed the room. Hell. The tousled sheets, the wedding pictures scattered across the room, the damned pink bear—it reminded him of her.

He'd box it all up. Or toss it in the bathtub. He should have just thrown it all away.

But he didn't.

Instead, he called Father Riley. "The annulment's off," he barked into his cell phone while opening his silver suitcase.

His switch stars were laid out in neat rows, cushioned in foam core.

He could hear the old priest chuckling on the other line. "Who's still married, son?"

Damien didn't want to have this conversation. "You wouldn't believe it if I told you."

"I don't know," the priest said in that frustratingly even tone of his. "I've seen some strange things in my day."

Time to change the subject. "My mission was a bust last night," Damien said, double-checking his switch star holster. It held five stars. The rest, he'd have to take in a backpack and hope security didn't search it. "I'm going back in."

The Council would contact him. When another opportunity arose, he'd be ready.

"Did you let her go?" the priest asked.

"Who?"

"You know who."

Damien gritted his teeth. Would it be rude to hang up on a priest? "I've got bigger problems."

Like what to do about a certain half-demon. He'd trapped Shiloh. She had to help him.

Damien tugged his sweater down, remembering the way she'd run her fingers along his chest. He sighed and shoved the thought out of his mind. As long as she didn't take him down, this might just work.

Shiloh sat at a patio table outside Starbucks and blasted a young hunk with a bolt of lust. He kept walking. She dug her elbows into the table, crunched her fists under her chin and willed him to turn around. *Look back. Feel me.*

Nada.

She sighed, glancing at her cold cafe misto. It had been two days since her quickie wedding. She needed to stop torturing herself. Her powers were tied up with Damien's. There was no getting them back, not until she gave the demon slayer what he wanted.

For all of her thousands of years on this earth, she wished she had an easier time with change. Frankly, she felt like a big scaredy cat most of the time. Dealing with full-blooded demons did that to a girl.

Now she was on call, waiting to meet up with Damien at The Seven Deadly Sins. They'd rendezvous in one of the theme rooms. She was rooting for Lust.

Never mind that Damien would still insist that he wanted her only for her access code. But she knew better. Shiloh had a few millennia's experience with men. She saw how he responded to her. And she found that fascinating.

As if thinking could make wishes come true, her phone buzzed. She dug it out of her purse. "Damien?"

"Don't use my name," he said, his voice low and sexy.

Oh please. "But it is you. I knew it was you." A niggle of unease touched her stomach. She didn't know how she knew. Perhaps their powers were more entwined than she'd realized.

"We have another opportunity. Meet me at your work. I'll request you."

That last part warmed her heart. He'd ask for her.

She snapped the phone closed. Of course he'd ask for her, she chastised herself. He needed her to break into Napthulo's inner sanctum. Still, it made her slightly breathless to know she'd see Damien soon.

Shiloh's heels clicked as she made her way down a long hallway at the back of The Seven Deadly Sins Casino.

Now that she was here, her excitement had been replaced with something else—the dripping fear that she was about to end her life as she knew it. She pasted a smile on her face.

Breathe.

Walk.

Act casual.

She was so deep in thought that she jumped as she pushed through the human-repelling energy shield.

Zap.

The static electric shock zinged her to her toes and reminded her to stay focused. She might not be trained like Damien, but she could keep her wits about her. This wasn't a game. Lives were at stake, namely hers, Fawzi's, Rufus's—even Damien's. Although she doubted the demon slayer would admit it.

Rufus the hellhound danced and barked at her approach and she gave him an extra long hug. He used it as an opportunity to lick her silly. "I've got you, hound doggie," she said, feeling the familiar comfort of his wiry fur against her skin.

She'd save him.

Shiloh gave the hellhound a final pat. He whined as she turned the corner toward the She-Demons assignment desk.

Jeebers the fairy raised his tiny little eyebrows at her as she approached. He adjusted his reading glasses. "Fine for you to show your face around here again."

Shiloh waved him off. "I was sick," she said, both of them knowing full well that succubi didn't get sick. She gave him her best pouty look. "I think I'll feel better if you put me back in Lust."

It was a long shot, she knew. But perhaps the case of Fitz's Root Beer had already arrived.

He scowled, dashing any hope of that. "I'm not putting you in Lust again. You ran off halfway through your shift."

"The client wanted to get out and enjoy Vegas," she

said, pretending not to know she'd violated about twelve casino rules.

The fairy looked down his glasses at her. "And then I got drunk calls at four in the morning. Please tell me you didn't actually set sail a hundred tiny paper pirate ships in the Venetian Grand Canal."

Oh no. Shiloh's stomach sank. "What else did you hear?" Her secret might already be out.

"Isn't that enough?" the fairy snapped. He jabbed at the computer keyboard in front of him. "If it's any consolation, you didn't completely ruin your chances with our newest client. He's requested you again, for whatever room you're in."

He said it as if he knew something.

Shiloh kept her face a blank slate. "Have you completed the background check on him?"

"No." The fairy kept typing. "Too tired from annoying phone calls."

Thank goodness. Damien's identity was safe. For now.

"Succubus number 14, I have you in Sloth tonight," he said, daring her to protest.

"Of course." Massaging men's temples. At least they would be Damien's temples.

"Fawzi's looking for you," he said, handing her the assignment slip.

Big surprise. The ifrit was probably going crazy. And now she had to convince him to hang out in Sloth and betray their boss. Good thing she had an idea.

Chapter Five

Damien rolled over in a massive beanbag chair in order to get a better view of *Wife Swap*. He used his arm as a pillow and fought back a yawn. Not that the television show was boring. It was an interesting bit of reality, far more addicting than he would have imagined an hour ago. No, the yawn was for the fact that he could already feel his body turning to mush.

Damien sank farther into the chair.

He was in Sloth, the least sexy room he could imagine. Therefore, it was the perfect place for his next run-in with Shiloh. He didn't want to think about kissing her, touching her, or the way her hands felt when she wrapped them around his shoulders.

Stop thinking about it.

Yeah right.

He fought his beanbag chair for a better position. His night in Lust had only been the most incredible night of his life. And that was the part he could remember.

He couldn't help wondering if Shiloh could be saved. He knew she'd been led to believe that she had to work with monsters like Napthulo. But she wasn't corrupt like him, or evil. Damien had seen the good in her. If she could live with those demons for centuries and still retain her goodness and vitality, then she was an incredible woman indeed, a woman worth saving.

Of course it wasn't his job to convert she-demons. He'd made quite a reputation killing them instead.

But Shiloh wasn't a true demon. She had choices, even if she didn't know that.

Yet another reason Napthulo had to be eliminated. Damien blew out a breath and focused on the task at hand. The Council had an agent observing Napthulo's inner sanctum. Once the coast was clear, Damien and Shiloh would make their move.

If Shiloh ever showed up.

Where were the she-demons?

He lifted his head and did a double check of the massive room devoted to laziness. Damien had chosen the beanbag area, only because he'd been way too tempted by the row of velvet recliners in the back. Then you had the water bed pit and the pile of pillows. Massive televisions lined the walls, spewing sports and junk television.

Damien had avoided college football, classic movies and anything else that would have normally intrigued him. Instead he went for reality television, hoping he wouldn't get drawn in. And now he found himself rooting for the fire-eating wife of a traveling circus lion tamer to give the daughter of the uber-strict pageant mom a makeover.

This place really was dangerous—with or without demons.

He ran a hand over his shirt and felt his hidden switch star holster. Five shots.

It should be plenty. A well-aimed switch star could slice through a demon and whirl back to Damien in under a second. If The Council's spy did his job, Damien wouldn't even encounter any spawn of Satan, not until he started sucking them back into hell.

He'd enter Napthulo's chambers using Shiloh's code. Once he located the portal, he'd reverse the energy and vacuum Napthulo, the she-demons and every single demonic creature back into the second level of hell. Then he'd seal them there for all eternity.

Except for Shiloh. Damien felt a twinge of guilt. He didn't think she'd go down, not if it hadn't happened the last time. And besides, he couldn't see her as damned.

Not really.

Or was he going crazy?

Damien pounded at the beanbag chair, trying to get comfortable.

What was taking Shiloh so long? He'd called her almost an hour ago.

Why was he so impatient? It wasn't as if he needed to see her. He certainly didn't miss her. But he would like to have her around. She wasn't bad company.

The hairs on his arms stood on end as the energy in the room surged. His skin tingled and he tensed, his body on high alert. A door creaked open behind the chain of recliners and Damien recoiled as he beheld a succubus in her true form.

He'd never seen one like that before. The she-demons he'd killed had already been feeding. That was how he'd spotted them.

But he knew from stories and from the overwhelming stench of sulfur exactly what he was seeing. She looked pale and plasticlike, as though she was a department-store mannequin. Gauzy hair wisped about her face and her entire body seemed to glow around the edges. Her features were as frighteningly regular as a plastic doll's. There were two more behind her.

Depravity hung heavy in the air, along with unmistakable, infectious evil.

He almost cringed as two more glided into Sloth. The true mortals in the room didn't seem to notice the way they seemed to float. These demons had almost no natural movement at all.

Shiloh entered last, petite yet resolute in a pale peach gown. She'd pulled on a pair of white evening gloves, most likely to hide the wedding ring on her finger. One glove drooped past her elbow as she hesitated in the doorway.

She didn't belong here any more than Damien did. She closed the door, purposely avoiding his gaze.

This might be the life she'd been forced to endure, but this wasn't what she was created to be. Damien could see it. Why couldn't she?

Damien caught her eye. She was so glad to see him that his mouth twitched into an encouraging smile. He couldn't help it.

She quickly hid her emotion and adopted a mask of seductive serenity. Shiloh held his gaze as she strolled toward him, knowing exactly what the sway of her hips did to him.

"Good to see you again," she said, sinking down next to him. She smelled like warm vanilla sugar.

Minx. "You made an impression last time."

Her eyes danced as she tucked a strand of blond hair behind her ear. "Would you like me to massage your temples?"

He cleared his throat. "That's okay. I think we can hold off on the touching."

"No," she said, sneaking a glance around the room. "I'm here to touch you. It's my job," she said under her breath. "So unless you want me to pick where I touch you . . ."

"Temples would be fine," Damien said quickly.

"I thought so." Delicate fingers touched him on either side of his head. "Although you have no idea what you're missing."

She was wrong. Damien had way too good an idea of what this woman could do to him. He wanted nothing more than to slip that pale silk gown from her shoulders and kiss those magnificent breasts. He'd tempt her. Tease her. Give to her. He wondered if she'd ever had the pleasure of being seduced. He doubted it.

She didn't have to live like this.

Her fingers slid through his hair and a small groan escaped him.

"You're such a puppy dog," she said, pleased.

"Woof."

She giggled at that.

He found he liked making her smile. "See? You don't need a hellhound," he said, glancing up at her. "You have me."

"Rufus gives me less trouble," she said, grinning.

"I can't argue there," he said, as she swatted at him.

He dug an elbow into the beanbag chair and sat forward. "Listen," he said, taking both of her hands in his. "I know this is rough on you, but I will take care of you." He squeezed her hands. "Rufus too."

He could see his promise pleased her a great deal. "Fawzi, too," she said.

"Anybody else?" he quipped.

She made a show of tapping a finger against her cheek. "Maybe I'll draw up a list."

He took her finger and kissed it. "You're going to be the end of me."

Funny how this felt like it was only the beginning.

Damien's mirth was cut short as he watched a succubus glide behind them. The creature stopped next to a short, stocky man two beanbag chairs down. Anger welled up in Damien as the succubus touched her client on the shoulder. The man groaned, arching like a cat as she fed off the briefest contact.

He itched to bury a switch star in her chest.

Shiloh planted her hands on his shoulders as they watched.

He'd dedicated his entire life to annihilating that kind of evil.

Shiloh sensed it too. "Damien—" she warned.

Remember why you're here.

He'd come to exterminate the entire roach's den, not pick a fight in Sloth. As great as it would feel to blow these she-demons straight to hell, one wrong move in this crowd and he'd have some dead humans on his conscience as well.

Still, watching them made his entire body burn with fury.

"It's wrong," he hissed.

"I know," she murmured.

As if in slow motion, he saw the succubus grip the other man's head. Her hand tightened as yellowed talons hissed and curled from an appendage that was more claw than hand. They weaved through the man's hair. Tendons and muscles worked under the creature's thinning skin.

She was a devil who feasted on men. A cunningly masked locust.

Shiloh's hands had moved to Damien's upper arms. She held him back against the chair as every nerve in his body vibrated with the urge to attack.

The air around the full-blooded she-demon shimmered with energy. Her pale body bloomed with life. Her shapeless gown wound into a red teddy, and her body morphed into a Victoria's Secret dream. Thick, black hair streamed down her back. Her cheeks were high, her lips full and seductive.

The man gaped at her, as if she were his deepest fantasy brought to life. Damien had no doubt she was.

The she-demon had hijacked the man's mind, rifled through his fantasies. And now she would feed on him.

Evil, pure evil. Damien triple-checked his switch stars, itching to hurl one through her skull.

Damien watched her siphon her victim's energy as she began massaging his feet. The man laid back and gave willingly.

Damien's fingers curled, his anger mounting.

"Not yet," Shiloh whispered in his ear.

The tickle of her breath aroused him and it pissed him off all over again.

Who was she to take up with these creatures? She should have stood up to them, or at least not taken part. But she was just as guilty as the rest of them. Using people. Feeding off people. These men had their wills and their very life forces weakened. Some turned to alcohol or drugs or sex after being with a succubus. They became addicts in a vain attempt to fill the hole that these creatures had dug inside them.

Some never made it out alive. They just disappeared. Lives were destroyed. Families were ruined. And for what? To enable men to pursue some sick fantasy—the seven deadly sins. There was a reason they'd been forbidden in the first place.

Sloth.

Greed.

Lust.

They weakened humans, made them susceptible to demons like Napthulo.

He couldn't wait to sink a switch star into the biggest locust of them all.

Damien's phone buzzed. It was a text from The Council.

Clear.

A dull satisfaction thudded in his chest. He refused to look at Shiloh as he tucked his phone back in his pocket. This was it. They had a straight shot at Napthulo's inner sanctum.

"Come on, demon," he said, shoving himself out of the beanbag. "I feel like taking a walk."

Chapter Six

"We can't leave," Shiloh protested as Damien walked straight for the door. "Not like this." He wasn't even ambling. He was charging through the Sloth room. She gripped his arm and almost fell backward in relief when he let her stop him.

"This way." She scanned the room, trying her best to act casual as she urged him past the pillows and to a curtained area behind the recliners. Luckily her coworkers were intent on their conquests. "Trust me."

An emotion that she couldn't quite place crossed his features. Indecision mixed with . . . what? Approval?

He took her hand and let her lead him to one of the hidden doors at the back of the room. She felt a burst of pleasure like a ray of sunshine burning bright. The powerful demon slayer was allowing her to lead him. For all of her doubts and worries about what would happen when he tried to take down Napthulo, his small gesture made her wonder if everything might just turn out right.

And even as she turned the knob, ready to sneak off with a client again, she couldn't help smiling.

He trusted her.

When had anyone else in her life given her this kind of a gift? She'd been desired, ordered about, bargained for and—in some centuries—feared. Trust was something new.

"Quiet now." Luckily, she was the first one to push through the door because a vicious hellhound waited on the other side. "Rufus," she whispered. The snarling beast turned into an eager puppy dog when he saw her.

"Ah, so this is the mutt," he said, closing the door behind them.

She buried her fingers in Rufus's thick, black fur and nuzzled him as he tried his darndest to lick her face, her arms, anywhere he could reach. He was the original cuddle beast. "Pet him."

"No thanks. I like having all my fingers."

She rolled her eyes at the big, brave demon slayer. "Come on, Rufus." The hellhound fell into eager step behind them as they made their way down the stark back hallway toward the service elevator.

They were out of range of the cameras, for now at least. That's why Shiloh had chosen to hide Rufus back here.

She felt a wave of excitement unlike any she'd felt for centuries.

"What are you smiling about?" Damien asked, glancing back at the hallway behind them.

"This," she said, enjoying the bemused look he gave her.

But truly, how could she begin to explain?

Yes, he was teaming with her to eliminate her boss. She couldn't forget that. But it was fun to have a partner, someone else to count on.

She'd been used for centuries. It was her job. But the way Damien treated her, the way he *saw* her, she was more than an object to him. She felt the difference down to her toes. And it was wonderful.

He moved to punch the button to the service elevator. "No," she said, and drew his hand back. Again, he let her. She gave his hand a small squeeze. "It's warded against outsiders," she explained.

Shiloh punched the button to the penthouse suite.

He checked the hallway behind them. "So far, so good."

She nudged against him. "That's because I'm good."

Shiloh had let it slip in the She-Demons dressing room that she was going to try to lure her client back behind the recliners for some Sloth room sex. The other succubi had laughed at her desperation and her inability to get a regular rotation in Lust.

Damien stood beside her, absently running a hand along her back as they waited. He didn't even want sex. He didn't want anything from her right then. Amazing.

She was scared to move, afraid to mess things up. The elevator chimed as the car clunked into place.

They both tensed as the bronze doors opened. It was empty inside.

"There will be cameras," she said, as he led her into the elevator. It was done in bronze art deco, with large lotus flowers and birds. Antique crystal sconces graced one wall and a gleaming chandelier hung overhead. Rufus curled around her legs, pawing the plush red carpeting as Shiloh pushed the code for the penthouse.

Damien laughed out loud. "6-6-6?"

She slid her arms around his shoulders and he stopped laughing. "Napthulo's lucky number. Now kiss me. We're on camera."

He hesitated. She could tell he wanted to.

She burned for a taste of him. He was an incredible-looking man. Still, she waited. She wasn't going to chase him anymore. This had to be his choice.

Anticipation snaked through her as he leaned forward, nuzzling her, his hot breath falling against the back of her ear. He stayed that way for a moment, drinking her in.

She almost broke. She wanted so badly to run her hands up over his muscular back and shoulders, to tempt him with a kiss that he'd never be able to refuse, to let him take her right here against the elevator wall.

She forced herself to hold still.

Wait for it.

Her body thrummed with anticipation as he took her by the chin and lowered his lips to hers. Slowly, almost reverently, he tasted her.

Shiloh moaned. This wasn't the kiss of a man who was pretending. He desired her, he needed her. He was willing to be vulnerable with her. It nearly did her in.

He caught the nape of her neck, entwining his fingers in her hair. His fingers tugged as he deepened the kiss.

She sank into him, reveling in the taste of him, the feel of him, the pleasure of connecting with him. His other hand caressed her side, just below her breasts, and she groaned out loud.

He gave her one sizzling nip. Then another. "Here's the plan," he whispered. "Are you listening?"

"Yes," she gasped as he trailed kisses down her neck. She was going to end up a puddle on the floor before this planning session was over.

He was hard as well. She could feel it. Her peach silk dress rubbed between them. She hadn't bothered with underwear.

"We'll enter using your code," he said, his breath harsh against her ear. "You stand watch."

"Stay close to me," she said on an exhale. "He won't spot you as easily with my energy as your shield."

Damien drew back, nipping at her lips. "He can't spot me."

Shiloh swallowed, running her fingers along Damien's jaw. "He will be able to sense you in his inner chamber."

"My sources say . . ."

She shook her head. "They're wrong." *Trust me.*

It was a test, one she sincerely hoped he passed.

He stopped, his cheek warm against hers. "Okay. We go in together."

His response nearly undid her.

The elevator clinked to a stop and he began to draw away from her. "Once I locate the portal, I'll reverse the energy and vacuum Napthulo and the rest of his minions to hell."

"Give me five minutes to get Fawzi and Rufus out."

"Be careful," he said.

She nodded. "You too."

The doors slid open.

A very angry Fawzi hovered on the other side. "Shiloh." He drew her name out like an angry father, shaking with indignation from his bald head to the wisp of smoke where his legs would have been.

Damien drew a switch star.

"No, wait," Shiloh protested. "This is my friend, Fawzi."

Damien blanched. "I'm saving *him*?"

"He's actually quite friendly," Shiloh said, inserting herself between Damien and the ifrit. "Sometimes."

Rufus started barking like a wild dog. Shiloh winced. They didn't need this kind of attention.

"I can explain," she said to Fawzi, glancing down the hallway on either side of Napthulo's massive front door. It was bronze, engraved with the demon's thirty-six legions of hell and framed with the skulls of his enemies. They gaped in bony, hollow-eyed terror, which was a pretty good idea when you were dealing with Napthulo.

"What have you done?" Fawzi thundered. "You banish me from the Sloth room. You make me hide in the master's private hallway and then you show up here with a client?"

"Will you let me explain?" she demanded.

At least the entryway was fairly contained. It cornered off after thirteen paces on each side. The demon was superstitious that way.

"You will be banished. Shamed." Fawzi stared at her gloved hand and went white from the tips of his ears to his smoky tail. "You will be killed."

Damien stared at the ifrit. "He can see through objects?"

Shiloh glanced at Damien. "Unfortunately."

"This could be good," he mused.

"Hush. I'm counting," she said, ticking off the skulls to make sure she got the right one. They were all the skulls of betrayers, but Judas was on the left, thirteenth from the top.

"Here we go. Judas Iscariot."

Damien about choked. "You mean Napthulo was the one who tempted—"

She knew where he was going. "No. He just won his skull in a card game."

Damien stood motionless, back to his old self. "I can see why a demon was needed to enter."

The comment hurt more than Shiloh cared to admit. "Yes. No pass code. Just evil-ness." The door locks clicked open.

She glanced up at Damien. "By now, the cameras will have a lock on us. Stay close and Napthulo will take longer to detect you." They had five minutes. Tops.

She opened the door to reveal Napthulo's ornate audience chamber. In here, he'd abandoned the art deco look in favor of the opulence of the kingdoms of old.

Rufus nosed his way past them.

The walls were done in gold gilt, engraved with scenes

from the many battles Napthulo had fought and won. Rich handwoven carpeting stretched across the room and curved up the stairs to an ornate throne made of gold, alabaster and—

"The bones of his enemies," Damien said under his breath.

"You catch on fast," Shiloh said, as the door closed with a boom behind them.

The cloying scent of incense mixed with sulfur hung low in the air. For the first time, she could feel the evil crawling over her skin.

Fawzi hovered beside her, his eyes wide with alarm. "We are not allowed in here."

"I'm a succubus," Shiloh said quickly, before she could agree with him.

Fawzi shook his head, his gold earrings slapping against his neck. "Yes, but you are a lesser—"

"Hey," Shiloh protested.

"You know what I mean. You are not a favorite and I am not a favorite . . ."

Yes, well they didn't have time to debate. "Can you sense it?" she asked Damien.

He'd drawn a switch star. Lovely. "It's around here somewhere," he said, moving like a predator.

She turned to Fawzi. "Where's Napthulo's portal?"

The ifrit gave her a bug-eyed look.

"We need to stay away," she lied.

"Yes." Fawzi scanned the room, his large copper-cuffed arms crossed over his chest. "Stay away from the mirrors on the ceiling of the bedroom. Do not even look at them."

Damien nodded.

"The bedroom is through that gold door," she told him. "The one with the Mongol invasion of Poland."

Fawzi grew as large as a bulldozer, his head touching

the ceiling of the audience chamber. "Stop," he commanded, his voice echoing.

Damien took cover behind the door and drew a switch star.

Fire shot out of the ifrit's fingertips. "I will smite you."

Shiloh wanted to smack her bodyguard. They didn't have time for this. "Do it and I go in there, Fawzi." She meant it. They were in too far to back out now.

She thought the ifrit was going to faint as Damien gave her a wicked grin and ducked into the bedroom.

This was madness. Fawzi wasn't going to cooperate. She was only making him suffer. Maybe if she could explain, but there was no time.

And so now, she'd end his suffering.

"Fawzi," she said, making her way to the ornate bar at the far end of the audience chamber.

"You are headed in the wrong direction." He hit his head on a chandelier and shrank back to normal size as he trailed after her. "We must leave."

"Yes," she agreed. "We must." She brushed past the top label alcohol, past the jars of eyeballs, innards and other intimate parts of Napthulo's enemies, and grabbed a gold ice bucket.

She caught the ifrit's tail. "I command thee enter."

Shiloh grimaced at the shock and anger on her friend's face as he was sucked down into the ice bucket. "I'm sorry," she said, placing the lid on top. "This is for your own good."

Fawzi didn't deserve to get mixed up in this drama. This way, if they were caught and Napthulo took his vengeance, her bodyguard would be blameless. And this way, she could get him out. Fawzi had never been real big on change. The ifrit hadn't even left the casino since it had been built. He needed a modern makeover too.

She carried the bucket under one arm and went to go find Damien. He was meditating.

"Hurry," she urged. "Napthulo will be able to sense you since you left my side. I'm not saying he's paying a lot of attention." Demons were notoriously cocky and Napthulo would have no reason to suspect a succubus would betray him. Still, the quicker they finished with this, the better.

"Got it." Damien climbed onto the bed. "You have to aim before shooting, or . . ." He trailed off.

Shiloh knew. Or he'd miss. She didn't even want to think of what would happen then.

Shiloh set down the ice bucket and followed Damien onto the bed, tamping down lustful thoughts as she admired his firm backside.

"Go. It will take me about five minutes to raise the power level." He gave her a steady look. "Run fast. I don't want you caught up in this." He raised his arms and she felt his power vibrate through the room.

She nodded, backing away, realizing she'd never asked him how he planned to get out.

"Run," he ordered. She saw the light then, pure and white as it radiated from his hands.

She fought for breath. Rufus stood next to her, barking.

Damien's arms began to shake. Something was wrong.

"Shiloh." It was both a demand and a good-bye. She saw it in his eyes. Something was terribly wrong.

A dull lump formed in her chest. This was it. The final stand. Even if he survived, she knew she'd never see him again. Tears threatened. *Run. Don't look back.*

She grabbed Fawzi from the floor and took Rufus by the collar. "Come on. Let's go."

She'd been ready to take down her boss, and it was nothing to her, but leaving Damien felt like a betrayal.

In a few minutes, it would all be over.

She stopped just short of the throne as she heard the front door locks slide open. Then she felt the overwhelming presence of the demon.

Damien.

The demon slayer's power swirled around her. He hadn't had enough time. The demon would find him and kill him. She fought her way back into the bedroom.

Wind whipped through the room. "What are you still doing here?" he demanded.

She slammed the door behind her. "Damien, he's back!"

He didn't question her. He didn't argue. Shiloh watched as he wound his power back into himself. Damien dropped to his hands and knees on the bed, his chest heaving.

Shiloh scrambled toward him. "We have to get you out of here."

Hope mixed with the cold reality of defeat. "Is there another way?" he asked, clutching his chest.

"No," she said, her heart sinking as she shielded him. It was a temporary measure at best. Napthulo had entered the audience chamber. He'd sense Damien at any minute, if he hadn't already.

"Shiloh," the demon uttered. "Show yourself."

She swallowed hard. "I'm waiting for you in the bedroom," she said, trying her desperate best to sound breezy and seductive.

Damien gave her a pained look.

What did he expect? She was a succubus. She only hoped the demon would buy it.

The demon snorted. "I don't lie with your kind."

And she was grateful for that. Despite her heritage, demons had always creeped her out. There was something about having a direct line to hell that Shiloh wanted no part of.

The demon approached. She could hear his footsteps and smell the overwhelming stench of sulfur.

Rufus growled and began barking.

The footsteps halted. "What is it, beast?"

The hellhound's barking grew more insistent, moving away from Shiloh. Oh Rufus! Her hope swelled as the front door opened and Rufus took off down the hallway barking.

Damien stood half bent over at her side. He encased her hand in his. "Did the demon follow?" he asked.

Worry tugged at her. "I don't know." But it was the only chance they had. "Come on."

Shiloh led him out through the audience chamber, and after a quick glance, down the hallway to the right. They turned the corner and she pushed open the door to the back staircase.

"Damn." He flinched behind her.

"Sorry." It was warded, but they didn't have a choice. She gripped his hand tightly, offering what protection she could as they ran.

She'd never raced down so many stairs in her life. She barely felt them as they took each circular level. Sixty-nine, sixty-eight, sixty-seven, lower and lower until they reached a back service exit.

"One last ward," she warned, clutching Damien's hand tightly and feeling the sizzle on her skin as they burst out into the moonlight pooling behind the hotel.

They'd been inside longer than she realized. She was momentarily disoriented, confused.

She fought for breath, her pulse pounding in her head. She tasted blood at the back of her throat.

"This way," he said as he grabbed her hand and dragged her along the outside of the massive hotel parking garage. He threw open the door to a black Jaguar parked in the alley. She slid into the passenger seat and with a hard jerk and a squeal of tires, they sped off into the night.

She choked back a sob as the lights of Vegas whizzed

past her window. They'd failed. Worse yet, she'd lost Rufus. And she'd left poor Fawzi locked in an ice bucket in the main audience chamber.

She'd never get him out now. Napthulo was surely onto her. Her friends were in worse danger than before. And a part of her heart had broken. It was all her fault.

Chapter Seven

Shiloh shoved her head back against the plush leather seat and stared at the ceiling of the black Jaguar. "We failed. I trusted you and we failed."

Jaw clenched, Damien focused on the road ahead. "We can go back in."

"Are you kidding?" Once was a risk. Twice was suicide. "We broke in his door. We left Fawzi in an ice bucket." Her voice cracked. "You created a firestorm in his bedroom."

Damien glanced at her. "You broke in his door."

"Hades have mercy." She buried her head in her hands.

Damien returned his focus to the road ahead. "He's not going to suspect a problem with a succubus in his bedroom."

She straightened at that. "Yes, well he's going to have an issue with all kinds of demon slayer powers flying around. What were you doing in there anyway?"

His power had surrounded him in a riot of blue. It was the most amazing thing she'd ever seen. Probably the most deadly too.

"I was reversing the portal. It's not pretty." His fingers gripped the steering wheel, then loosened. "I basically had to pit my power against the demon's. I was using my strength to neutralize his and create a vacuum."

She'd heard of that kind of power, but had never seen it. "Isn't that dangerous?"

He gave her a look like she had to be kidding.

Undeterred, Shiloh shifted in her seat. "What I mean is that you were trying to neutralize Napthulo's strength by using your own." They drove in silence for a moment while she thought and he acted like a big brick wall. "You're not stronger than Napthulo," she finally said. He couldn't be.

"No." He wasn't going to make this easy.

The truth of it seeped over her. "You were going to kill yourself."

This brave, smart, powerful man was going to end his existence to destroy a creature like Napthulo. What a waste. Napthulo would live. In hell, of course. But it wouldn't be the end of the demon, only the slayer.

Damien kept his eyes on the road. "What do you care?"

Shiloh wanted to say she didn't, but she couldn't quite bring herself to be that cruel.

She settled on a half-truth instead. "Well, if you don't get them all, it would be nice to have someone to hide behind as Napthulo blasts my butt."

He leveled a stern gaze at her. "I told you to run."

She'd wanted to. She still wanted to. Shiloh would love nothing more than to run and keep going.

"How close were you?" she asked.

"I don't know." He shook his head. "I was ready to reverse the portal, but something was blocking me."

"What?" she demanded.

He looked worried. "I don't know."

Lovely. He might not even be able to pull this off. She didn't know what she'd been thinking. Napthulo was too powerful to be bested by a demon slayer.

Shiloh was screwed either way. If Damien created the portal, he'd most likely kill himself and leave her alone to pick up the pieces. If he failed and survived, Napthulo would take them both out.

She gazed out the car window. They'd reached the end of The Strip. The desert lay beyond. Worry niggled at her. "Where are you taking me?" She'd assumed they'd hole up in his hotel room.

His lips curved. "Trust me."

Hades help her, she did. Damien had proven that he'd do what he could to keep her safe. But she wasn't so sure she trusted him to keep himself out of trouble. More and more, she was seeing that this drive to take down Napthulo could turn into a suicide mission for the slayer. She didn't understand it.

Shiloh stared out at the shadows of scrub brush and cacti in the blackened desert. "Do you want to die?" She shouldn't care, but she did.

A tense silence stretched between them. "Of course not."

It was harder to gauge his reaction now that they'd left behind the lights of the city. The inside of the car was awash in darkness. "Then why?" she asked.

"Sacrifice yourself," he said simply. "It's one of the three truths of the demon slayers."

She couldn't believe what she was hearing. "It's a wonder you're still alive."

He shot her a look. "You must sacrifice yourself, step outside who you think you should be, or you'll never truly live." He paused for a moment, with an intent look about him, as if he'd made some kind of discovery himself. "Demon slayers can't hold back," he said, almost to himself.

Shiloh shifted in her seat. "Well, it's a dumb rule."

He made a hard left down a bumpy dirt road. "Why? What rules do you live by, Shiloh?"

Apprehension snaked through her. "I do what pleases me."

"No, you don't," he said. "Does it please you to be a virtual slave to a demon? Does it please you to be used every night?"

What did he care? "Stop it."

He took another hairpin turn down a winding path through a canopy of prickly bushes that reached out, clawing at the car. Branches scraped the windows. Shiloh felt trapped. Damien refused to let her hide. "Does it please you to have no life of your own? No other way of living?"

The car ground to a halt. He turned to her then, intent in the darkness. "You're better than that, Shiloh."

She didn't know where she was. What to think. She felt completely removed from her world and everyone in it. "Am I? What makes you think you know anything about me?"

He reached out to her. "I know enough."

She drew back. "Where are we?"

He clicked open his door, allowing her distance. "This is a safe house," he said, getting out. "I don't trust the hotel. Not after what we tried to pull."

She tried to see it through the window, but could only make out spindly bushes and blackness. "What is this, like a secret demon slayer base or something?"

He opened her door for her. "Yes," he said, looking down at her.

"And you're bringing me?"

"You're not like them, Shiloh."

As she emerged from the car, she could see a small stone house that seemed to be built into the desert itself. It was covered in desert scrub and, she imagined, invisible until you were right up on it.

She watched Damien work a silver padlock on the door, then say a few incantations before turning the weathered door handle.

He was bringing her into his inner sanctum.

If she wanted, she could tell Napthulo. She could deliver him a demon slayer, and his hideout. Who knew what kinds of weapons Damien had stored in here? The intelligence information alone could be priceless.

Her stomach quivered. But where would betrayal get her? A lifetime of service to the demon. She already had that. She'd always wanted something more. Yet wanting and doing were two vastly different things. Taking that step frightened her more than she'd ever imagined.

"Shiloh?" He stood in the rectangular entry way. "It's okay."

She shivered in the darkness. It wasn't okay. None of this was okay.

She crossed her arms to stay warm. "Are you sure going inside won't blast me to hell or something?"

"I'm sure," he said, wrapping a comforting arm around her. A smile played across his features. "Come on," he said, picking her up and carrying her across the threshold like a newlywed.

She laughed, bracing herself for a zap like the one she got every time she went to work at the casino. Instead, all she could feel was his warmth against her. It was strange.

"What do we do now?" she asked as he set her down gently. She was like a fish out of water, a half-demon in a demon slayer's lair.

He switched on a single overhead bulb to reveal a small square room with a table and chairs near the door and a futon in the back. There was a dirt floor and stacked white stones forming the walls. It smelled like a cave. "We wait for our chance to go back in. We save your friends."

Tears threatened as she nodded.

He touched her on the chin, tipping her face close to his. "Come on. This place isn't that bad."

She sputtered out a half-laugh, half-cry. "It's awful."

"I'm no Martha Stewart, but it'll keep us safe." He kissed her lightly on the lips, more of a comfort kiss than anything else. "We can do it, Shiloh."

She felt her blood heat at his closeness. "I hope so." She didn't want to fail again. She didn't want to see anything happen to Fawzi or Rufus, or even this demon slayer. She wanted to start over with all of this behind her.

"Trust me," he murmured against her lips.

The crazy thing was, she did.

Damien's breath grazed her lips, his mouth a fraction from hers.

He could tell she was tired of running. So was he.

Damien let himself taste her once. Then again. He bent, pulling her flush against him.

"Damien," she sighed as he trailed kisses down her sweet jaw and tangled his fingers in her soft curls.

He was all about the job. The duty. He'd been ready to die in the demon's chambers. He'd made an oath to sacrifice himself, to give it all up.

But he couldn't give up on her. She was so brave, so forthright, so full of life. *Trust me, Damien.* Didn't she understand she needed to trust him too? He could help her. He could protect her. He could save her.

"Damien?" She pulled back slightly, her gown rumpled, her mouth wet from his kisses. Seeing her like that nearly undid him. She wasn't a sex demon on a rampage. She was Shiloh, a warm and willing woman.

Her eyes flickered to the dirt floor, then back at him. "We don't need to do anything but kiss."

He ran his fingers along her jaw. She was so soft, so vulnerable. And she would stop if he asked her.

But he didn't want to stop tonight. He'd gone too long alone, pushing himself, driving himself, never stopping to even see if there was another way. Tonight would be different for both of them.

Damien closed the distance between them and kissed her hard. His body tensed and then yielded to her as she ran her soft hands up his back, over his shoulders, pulling him to her. He devoured her mouth, hungering for more as he walked her backward to the blanket-draped futon.

They went down in a heap, Shiloh crawling over him and pulling his shirt off. He let her, releasing the tie at the back of her gown so that the whole thing went down in a pool of silk at her waist. Oh man. She wore nothing underneath.

He stopped and simply looked at her, drinking her in. She'd done something to him that went beyond the meshing of powers. She'd somehow gotten inside him and freed that part of him he'd tried so hard to restrain.

He cleared his throat, trying to find his voice. "You're beautiful, Shiloh. You know that, don't you?"

She looked away at that, unable to face him. But he'd seen how her eyes shone with happiness.

Damien trailed his fingers up her sides until her nipples puckered and goose bumps rose on her skin. Somehow this slip of a half-demon had wound herself into his life.

"Are you afraid of what happened last time?" she asked shyly.

"I padlocked the door." It wasn't necessarily a joke. He had locked them in tight. And this place was warded like Fort Knox.

She chewed at her lip. "I'm not drinking any more of your concoctions."

"That's a shame. I liked how you did it."

She grinned at that and tried to roll him onto his back.

"No, Shiloh," he said, pulling her under him.

He had a feeling that all of her life she'd been the seductress, the siren, the one who had to work during sex.

He stretched over her. "Have you ever been seduced?"

Her eyes widened and her lips parted slightly. "No."

"Lucky me."

Her breath tumbled into his mouth and he drank it, the heated charge spiraling through him like liquid lightning.

He found her collarbone, her breasts, the little valley of skin above her navel. He flicked her, teased her and licked her until she shuddered with the pleasure of it.

Damien drew her dress down over her hips and spread her legs wide. "I never—" she panted, unable to finish the thought.

He was coming unglued and so was she. She jerked as he found the very center of her.

She deserved it. She needed it. As much as it stunned him to admit it, he needed it too.

Damien kissed her and loved her with the pent-up passion of a lifetime of denial. He felt the power building between them and grew even harder. It felt so good, so right, so natural to be here with Shiloh spread beneath him.

She shuddered with every lick and caress. She moaned his name and thrashed under him. He explored her until she let out a scream and a shudder of release.

"Damien—" She arched her back, her hands buried in his hair. "I need you inside me. Now."

Her words excited him beyond measure. This beautiful, brave woman wanted him. Needed him. The power of it hummed against his skin as he rose up over her.

Last time, they'd been blind to this moment, their energies wild with the drug he'd given her. Now, he was aware with every fiber of his being what was about to happen.

He dragged his body up over hers, skin-to-soft-sweaty-skin. She threw her legs around his hips and drew his cock against her. He let out a groan.

She ground against him. "Now."

He pulled back, nibbling on her ear. "You deserve it slow."

She laughed at that. "I don't deserve you at all."

Ah, but that was where she was wrong. Shiloh deserved to be well loved. She deserved the freedom to make her own decisions and to live her own life. If only she could see it as clearly as he could at that moment.

He looked down at her then, soft and vulnerable and panting with desire. "I'll set you free."

"You don't know what will happen," she said as the tip of him found her entrance.

He felt the power surge between them.

True, he didn't know the consequences. He couldn't believe they would be bad. Shiloh wasn't evil. "This isn't wrong."

Damien rose above her. He was a demon slayer.

Sacrifice yourself.

He would take her and savor her and show her just how much she deserved to be loved.

They both gasped as he drove into her. She wept with the power of it as he made love to her, slowly at first, then with mounting passion.

You are beautiful.

You are strong.

You are loved.

"Damien," she gasped, raw with emotion. "It's too much."

He kissed her hard before she buried her face in his chest.

She clutched his back, tears streaming from the corners of her closed eyes as the power of their joining raged between them.

He felt it, pure and blinding, as they both shuddered with release.

Sweet heaven. He held himself above her as they both came down to earth.

He'd never known a joining to be so powerful. His heart skipped as she urged him down next to her. Then again, this was only his second time.

She snuggled against him, warm and soft. "I don't know what to think."

He tucked her into the crook of his arm and held her close. "Good," he murmured into her hair.

They'd strengthened the power flowing between them. He wondered if she felt it too.

"So what happens now?" she asked.

"I'll protect you." She was good. She was his to look after.

Damien pulled a blanket over them, eyeing the locked door and the low walls of their hideout. He didn't know what the morning would bring.

He settled back down with her. "I'll save you," he said against her hair.

She shifted against him, drawing even closer. "Don't make promises you can't keep."

His mouth set in a determined line. "I don't."

Chapter Eight

The call that the coast was clear came the next morning.

"This is a mistake," Shiloh warned him as he eased his black T-shirt over a fully loaded switch star belt.

"I know," he said simply.

He wore black leather pants and had a black leather jacket draped over one of the hideout's rickety chairs. She didn't know why he was wearing black. It wasn't like they'd be able to hide anymore.

Sure, she liked men studly and brave, but not suicidal. "If it's a mistake, then why are we going back in?" The way Damien had been tossing power around last night was bound to have alerted the demon.

She paced beside the futon, her peach gown swirling at her ankles. "This is too quick to be another chance opportunity. This is a trap."

"Exactly," he said, fastening the clasps on the silver switch star case. "Now we get to face Napthulo."

"On his own terms. At his casino. And I'm willing to bet he's pissed."

He pulled on his leather jacket. "I'm not feeling too generous myself."

"This is the demon who plays Tiddlywinks with the spine bones of his enemies."

He closed the distance between them. "What else do you suggest I do?" he asked, running a thumb along her chin, blazing a heated path straight to her core.

She licked her lips, fighting the urge to kiss him. "I don't know." She hadn't thought that far. "Run. Leave." *Take me with you.*

He gave a small smile. "I can't do that, Shiloh." His expression hardened. "We don't have a choice here. I have to go back in and destroy that portal before your boss blasts Vegas to hell."

It was happening too fast. There had to be another way.

He ducked out the door and she followed him, gold heels in hand. "You can't be sure that The Fire Storm Hotel is going to transport souls to hell," she argued. Hard desert rocks pricked her feet as she followed him out to the car. "Be logical," she pleaded.

He turned, stony determination etched across his features. "You're right. I don't know what Napthulo is going to do. But I do know he needs that portal."

Exactly. "The portal that you couldn't seem to grab."

He opened the door for her. She slid in with a huff. Shoulders squared, he locked the door to the demon slayer refuge, ducking under the low-hanging desert vines. Every bit the soldier. He slid into the front seat next to her and placed the switch star case between them.

"I don't know why I couldn't get a hold on that portal last time. But I promise you, Shiloh. This time will be different."

"How?"

"I have to give more of myself." He steeled himself like a soldier. "It's all I can do."

The horror of his plan sank in. "It's going to kill you," she whispered.

Tears welled up. She shouldn't care. Shiloh didn't need to care about anybody but herself. She was alone and she always would be.

So why did the idea of losing him hurt so damned much?

Every instinct screamed for her to protect him, but she had no idea how she of all creatures would stand a chance against Napthulo.

He reached across the silver case to caress her cheek. His expression was intent as his fingers found her chin and tipped her face up to look at him. "We don't have a choice, Shiloh. It's the only way to destroy Napthulo and keep you safe."

Her throat felt tight as he reached across and kissed her forehead.

Damn the man, why did he have to be so honorable? She'd never been able to count on anyone in her life and now that she'd found someone who actually cared about her, he was going to sacrifice it all for her—a she-devil. She would have laughed if she wasn't afraid she'd start crying.

They drove back to the casino in silence, Shiloh too upset to speak and Damien focused on what he had to do to bring down the demon. He squinted against the rising sun as he formulated his plan.

The last time he'd entered Napthulo's inner sanctum, he'd felt strong resistance. It made sense. The demon's powers and his own were like oil and water. But there was another problem Damien hadn't anticipated. Something had blocked his power when he'd tried to get a grip on the portal.

He pulled on a pair of black shades.

He basically needed to flip the portal inside out and reverse the energies.

The demon slayer before him had done this in the Great Vegas Cleansing of 2009. She wasn't a born slayer, like him. She was a made one. And she hadn't even finished her training.

If Lizzie Brown could do it, so could he. So why had it been impossible for him to grab hold of the portal? Something was holding him back.

He had to believe it was his willingness to sacrifice himself. He had to let go of this idea that he could be with Shiloh. It was tying him to this life, making it harder for him to accept the fact that he might need to die.

"Damien?" Shiloh's voice broke through his dark thoughts.

He swung the black Jaguar into a spot at the back of the hotel. "Yes."

She gazed out the window at the towering Seven Deadly Sins Casino. "How are we going to get in there?"

He killed the engine. "I was hoping you knew a back way."

She blanched. "I don't."

He took a moment to think as he got out of the car. "Secret entrance?" he asked, surprising her by opening her door for her.

"Sorry."

He was afraid of that. He surveyed the towering gold casino, gleaming in the morning sun. "Then we'll have to go in the front."

She almost fell sideways. "No." She gripped his arm. "We'll go in the employees' entrance."

He left the silver case in the car, opting for speed and

stealth over firepower. Damien was counting on Shiloh's back entrance to buy them some time. The demon might know they were coming, but he didn't know when.

Shiloh tugged on her gloves, hiding her wedding ring as they hurried together toward the back of the casino. "You were hoping I'd sneak you in," she said, as if she'd caught him at it.

It was true enough. "My wife is smart."

She nudged him in the ribs. "I just want to let you know I'm on to you," she said as she dialed the access code on a gray door at the back.

He supposed that was fair enough. "I'm a man of simple desires, Shiloh." He wanted to do his job, keep his integrity and well, maybe that was enough.

They hurried through the employee entrance, down the long back hallway, cringing together as the human repelling ward zapped them.

"Rufus!" Shiloh greeted an eager hellhound. Damien reached down and gave the beast a scratch behind the ears.

"Whoa," Shiloh said, petting the hellhound under the collar. "You're a Rufus fan, now?"

"Are you kidding? This guy saved our skin." He grinned at the beast, and then at his lovely partner in crime. She deserved a dog and so much more.

"What?" she asked, her face falling when she saw Damien stiffen with alarm. The battered brown She-Demons assignment desk stood empty. They were just about to skirt their way past it when a strange little fairy burst out from behind the desk. "What are you doing here? Go away."

Shiloh and Damien halted as the fairy shoveled papers into a red briefcase.

He could switch star the fairy, but he hated to do it to a non-demonic being. And he really didn't want to expose his powers so early.

"Damien, meet Jeebers," Shiloh said, by way of introduction. "Jeebers, Damien."

Oh great. Now he knew the creature's name.

The fairy's eyes were wide with fear. "That's Mr. Jeebers to you, and I told you to leave."

"Got an assignment for me?" Shiloh asked, acting as if they weren't about to blow her boss to hell.

The fairy snapped his case shut. Dragging it behind him, he headed out the back hallway toward the parking lot. "I'm taking the day off and you should too."

Shiloh glanced at Damien. "That was weird."

"Not so much." Damien had a feeling he'd just met The Council's source on the inside. And if the fairy was hightailing it out of there, then Shiloh and he were indeed walking into a mess.

Damien tilted his head toward the nearby Video Surveillance room. "Who runs that?"

"The fairies," Shiloh answered, as they headed for the elevator.

He tried the door. It was locked.

No wonder their presence in Napthulo's chambers hadn't been reported right away. The Council had done its job. Now Damien just needed to do his.

Shiloh sensed Napthulo the moment she set foot in his casino. She could smell him too. The raw stench of sulfur assaulted her. Her eyes watered and she sniffed as they entered the elevator that led up to his private chambers.

Rufus followed, winding around her legs like an overgrown cat.

Damien touched her on the arm. "Are you okay?"

She leaned into him, fully aware he needed to be able to draw weapons at any moment. "This place is getting to me today."

Something had changed. She felt it down to her toes.

Was it the anger of the demon or was it her? *Them?*

Something had happened last night when they'd made love. She'd felt their shared power flowing between them. It was unlike anything she'd ever experienced. It had happened a second time, and a third time just before dawn. Her body warmed as she thought back to their lovemaking. It had been so pure, so honest. So good.

"Shiloh"—he rubbed her back—"are you listening to me?"

"Yes," she lied.

He looked down on her, intent. "Remember. All you need to do is open the door. I'll get Fawzi for you. Then you take your friends and you get out of here."

She nodded but a hollow spot opened in the pit of her stomach.

Hell. He was so good, so noble.

"I need you to do exactly as I say, Shiloh. I don't want to have to worry about you if things go bad in there."

He didn't want her to see him die if it came to that.

He gave her one last, lingering kiss. "Promise me," he said against her lips.

The elevator clunked to a stop. "I promise."

The doors opened to an empty hallway. Damien took the lead, followed by Shiloh and Rufus. The dog sniffed at the bottom crack of the door as Shiloh wrapped her hand over the skull of the betrayer.

The door opened. And there, on the throne of human bones, sat Napthulo.

His leathery skin crackled as he showed a row of hideous white teeth. He'd had them capped and bleached. Spittle sizzled against the veneers, dripping down onto a gold leaf club shirt. He held an ivory goblet in one hand and planted a booted foot on the antique ice bucket Shiloh had used to trap Fawzi.

Her stomach sank as the demon leered at her.

He wasn't supposed to be there. This was supposed to be an empty room, another opportunity. But even as the thought formed, Shiloh realized that this was what had to happen all along. Damien had come to face the demon. Heaven help them.

"Enter," Napthulo crooned, all too pleased with himself. "You as well, Succubus 14." The door slammed behind them.

Chapter Nine

A haze of death, rot and sulfur swirled throughout the chamber and Shiloh had to work hard not to gag. She'd seen the smoke before, but had never felt it like this.

Napthulo sneered, a trail of sulfuric smoke circling from his nose. "It's about time you stopped sneaking around." His voice rubbed her like tiny needles digging into her skin.

Damien fired a switch star at the demon's head. Napthulo caught it, the blades sizzling against his thick hide.

The demon chuckled as Damien made a dash for the portal in the bedroom.

"By all means, go ahead," Napthulo called from his chair like a lazy host. "Fight before I suck you down to hell."

Shiloh fought down a wave of panic. Damien wouldn't know what to do in hell. Neither would she, but at least she wouldn't be an unarmed walking target for the damned.

She wanted to go to him. To run, to flee, but shock left her unable to move. She was alone in the demon's lair.

Shiloh's head swam and she tried not to hyperventilate. Napthulo was too confident. He had it rigged. They'd failed. He'd kill Damien. She hoped he'd kill her. She didn't even want to think of the alternatives.

Napthulo scoffed at the switch star, bent and smoking in his hand. "What a fucking mess." He leaned forward and speared it into the ice bucket.

"Fawzi!" Shiloh gasped.

The bucket shook as the switch star lay smoking, half-buried in the lid.

The demon snarled at her. "He's not getting off that easy." His yellow eyes took on a sickening glow. "Neither are you." He regarded her with unadulterated hate. "First I'll rip your fingernails out, one by one." His awful eyes raked over her. "I'll skin you," he said with relish. "And when I grow bored lapping at your blood, I'll boil you alive for eternity."

She splayed a hand on her chest, trying to get hold of herself as blue lights flashed from Napthulo's bedroom. Damien was at work.

The demon laughed. "You want to watch him fail first? Yes, I think you deserve that."

"No," she whispered.

"I can feel his soul opening up." Napthulo rumbled. "Give him a moment longer and I can have that too."

Horror speared Shiloh. Damien's power had turned electric blue. "He's going to kill you," she said on a shaky breath.

"I thought you knew better than that," Napthulo said, grasping her by the wrist, his cold grip seeping through her as he dragged her toward his throne. "Then again, you are a lesser." She felt his sticky breath against her cheek. "No, I'm afraid your demon slayer was destined to fail." He trailed a single taloned finger down her neck and on to her breast, drawing blood. "If a slayer wants to reverse a demon's power, he needs to use the demon's power."

Shiloh couldn't stop shaking. She wet her lips. "Lizzie Brown did it." That slayer had almost destroyed them all.

"An unfortunate mistake," Napthulo said, watching the blood stain her peach gown. "Careless. That slayer took demon power into herself. The slayer in there has nothing."

Shiloh's heart thumped against her chest. Damien had her demon's power. But would he know how to use it?

Hope flared within her.

She could help him use it.

Napthulo would never suspect. Demons were incapable of connecting, of sharing, of love. But she'd bonded with Damien. Their powers had meshed. And they'd only strengthened the connection last night when he made love to her. She'd felt it down to her toes.

Now Damien needed her to complete the bond and take hold of hell.

Shiloh grabbed the ice bucket and smacked Napthulo upside the head with it. "Die, demon!" Her sweaty hand clutching the handle, she dashed into the bedroom, the demon's cackle echoing in her ears.

"Damien," she gasped.

He stood with his arms outstretched in a storm of blue power that almost knocked her backward. "Damien!" She fought through the winds that seared her skin and buffeted her body.

She could see his muscles straining, feel the weight of the portal above them. There was no way he could hold on much longer.

He saw her and the agony on his face nearly made her swoon. "Leave, Shiloh. Run!"

"You need me," she hollered, battling her way to his side. He was fighting for his soul and he was going to fail unless she could make it.

She didn't know how she was going to reach him. His power tore at her. "Trust me," she begged.

He lowered his hands a fraction and she pushed through the last layer of resistance, climbing up to his side. She threw her arms around him, touching him, kissing him, feeling her dark strength well up inside her.

"Take it! Take power from me." She threw her demon energy into him as she drew him down for a searing kiss.

God, she hoped she was right.

The power sizzled between them, twining together, mixing and flowing. She ground against him as their energies melded and grew. He drew one arm around her, in a desperate, eating kiss that consumed them. The power storm howled around them, spinning into a massive cyclone above the bed. Then she felt it expand and shift.

The mirror flashed as the vortex flipped and opened.

Napthulo stormed into the room, eyes wide with panic. Claws out, teeth bared, he dove straight for her. The demon howled as the winds caught him, sucking him up into the portal and straight to hell.

Shiloh clung to Damien, kissing him with the pent-up passion of a lifetime as her sister succubi screeched past her. The minions went next, dark masses clamoring and hissing. Shiloh gasped as Fawzi's ice bucket sailed past.

Damien caught it by the silver handle and brought it down to her, wrapping her shaking fingers around the mangled silver handle. "Don't cut yourself," he said, pointing the crushed switch star away from her.

She almost cried with relief. Shiloh clung to Damien as she felt Las Vegas empty itself of demons once more.

She sank into Damien, amazed. They'd done it. They'd actually pulled it off. And just when she was about to tell him so, she felt the portal grab her.

It drew her up by the arms. She felt the stinging cold of hell as she gaped in horror at the swirling blue light above her.

"Shiloh!" Damien's hands gripped her waist.

Shiloh choked with fear. "I'm evil." Just like the rest of the demons. She was going to hell.

"Damn it, Shiloh. Hold onto me." The vortex was growing stronger. It wanted one last demon. She felt Damien's hands slip.

His goodness surrounded her. As she'd emptied her demonic power into him, so was she filling up with his goodness.

"Hold on," he yelled as the churning mass swirled above her.

He clutched her by the ankles now as the icy grip of hell chilled her to the core. Her breath came in gasps, and she stared down at Damien. She could feel the heavy weight of contentment, understanding, love as they began to take hold inside her.

And then the warmth.

"Let it in, Shiloh," he pleaded. "You have a choice."

She almost swooned with the beauty of it. She'd never had a choice. She'd existed to be ordered about, used.

He was the pure one, the noble one. If she could choose, she'd want to be with a man like Damien. "Stay with me, Shiloh."

"I will," she said, focusing on the powers that bound them, seeking out the good and the honest and the real affection she felt for this demon slayer.

She imagined him as he was that morning, hair tousled and warm as he slept next to her. She thought of their tacky wedding pictures, making lion faces outside the MGM Grand and even the stupid stuffed pink bear.

"That's it," he said, his affection for her plain on his face as the portal loosened its grip.

She accepted his goodness into her body and her heart. It drew her toward him, weaving them together.

She imagined him as he'd been in the Sloth room, putty under her hands as she massaged his temples and made bad jokes. She thought of how he'd taken her to his special place. And she thought of what an amazing day it had been when Damien had walked into her life.

She slid down the length of him as the portal faded and

disappeared. "Kiss me," she said, wrapping her arms around his neck. He did.

A few remaining winds buffeted the room as Damien folded her against his warm chest. "Your hands are cold," he murmured.

"I've been to hell and back," she said against his warm skin. He held her as if she was the most precious thing he'd ever found.

His heart was beating as fast as hers. "I thought I was going to lose you."

"Me too," she mumbled against his chest, content and safe for the first time she could remember. "I'm good," she said, hardly believing it herself.

He gave her a small squeeze. "Told you I was going to save you."

She drew back. "Rub it in." She tried to frown but ended up smiling as much as he was. "You know, for the record, I saved you too."

He flexed his hips against hers. "However will I repay you?"

"We'll think of something," she said, sliding a warmed hand up under his T-shirt.

He'd just lowered his head to kiss her when a man cleared his throat in the doorway.

They looked up to see an aged priest holding a large cross and a bucket of holy water. Rufus had followed him in, tongue lolling. "I see you closed the portal."

Father Riley. This man had sent at least a dozen demons to hell. Shiloh's throat contracted. "Don't kill me."

The priest set down the bucket. "Don't worry," he said, "You've done good."

"How do you know that?" she asked, trying to casually move behind Damien. It was just like an exorcist to be tricky.

The white-haired priest shook his head as Damien helped a reluctant Shiloh off the bed. "Evil is not about our birth. It's about our choices." He held a hand out to Shiloh and she took it gingerly. "You've made good choices," he said, giving her hand an extra squeeze.

Shiloh stared down at their joined hands. She never would have imagined this in a million years. "What do I do now?"

The priest grinned. "Well, I suppose the first order of business would be to let your friend go."

They looked down to the shaking ice bucket Shiloh held.

She closed her eyes. "Oh no. Not Fawzi. He's going to smite me."

"Why?" Damien asked. "You freed him from Napthulo, just like you said you would."

She grinned. She had, hadn't she?

Rufus jumped up on the bed in crazed dog affection, licking them wherever he could reach.

Shiloh scrunched his fur between her fingers. "Oh, I'm so glad you're okay, sweetie."

Damien crouched and let Rufus attack him with affection. "He was never a bad dog, Shiloh. He just needs a good owner."

"Me," Shiloh said, capturing Rufus in a big hug. At last, she'd have a hellhound of her own. "I can hardly believe it."

"You deserve it." The priest grinned as he sprinkled holy water around the edges of the room.

Shiloh was shocked to realize she didn't even mind the holy water. In fact, it made the room smell a whole lot better. The sulfur faded, replaced by a pure unearthly scent. "Amazing," she said to herself.

"Stick with me," Damien said, drawing her to his side.

The priest straightened from where he'd been sprinkling holy water behind a large fire pit. "No annulment?"

Shiloh's breath caught. Was he really suggesting what

she thought he was? The demon slayer wanted to stay married to her, to be with her?

Damien pushed her hair off her shoulders and drew her close. "Why are you so surprised? I can give you freedom, love." They both smiled as Rufus inserted a wet nose between them. "A hellhound . . ."

Shiloh's heart swelled with love. She couldn't think of anything she wanted more.

"Maybe we should renew our vows," Shiloh said, wrapping her arms around Damien. "I'd like to remember them."

He grinned. "Lucky for us, there's a priest right here."

The Bride Wore
Demon Dust

Lexi
George

To my writers' group—cheerleaders, whining boards, promotional team, and friends, all wrapped up into one.

To Melissa—an extra pair of eyes when I needed them. Thanks for sharing the joy of this adventure.

To Erin, my crit partner and sister from another mother: Love you, chicka.

Chapter One

Bunny's wedding was perfect—until her husband tried to kill the photographer.

Her strapless, white tulle gown with the silk taffeta sash fit her like a dream. The bridal bouquet of white roses and calla lilies was the picture of simple elegance. And the quaint old church by the river had provided the perfect setting, with its heart pine floors mellowed and warped with age, beadboard wainscoting and hand-stenciled blue-and-white ceiling.

Even the weather had cooperated, gracing them with a cloudless sky, a gentle breeze and temperatures in the low eighties, an unusual occurrence for late September in the Deep South.

Bunny thought she might die of happiness as her daddy walked her down the aisle between rows of smiling friends and family to the altar where *he* had waited for her. Rafe Dalvahni, six foot four inches of hard-muscled masculine perfection in a black tuxedo, a man so mouth-wateringly gorgeous half the females in the church swooned just looking at him. His handsome features were schooled in his usual expressionless mask, but the look he had given her as she floated toward him could have melted concrete. It made her feel shivery and weak. *He* made her weak.

It was hard to believe this beautiful, sexy man with the stern manner and the hot mouth and gentle, roving hands that drove her wild would soon belong to her, Bunny Nicole Raines, small-town librarian with a double stripper name.

The past few weeks had been a blur. First, she had been attacked at the library late one night. Bunny remembered little of what happened, only searing pain and blackness. Then waking in Rafe's arms and knowing, *knowing* this was the man she'd waited for her whole life. A dizzying, whirlwind courtship followed . . .

Culminating in the Big Day.

Vows were spoken and they were married. Bunny felt a surge of giddy happiness as they walked out of the church and into the late afternoon sunshine. She was his and he was hers, husband and wife, Mr. and Mrs. Rafe Dalvahni, forever and ever amen. Now they could begin their happily-ever-after.

Arm in arm, Bunny and Rafe stood at the foot of the steps and greeted their guests as they left the chapel. After directing everyone to the white tents down by the river for the reception, they slipped into the rose garden at the back of the church to take a few more pictures.

And that's when Bunny's perfect wedding had morphed into a nightmare and her dreams of a quiet, ordinary life with the man she loved went up in smoke.

Or demon dust, to be more exact.

"Oh, darn, my battery's dead," Spence Hardy, the photographer, said after the first few shots. "I've got some extras in my car. You two lovebirds stay here. I'll be right back."

He hurried off, leaving Bunny and Rafe alone in the rose garden.

Rafe pulled her into his arms and kissed her. Bunny caught an intoxicating whiff of his cologne, something green and spicy and earthy. God, he even smelled beautiful.

He nuzzled her neck. "I missed you."

"It was only one night," Bunny protested, shivering in response. Lord help her, she was a goner for this man. Rafe touched her and she went up like a Roman candle. It had been like this from the moment they met. "How was the big bachelor party? Did you get drunk?"

"The Dalvahni do not get drunk. We are not affected by alcohol and other drugs."

She smothered a giggle. She thought it was cute the way he referred to himself and his brother, Brand, in the plural. "The Dalvahni" this and "the Dalvahni" that, like they were a breed unto themselves or something.

And maybe they were. Bunny had never seen anything like the Dalvahni brothers. Tall, green-eyed, stacked with muscles, they were both inhumanly handsome, although Brand had dark hair and Rafe's was the blood-red color of garnets.

Bunny found Rafe's older brother grim and intimidating, but her friend, Addy Corwin, seemed to like him just fine. Brand and Addy were a hot item. Bunny thought there was something lethal and predatory about Brand, but she kept her thoughts to herself. After all, Rafe put up with her older brothers, Cam and Coop, and they were an acquired taste.

"Your brothers drank a large quantity of ale. I took them home," Rafe continued. "I do not understand the human affinity for substances that make them lose control."

She smiled up at him. "What about you, Rafe? Do you ever lose control?"

"Only with you, *cara*," he said, kissing her.

It was a lovely thing to say, Bunny thought wistfully, although she suspected it wasn't true. Rafe always seemed to be in perfect control. Sometimes his perpetual calm bothered her. He was so disciplined and she was all over the place with her emotions, especially lately.

Rafe deepened the kiss and Bunny forgot everything but the heated joy of his touch. His tongue brushed hers and she tasted honey and spices. The taste of him, the heat radiating off his big-muscled body and his special, masculine scent made her light-headed with longing. A delicious ache started in her breasts, then spread to her belly and between her thighs. She wanted him now. Heck, with a little encouragement, she'd do him right here in the rosebushes behind the Mount Carmel Methodist Church, with half the town and her entire family within shouting distance.

Not exactly the photo spread she'd envisioned for the Hannah *Herald*.

The *crunch* of approaching footsteps brought her to her senses; Mr. Hardy, returning with the fresh batteries. Blushing, she slipped out of Rafe's embrace and turned to face the older man with a welcoming smile.

Her smile quickly faded. A pleasant, round-faced man with thinning silver hair, Spence Hardy was Hannah's unofficial photographer, even though his business was thirty miles away in Paulsberg. He had taken her baby pictures and the gap-toothed photograph of her in the first grade. The formal portrait of her in a white dress at sixteen that hung over her parents' mantel was a Hardy original. He was there when she and her classmates graduated high school, taking snapshots of them in their caps and gowns. But the person walking toward them looked nothing like the man she'd known all her life. His skin was sickly gray, his facial features stretched and rubbery.

And his eyes . . .

His eyes were blank, dark pools above his grinning slash of a mouth.

"Mr. Hardy?" Bunny squeaked.

To her shock and surprise, Rafe produced a lethal-looking battle-ax out of nowhere and stepped in front of her. He twirled the battle-ax, and the thing wearing Spence Hardy's skin hissed.

"Did you think to find me unprepared, fiend?" her new husband asked Mr. Hardy in a cold, dangerous voice she'd never heard before. "I protect what is mine."

Fiend? Unprepared? What on earth was he talking about?

She peeked around Rafe. Mr. Hardy looked bad, really bad, like something out of a horror movie. But monsters don't exist, so he must be sick. Yeah, that was it. Mr. Hardy was ill. Maybe he was coming down with the flu.

Or he had something worse like the plague, the nasty, flesh-eating kind that made random body parts fall off.

Oh, good Lord, she'd hired a plague-infested photographer. Everybody at her wedding was going to die of a pernicious, infectious disease, and there would be dead bodies and stray body parts everywhere.

Eww.

The caterer would be pissed. She'd probably lose her deposit.

She tapped Rafe on one broad shoulder. "Rafe, what are you doing?"

"Anon, Bunny. Stay back. I will deal with this foul creature."

Anon and *foul creature.* His speech was always formal and proper, a bit stiff and old-fashioned, and he never used contractions. He reminded her of something out of one of her books, a knight errant of old. Usually, she found it charming, but not in the face of an honest-to-goodness, bona fide wedding emergency.

Bunny stepped around Rafe. "Mr. Hardy, you obviously aren't feeling well. Why don't you go ho—"

Mr. Hardy rushed at her with a horrible gobbling noise.

Rafe waved his hand, and Bunny shrieked as she was tossed into the air and turned end over end. She lost a shoe on the third rotation. When she stopped spinning, she was hanging upside down. The voluminous skirts of her wedding dress and petticoat fell down, covering her head in a suffocating swathe of tulle and netting. It was hard to think with the blood pounding in her temples. What was happening?

A cool breeze fanned her nether regions. *Good Lord*, she realized with a spasm of mortification. *I'm mooning half of Behr County.*

She wasn't wearing much. A scrap of lace here, a couple of bows there, held together by a narrow strip of ribbon and not much else. She'd spent a great deal of time picking out this particular pair of panties and imagining Rafe's reaction to them on their wedding night. This was not the "reveal" she'd planned. But who could plan for a thing like this?

"*Rafe*," she said, equal parts terrified and humiliated.

If she hadn't been so scared and confused, she would have cringed at the shrill sound of her voice. She sounded like a squeaky toy in the jaws of a frustrated boxer.

Without warning, she turned right side up. Slapping her skirts back into place, she swatted the gauzy folds of her wedding veil out of her face. Her stomach did a queasy flip-flop. She was suspended high in the air with a bird's-eye view of the river and their wedding guests milling around the white tents.

Bunny hated heights. It was all she could do to climb a ladder to reshelve books in the stacks. She always sat on the bottom row of bleachers, she avoided balconies and she *never* had dreams of flying.

"Oh God, oh God, oh God," she said, flailing her arms and legs about in panic.

To her surprise and relief, her clumsy movements propelled her forward. She floundered weightlessly through the air until she reached the church steeple. She grabbed it and held on. Looking down, she saw her family and friends mingling around the champagne fountain. A line of live oaks separated the church from the river. No one at the reception could see the drama unfolding several hundred yards away. The orchestra was playing. The party had started, but the bride was stuck on the roof like an abandoned Frisbee, and the groom . . .

The groom and The Thing That Was Mr. Hardy were engaged in a death match in the rose garden. Or what was left of it. Rosebushes, statuary, great clumps of dirt and sidewalk pavers exploded as Rafe and the possessed photographer hurled lightning bolts at one another.

"*Rafe*," Bunny screamed, terrified for him.

Terrified *of* him, this godlike creature with the blazing eyes who hurled death from his fingertips.

The ornate, three-tiered fountain at the center of the garden flew through the air and crashed to the ground at Rafe's feet, narrowly missing him.

He's going to be killed. He's going to be killed. The singsong litany ran through her mind.

Rafe threw his double-headed ax. It sailed across the garden toward his opponent. *Bloop*, Mr. Hardy disappeared from sight with a high-pitched giggle. With a metallic whine, the ax made a wide circle and returned to Rafe's outstretched hand. *Bloop*, Rafe disappeared, too. *Bloop, bloop*, he and Mr. Hardy reappeared on the other side of the garden.

This was a nightmare. It couldn't be real. Spence Hardy was a gentle man who filled his pockets with Tootsie Rolls and Smarties for the kids. At Christmas, he would set up a backdrop in front of the hardware store and take pictures of people in a sleigh pulled by eight basset hound reindeer wearing jingle bells and felt antlers.

This was not the Spence Hardy she knew.

This was not the Rafe Dalvahni she knew either, this hard-faced man with the glowing eyes and the supernatural powers.

He was unrecognizable, a stranger, and that frightened her most of all.

To Bunny's shock, Brand materialized on the roof beside her. As Rafe's only family, he was a member of the wedding party. He looked sinfully handsome in his tuxedo—in a dark and deadly I'll-kill-you-if-you-so-much-as-look-at-me-cross-eyed kind of way. His long, dark hair gleamed in the sunlight.

"I heard a noise over the obnoxious clamor that passes for music here." He briefly observed the mini-war being waged below them in the devastated garden. "I see my brother has things well in hand."

To her astonishment, he vanished. Left her on the roof with no explanation and without offering to help her or Rafe. Like possessed photographers and fireball-wielding grooms and people popping in and out of thin air were everyday occurrences. They were so *not*.

To add insult to injury, he had dissed her wedding band.

"Obnoxious clamor?" She shook her fist at the empty spot where he'd been standing a moment ago. "Do you have any idea how lucky we were to get a band *at all* on such short notice?"

Brand was long gone, but yelling made her feel better.

Her relief was temporary. Clinging to the steeple, she returned her attention to the fight below. Super Rafe was stalking his enemy. *Bloop,* he popped into view near the rear entrance of the church. *Bloop,* the Hardy monster materialized in the far corner of the garden. The monster was outmatched and his powers seemed to be waning. His arms hung limply at his sides, and he no longer threw fiery orbs of energy. His gray mouth hung open and he was heaving from exertion. Some of Bunny's terror for Rafe eased. It was going to be okay. It was all going to be okay.

Rafe blinked from sight and reappeared next to Hardy. He swung his ax. The blade whistled through the air in a shining, silver arc.

It was *soooo* not going to be okay.

Her husband was about to commit murder on their wedding day. Not an auspicious beginning for a marriage, any way you sliced it.

Somehow, Bunny was off the roof and running across the garden.

"Rafe, *no.*"

The blade came down. It missed Mr. Hardy and shattered a marble statue of Saint Francis instead.

Bunny skidded to a halt, staring in horror at Mr. Hardy. His head swelled, his mouth fell open, and his lower jaw stretched to the ground. Black smoke poured out of the gaping hole. Mr. Hardy's body crumpled to the ground like an empty balloon. With an eerie howl, the column of smoke flew over the church and disappeared in the direction of the river.

The battle-ax in Rafe's hand winked out of sight.

Mr. Hardy groaned and sat up. "What happened?"

Rafe made a slashing motion with one hand. "You will sleep."

Mr. Hardy's eyes rolled back and he slumped over.

"Mr. Hardy!" Bunny cried, running over to the photographer. She glared at Rafe. "What did you do to him?"

"He is unharmed. When he awakens, he will remember nothing of this."

"Lucky fellow." Bunny checked Mr. Hardy's pulse. It

was steady. "I don't understand anything that just happened."

Rafe stalked over and yanked her to her feet. "I will tell you what happened. You interfered where you should not have. You will not do so again."

Bunny gasped. "You almost killed Mr. Hardy!"

"'Twas my intent to kill him. I would have succeeded but for your screeching."

"You can't go around killing people willy-nilly, especially at a wedding! It's bad luck!"

"I do not kill in a random fashion—"

"The proper response would be *I don't kill people at all*!"

"—but in accordance with my preordained purpose. This was not a person. It was a demon in the Hardy human's flesh, likely the same demon that attacked you."

Bunny tried to process what he was saying, but it was difficult. Too much had happened, too quickly.

"Attacked me?" she repeated, frowning. "Are you talking about that night at the library? You told me it was a mugger."

He glared down at her. "It was not a mortal assailant. You were attacked by a djegrali. A demon, you humans would call it."

She shook her head in growing confusion. This was all unreal. She couldn't process any of it. Her brain was mush. She must be in shock. Or maybe she'd had a stroke. Yeah, that was it. She'd had a stroke. That would explain a lot.

"You say 'you humans' like you're not one."

"I am Dalvahni."

Bunny stamped her foot. "I know who you are, for crying out loud! I'm *Mrs.* Dalvahni. I married you."

He gripped her shoulders. "Dalvahni is not my name, Bunny. It is what I *am*. The Dalvahni are demon slayers, warriors who seek the djegrali through space and time.

Kill them, if need be, lest they wreak havoc upon innocent beings."

"I thought you worked for INS!"

"I am unfamiliar with this term."

She twisted free of his grasp. "Immigration Services? You told me you rounded up aliens, for Pete's sake!"

"So I do. The djegrali are alien to this world."

She stared at him in disbelief. "You're telling me you're not human."

"I am not human."

"And that you don't work for the federal government."

"I do not."

"And you're a demon slayer."

"Yes," he said.

She took a deep breath and blew it out again. "I'm not listening to any more of this."

She spun on her heel and stomped off. Her exit would have been more dramatic if she weren't limping on one shoe.

"Stop. That is not all," he called after her. "The demon inflicted a mortal wound upon you that night. If not for my intercession, you would have died." She limped faster. His voice rose, following her. "Do you hear me, Bunny? I gave you a portion of my essence. You are no longer human."

Bunny picked up her skirts and ran.

Chapter Two

Rafe watched Bunny flit down the tree-lined path away from him, the train of her white dress trailing behind her.

He scowled. She was running from the truth.

She was running from *him*.

The knowledge made him feel hollow inside.

He shrugged the thought aside. The Dalvahni did not have *feelings*. They were immortal demon hunters, created for that purpose alone. They experienced battle lust and sexual desire—particularly in the wake of battle—but little else in the way of emotion.

Sentiment had no place in their existence. Feelings were a human indulgence.

Rafe still found it unbelievable that Brand had fallen so completely under a woman's spell. Never before had a warrior surrendered to sentiment. That it had happened to *Brand*, a stalwart, courageous warrior, ferocious in battle and unswerving in purpose, sent a ripple of unease through the ranks of the Dalvahni.

It was the reason Rafe accepted this assignment from

Conall, the captain of the Dalvahni. He needed to find out for himself why one of their finest warriors had done something so unprecedented.

He had filed his initial report. Brand's passion for Addy Corwin was an anomaly, he informed Conall, a form of madness confined to Brand. The incident was unfortunate, but it would not happen again.

His decision to marry Bunny was the practical solution to a problem: he could keep her safe from the demon that attacked her. Nothing more. True, he enjoyed coupling with her, but that was an added benefit. The pleasure they shared was physical and of little consequence. He, in turn, protected her from the djegrali.

Having marked her, the creature would be irresistibly drawn to her. When it came for her, Rafe would be there to slay the demon. Once Bunny's safety was ensured, he would return to the Hall of Warriors.

Yes, his marriage to Bunny was a simple business arrangement. Certainly, his *emotions* were not involved.

His scowl deepened as she disappeared from view. Bunny still did not fully comprehend the situation. She had received a severe shock. He would give her time to think things over. Then they would discuss matters in a calm, rational manner.

Calm, rational, unemotional, that was the Dalvahni way. Now that Bunny was Dalvahni, it would be her way too.

He felt an enormous sense of relief at the prospect. He had been off balance since he met Bunny, a feeling of disorientation he attributed to the unusual amount of demonic activity in this place and the circumstances of their initial encounter.

He had been on the trail of one of the djegrali the first time he saw her. Stalking the creature through the streets at dusk, he had noticed a small building ablaze with lights not far from the center of town. Curious, he had paused in front of the structure and spied Bunny through the window.

That first glimpse of her had been like a hammer blow to the head. His already heightened senses sharpened and his body tightened in awareness.

Ah, he remembered thinking. Something buried deep inside of him stirred to life, as though he'd waited for this moment throughout the long, dark tunnel of his existence. It was a ridiculous notion, of course. Proof positive that unwholesome forces were at work.

He could see her from the waist up. She had her back to him. Standing on tiptoe, she placed a book on a shelf. The small movement made the muscles of her back and narrow shoulders bunch against the thin fabric of her blouse. His throat went dry. By the sword, he needed to slake his lust in the House of the Thralls if the sight of a woman's back was arousing him. And a fully clothed female at that.

He moved closer to the window, wanting to see more of her.

She was not to his usual taste, too slender and pale. Not golden-skinned and sumptuously curved like Xedra, his favorite thrall.

But her hair was glorious, like dark silk. She wore it in a careless knot on top of her head. A few wispy curls escaped their moorings to dangle at the back of her neck. He stared resentfully at those silky ringlets, fortuitously positioned against her tender nape. *He* wanted to whisper kisses along her creamy skin, lick the delicate shell of her ear, and feel the teasing caress of her dark locks upon his naked body.

She turned, as though she sensed his scrutiny. She could not see him. He was Dalvahni and invisible for the hunt. Still, he felt her gaze upon him like a physical touch.

And her eyes . . .

They were large and round, surrounded by a fringe of dark lashes. He could not tell their color.

Frustrated and curious, he moved closer still. She came to the window to look out. They were face-to-face. All that separated them was a pane of glass. The light was behind her, her face in shadows. He gazed at her, fascinated by the satin planes of her high cheeks and the soft curve of her wide mouth. With his finger, he traced the outline of her lips on the glass, memorizing their lush shape. She was not a beauty, perhaps. Her face was more heart-shaped than oval, her chin too stubborn, but she was fascinating to him all the same.

She stared out the window for a long moment, searching the darkness before turning back to her cart of books. He suppressed a growl of displeasure. She had abandoned him.

Abandoned him? Where had such a notion come from? A Dalvahni warrior was a rock, unworn by time, need or loneliness, an island fortress complete unto himself.

Shaking off his uncomfortable thoughts, he retreated into the shadows. A good hunter possessed patience. And, like all Dalvahni warriors, he was a very good hunter. The djegrali forgotten, he settled down to await his new prey. She would emerge from the safety of her den eventually and then he would . . . what?

Follow her home like a lovesick swain, an unseen escort protecting her from an evil she would neither accept nor comprehend? Step out of the night and introduce himself? But to what end? Congress between humans and the Dalvahni was impractical, to say the least. Humans were frail, insubstantial creatures, their lives but a brief flutter of candlelight in the dark reaches of eternity compared to the immortal Dalvahni.

The minutes stretched by and he grew uneasy. His instincts told him some mischief was afoot. He prowled the perimeter of the building, searching for signs of the djegrali, but found none. He could enter the building. Ascertain her well-being and slip out again undetected. No lock or key was proof against the Dalvahni.

He hesitated, reluctant to give in to this unaccustomed weakness. He was acting like an old woman, afraid of the dark and jumping at shadows. Annoyed with himself, he crossed the street and stood on the other side. He needed distance from the woman.

A man pulled up in one of the modern wheeled conveyances used by humans. Rafe could not remember the word for this particular contraption. The horse and carriage were still in use the last time he hunted the djegrali on Earth. He searched his word bank for the appropriate word. Ah, yes, the thing was called a "truck." The vehicle had a sign on the side with some lettering. Rafe concentrated. The gift of languages was another Dalvahni talent, a necessity in their travels between worlds. After a moment, the strange squiggles rearranged themselves into something recognizable. PRINGLE JANITORIAL SERVICES, the sign said.

The man pushed a wheeled cart up to the front door of the building and pressed the buzzer.

"Hey, Mr. Pringle, come on in," the woman said, opening the door to the man with a smile. "I'm still putting up books, but I'll be out of your hair in a minute." She wrinkled her nose. "Good gracious, they must be burning tires out at the dump again. Something sure smells bad."

The cart rattled as the man followed her inside and shut the door.

Rafe stood unmoving in the darkness. His blood pulsed hot in his head and in his groin. That voice, that throaty, slightly breathless voice, unexpected from a creature so sweet and demure in appearance. It conjured up images of heated bodies and sex-drenched sheets.

He wanted her. He needed her. Now.

Cursing his bewildering and unruly lust for the human female, he strode across the street. As he approached the entrance he detected the faint but unmistakable rank odor of the djegrali.

She had opened the door and let the demon in. She would be helpless against it.

A kind of madness seized him. With a roar of anguish, he flung his arms wide. The door tore off the hinges. Moving with the preternatural speed of a predator, he raced inside and found her, lying on the floor beneath the djegrali amid a jumble of books. There was blood on her blouse, on the books, and on the demon's human shell. Rafe threw his ax. The demon snarled and leaped unharmed through a window, disappearing into the night.

There was no thought of pursuit. All of Rafe's being was focused on the broken figure lying on the floor. Her arms and legs were bent at odd angles and her throat was torn and bloody. He fell to the floor beside her and pulled her into his lap. A weak pulse beat in her savaged neck but she was near unto death. The beast had torn her jugular and she had lost too much blood.

She was dying. He could feel her slipping away from him.

"No, you will not leave me." His voice sounded rough to his own ears. He shook her. "Do you hear me? You will not leave."

Without thinking, he placed his hands on her and poured his essence into her body. The gaping wound at her neck closed and some of her color returned. Her eyelids fluttered and lifted.

Gray, he noted with bemusement. Her eyes were gray with turquoise rims. Beautiful, liquid, starred with flecks of silver. He fell into them.

"There you are." She looked up at him in wonder. "Where have you been? I've been waiting for you."

Her words startled him. She did not know what she was saying, of course. She could not. How could she be waiting for someone she had just met? It was irrational.

"Be at ease, you are safe," he said gruffly, even though she did not appear to be alarmed. "I will protect you. You have my word."

The next day, he hunted down the man called Pringle with the intention of disposing of the djegrali once and for all. It was the only way to keep Bunny safe. But the demon had abandoned its human host and there was no trace of it. He could not predict where it might be or in what form.

The demon had marked her. It would come for her again. Rafe was certain of it.

And so he had married her. It had been an easy enough thing to accomplish. She was so in love with him. He'd planned the matter most carefully, laying siege to her with tender words and passionate caresses one night in her bedroom until she was panting and eager for him.

"Rafe, please," she'd said, arching against him. "I love you."

Meaningless words to a Dalvahni warrior and, yet, he hoarded them away like a beggar stores scraps of food for a cold, hard winter. He was sweating with the effort not to take her. It was always like this with her, a fever of desire he did not understand.

But he held back.

"I need you, too." Lifting his hips, he rubbed the head of his shaft between her tender folds. Gods, she was damp and ready for him. He gritted his teeth to keep from sliding inside her.

"I want to make you mine," he said, "to keep you safe and protect you. Say yes, Bunny."

Her beautiful eyes widened. "Are you asking me to marry you?"

Marriage: a rite wherein one human is bound to another in a consensual, contractual relationship recognized by law.

Bunny would be his.

"Yes, I am asking you to marry me."

It seemed the most expedient way to keep her safe, Rafe reflected as he followed his runaway bride down the path. He desired Bunny, this he freely admitted, but love had nothing to do with it. A Dalvahni warrior did not suffer the pangs of human emotion.

His steps flagged. A Dalvahni warrior also did not chase after a woman like a lovesick boy.

But how can you protect her if you are not with her? a traitorous voice whispered inside his head. *The djegrali could return. The fiend could be at the river, disguised as one of the guests. She is not safe.*

His gut clenched at the thought. He took a steadying breath and started after her again.

He said he would protect her and he would.

It was his duty, and a warrior always fulfilled his duty.

Chapter Three

Bunny ran, but she could not escape her whirling thoughts.

Demon . . . I am a demon slayer . . . a warrior who seeks the djegrali through space and time.

She had married a stranger. The man she'd fallen in love with did not exist. It was all a lie.

None of it made sense. This couldn't be happening. Not here. Not in *Hannah*, a town so quiet you could hear an ant fart.

Heedless of her missing shoe, she raced down the tree-shaded path that curved around the building to the front of the church.

She couldn't face Rafe right now. She needed time to think.

Think? Think about what?

Think about dear, sweet Mr. Hardy turning into a denizen from hell? Or the fact that she'd married a super-human escapee from another universe?

Think about the hundred-year-old rose garden Rafe the Newlywed Destroyer had turned into a scorched wasteland?

Or perhaps she should think about Rafe's stunning pronouncement that she was no longer human.

Which meant the precious, new life growing inside her might not be human either.

Her mind balked.

No. No. *No.*

Think about that and she'd go stark, staring mad.

She needed a drink.

Oh, hell, she couldn't drink. She was pregnant.

Sugar. She needed sugar and lots of it.

She veered across the front lawn of the church. Grass, trees and the river went by in a blur and somehow she was at the reception, from point A to point B in a split second. It was like she acquired super powers, or something.

Weird, but she wouldn't think about that either. She'd had more than enough weird for one day. Enough to last a lifetime.

She'd think about wedding cake instead. Mounds of it loaded with fluffy frosting. Five tiers of luscious lemon pound cake topped with buttercream icing and garnished with delicate white gum paste roses and calla lilies, sweet salvation calling her name from beneath the centermost tent.

Pushing her way through the crowd to the table, she grabbed the top layer of the cake and buried her face in it.

"Yum," she moaned between bites, quivering with bliss. "Thish ish sum wumphful cake."

Holding what was left of the slab of cake in one hand, she picked up a crystal bowl of butter mints and dumped them into her mouth. The mints were smooth and cool and creamy. They melted on her tongue and slid down her throat in a sugary cascade of deliciousness. She swallowed and jammed the rest of the wedding cake in her mouth.

She had icing and lemony bits of cake on her hands

and under her newly manicured fingernails. Her nose was coated in icing and buttercream frosting ringed her mouth and dripped from her chin. A blob of cake dropped off her hand and landed between her boobs.

No problem. More cake for later.

The sugar entered her bloodstream and shot straight to her brain. The fog cleared. Oh, good God, what was she doing? People would think she was off her nut. Her family would have her committed.

And rightfully so. How many brides took a swan dive into their wedding cake?

Cringing in mortification, she glanced around, expecting to be the center of horrified attention.

To her surprise, no one seemed to be paying any attention to her. Guests wandered the manicured grounds that gently sloped down to the river's edge, and swarmed around the refreshment tables and the low stage and dance floor that had been set up for the band.

Her sense of relief was short-lived. A man's raised voice drew her attention to a nearby card table stacked with presents.

"—and the reason those pants make your ass look big, Doreen, is 'cause you got yo'self a big old *ass*," George Nesbitt, the henpecked pharmacist from Hannah Drugs, said to his wife.

"I got your fat ass right here." Doreen whopped George upside the head with her oversized purse. "I'm glad Junior looks like the air conditioner repairman, 'stead of you, praise Jesus. I may be fat but I can lose weight. But you ain't never gon' be nothing but ugly. You got a puss on you that would sour milk."

She hit him again with her purse for good measure. Goodness, whatever possessed Mr. Nesbitt to talk to his wife like that? He ought to know she was mean as a snake in heat and would squash him like a bug.

Bunny started as another loud voice assailed her ears.

"—been cheating on my taxes since '02," Eugene Huggins said in a booming voice from the next tent. He balanced a loaded plate of food in one hand as he addressed Carl E. Davis, the chief of police. "And socking away a little moolah so me and the girlfriend can take us a vacation while the wife's away at that family reunion of hers. Nothing like a little strange to keep the lead in the old pencil, if you know what I mean. That and Viagra. I'm telling you, Carl, that little blue pill is a pecker picker upper."

Bunny flushed. Mr. Huggins was a regular at the library. He enjoyed nonfiction books on history, the occasional mystery . . . and, apparently, a little nookie on the side. Good Lord. How was she supposed to look him in the face the next time he came in to check out a book?

The steady *wump wump wump* of a big engine made her forget about Mr. Huggins.

"Oh, no," Bunny gasped, looking up the grassy slope toward the church.

Darryl Wilson was doing doughnuts on the lawn in his old Chevy. Chunks of grass flew from his spinning tires. His girlfriend, Raeleene, was hanging out of the passenger side window, her dress hiked up around her tanned thighs. She had one fist in the air and she was whooping at the top of her lungs.

Holy cow, what was happening? Had somebody slipped something in the punch? People were acting crazy.

Then Bunny heard someone sobbing. She followed the sound to where her daddy was sitting in a folding chair under a tree. He held his head in his hands as he cried. Her mother hovered over him, offering him support. Mama looked shell-shocked too. Bunny knew exactly how Mama felt.

She hurried toward her parents only to stop short at the sound of a familiar male voice.

"Whoo hoo, this water's colder 'n a well digger's butt," the voice said.

"You can say that again," someone else said. Someone she *knew*.

"Whoo hoo, this water's colder 'n a well digger's butt. There, you happy?"

"You are such a smart-ass, Cam."

"Kiss my ass, Coop, and get smarter 'cause you're dumb as a bag of hammers."

Oh, no, they wouldn't.

Bunny whirled around. Oh, yes, they would.

Her big brothers, Cam and Coop, were swimming in the river.

Naked.

Bunny loved her brothers. She really did. But she could go the rest of her life without seeing either one of them without their clothes on, especially at her wedding.

And that sentiment was doubly true for Herbert Duffey and Jefferson Davis Willis. They were friends of her grandparents, eighty years old, if they were a day, and skinny-dipping at her wedding, for Pete's sake! The old guys' pouches were saggy and the "boys" were hitting the water. So were Mamie Hall's tube sock boobies. Miss Mamie was older than dirt, too.

Bunny shuddered and turned her back to the river, but everywhere she looked she saw more craziness. Over to her right, Billy James Overton, a teetotaling Southern Baptist, had his head under the champagne fountain guzzling bubbly like a frat boy at a keg party. To her left, Mr. Overton's wife, Lou Lee, was doing a burlesque bump and grind in the middle of the stage. She was dancing to an imaginary tune, because the band had broken out in a fistfight.

Directly in front of Bunny, Mayor Tunstall, a career Republican, was committing political suicide by telling anyone and everyone who'd listen that his daddy was a

Yellow Dog Democrat. Less than ten feet away from him, the Judson twins, prim, retired schoolteachers and soloists in the Methodist church choir, were speed cussing.

"—hasn't touched me in over a year," someone said.

Oh, Lord, she knew that whiny, unpleasant voice. It belonged to Meredith Starr Peterson, bitch extraordinaire and wife of Trey Peterson, scion of one of the richest and most socially prominent families in town.

Meredith had made Bunny's life miserable in high school. Made fun of her because she was a straight A student and called her the Princess of Poop because her daddy ran a successful plumbing business.

Bunny *hated* Meredith.

But then pretty much everybody hated Meredith. She was an equal opportunity pisser-offer. Bunny invited her to the wedding for her family's sake. You couldn't operate any kind of business in Hannah and alienate the Petersons.

Meredith stood by the punch bowl. She was wearing an ice-blue silk designer suit and matching heels, and holding court with a group of her sycophants.

"Twenty-eight years old and limp as an overcooked noodle." Meredith fluffed her perfect blond bob with a manicured hand. The big diamond on her ring finger sparkled in the sunlight. "He was Mr. Big Stuff when I married him, but he couldn't get it up now with a cable and winch. If it wasn't for that vibrating radish I got at my cousin Debra's sex toy party, I'd be dry humping a fire hydrant by now."

"Shut up, Meredith," her husband Trey said, just before he dumped the bowl of lime sherbet punch over her head.

Green foam dripped from her hair and down her face. Meredith screeched and launched herself at Trey like a spider monkey. He grunted in surprise at the impact and stumbled back. Wrapping her legs around Trey's waist,

Meredith grabbed a double handful of his hair and yanked. He bellowed and tried to pull her off.

Trey was wasting his time, Bunny thought in dazed amusement, as she watched the couple stagger around the lawn. Meredith had a leg lock on him a can of WD-40 and a crowbar couldn't pry loose.

They lurched past Bunny, got their feet tangled together and crashed into the wedding cake. The table collapsed and the cake exploded in a fountain of yellow-and-white goo. Snapping and snarling, the Petersons rolled around in the remains of Bunny's once-beautiful wedding confection.

"My cake!" Bunny shrieked in anguish.

"Ooh, cake rassling." Looking gorgeous in a sleek, deep red dress that hugged her curvaceous body and showed off her killer legs, Bunny's friend Addy Corwin strolled up to watch. Addy's white-blond hair hung in soft curls around her toned shoulders. The platinum do was a new look for Addy, and Bunny thought she looked stunning. "You sure throw a fun wedding, Bunny."

"Fun? It's a freaking disaster."

Addy's mocking expression softened. She put her arms around Bunny and gave her a swift hug. "Don't look so woebegone, Bun Bun. It'll be okay."

"No, it won't. My parents paid a wad of money for this train wreck. Have you seen my poor daddy? He's *crying*. And Mama looks like she wants to throw up. I feel like hurling myself."

"Ah, it's not so bad." Addy picked up a monogrammed napkin and dabbed at the icing on Bunny's face. "Looks like you got caught in the fallout. That cake went up like Krakatoa."

Bunny jerked away. "Not so bad? It's mass insanity. Half the town's acting certifiable."

"I wouldn't worry about it too much. It's probably the demon dust."

"Demon dust?"

Addy raised her finger and pointed up.

With a feeling of dread, Bunny stepped from under the white awning. A glittering, black mist hung over the wedding guests like an evil spell cast by a vengeful fairy.

There was a buzzing noise inside her head. *Demon dust*. Addy had said it casually, like demons were no big deal.

And maybe they weren't to her. Addy's flinty-eyed boyfriend, Brand, was Dalvahni too. That meant he was a demon hunter from another dimension. Like Rafe, her new husband, the other life form she'd married.

Addy followed her out of the tent. "Looks like the Wedding Crasher from Hell left you a little present, but don't worry. The demon funk will wear off in an hour or so, and everybody will go back to normal." Addy gave Meredith a sour glance. "Except for Meredith, of course. Being a pain in the ass *is* normal for her. Brand and Rafe will fix everything. All anyone will remember tomorrow is having a really good time."

The buzzing noise in Bunny's head grew louder. She shook her head, trying to clear her thoughts, but everything was fuzzy. She couldn't breathe.

Get away. She had to get away.

Addy looked worried. "Say, Bunny, you don't look so good. Rafe explained things to you, didn't he? He promised me and Brand he would talk to you before the wedding."

"Oh, sure," Bunny lied, giving Addy a bright smile. She wasn't about to tell Addy her husband had kept something so important from her. Of course, *she* hadn't told him about the baby, which just about made them even. "Gee, would you look at the time!" She edged farther away from the tent. "Nice talking to you, Addy. If you'll excuse me, there's something I need to do."

Like get the hell out of Dodge before she had a complete mental breakdown.

She turned away from the line of live oaks that separated the river from the church and hobbled up the hill on the other side, nodding and smiling at friends and acquaintances she passed. Not that they noticed, she reflected darkly. They were too busy vacationing in Loony Land, thanks to Rafe and his demonic buddy.

Rafe. Oh God, *Rafe.*

She walked faster. She needed time alone to decide what to do, and that meant time away from Rafe. She couldn't think when he was around. One look in his green eyes and her brain shut down and another part of her anatomy took control.

How many times had she heard her daddy tell Cam and Coop to stop thinking with their little head and use their big one?

Daddy should have given her the girl version of the same lecture. She and her brothers had different equipment, but her hootie had been driving the Bunny Mobile for the last six weeks.

It was high time she took back the wheel.

She reached the long, gravel driveway at the top of the rise that led to the church some two hundred yards in the distance, and broke into a run.

There, parked in front of the church, was her wedding chariot and means of escape: Her sister-in-law Audrey's pink Mary Kay car, on loan to the happy couple for the honeymoon.

Happy couple, hah!

The big sedan was festooned fender to fender with shaving cream, ribbons, bows and flowers. A large, heart-shaped sign attached to the front bumper said JUST MARRIED, and tin cans, aluminum plates, old shoes and a string of cowbells trailed from the back.

She flung open the driver's side door. Good grief,

someone had rolled the inside of the car from top to bottom. She couldn't see the seats.

Wadding up the voluminous skirts of her wedding gown, she shoved aside the mountain of toilet paper and climbed in. The keys were in the ignition, thank goodness.

The windows had been left down so the interior of the car wouldn't overheat. Bunny stripped off her torn stockings and her remaining shoe and tossed them out the window. She cranked the car and roared off down the drive in a clatter of tin cans and cowbells, toilet paper streaming like parade confetti from the open windows of the pink pearl Cadillac.

Chapter Four

Rafe strode down the hill and through the trees to the gathering by the river. A grimy cloud of demon dust lingered above the white tents. It had the expected effect upon the humans, though he paid little attention to their antics. He needed to find Bunny. They would discuss matters in a sensible manner. She would understand, and things would return to their former state.

He pushed his way through the crowd looking for her, but did not see her. The gnawing ache in his chest grew worse. Where was she? What if the djegrali had taken her? He had the sudden inexplicable urge to smash something.

Brand stood near one of the tents on the riverbank talking to Addy Corwin, the leggy, blond sorceress who'd bewitched him. Not an unusual occurrence, Rafe reflected sourly. Brand was seldom far from Addy's side. He hovered near her now, his gaze hot and possessive as he looked at her. By the sword, Rafe pitied him. Brand had been a fearsome warrior, the scourge of the djegrali, until he was enslaved by his *feelings* for the female.

He shrugged aside his distaste. Addy and Bunny were

good friends. Perhaps she knew where to find Bunny. The need to find her grew stronger with each passing moment.

Rafe stalked up to them. "Where is Bunny?"

Addy scowled. "You're in deep doo doo, jerk wad. You lied. You promised to tell Bunny what you are *before* you married her."

The female Addy's speech was frequently incomprehensible to Rafe, but his brother warrior seemed to understand her.

Brand slid a protective arm around Addy. "Adara's acerbic manner belies a tender heart. She is troubled for her friend."

"Don't try to sugarcoat it, dude," Addy said. "I call 'em like I see 'em. And I say this guy's a jerk wad for playing Bunny like a fool."

Rafe frowned, trying to sort through her words. The Dalvahni gift of languages had its limits. It did not account for accent, local expressions or speech patterns. The humans in this locale were particularly fond of euphemisms, exaggerated speech and random odd terms called "Southern-isms," that made the language hard to follow. He grasped onto the one word he thought he understood.

"You think I have made Bunny appear foolish?"

"I think you've made her *feel* foolish! How would you like to find out the man you married is an immortal demon hunter from another dimension?"

"I would not marry a man, so such a supposition is pointless."

Addy rolled her eyes. "Can you *try* to have a little imagination here, Mr. Literal? Put yourself in Bunny's shoes and think how you'd feel."

"Why would I put myself in Bunny's shoes? They would not fit."

Addy threw up her hands. "He's worse than you, Brand.

You explain it to the meathead. I give up." She stomped off muttering to herself.

"She is a most volatile female." Rafe scanned the crowd again, searching for Bunny. "I find her difficult."

Brand crossed his arms on his chest. "Adara is concerned for her friend and so am I."

"Bunny is my concern. I will protect her."

"Ah, but who will protect Bunny from you?"

Rafe stiffened. "I would never hurt Bunny."

"I fear you may already have. I see the way Bunny looks at you. She loves you. Yet, you were not truthful with her before you bound her to you in the human ritual of marriage. You gave her no choice. That was not well done of you."

The back of Rafe's neck burned at the censor in Brand's voice. "There was no time," he said through his teeth.

"No time?" Brand's tone held a hint of steel. "I think not. A Dalvahni warrior does not lie, especially to himself. You care for Bunny. You were afraid of losing her. That is why you did not tell her the truth."

"Do not think to lecture *me*. You no longer know what it means to be a warrior thanks to this . . . this *affliction* of yours."

"Affliction?"

Rafe made an impatient gesture. "Your emotional involvement with the female Addy Corwin. She is responsible for your deteriorated state."

To Rafe's surprise, Brand grinned. "Deteriorated, am I? What about you, brother? I assumed you suffer from a similar condition."

"You assumed wrong."

"Then why did you marry Bunny?"

"To protect her from the djegrali, of course."

"I see. You do not love her?"

"Of course not." He shrugged. "Love is a human emotion."

Addy sauntered back up. "You 'bout done trying to talk some sense into this guy, babe?" she asked Brand. "I'm ready to blow this Popsicle stand. The cake's history, thanks to Meredith and Trey. Billy James has sucked up all the champagne, and most of the town's nekked and in the river. It's like Field Day at a nudist colony around here." She shuddered. "You know, if I've heard Mama say it once, I've heard her say it a thousand times. Most people look better with their clothes on. Hate to admit it, but she's right." She gave Rafe a curious glance. "What's the matter with Red? He looks like he ate something that disagreed with him."

Rafe felt a prickle of annoyance. "My name is not Red."

"To the contrary, *cara*," Brand said. "Rafe thinks I am unwell. He fears I am in a decline and you are the source of my illness."

Addy's eyes narrowed. "Is that so? Look, bub, I'll have you know—"

"—but fear not that he suffers from the same dread disease," Brand continued.

"Disease, is it?" Addy said. She narrowed her eyes at Rafe. "Why I ought to—"

"—because he married Bunny out of a sense of duty and nothing more. Or so he assures me. He does not love her. Such a thing is beneath a Dalvahni warrior." Brand shook his head. "I fear I am a disgrace to the brotherhood. Fortunately, Rafe is made of sterner stuff and will not succumb to my . . . er . . . abominable weakness."

"Well, big whoopee doo deal. Let's hear it for Rafe, the Dalvahni dickhead." Addy propped her hands on her hips and glared at him. "Personally, I think you're full of it, Red."

"You seem to think I have done Bunny a disservice by marrying her," Rafe said. Someone at the top of the hill was ringing a bell—several bells, in fact. Angrily, he pushed the irritating sound to the back of his mind. "I assure you it is my intent to—"

Addy held up her hand. "I know, I know. You're *concerned* for Bunny, but you don't love her. You'll keep her safe from the nasty old demon that tried to kill her, but all you feel for her is a sense of responsibility. Honor. Duty. The Dalvahni Way. I get it." She turned to Brand. "So, babe, since Red here isn't emotionally involved, I suggest *you* go after Bunny. He can stay here and clean up this mess. It's his wedding after all."

"Go after Bunny?" Rafe demanded sharply. "What do you mean?"

Addy shrugged. "See the big, pink Caddy leaving in a cloud of dust, the one with the long, white cloth streaming out the driver's side window? That's a wedding veil, Red. Since Bunny's the only bride here today, I'm guessing she's behind the wheel. Looks like she decided to start the honeymoon without you."

Bunny drove blindly. It wasn't until she wheeled onto Highway 31 and turned south that she realized she was headed for the beach house where she and Rafe were supposed to spend their honeymoon.

The beach house had always been her special place, her refuge in any moment of crisis. Marrying a demon slayer from another dimension certainly qualified.

This wasn't about running from Rafe. No, not at all.

Okay, maybe it was the *teensiest* bit about running from Rafe. But it was also about having the time and space to think things over. She probably didn't have much time. If Rafe saw her leave, he'd be right behind her. And if he couldn't figure out where she was going, her family would tell him once they sobered up.

The beach wasn't far from Hannah, seventy miles or so, little more than an hour's drive in the early sixties when her grandparents bought the cinder-block cottage by the ocean. That same seventy miles took considerably longer to drive now, what with the real estate boom in Gulf Shores and Baldwin County in the eighties and the influx of tourists and snowbirds.

Her parents were married in 1968 and had honeymooned in that little cottage. Growing up, Cam and Coop spent summers there. Bunny loved the old family photos of her brothers, stick thin and berry brown, posing in their bathing trunks on the sugary sand with the Gulf of Mexico shimmering behind them. But that was before September of 1979 and Hurricane Frederick, the storm that took out the dunes and most of Gulf Shores, including the little house by the sea.

Her parents' plumbing business was doing well by then, and they bought the lot from her daddy's parents and rebuilt. The "new" beach house was bigger and nicer. A raised foundation, four bedrooms and two and a half baths, a wraparound porch, dormer windows and a boardwalk leading down to the beach. It was completed in 1983, the year Bunny was born. She spent every spring and summer vacation there as a girl and a few Christmases and Thanksgivings, too. As an adult, it was her home away from home. She loved sitting on the porch, feeling the kiss of the sea wind on her skin and in her hair, inhaling the briny scent of the ocean and listening to the shrill cries of the circling gulls.

Honeymooning at the beach had seemed like the perfect way to start her new life with Rafe. Serendipitous, the circle completed from her parents' honeymoon.

Rafe seemed fine with the idea when she suggested it.

"I do not care where we go, as long as I am with you, *cara*," he told her in that dark, smoky voice of his. "I am not from here, so I will leave the decision to you."

Not from here? Yeah, you think? Talk about your understatements. He'd been vague about his past and she'd been too smitten to ask questions.

Her grip tightened on the wheel.

No, not too smitten. Too afraid.

Deep down, she knew it was too good to be true. Rafe was sexy, gorgeous and attentive. With him, she became someone else, someone daring and wild, a tigress, not a bunny. He made her feel beautiful. He made her shiver and weep with joy and desire. Guys like him didn't fall from trees, especially in Hannah.

She was crazy mad in love with him and he was a *demon slayer,* for Pete's sake.

And she was having his baby.

Oh God, oh God, oh God.

Bunny drove faster.

Chapter Five

"Bunny," Rafe shouted, running after her.

The pink vehicle sped down the dirt road and disappeared in a cloud of red dust.

She was gone. She left him.

She *left* him.

With a bellow of frustration, he hurled a lightning bolt at a nearby pine tree. It exploded in a shower of wood.

"Way to go, genius." Addy walked up the hill with Brand. "If this is you being unemotional, I'd hate to see you riled up."

"She's gone."

"A master of the obvious, aren't you? Well, don't just stand there murdering innocent trees. Go after her."

"How?" Rafe snarled.

"*Hel-lo,* you're a Dalvahni super dude. Use your woo woo."

Rafe's head began to pound. Bunny was gone. His gut burned, his chest ached like he'd been gored by a three-headed Gorthian bull, and this irritating female was speaking nonsense.

"I do not understand," he said through his teeth. "What is 'woo woo?' "

"Your super powers, Red. You know, *pfft* you're here. *Pfft* you're there. *Pfft pfft*, you're everywhere."

"It is not so simple, Adara," Brand said. "Rafe cannot teleport to Bunny if he does not know where she is going."

"I bet I know where she's headed," someone said behind them.

"Yep, me too."

"Oh, goody, man boobs," Addy muttered as Bunny's brothers, Cameron and Cooper Raines, huffed up the grassy hill from the river. "At least they're wearing pants." Addy raised her eyes skyward. "Thank you, Lord Jesus."

Rafe eyed both men with disapproval. They had, indeed, donned their breeches. But they were shirtless, leaving their distended bellies and hairy chests exposed. He liked Bunny's brothers well enough. But he could not understand how they allowed their bodies to deteriorate in such a manner. Cam and Coop were fleshy and unfit from too much food and ale and too little exercise.

The Dalvahni stayed in peak physical condition. Anything less was unacceptable. Anything less would get them killed.

Addy gave them a bright smile. "Have a nice swim?"

Cam looked perplexed. "You know, it was the damndest thing. I don't remember getting in the river, but I looked down and the old anaconda was out of the cage and going for a swim, if you know what I mean."

Addy's smile faded. "Unfortunately, I do. Thank you for that image. So, you know where Bunny might have gone?"

"Sure," Cam said. "Ten to one, she's gone to the beach house. She loves that place, has since she was a little bitty thing. She calls it her happy place."

Rafe felt a surge of adrenaline. His hunter's instincts sharpened. The Raines' second home on the ocean, the place where he and Bunny were supposed to engage in the postmarital ritualistic period of harmony referred to by humans as the "honeymoon." She had run from him, but she had not run far. Viewing the circumstances in the best possible light, she had, in reality, run *to* him. A little of the tightness in his chest eased.

"I will find her." He took a deep breath. "Much as it pains me to admit it, you are correct in one aspect, Addy. I did not explain things to Bunny as I should have. I nailed up."

Addy's eyes twinkled. "You *screwed* up, Red."

"Whatever." He waved his hand in a gesture of dismissal. "I will rectify my mistake. I will find Bunny and make her understand. She is mine now."

"Ooh, possessive," Addy said. "Boy, for an 'I'm-in-control' kind of guy who would *never* do something as humanly pathetic as fall in love, you seem mighty interested in our Bunny."

Rafe ignored her. She was not a warrior. She could not understand the warrior way. His desire to shield Bunny had everything to do with duty and honor, and nothing to do with *love*.

He turned to the brothers. "You have some means of transport here?"

"I rode with the wife," Cam said. "But Coop's got his truck."

Rafe held out his hand. "You will give me the keys to this vehicle."

Coop eyed him with uncertainty. "Do you know how to drive a five-speed?"

"No, but that will not be a problem."

Coop shook his head. "Damn straight it won't be a problem, 'cause I ain't giving you my truck."

Something inside of Rafe snapped. He snarled and seized Coop by the throat, much to Cam's apparent delight.

"But I'll take you wherever you want to go," Coop wheezed.

Rafe released him. "That is good. Where is this truck of yours?"

Rubbing his throat and glaring at his chortling brother, Coop pointed to the grassy field where the guests had parked their cars. "Over there, the red Ford with the big toolbox on the back."

Coop gave a startled yelp as Rafe grabbed him by the arm and teleported them across the lot.

Coop swayed and grabbed the side of the truck for support. "Whoa, musta had more to drink than I thought. Thing is, I don't remember drinking anything. Last thing I remember is leaving the church for the reception and the next thing I know I'm standing in the river naked as a jaybird." He shook his head. "Man, I'm gonna catch hell from Audrey when she hears about this. Good thing she's in Mobile at the hospital with her mama. I wouldn't wish a heart attack on anyone, but if Audrey was here and caught me with my Johnson hanging out at my sister's wedding, *I'd* be the one in the ICU."

Rafe opened the door and climbed into the passenger side of the truck. "Do not trouble yourself. Your wife will not hear of this. Take me to your sister."

"*Take me to your sister.*" Coop slid into the driver's seat and turned the key. The truck engine rumbled to life. "You sound like a little green man from one of those cheesy science fiction movies." He made a wide circle on the grass and pulled onto the narrow, winding dirt road that led from the church, through the woods to the highway beyond. "'Cept they say 'take me to your leader,' not 'your sister.'"

"I am not green or little," Rafe said.

"You can say that again. You and that brother of yours are big sonsabitches." Coop's belly jiggled as the truck bumped down the tree-lined road. "So are you, or aren't you?"

"Am I what?"

"An alien."

Rafe sighed mentally. He knew Cooper was joking, but he was in no mood for levity. He would tell him the truth and erase his memory later.

"I am not from Earth."

Cooper slammed his palm on the steering wheel. "Not from Earth, that's a good one. Do you lie to your mama out of that same mouth?"

"The Dalvahni do not have mothers. We are an immortal warrior race created some ten millennia ago by the god Kehvahn to keep the djegrali in check."

"The what?"

"Demons, you humans call them."

Coop chuckled. "Demons and a god named Kevin. Hoo boy, you're a strange one. You know that?"

Rafe remained silent, his thoughts on Bunny. He stared out the windshield at the road, willing the truck to go faster. Bunny was somewhere up ahead. What if the djegrali had followed her?

He clenched his fists. No. He would find her first and slay the djegrali.

She would be safe.

He would destroy anyone or anything that tried to harm her.

Brand's words floated through his mind. *But who will protect Bunny from you?*

What would Bunny do when he left her? She loved him. She had told him so many times in words and in a thousand other ways. It was in her beautiful eyes every time she looked at him, and in the way she came apart in his arms. In truth, his empty soul drank in the sweet words like a rain-parched flower. She was so open and gentle and loving, so generous and giving. After he left, would she turn to another for comfort?

A tortuous image formed in his mind of Bunny in someone else's arms, her white limbs wrapped around another man's waist as he moved in and out of her . . .

A red haze seized his brain and his mind slammed shut. No, he would not think about that. Bunny was his . . . at least for now.

Emptiness loomed ahead of him at the thought of living without her. Absently, he rubbed his aching chest but the pain did not subside. The Dalvahni were immune to sickness and healed quickly. This hurt, whatever it was, would soon be gone.

He would not think about leaving Bunny. He would think about the hunt and keeping her safe.

What she did after he returned to the Hall of Warriors . . .

He would not think about that either.

The two-lane highway cut through the gently rolling farmland of Behr County. Cattle grazed in open fields, and pines and hardwoods jostled with one another to reach the side of the road. Bunny usually enjoyed this drive but today she saw none of the pastoral beauty of South Alabama. Her beautiful wedding and her beautiful husband were the shattered dreams of a naïve fool. She alternated between tears and anger. All she could think about was getting away, driving faster. Drive fast enough and Audrey's pink Cadillac would abandon the highway and soar into the clouds like Chitty Chitty Bang Bang, taking her away from her life and her problems.

She was going eighty miles per hour when she crossed the line into Baldwin County. She barely noticed the gray trooper car parked at an abandoned gas station. The wail of the siren jerked her out of her misery. She looked in the rearview mirror and saw the blue light.

"Shoot, oh shoot," she said, pulling onto the grassy berm.

The state trooper got out of his vehicle and walked up to her window.

"I clocked you doing eighty-five in a fifty-five-mile-per-hour zone, ma'am. What's the big hurry?"

Bunny dropped her head onto the steering wheel. "I— I'm a little upset, Officer. I didn't realize how fast I was going."

"Uh-huh. That's no excuse to break the law. I'm going to have to write you a ticket."

"Great," Bunny mumbled.

"Just got married, huh?" The officer chuckled. "Most people take their husband along for the honeymoon. But I don't see yours. 'Course, he could be buried under all that Charmin in the backseat."

Oh, brother. Of all the troopers in Alabama, she got the funny guy. Bunny sighed and lifted her head.

"Darn." Wiping her eyes, she looked up at the officer through the open window. "I knew I forgot something."

He was younger than she expected, maybe in his mid-thirties, with warm brown skin, strong features and a wide, pleasant smile.

His friendly smile faded and his mouth fell open. What was the matter with him? She'd been crying but, jeez, she couldn't look that bad. She felt a spasm of alarm. Oh good God, surely he wouldn't arrest her?

"Is there a problem, Officer?"

"Duuuh," he said.

She took a quick peek in the rearview mirror. Nope, her mascara was fine, though she did have a few spots of icing here and there.

"Pretty," the trooper said, giving her a goofy grin.

"Look, Officer, I know I was speeding and I'm sorry. I promise to slow down. So if you'll just write me a ticket, I'll be on my way and—"

"Pretty," he said again.

She waved her hand in his face. He looked back at her without blinking.

"Uh, thanks. Can I please have my ticket now? I'm kind of in a hurry."

He shredded the ticket and handed it to her. "Wedding present. Pretty."

Bunny felt certain he wasn't supposed to do that, but she wasn't about to look a gift horse in the mouth.

"Gee, that's awfully nice of you, Officer. Well, if you don't mind, I'll be going." Giving him a bright smile and a wave, Bunny eased her car back onto the road. "Bye now," she called out the open window. "I'll watch my speed, I promise."

As she drove off, she checked him in her rearview mirror. He stood by the side of the road gazing after her with a hangdog look on his face, his shoulders slumped in a mournful fashion.

"Like a kid at Christmas with a broken toy." She shook her head. "Weird."

Not so weird if you think about it, dummy, a voice inside her head said.

Bunny groaned aloud. She knew that voice, although she hadn't listened to it much lately.

It was Smart Bunny. Smart Bunny kept her out of trouble. Smart Bunny was . . . well . . . *smart*.

Dumb Bunny . . . ? Eh, not so much. And Dumb Bunny had been running the show since she met Rafe.

Remember the gaggle of teenage boys that have been hanging around the library for the past few weeks? Smart Bunny asked. *You wrote it off as boredom and interest in that cute little Betsy Phillips who's been volunteering in the afternoons.*

"She's sixteen and homeschooled," Bunny protested. "She's a new girl for them to flirt with."

Uh-huh, and what about Horace Clement? He brought you all those roses.

"He grows roses. He had a bumper crop this year."

Smart Bunny made a rude noise. *Bumper crop, my ass. He stripped his prize rosebushes down to the nub for you. And how do you explain Jackson Pritchard and the lemon meringue pie he's left on your desk every Monday for . . . oh, let me see . . . THE LAST SIX WEEKS? Rat Godwin down at the garage, the druggist, the guys down at the hardware store*—Smart Bunny's list seemed to go on and on—*your parents' yardman, your brothers' friends— their MARRIED friends—they've all been coming on to you.*

Bunny shifted in her seat. Being a single female in a small town, she had her share of admirers. But lately she seemed to attract anyone with a moving part.

And a few without a moving part, as well, Smart Bunny said. *Deanna Wilkerson down at the Kut 'N Kurl put the moves on you big-time when you went for a pedicure. DEE! You've known Dee since kindergarten.*

Smart Bunny was right. It was as though she'd morphed into some kind of sex goddess, shedding pheromones wherever she went, like a Lab blowing its coat. She hadn't paid much attention to it. Too busy living in Dopeville strung out on a certain hunk.

A handsome hunk from another dimension who claimed to be a demon hunter.

A demon hunter who claimed to have changed her.

She could still hear his words. *I gave you a portion of my essence, Bunny. You are no longer human.*

She began to shake.

Oh God. She needed sugar. A buttload of it.

She swerved the car into the parking lot of a Gas 'N Gulp and rushed inside.

Chapter Six

Bunny threw the train of her wedding dress over one arm and cruised up and down the aisles of the Gas 'N Gulp. She stuck a two-liter bottle of Dr Pepper under each arm, grabbed several packages of powdered donuts, a large bag of Skittles, two boxes of Hot Tamales, a giant Sweet Tart and a PayDay, and hurried to the register. After plunking her items on the counter, she selected a giant-sized Butterfinger from the display rack, then put it back. The thought of eating chocolate made her queasy.

Strange. Usually she was all about the chocolate.

The row of Good & Plenty boxes caught her eye. She hated licorice. But for some reason it sounded good today. Better than good; essential. She added three boxes of Good & Plenty candies to her cache of sugar and threw in two bags of barbequed peanuts for good measure. A little salt to balance out the sugar, she rationalized.

The woman behind the counter sported a female mullet—buzzed, short hair in front and on the sides and long and scraggly hair in the back. She regarded Bunny with a curious expression over her double chins.

"Nice dress," Mullet Woman said. "Getting married, huh?"

No, I wear this to clean the toilets, Bunny thought irritably, gazing longingly at the licorice candy at the top of the pile.

Oh, what the hell. If she didn't have some sugar soon she'd go ballistic and twirl Mullet Woman around by the hair.

The hair in the back, of course. That fuzzy stuff in front would do a Marine proud.

Bunny picked up the nearest box, tore it open and dumped the contents in her mouth, chasing it with half a liter of Dr Pepper. She burped and smiled as the sugar euphoria took hold.

Her desire to throttle the woman behind the counter abruptly faded. She handed the cashier the empty candy box and the opened soda bottle. "You can ring me up now, please."

The woman shook her head and started totaling the purchases. "Honey, you got man troubles if ever I seen 'em. Wuddee do, hitcha?"

"No, nothing like that. I found out he lied." Bunny wrinkled her nose. "No, that's not fair. He didn't *lie*. He just didn't tell me everything. Lots of things. *Important* things."

"*Deceive me not by omission, love,*" Mullet Woman said. "*The heart is pierced as deeply by silence as e'er by spoken lies.*"

"Why, th-that's beautiful," Bunny said, fighting back tears. God, her hormones were all over the place. Homicidal to maudlin in a nanosecond.

"I write poetry sometimes. Keep one of them composition books by my bed."

Bunny blinked in surprise. "You wrote that?"

"Yeah. Come up with it after I found out my second husband, Travis the Louse, had him another wife and kids in Loo-zee-anna." She gave Bunny a narrow-eyed stare. "He was a truck driver, see. Traveled a lot. Your husband ain't a truck driver, is he?"

"No."

"Good. I was a prize idiot. Got stuck with the payments on Travis's boat and truck when he left."

"That's awful," Bunny said, tearing up again. Good grief, she couldn't stop crying.

"Yeah, Brittany got Travis and I got the bills. That's why I'm working here. Sucks, don't it?"

"Sucks the big one," Bunny agreed. She grabbed a napkin off the deli counter and blew her nose.

"Haven't been able to stand the name Brittany ever since." Mullet Woman gave Bunny another hard look. "Your name ain't Brittany, is it?"

"No, my name's Bunny."

"Bunny? What kind of name is that?"

"Mine, I'm afraid."

"Is it a nickname?"

"Unfortunately, no. I was born on Easter."

"Huh," Mullet Woman said. "You don't look like a Bunny. Look more like an Emma or an Olivia, to me. No disrespect, but your parents screwed the pooch on the name thing."

Bunny slapped her hand down on the counter. "I *know*. I could have been Elisabeth or Jane or Grace." She made a face. "Instead, I get stuck with Bunny. And if that isn't bad enough my middle name is *Nicole*." She shuddered. "Isn't it awful? Bunny Nicole. Sounds like a pole dancer."

"My name's Nicole."

Bunny gaped at her. It felt like all the blood in her

body rushed to her head. "Uh . . . yeah . . . well . . . um . . . you don't look like a pole dancer either."

"I worked at Bobby's Booby Trap in Pensacola for three years. That's where I met Travis."

Mullet Woman the poetry-writing pole dancer. Huh.

Bunny gave her a weak smile. "Your name's Nicole. Isn't that the funniest thing?"

"Yeah, a real stitch." Mullet Woman shoved the bag of junk food at Bunny. "That'll be $18.29."

That's when it hit Bunny. She didn't have any money. Or a purse.

"My purse," she cried. "I forgot my purse! Oh, my goodness, I've been driving without a license."

"You ain't got no money?" Mullet Woman pulled the bag back across the counter. "I'll put these things back then."

Bunny grabbed the other end of the sack and held on. "Wait. You don't understand. I *need* this stuff."

"I need a lot of things, sugar, including $18.29 from you. You can't pay, you don't get the goods. This is a gas station, not the Salvation Army. You'd best be worrying about how you're gonna pay for the candy you ate and the half a bottle of Dr Pepper you drank. I can't put that soda bottle back on the shelf. It'ud be unhygienic."

"But . . . but," Bunny stuttered.

"Bunny Raines, is that you?"

Bunny whirled around. A woman wearing skintight jeans, a camisole that exposed her golden cleavage, a bright orange cropped jacket and high-heeled sandals stood in the doorway. She regarded Bunny from behind a pair of Dolce & Gabbana sunglasses.

"Trish Russell," Bunny said, her heart sinking.

Great, just what she needed. Trish and Meredith Peterson had run around together in high school. They made fun of everybody who wasn't in their clique, snaked other girls' boyfriends just 'cause they could, flirted with the male teachers—and slept with some of them, according to rumor—and generally made life miserable for the un-cool kids at Hannah High, a number that had included Bunny.

"In the flesh." Trish clicked over to the register on her high heels. "Only it's Trish Baughman now. I married an orthopedic surgeon five years ago with a practice in Fairhope. Maybe you heard about it? It was in all the society papers."

Oh, yeah, she heard about it. Trish was a receptionist at the doctor's office until the first Mrs. Baughman caught Trish and her husband making the beast with two backs in one of the examining rooms. Gave a whole new meaning to the term "bone doctor." One nasty divorce later and Trish Trash Russell was the second Mrs. Baughman.

Trish twirled a lock of her honey-blond hair. "My Jimmy Wimmy is crazy about me. Spoils me something rotten." She looked Bunny up and down. "So, what's with the getup? You finally get married or is this what passes for plumber chic in Hannah?"

Still with the cracks about her dad being a plumber. Bunny refused to take the bait. She caught a whiff of something unpleasant and looked around. "Is something burning?"

"I don't smell anything." Trish examined her painted nails. "You headed for the beach?"

"Yes," Bunny said.

"Awesome. My Mercedes broke down. You know how it is with these expensive luxury cars. They are *soooo* temperamental. Would you be a doll and give me a ride to Foley?"

"Well . . . I . . . uh," Bunny stammered, trying to think of an excuse. *Pfft*, the sugar rush from the Good & Plenty candies evaporated, leaving her sucrose-starved brain unable to form an intelligent thought. "Uh, yeah. Sure. I guess."

Was she out of her mind? Be locked up in a car with the bitch from hell for forty miles? Great, couldn't she just poke her eyes out? If she was blind, she couldn't drive, right?

The cashier cleared her throat. "Why don't you get your friend to pay for your groceries in exchange for a ride?"

"Thanks, Wide Load. That's a good idea." Trish slapped her platinum card on the counter. "Hold on while I get something to drink."

"Her name is *Nicole* and she's a poet," Bunny said as Trish clattered off in the direction of the coolers, jean-clad hips swaying.

Trish waved one manicured hand. "Whatever."

Nicole shook her head. "That there's a Brittany if ever I saw one. Sure you don't wanna hang out here until your man shows up? I'm working three to eleven."

Her man. Bunny's stomach fluttered nervously. Holy mackerel, she still found it hard to believe she was married. For better or for worse, only her "worse" included demons and a supernatural hunk for a spouse.

She grabbed the PayDay out of the bag and bit the end off of it, paper and all. She chewed frantically. "I appreciate the offer, Nicole, but I'm not sure he'll come after me."

"Are you kidding? He'll be on you like white on rice. You got that sweet, helpless thing going for you. Men love that shit."

"I am *not* helpless . . . or . . . or *sweet*. What a horrible thing to say."

Nicole shrugged. "I call 'em like I see 'em. 'Course, it don't hurt none that you're gorgeous. I noticed that right off soon as you walked in the door. You look like something off one of them romance novels, all soft and elegant and refined-looking. Not that I'm hitting on you or nothing like that. I don't swing that way. I'm just saying you're a mighty purty woman. You ever thought of taking up exotic dancing?"

"Uh . . . no."

"Too bad. You could make a killing." She waved her hands around, causing a ripple effect up and down her fleshy arms. "You could call yourself Bunny Love. That 'ud be your stage name, see?"

"Thanks, I'll keep that in mind."

Trish sauntered back up to the counter, a bottle of cheap wine in each hand. "I'll take these and two of your chili dogs. Extra onions," she said.

Strawberry wine and chili dogs? Bunny's stomach roiled. The stench that permeated the little store didn't help, either.

"Whew, what *is* that smell?" The cashier produced a can of air freshener and sprayed the area behind the counter. "That dang sorry Luther musta left the garbage in the storeroom again."

She bagged the wine and Trish's chili dogs and handed Trish her credit card and the receipt to sign. "Anything you want me to tell that man of yours in case he shows up here looking for you?" she asked Bunny.

Rafe. Oh God, Rafe.

Rafe with his magic hands and mouth, and his sexy bedroom voice, deep and full of sultry promise as a hot summer night. Just the thought of him left her weak and willing. Willing to do anything he wanted.

She felt a spasm of self-disgust. There she went again, listening to her hootie. It had to stop. There was the baby to think of now.

"No messages," Bunny said. She ripped open a pack

of powdered donuts and jammed two of them in her mouth. "I doubt you'll see him anyway."

Trish handed Nicole a card from her wallet. "But if he does come in, give him my card." She gave the cashier a glittering smile. "Be sure and tell him *I'm* with Bunny now, and that I'm going to take good care of his sweetie."

Chapter Seven

Bunny clutched the bag of junk food to her chest and hurried out to the pink Caddy. The pavement of the parking lot blistered her bare feet, but she hardly noticed. Stuck in the car with Trish Trash Russell for the better part of an hour? Somebody shoot her. Please. Things couldn't get much worse.

She pulled the bag of Skittles, the Hot Tamales, and the partially emptied bottle of Dr Pepper out of the sack and deposited the rest on the floorboard within easy reach. If she was going to do this, it would have to be under the influence of sugar.

She climbed into the car, wadded her dress up around her thighs, and jammed the soft drink bottle between her legs. Tearing a hole in one corner of the Skittles bag, she poured a third of the contents into her mouth and chewed. The sugar euphoria took hold. She closed her eyes and concentrated. She could do this.

The car door opened and Trish slid into the passenger side seat in a cloud of chili dog and onion funk. Good thing the windows were down or Bunny might have hurled. She took a hearty slug of Dr Pepper and scarfed down some more Skittles. *I think I can, I think I can, I think I can,* she chanted mentally.

"Ooh, this is going to be so much *fun,*" Trish crooned. She took a bottle of wine out of the plastic sack and set it on the seat. "Just like old times."

"Old times?" Bunny cranked the car and pulled back onto the road. "What 'old times' are you talking about? The time you stuck sardines in my locker or the time you announced over the loudspeaker during cheerleader try-outs that my favorite hobbies were catching farts in a jar and giving Principal Chambliss blow jobs during study hall?"

"My, you were an industrious little girl."

"I didn't *do* those things. You lied!"

"I did?" Trish took a huge bite out of a chili dog. "Oh, well, water under the bridge."

"Have to be a mighty big bridge," Bunny muttered.

She kept the windows down because of the smell. Her beautiful upsweep hairdo was toast by now anyway. Trish's highlighted tresses whipped around in the wind from the open windows, but she seemed oblivious to anything but her chili dog.

Bunny shuddered. She didn't know which was worse, the greasy, burned smell of the hot dog or the little grunting noises of enjoyment Trish made as she ate it.

Trish finished off the first chili dog and unwrapped the second one. Setting the foil wrapper in her lap, she opened her purse and fished inside it. "Ah, here they are," she said, brandishing a bag of M&Ms.

She ripped open the package and sprinkled the multi-colored candy on top of the waxy smear of melted cheese.

Bunny's stomach lurched again. Gross. She eased the accelerator down a notch. The faster she got to Foley and ditched Trish, the better. They sped through the green countryside, passing the occasional house and seedy-looking gas station. A metal sign said BAY MINETTE 8 MILES.

Trish waved the M&Ms sandwich in Bunny's direction. "Wanna bite?"

"Uh, no thanks." She gave her passenger a sideways glance. Trish's sunglasses moved up and down on the bridge of her nose as she munched. "I don't believe I've ever seen anyone eat a chocolate chili cheese dog before."

"Really? I like to mix my pleasures, in spite of the sometimes unpleasant consequences."

"Consequences?"

"Broken bones, cirrhosis, venereal disease, heart attack." Trish shoved the last of the bun in her mouth. Unscrewing the bottle of strawberry wine, she drained half of it in one swallow and belched. "Ooh, and heartburn. Mustn't forget that one. That's the trouble with humans." Her voice deepened to a harsh bass. "Your bodies wear out too quickly. It's a nuisance, really, having to constantly change from one carcass to another."

"Holy shit!" Bunny shrieked, swerving across the yellow line and back again.

She shot a startled look at her passenger. Trish's sunglasses were gone and her eyes were dark pools of purple gunk. As Bunny watched in horror, Trish's face distorted and the hands gripping the wine bottle grew twisted and gnarled. Wicked claws sprouted at the end of the demon's grotesque fingers.

The thing on the other side of the car gave her an evil grin. "What's the matter, little rabbit, afraid of the Boogie Man?"

"Oh God, you're not Trish. You're a demon!"

The Trish-thing chuckled, a low, rumbling sound that crawled up Bunny's spine and paralyzed her with fear. Holding the bottle in a two-fisted grip, the demon took another long swallow of wine and wiped its mouth with the back of one misshapen, warty hand. "Not the brightest star in the universe, are you? But I doubt it's your intellect that attracted the Dalvahni. I can't say as I blame him." The demon trailed a crooked, black nail down Bunny's bare arm. "You are a delicious little thing."

"Don't touch me," Bunny cried, shrinking against the driver's door.

The car careened over the yellow line again and she jerked it back into the right lane. She stared straight ahead, willing her frozen brain to think. What should she do? Drive faster? Slower? Slam on the brakes and throw herself out of the car?

No, couldn't do that. She might hurt the baby.

The demon went on talking in that deep, horrible voice. "I thought you were succulent the first time I saw you." The monster took another pull on the wine bottle. "But now you're even more delicious. Sweet and creamy, my very own Bunny Shake."

"The first time you saw me? Wait, you're the demon that attacked me at the library?"

"Right again, little rabbit." The demon tossed the empty wine bottle out the window and broke open the second one. "Thought I killed you, to tell you the truth. You must be tougher than you look."

No, not tougher. Rafe saved her, thank God. But he wasn't here to save her now. And that was her fault for running away.

Bunny kept driving. She didn't know what else to do. She was too terrified to think. If she jumped out of the car and ran, the thing would probably catch her. Her only chance was to keep talking, to keep *it* talking, and hope it would buy her some time until she could think of something to do.

"What do you want?" she asked, clutching the wheel with terror-stiff hands.

"I'm going to use you to trap the Dalvahni. Then I'm going to kill him and drain him dry of his powers. When I finish with him, I'm going to feast on that sweet little meat sack you call a body."

Use her to hurt Rafe? Not no, but *hell* no. Maybe it was hormones or maybe her sugar high had worn off, but Bunny was no longer afraid.

She was pissed.

"Oh yeah?" she said. "I got your meat sack right here, bitch."

Taking her right foot off the accelerator, she lifted her leg and executed a perfect side kick over the center console. Bunny had never been particularly athletic, but this side kick was a thing of beauty. Jackie Chan couldn't have done better. *Wham!* Her right foot connected with Trish with the force of a battering ram. The blow took the passenger door off its hinges and knocked the demon out of the car.

"Whoo hoo," Bunny shouted, pumping her fists in the air. "That's what I'm talking about!"

Exhilaration coursed through her veins. She felt strong and invincible. No more Miss Nice Bunny.

She was Bunny to the max, Bunny with an attitude.

She was freaking Super Bunny.

She looked in the rearview mirror. The demon rolled down the side of the highway and came to rest in a grassy ditch.

Bunny slowed the car. "Crap."

Trish might be a brass-plated bitch, but she didn't ask for this. Bunny couldn't in good conscience drive off and leave her on the side of the road without making sure she wasn't hurt. That would be rude, especially if the demon was gone.

And even if it wasn't, she still had to check. It was the right thing to do.

Shoot a monkey.

She put the car in reverse. The broken door dragged in the dirt as she backed up. "You all right, Trish?"

Trish groaned and sat up. She'd lost her sandals, her hair looked like it had been attacked by a rabid Flobee and her clothes were covered in dirt and grass stains. But nothing seemed to be broken. A pair of wobbly purple eyes focused on Bunny with an obvious effort. Recognition dawned. The fiend roared, buffeting Bunny with a gale force wind that reeked of onions and canned chili.

"Whew." Bunny waved her hand in front of her face. "I'm taking that as a yes."

Trish's jaw expanded grotesquely. A long, black tongue as thick as a man's arm whipped out of her mouth and snaked through the air toward Bunny.

Uh-oh. Something had its demonic panties in a bunch.

She'd done the polite thing. She asked, "You all right, bitch?" and Trish had answered. The rules of Bitch Etiquette had been satisfied.

Bunny gunned it. The damaged passenger door swung crazily on its busted hinges. With a loud metallic screech, the demon snagged the broken door with its tongue and ripped it off the Caddy.

Yeow.

Audrey was going to have a kitten when she saw her car.

Coop was singing along with the musical device called a radio.

Git your dawgs off my porch.
Git your Chevy out my drive.
Git your Redman off my table,
'Cause I done found out you lied.

Rafe gritted his teeth. His head pounded with images of Bunny. Bunny trapped and at the mercy of the djegrali, Bunny broken and bleeding, the life's blood pouring out of her while he sat confined in this wheeled conveyance with her idiot brother. Granted, the vehicles of today were faster than the horse and carriage, the mode of transport used by humans the last time he had hunted on Earth. And the roads were vastly improved. But their progress seemed agonizingly slow.

His muscles tightened with repressed rage. He wanted to kill someone or something, maybe Coop if he did not shut up.

He scowled and waved his hand at the radio, and the annoying racket Cooper called "music" abruptly ceased.

"Hey!" Coop fiddled with the noisemaker. "The radio quit working. Damn. I like that song."

He swerved the truck off the road and pulled up to a metal box in front of a single-story building.

Rafe glared at Coop. "Why are we stopping?"

"We need gas. Only got a quarter of a tank. I wasn't planning on driving to Gulf Shores."

"I see." Rafe tightened his hold on his temper. He was a warrior. A warrior remained calm and rational. This delay could not be helped. Why then did he feel so murderous and on edge? "I will pay for your fuel."

"Nah, man, don't worry about it."

Rafe removed a leather pouch from his jacket pocket and handed Cooper a wad of bills. "I insist."

Coop counted the money. He looked up, his expression incredulous. "Are you crazy? There must be a thousand bucks here."

"If that is not sufficient—"

Coop shoved the money back at Rafe. "Sufficient? It's way too much."

"It is not too much," Rafe said stiffly. "I would recompense you for the use of your truck."

"Recompense? Now there's a twenty-five-dollar word if ever I heard one. No wonder Bunny fell in love with you. Smart as a whip, my baby sister, but I can't understand half of what she says. Always got her nose in a book. 'Course, she *is* a librarian."

Rafe tried again. "At least allow me to pay for the fuel."

Coop unhooked a long, black tube from the metal box and stuck one end of it in a hole in the truck. Rafe stared at the contraption. What was it called? Ah yes, a gas pump.

"Nope," Coop said. "You're family now. Your money don't spend with me."

A curious sense of warmth stirred in Rafe's chest. "Family?"

"Sure. You married my baby sister. That makes you family. That is, if you can patch things up with Bunny. What'd you do to make her so all-fired mad, anyhow?"

"I told her the truth about me."

"Not your first lap around the racetrack, huh?" Coop rolled his eyes. "No wonder she's pissed. It's your wedding day. She wants butterflies and roses and all that romantic shit. She don't want the *truth*. Listen, I been married nearly fifteen years. If in doubt, apologize, even if you got no idea what you did wrong. Even if you didn't *do* anything wrong, say you're sorry. It'll get your nuts out of the blender."

Rafe processed this bit of information. "I will endeavor to remember that."

"Good. Tell you what, Mr. Money Bags, why don't you go inside the store and get me a bag of pork skins and a Co-cola. I'm thirsty."

"Very well," Rafe said.

He strode into the low building. As soon as he stepped inside he detected Bunny's delicate floral scent and the unmistakable stench of the djegrali. He opened his senses. Gone, both of them; whether together or separately, he could not tell.

Bunny could be safe or she could be hurt or dying at this very moment.

An unfamiliar emotion shook him to the core and turned his bones to water.

"Are you real or am I hallucinating?" The question shook him from his roiling thoughts. A woman wearing a thin, sleeveless garment that exposed her fleshy arms and heavy bosom leaned across a partition at one end of the store. She gawked at him. "I ain't never seen a man as pretty as you in all my born days."

Rafe stalked up to her. "You are the proprietress of this establishment?"

"Oh yeah."

"I am looking for a woman."

"My lucky day."

He gritted his teeth. "The woman I am looking for is my wife."

His wife; he felt a surge of fierce possessiveness at the words. She was his, and no one, man or demon, would take her from him.

"Ah, hell, you're Bunny's old man, aren't you?" She straightened with a sigh. "Figured as much, you wearing a tux and all. But a girl can hope. You just missed her. She left a few minutes ago."

"She was unharmed when she left?"

"Seemed fine to me, except for a major sugar Jones. She bought enough candy to choke a horse." She shook her head. "It ain't fair, her being able to eat like that and stay skinny as a straw-fed hog."

"Did she leave alone?"

She made a face. "Nah, she left with a woman named Trish. Your wife seemed to know her. A real piece of work, this Trish. I'd call her a bitch, but that would be an insult to bitches everywhere. She left you her card."

She held out a small, rectangular piece of paper. The moment Rafe touched the card it dissolved in a puff of greasy, black smoke. The smoke formed into a gaping maw. A rasping, sinister voice spoke from the dark abyss.

"*Mine, Dalvahni,*" the voice said.

Rafe's mouth went dry and his insides twisted. Fear, he realized with a sense of shock, finally able to put a name to the strange sensations he'd encountered since entering the shop. He was afraid. He'd heard humans speak of fear many times, but he'd never experienced it until now. He tried to examine the sensation with calm detachment and failed. He could not remain detached when it felt as though a demon had pulled the heart from his chest.

The djegrali had Bunny.

Chapter Eight

Rafe materialized behind the wheel of the truck.

"Whoa, where'd you come from?" Cooper jerked open the passenger door. "And what do you think you're doing? You can't drive a stick."

"I do not have time to argue with you, Cooper." Rafe gripped the steering wheel. "Get in or stay put. I do not care."

"Now see here, Rafe. This is my truck. You can't just—"

Rafe turned his head and looked at Coop.

Coop jumped back. "Jesus, man, your eyes are glowing."

Without a word, Rafe waved his hand. The engine started and the truck jerked into gear.

"Okay, okay, hold your horses." Coop scrambled inside the moving vehicle. "How do you think you're going to find the beach house without me anyways? You need me, man." The truck careened onto the road, narrowly missing an oncoming van. Coop gave a frightened yelp. "What the hell do you think you're doing? Put your hands on the wheel before we have an accident. This is a brand-new truck."

"We will not have a mishap. But in the unlikely event that I do damage your truck I will purchase you a new one."

Coop clutched the seat as the truck accelerated. "I don't want a new one. I want—Hey, slow down, you're going ninety miles an hour and—Watch that old lady in that . . . Oh God, you're going around her. Oh, shit, there's a beer truck coming—Move over, dude, move over. Wrong side of the road, dude. *Wrong side of the—*" Coop threw his arms over his head. "Oh, man, we're gonna die."

Rafe ground his teeth. He wanted to leave Coop on the side of the road. But, as much as it galled him to admit it, he needed Coop to find Bunny.

Coop lowered his arms as the driverless vehicle sailed around another slow-moving car. "You weren't kidding, were you? You really are an alien."

"I suppose that is one way of looking at it."

"What do you want with my sister?" Cooper was pale and sweating. But his gaze was steady and he looked Rafe in the eye without flinching. "You ain't going to suck all the blood out of her or turn her into jelly, are you? 'Cause I can't let you do that."

Rafe felt a grudging respect for the man. Cooper was obviously bewildered and frightened, but his concern and determination to protect Bunny were genuine. In this, at least, they were united.

"I would die before I hurt your sister."

"Glad to hear it, 'cause the way you're driving that's gonna be any time now."

"The Dalvahni are extremely hard to kill."

"Oh, yeah? Well, the Raines aren't, and you're scaring the bejesus out of me."

Opening a compartment in the truck, Coop took out a neatly folded white dress shirt and started putting it on.

"What are you doing?"

"What does it look like I'm doing? If I'm going to die, I'd better be dressed. Audrey would kill me if I was to die without a shirt on."

Rafe did not try to follow the logic in that. Humans were sometimes indecipherable. "You are not going to die, Cooper. At least not today."

Cooper tucked his shirt into his pants and buckled his safety device. "So, you're a demon hunter."

"Yes."

"And you're not from Earth."

"No."

"And you're here, so I'm guessing you're after a demon."

"Yes."

Coop took a deep breath and blew it back out. "I know I'm gonna be sorry I asked, but what does Bunny have to do with this?"

"A demon attacked her the first night we met. I intervened."

Rafe decided not to tell Cooper about the change in his sister. The man could only handle so much. Besides, Bunny needed time to adjust to her new self. Later, she could tell her family, if she so desired.

Later. After he left.

The thought of a future without Bunny sent a blinding spasm of pain through Rafe. The years without her stretched ahead, lonely and endless, a dull, meaningless blur. When had she become so necessary to him?

Coop was talking.

"You mean the mugger?" he said. "Oh, boy. You think this demon is still after Bunny, don't you? That's why you've been acting so squirrely."

"Yes."

"Oh, boy," Coop said again. "Do my parents know any of this?"

"No."

"Good. Don't tell them. They'd never understand. Good folks, my mom and dad, but real down to Earth. Don't believe in all that boogedy woogedy stuff."

"And you do?"

Cooper shifted on the seat and looked uncomfortable. "Going to tell you something I never told nobody, not even Cam. Promise not to laugh?"

"The Dalvahni rarely indulge in mirth."

"No kidding. I noticed."

"What did you want to tell me?"

"Know it sounds crazy, but I saw a werewolf when I went boar hunting a few years back. I was on my way home, and I took a shortcut through Froggy Bottom. This weird mist rolled in and I got lost. By the time I got my bearings, it was dark and the moon was up. I heard a noise in the bushes over to the yonder of me, like an animal thrashing around. I sneaked up, real quiet like, and that's when I saw it, standing in a little clearing on its hind legs. Must have been eight feet tall. All jaws and teeth." Coop gave a shaky laugh. "Scared the hell out of me. Haven't been hunting by myself since."

Rafe felt a surge of satisfaction. Conall had been right to send him here. There was more to this backwater hamlet than met the eye. Perhaps he should request assignment in Hannah. Exhilaration filled him at the thought. For the first time in weeks, some of the perpetual tightness in his chest eased.

His elation sprang from an eagerness for the hunt, of course. He was *needed* here. It was his duty to investigate unusual demonic activity.

His desire to remain in Hannah had nothing to do with Bunny or his *feelings*.

"Probably the werewolf you saw was a demon," he said. "The djegrali take on many shapes, though it is taxing on their hosts."

"Hosts?" Coop swallowed. "You mean humans, don't you? Why do they need us, if they're so all-fired powerful?"

"The djegrali are amorphous creatures of the spirit world and lack substance. A human host satisfies their thirst for the physical sensations they crave. In human form, they can eat, drink, kill and have sex. Unfortunately for those they possess, they often indulge in sensual pleasures in excess, draining the humans of life. When the shell they occupy is spent, they seek another and the human dies."

Coop shuddered. "Shit, the damn things are like ticks. I hate ticks." He peered over his shoulder as the truck sped past a vehicle with flashing lights parked on the side of the road. "Hey, that looked like Trish Russell back there sitting on the ground. Wonder what happened?"

Rafe brought the truck to a screeching halt. "What did you say?"

Coop made a strangled sound. "Seat belt," he said with a gasp, loosening the safety device. "What's the big idea putting on the brakes like that? You dang near cut my windpipe in half."

Rafe turned the vehicle around. "The woman back there, you recognize her?"

"I told you, that's Trish Russell. Her daddy's the president of the First National Bank of Hannah."

"Bunny knows this person?"

"Sure, sure. They went to high school together. I ran into Trish at the drugstore yesterday. She was in town visiting her folks. She lives in Fairhope now, I think."

Rafe parked the truck across from the vehicle with the flashing lights and got out. Cooper got out, too, and they walked across the road.

"The female is injured?" Rafe asked a police officer standing next to the vehicle.

"I found this woman wandering down the side of the road. She seems disoriented. You know her?"

"No," Rafe said.

"Then move along, buddy. We don't need rubber-neckers."

"I know her, Officer," Coop said. "Her name is Trish Russell and she's from Hannah."

The man in the uniform scribbled something on a pad of paper. "Thanks. I think she's suffering from a concussion. Her eyes are dilated and she's complaining of a headache."

Rafe listened to them with half an ear. The woman on the ground appeared bruised and shaken, but otherwise unharmed. More importantly, though, he detected the residual stink of the djegrali on the human. The demon was gone.

By some miracle, Bunny had escaped the clutches of the djegrali.

He wanted to shout with relief. And on the heels of that sensation was a driving need to be with Bunny again, to hold her and kiss her. To run his hands over every inch of her satin skin until he was satisfied that she was unharmed, to mark her as his with his teeth and body.

He wanted to make love to her until she lay pliant and weak in his arms. Until his damnable addiction to her was satisfied once and for all.

He wanted to shake her until her teeth rattled for putting him through this hell.

By the sword, she would not run from him again.

Chapter Nine

It was late afternoon by the time Bunny got to the beach house. She parked the car under the wraparound porch and walked barefoot down to the beach. Sitting on the sun-warmed sand, she listened to the shrill cries of the gulls and the steady wash of the waves against the white shore. The sun slowly set, melting into the ocean in a glorious puddle of orange and pink. Her earlier anger was gone, leaving her feeling sad and drained.

Nothing about this day had turned out as expected.

Her big, fat supernatural wedding had been a fiasco. Instead of Prince Charming and a happily-ever-after, she was married to an inter-dimensional bounty hunter and pregnant with ET.

Audrey's beloved pink Caddy was missing a door. Bunny cringed at the thought. She was going to have a hard time explaining that one, much less paying for it.

Her beautiful wedding dress was damp and full of sand. Her carefully coiffed hair was in tatters and so was her heart. She had a hoedown throw down with a demon with a taste for junk food and—oh, yeah—her body and her husband's super powers.

Worst of all, she was on her honeymoon alone.

Not the wedding night of her dreams.

Would Rafe come after her? She couldn't blame him if he didn't, not after she had run away.

She couldn't call him, because she didn't have her cell phone. Rafe didn't have a cell phone anyway.

He was a demon hunter. He probably communicated by owl or something.

She could drive back to Hannah, but she had a feeling he was long gone. Her bottom lip trembled.

He was probably back on Planet Hot Stuff or wherever it was he hung out when he wasn't kicking demonic booty. She doubted she'd ever see him again.

A suffocating ball of sadness welled inside her and she began to cry. She cried for a long time, until she was exhausted and her eyes felt dry and sandy. She wiped her wet cheeks with the back of her hands. She didn't have to look in the mirror to know she was a pink, swollen blotchy mess. She was *not* a pretty crier.

She got up and plodded to the house. That's when she remembered she couldn't get in because she didn't have a key. She almost sat down on the porch steps and cried all over again, but tried the door instead. To her surprise, the knob turned with a muffled *snick*. Stepping inside, she flipped on the lights and gasped. The wedding fairy had paid a visit, transforming the beach house into a honeymoon paradise. Bunny's eyes filled with tears. Her parents, her sweet wonderful parents, had done all of this. There were candles and fresh flowers in the foyer. In the kitchen, she opened the refrigerator. It was stocked with milk, juice, beer, white wine, eggs, cheese, steaks and salmon. On the kitchen table were a basket of chocolates, an arrangement of fresh fruit and two bottles of champagne. Bunny examined the bubbly. Wow, it was the good stuff, not the grocery store kind that gave you a headache.

She went into the great room and did a double take. A faux fur rug, complete with a snarling tiger head and outstretched paws, sprawled in front of the fireplace. Silk cushions littered the floor. Draped across a chair was some kind of filmy garment. Good grief, it was like something out of Arabian Nights.

Scratch that. This was Alabama. More like Ali Bubba and the Ford-y Thieves.

A remote control sat on a table behind the couch. Beside it was a place card with an arrow pointing to the device. Bunny picked up the card. *Push Me* the card said in her mother's handwriting.

Bunny pressed the button. Ravel's *Bolero* blared out of the speakers on the wall.

Ugh, she had the uncomfortable feeling she'd just gotten a glimpse into her parents' sex life.

Double ugh.

She turned off the music and headed for the back of the house. As she passed the master bedroom she did a double take and backed up. The room had been completely redecorated. Gone were the worn bed and serviceable chest of drawers her parents had used for more than twenty years. A path of rose petals led to a sumptuously appointed four-poster bed with a sheer canopy. The covers were turned back, exposing crisp, linen sheets. More rose petals were strewn across the sheets and pillows. Candles beckoned from the heavy wall sconces on either side of the bed and from the bedside tables and dresser.

It was a love nest, romantic, sensuous, evoking images of heated caresses and panted entreaties. But Rafe wasn't here. He was gone and her love nest was empty.

In more ways than one.

She couldn't sleep here. Not without Rafe. She fled down the hall to her old room. To her relief, her bedroom remained unchanged. Same soothing green-and-white decor. Same pale furniture. She opened one of her dresser drawers, took out some of the extra clothes she kept at the beach, and headed for the shower.

She washed and dried her hair and slipped on a pair of cotton panties and one of Coop's old T-shirts. Going back onto the porch, she watched the last, silver light of dusk fade, leaving the shore clad in velvety darkness, and wondered what to do. In retrospect, maybe running away hadn't been such a good idea. For one thing, in spite of everything, she still loved the big jerk. She couldn't imagine life without him. But she'd screwed it all up and now she didn't know how to fix it.

The beach had been quieter and less crowded since the BP oil disaster. The kids were back in school, and the summer tourist season over. Gulf Shores was once more a little town that happened to be on the ocean; empty, except for the locals and the snowbirds from Ohio, Michigan, and Wisconsin who wintered here. But the snowbirds mainly stayed in campers, RVs or condos farther down the strip. The private homes along this stretch of the shore were dark and vacant.

Bunny normally liked Gulf Shores this time of year. Things moved at a slower pace. The beaches and restaurants weren't as crowded or the streets as congested. But now it seemed desolate and lonely.

She heard the dull *thunk* of a car door. Her senses sharpened and her skin tingled in warning. Someone was here.

She leaped to her feet, her heartbeat thudding in her ears. Alarm skittered along her nerves. Danger; danger had found her. She could feel its approach. The air throbbed with rage and suppressed violence and raw, primal hunger. Oh God, the demon.

Run. *Get away before it finds you.*

She raced down the steps. A formless shape, darker than the surrounding night, blurred and materialized on the path in front of her. She screamed and ran back up the steps. The house, she thought, panicking. *Get inside the house and lock the door.*

She reached for the doorknob.

"Bunny."

The sound of that deep, magical voice stopped her in her tracks and made her shiver with longing.

Rafe. He was here. Oh thank goodness, he was *here.*

She whirled around with a cry of delight and gasped. He stood at the foot of the steps. The black tuxedo jacket and bow tie he'd worn at the wedding were gone, and his white shirt was unbuttoned, exposing his muscular chest and ridged abdomen. His chiseled features appeared strained and harsh in the dim light from the porch and his eyes . . .

They glowed in the darkness, feral green, like a jungle cat's on the prowl.

And she was his prey.

Good Lord, the dark, throbbing menace she'd sensed just now was *Rafe*, not the demon. Even during the heat of the battle in the rose garden, he had not seemed so fierce and intimidating.

He stalked up the steps toward her, his gaze on her face. She backed away. Energy pulsed around him in jagged black and red currents. She felt the porch rail against the back of her thighs and stopped moving.

He halted a few feet away from her. His hard, shining gaze moved slowly over her bare feet and legs and drifted past the worn T-shirt. Her skin burned and tingled from the blistering contact.

"You are well?"

There was a hard, gruff edge to his smoky baritone that she did not recognize.

"Yes, Rafe, I'm fine. Listen, I want to tell you that I—"

"The djegrali did not harm you?"

Her heart sank. He looked so stern and rigid . . . so *angry*. But at least he was here. She thought she'd lost him.

Thought she'd never see him again. This was her chance to explain, to try and make him understand.

"No, I'm not hurt. Listen, Rafe. I know you're angry with me, and I don't blame you. But if you'll just—"

"I am not angry. There are no words in your language to describe what I am. The Gorthians call it *hrul chathka,* the black flame that devours. But even that is inadequate." He took a step closer. "Do you have any idea the torment I have suffered imagining you helpless and at the mercy of the djegrali? Terrified that you might already be dead? You left me. To make matters worse, I have been forced to spend an eternity of an afternoon with that idiot brother of yours because he knew where to find you."

"Which idiot brother?"

Bunny jumped as Rafe threw back his head and roared, the veins in his neck bulging. "Never mind which brother! Did you hear what I said? I was afraid. I, a Dalvahni warrior! I have faced death countless times and in many forms, but I have never known fear until I met you."

Bunny felt a wave of remorse at his words. And at the same time a flicker of hope. He had come after her. He was afraid for her. Surely that meant he cared for her a little.

"So, you and Cam followed me here?"

"'Twas Cooper."

"He dropped you off and went back home?"

A muscle worked in his jaw. "Yes."

"I'm glad you came after me." She smiled up at him. "And I'm sorry you were worried. But I had a few things to think about."

His eyes glittered, fever bright. "You left me."

"I know. But it's not every day a girl finds out her husband is a demigod and she's had a supernatural makeover."

"I am not a demigod."

She waved her hand. "Close enough for government

work. The point is, I've had a bad day, but that's no excuse. I shouldn't have run away."

"No, you should not have."

"And I'm sorry."

"You should be. You will not run from me again."

It was a statement, not a question. She straightened her shoulders. "Of course not. I learn from my mistakes."

"That is good to know. Now take off your shirt."

Bunny blinked. "What?"

"I can see your nipples and the soft sway of your breasts through the thin cloth of the garment you are wearing. I have had a bad day, too, Bunny. If you are truly sorry, take off your shirt."

Chapter Ten

Her eyes widened and her soft mouth went slack with surprise. Fury, relief and raw, aching need churned within him. He ached to bury himself in Bunny's tender body and spill his hot frustration into her sweet flesh. Only Bunny could soothe his torment. He clenched his jaw to keep from howling. He was rock hard and ready to explode. Never had he felt so out of control. What was happening to him?

She was afraid and bewildered. Moments ago, he'd sensed her fear and uncertainty as he stalked her across the porch. Part of him exulted in it. He wanted her to know some portion of what he'd felt since meeting her.

Rage was good, a natural response to danger and adrenaline. Rage he understood. He fought to hold onto his anger. It was his lifeline in the turmoil of emotion this woman wrought within him.

She stepped away from the railing and, in one fluid motion, pulled her shirt over her head and tossed it aside. His throat tightened as he drank in the sight of her. She was balm to his thirsty soul, a moon goddess with her shining hair floating around her shoulders and her pale, smooth skin gleaming in the darkness. She stood proudly before him, her small breasts high and firm and round. They would fill the palms of his hands perfectly, he knew. Her rosy nipples taunted him, begging him to take them in his mouth. He longed for the taste of them and the soft, breathy sounds of pleasure she would make as he licked her creamy flesh.

Below her high rib cage, her tiny waist flared above slim hips. A triangle of white cloth covered her mons. His gaze lingered there and his mouth went dry. She would be tight when he entered her and she would give him pleasure. Such pleasure. Like he'd known with no other.

Soon, very soon, he would have her again. But first he must regain control. A Dalvahni warrior knew discipline and restraint. A Dalvahni warrior did not fall upon a woman like a ravenous beast, no matter how great his need. He could do this. He would have Bunny, ease some of his burning lust and empty himself of these damnable feelings.

Lust; that is all this is, he thought through the roaring in his ears. He needed sex. The Dalvahni were known for their sexual prowess and it had been hours since he and Bunny had lain together.

He would request assignment in Hannah to protect Bunny and her loved ones. He would enjoy the company and pleasure of his wife. But he would remain detached.

His wife. She was his. The knowledge blazed through him.

"Turn around," he said through clenched teeth.

Control. He must maintain control.

Stepping up to him, she pushed the open shirt off his shoulders and rubbed her palms across his chest. "Bossy."

He nearly groaned aloud at her touch.

"But I think I like it." His shirt drifted to the floor and her hands moved to the top button of his trousers. "You are something else, Rafe Dalvahni. All hard muscle. So sleek and powerful. Totally yummy. Have I ever told you that?"

He gritted his teeth as her fingers stroked him through the fabric of his trousers. "Bunny, how can I restrain myself if you continue to—"

He forgot everything. Forgot not to groan, forgot the demands of discipline and his Dalvahni detachment. Forgot what he was about to say as she dropped to her knees, unzipped his pants and took him in her mouth. "Bunny, *cara*," he said as her tongue worked the hot length of him.

It felt so good, the heated, wet warmth of her mouth and tongue and teeth upon him. Almost more than he could bear.

"Did I mention I am sorry?" She looked up at him, his moon goddess, through her lashes as her wicked tongue laved his hardness. She trailed the flat of her tongue along his hot flesh. The combination of her mouth and the soft, cooling caress of the salty breeze from the ocean nearly sent him over the edge. "Really, really sorry?"

He clenched his jaw. He could do this. He was Dalvahni. He would not lose control. He would not—

She gave him a last, torturous lick and suckled him. The steady, intoxicating pull of her mouth nearly brought him to his knees.

He looked down at her. She had one hand wrapped around him while her eager tongue circled the head of his shaft. It was too much, seeing her on her knees with her sweet mouth on his cock. It made him feel powerful and tender, all at the same time.

It made him crazy.

He jerked her to her feet. Wrapping his hand in her long hair, he tilted her head back and kissed her, his tongue ravaging her open mouth. She tasted sweet as honey and he was a starving man. He could not get enough of her.

Too rough, too rough, a distant voice warned, but he

was too far gone to pull back from the precipice. He needed her, needed her now or he would lose his mind.

She pressed her naked breasts against him and kissed him back. She was heaven. She was sanctuary. She was his salvation. The tips of her nipples grazed his chest and her hair was glossy silk between his fingers. He breathed in the scent of her soap and the warm, heady fragrance that was hers alone.

His roving hands slid down her naked back to the slim curve of her bottom. He hooked his thumbs inside the scrap of cloth at her hips and tugged. The flimsy garment fell to her ankles.

She kicked it aside with a flick of her foot. Her flawless skin was milky in the moonlight. The wind off the water stroked her naked body, tightening her nipples to puckered buds. She smiled up at him, the promise of fulfillment and untold delight in the curve of her ripe mouth.

Something twisted deep inside of him. "I cannot wait, Bunny. I need you now." The blood pounded in his head and in his cock. "I fear I cannot be gentle."

"Shh." She traced his bottom lip with her finger. "I'm a big girl. You won't break me, but I sure as hell want you to try."

He gave a shaky laugh. "Is that a command, milady?"

"Damn straight it is."

He set his hands on her waist and turned her around. She was so soft, so fragile, the essence of femininity. And yet she had the power to leave him weak with lust and longing for things he did not understand.

She grabbed the porch railing and arched her back. Her legs were slightly spread and the sweet, pink flesh between her thighs beckoned. He cupped her and nearly shouted with relief. She was wet and ready for him, thank the gods.

With a growl he thrust inside her. She clenched him tight as a fist. The sensation was so exquisite he nearly spent himself right then and there. Murmuring words of endearment and encouragement, he began to move. She answered back with a breathy moan. He moved faster and she moved with him, stroke for stroke.

"*Rafe*," she cried. The muscles of her snug channel tightened around him.

He looked down at them. His bronzed hands gripped her alabaster bottom. She was beautiful, so beautiful, and they were connected flesh to flesh.

He pulled out and sank back in. The sight of him entering her softness was the most erotic experience of his centuries-long life.

He felt a sudden, savage urge to mark her as his. Though it nearly killed him to stop, he pulled out again. Leaning over, he brushed her long hair aside and nipped the back of her neck.

"Do you like the things I do to you, Bunny?" he murmured against her ear. "Do you like the way I make you feel?"

"Yes, Rafe. You know I do." She twisted in his grasp and tried to turn.

He put his hands on her hips. "No, be still." He stroked the delicate curve of her back. "If you want me, tell me."

"Dammit, Rafe, I—"

"Tell me."

She was panting. "I want you, Rafe."

With his tongue, he soothed the red spot he'd made on her neck and nipped her again. "I like it when you say that, Bunny. I like it very much. Say it again."

She arched against him. "I want you, Rafe. Please. Now."

He plunged inside her. With a cry, she pulsed around him.

It was his undoing.

With a hoarse shout, he spilled himself into her body.

She climaxed again in a long, rippling spasm and went limp.

He lifted her against him, his chest to her back, and wrapped his hands around her plump breasts. He could feel the rapid flutter of her heartbeat against his palm. A bittersweet ache bloomed in his chest.

They were still joined.

He closed his eyes.

It was not enough.

It would never be enough.

Chapter Eleven

Bunny tilted her head against the side of the garden tub and closed her eyes. The warm water felt wonderful. She and Rafe had been doing it like . . . well, like bunnies, for the past four days. He was insatiable. He couldn't seem to get enough of her.

She couldn't get enough of him either. He was her own personal drug, exhilarating, intoxicating and highly addictive. The more she had him, the more she wanted him. They'd made love all over the house. In the master bedroom's big four-poster bed, in the living room on the faux fur rug, in the shower, on the kitchen table and on the beach under a canopy of stars.

The memory of their wedding night still made her shiver with delight. Rafe stalking her across the porch, his beautiful features taut with strain. The hot words he whispered in her ear as he drove his body into hers, sending her over the edge. It was always the same way with him. One touch, one word, one look, and she was history.

Who would have thought that boring little Bunny Raines, small-town librarian, would turn out to be a world-class nympho?

Only she was Bunny Dalvahni now. She kept forgetting she was a married woman.

She frowned. Why was that? Was it because she didn't love her husband? Nah, she was crazy about the big galoot.

The answer drifted up from her subconscious.

You don't feel married because you know it's not going to last. He likes having sex with you, but he doesn't love you. He's going to leave you and break your heart to smithereens.

Bunny shifted uncomfortably in the tub. Smart Bunny was running her mouth again. For the past few days, Dumb Bunny tried very hard to keep Smart Bunny locked tightly behind a big steel door in the back of her mind.

Unfortunately, in addition to being a know-it-all, Smart Bunny was an escape artist. Every now and then, in spite of Dumb Bunny's best efforts, Smart Bunny picked the lock, broke free and ran her smart-aleck mouth.

You keep hoping he'll fall in love with you. Be honest. You married him to buy yourself some time. That's why you haven't told him about the baby. You want him to love you, but you don't want to trap him. Grow up and stop being such a hopeless romantic. Tell him and he'll stay.

"You are frowning. What has made you unhappy?"

Bunny's eyes flew open. Rafe stood near the garden tub looking down at her, his arms crossed on his bare chest. She hadn't heard him come in. No surprise there. The man moved like a freaking ghost.

She soaked in the sight of him. Wow, he was gorgeous. He wore a pair of shorts that rode his lean hips and no shirt. Turned out their suitcases were in the back of the Caddy the whole time, along with her purse. She never thought about looking in the trunk.

Duh. Sometimes she really was a dumb bunny.

"Just thinking." Her gaze moved from his bare feet

and up his powerful legs to his muscular abdomen. She wanted to pour champagne on his stomach and lap it out of the ridges. Too bad she couldn't drink. "Where have you been?"

"I went to the market to purchase a few things."

Her cheeks burned. She'd gone on a binge after one of their lovemaking marathons and cleaned out the refrigerator. These pregnancy cravings of hers were off the charts.

Luckily, they were infrequent. Otherwise the grocery bill would have been astronomical. She ate like a squad of football players at an all-you-can-eat buffet.

How embarrassing.

"That's sweet, Rafe, but I would have gone to the store." A sudden thought made her sit up in the tub. "Wait a minute. Did you go to the store like *that*?"

His gaze shifted to her naked breasts and stayed there. "Like what?"

"Like not wearing a shirt."

"Yes. Is there a problem with my attire?"

"Damn right there's a problem. You can't go around wearing nothing but a pair of shorts."

"I cannot? Why?"

"Because you're a vagina magnet, that's why. It's a miracle you didn't get molested. You're sex on a cracker. You're gonna give some poor woman a heart attack. A whole *herd* of women. Do you want that on your conscience?"

"I suppose not."

She waved her hands. "Besides, it's not fair to me. Some chick lays a paw on you, and I go to jail."

He lifted his gaze from her breasts to her face. Finally. Sheesh, he was such a guy.

"Bunny, are you, per chance, jealous? I have heard of this emotion."

She rolled her eyes and slid back down in the tub. "Jealous, me? Why, just because you're crazy hot and an orgasm walking? No way."

"Have you finished your bath?"

"Yes."

"Stand up and I will dry you off."

The hot look in his eyes made her shiver with anticipation. She knew that look. He wanted her. And God knows she wanted him. She'd been living in Nympho Land since they met.

She rose, dripping, from the tub.

"Stop," he said.

He stepped closer and licked the tops of her breasts, his tongue brushing her damp skin in a wicked, sensual dance.

His restless fingers teased the underside of her breasts. His hands were big and strong, like the rest of him. The rough stroke of his skin on hers was sweet agony. God, he got her going. Little pulses of desire throbbed in her belly and between her legs. Bending his head, he touched one of her nipples with his tongue, and then the other. Her breasts tightened in response and the throbbing between her legs increased.

"What are you doing?" she murmured, swaying toward him.

"Drying you off."

"With your tongue?" Her knees nearly buckled as he dragged an open-mouthed kiss along her collarbone and down her wet shoulders. "Don't you think a towel would be faster?"

"Faster is not always better." He lifted her out of the tub and set her on her feet. "Or as satisfying."

Bending his head, he nibbled and licked the tender skin of her wrists and kissed his way up her arms to her throat.

"Turn around," he said in her ear.

The deep, husky sound of his voice wrapped her brain

in a sensuous haze. Her breath quickened and her skin tingled.

"Bunny?" Her knees threatened to buckle as his hot tongue explored the skin along her jaw. His teeth grazed her earlobe. "Are you going to turn around?"

"I . . . I don't think I can."

He chuckled and, placing his hands on her shoulders, spun her gently around. Then he proceeded to devote equal and meticulous attention to licking and kissing the moisture off her back and the curve of her rump. At last, when she was weak and shaking with need, he turned her to face him once again. Dropping to his knees in front of her, he pressed his cheek to her stomach.

"Rafe." She stroked his garnet locks with trembling fingers. "Rafe, I love you so much."

It was the truth, though she'd promised not to say it. Not anymore, not for his sake. It was unfair to burden him with the weight of words and feelings he could not return.

But she loved him with all of her heart. She was overflowing with love for him, and she wanted him to know, to carry the knowledge with him when he left.

Oh God, when he left.

He seemed to sense her distress, because his arms tightened around her. "Shh." He moved his head back and forth, dragging his lips and tongue across her abdomen. Her muscles twitched in response as he circled and licked the shallow indention of her navel. "No words. There are no words."

Yes, there are. But you won't say them. You can't say them. In her experience, it was hard for most men to express their feelings. Her daddy and her brothers loved her, she had no doubt. But they had a hard time saying the words. Just her rotten luck to fall in love with the most emotionally handicapped male of them all. Tears burned the back of her eyes.

She forgot her aching heart. Forgot everything as Rafe's mouth moved down her stomach and his questing tongue probed the sensitive seam between her legs.

"*Rafe*," she gasped.

This time her knees did buckle. He caught her as she fell. Lifting her against his hard chest, he carried her into the bedroom and tossed her onto the bed.

She landed on her back. Dazed and lust-drunk, she gazed up at him. God, she was so pathetically in love with this man.

"Open your legs, Bunny," he said. "Let me see you."

She smiled. "Uh-uh. First you have to undress." She lifted her leg and rubbed the arch of her foot against the hard ridge at the front of his shorts. "You, sir, have me at a disadvantage."

He gave a shaky laugh. "To the contrary, milady. I am like a raw recruit in your presence. Eager. Reckless. Liable to go off half-cocked." He looked down at his bulging erection. "Only 'twould seem I stay fully cocked around you."

Bunny sighed. It wasn't a declaration of love exactly. But it was something. He wanted her and she wanted him like crazy. So what was she waiting for? Who knew how long they had together? Panic flared at the prospect of life without him.

No. She would not think about that. She would think about The Now. It might be all they had.

She parted her legs.

He looked down at her. His eyes glowed, a bright, hot green. She didn't remember them looking like that before they were married. But they glowed now, whenever he was aroused. It should have freaked her out, but it didn't. She liked it. Liked knowing she turned him on, because God knows he got her engine going. The Bunny Mobile stayed on idle all the time, a low, soft hum that throttled to a full roar whenever he looked at her or kissed her or said her name.

Or touched her like he was touching her now with his hand between her thighs, parting the damp, slick folds to slip his finger inside.

"Rafe," she said, clenching around him.

"No, do not tense up. Relax. I like touching you."

She scowled up at him. "Easy for you to say. How can I relax when you do things like—"

He pushed her thighs apart and put his mouth on her.

"—that," she sighed.

His tongue found the sensitive bud between her legs and worked it.

She went still, her entire being concentrated on what he was doing to her with such skill. A lick, a nuzzle . . . a teasing flick and she came apart.

Yep, she was a nympho-buniac. No doubt about it.

She was still pulsing when he came down on top of her and pushed inside, filling her with his rock-hard, heated thickness. But he did not move.

She opened her eyes to find him looking down at her, a bewildered expression on his beautiful face.

"Bunny," he began. "I . . . I . . ." His face twisted.

She smoothed her hands down his muscled back. "Shh, it's all right. No words, remember?"

Her fingers moved lower to toy with the hard curve of his butt. God, he was built.

She found the edge of his waistband and smothered a giggle. His shorts were bunched around his thighs. Mr. Calm, Cool and Collected was in such a hurry he forgot to take off his pants.

Nice to know she got his motor going too.

She forgot to be amused as he began to move. She moved too, her body and soul straining to meet him, to merge as one. Each stroke sent her higher and higher.

He murmured something hot in her ear and she shattered into a million, glittering pieces of joy.

With a harsh cry, he followed her into the abyss.

Smart Bunny was running her mouth when she floated back to consciousness.

He almost said it. Why'd you stop him? You really are stupid, you know that?

"Oh, shut up," Bunny said irritably.

Rafe rolled over and took her with him. "I beg your pardon? I did not say a word."

Bunny laid her head on his chest. "Not you. I was talking to myself."

He smoothed her hair back and kissed her on the forehead. "I cannot allow anyone to talk to my wife like that, not even you."

"Yes, sir."

"What is this, meekness from my fierce little Bunny? Dare I hope that you mean to be an obedient wife?"

"I wouldn't hold my breath, if I were you."

"Ah. I feared it was an anomaly."

He yawned. A moment later, he was asleep.

Bunny listened to the thud of his heartbeat beneath her ear. He might be a Dalvahni warrior, but he had a heart. And that meant there was hope.

She would wait for him. He was worth it.

Idiot, Smart Bunny snorted.

Dumb Bunny slammed the door in Smart Bunny's face and triple-locked it.

Chapter Twelve

Bunny stepped out onto the porch to take a last look at the gulf. The ocean glittered in the midafternoon sun like bits of glass. The salty breeze tugged at her sundress and tickled her bare legs and sandaled feet. With a harsh cry, a gull swept low over the waves. The lonely sound perfectly fit Bunny's wistful mood.

The past few days with Rafe had been bliss, but her vacation was almost over. The Fall Art Show opened at the library tomorrow and she needed to be there. It was their biggest fund-raiser. She'd worked overtime the week before the wedding to have everything set up and ready to go when she got back. Still, she had had no business leaving work at such a busy time.

But she hadn't planned on meeting and falling in love with Rafe Dalvahni.

Or marrying him, for goodness sake.

Or having his baby.

Her hand crept to her stomach. A child, conceived and born of her love for the father; she loved their baby already. It was a boy, she was sure of it. He would be red-haired and strong and handsome, like his father.

When Rafe . . .

Grief stabbed at her. She pushed it aside. She had to be strong, for the child's sake.

When Rafe left, she would have their child to love and remember him by. It would not be enough, not nearly enough, but it would be something. A wonderful something.

Shrugging off her gloomy thoughts, she picked up her suitcase and almost dropped it in surprise. It felt empty. She set the bag on the porch and unzipped it. The lid popped open. Clothes bulged against the inner straps. She was notorious for overpacking.

The suitcase should have been heavy, but it was not.

She closed her wheeled upright and grabbed Rafe's duffel bag. Weightless, like hers. How odd.

Shaking her head, she carried the luggage down the steps to the parking area beneath the porch. She saw the pink Caddy and winced. She'd been so happy and loved up by a certain fellow she'd forgotten about the missing door. Until now. Audrey was going to go nuclear when she saw her car.

"What are you doing?" Rafe said.

Bunny shrieked and spun around, the suitcases swinging wildly in her hands. "Rafe, you scared me to death!"

The blue polo he wore hugged his muscular shoulders and broad chest and his massive biceps strained against the short sleeves of the shirt in a most fascinating manner. Bunny tried not to stare, but yowza! He was totally built and totally gorgeous. And how his lower body looked in a pair of jeans ought to be illegal.

He took the bags from her. "I was going to get these."

She followed him to the back of the car. "No big deal. They aren't heavy." She watched him open the trunk and toss their luggage in. "I guess one of us will have to sit in the backseat. Do you drive? I mean, *can* you drive?"

"I can operate this machine, but why cannot we sit together?" He grabbed her and pulled her close, nuzzling her on the neck. "I do not like to be away from you."

Didn't like to be away from her, huh? That was promising, at least. Maybe he would visit her and the baby every now and then between assignments. It would be kind of like having a husband overseas in the military. Her spirits lifted.

"The front passenger door is missing." Bunny shivered. She put her hands on Rafe's sinewy shoulders and held on as he nibbled his way up her throat to her ear. "Remember?"

In the past few days, Rafe had grilled her at great length regarding her encounter with the demon. Not that there was much to tell. She had kicked the demon out of the car. End of story.

She figured it was adrenaline. People did strange and unbelievable things under stress. Picked up cars. Moved trees. Lord knows being around Trish was stressful enough to give the Dalai Lama indigestion. And this particular demon had been foolish enough to threaten her and Rafe while wearing a Trish Russell suit. Big mistake.

Taking out Trish *and* the demon was a twofer, as far as she was concerned.

"The door will not be a problem," Rafe said. "I have cleaned and repaired the automobile."

"What?" Bunny said.

Stepping out of the circle of Rafe's arms, she slowly backpedaled around the Cadillac. The car was spotless, inside and out, the chrome bumpers and trim mirror perfect. More importantly, the missing door was back in place.

"I don't understand." Bunny opened and closed the passenger side door. It was as good as new. "Somebody did a nice job, but the color's not right. Audrey will be sure to notice." She grimaced. "I wonder how much a new paint job is going to cost me."

"What is wrong with this color? It is pink."

"Yeah, but it's not Mary Kay pink." She waved her hand at the car. "This is more of a bubblegum color. Mary Kay pink is pearlier."

Rafe scowled. "Pink is pink."

"Hey, don't worry about it. Mary Kay pink is hard to match. How on earth did you find a mechanic who could fix the car on such short notice?"

"I repaired the machine myself."

"That's impossible."

"It is?"

"Yes, it is." She ran her fingers over the passenger side door. The finish was mirror smooth. "You'd have to order the door, and besides, you don't have the equipment."

His brows rose. "I do not? I am wounded."

"Don't start with me, Rafe Dalvahni. You know very well I'm not talking about *that* equipment." Her face got hot. "That equipment works just fine."

"I confess I am relieved to hear it."

Her cheeks burned . . . and other parts of her as well. Man, he had a sexy voice. "Stop teasing me, Rafe, and tell me the truth!"

"I am. But, since you obviously do not believe me, I will prove it to you."

He waved his hand and the front doors came off the Caddy. One door spun through the air and smacked into the storage room wall. The other one landed forty feet away in the sand.

"Are you crazy?" Bunny's voice rose to a shriek. "Look what you've done to Audrey's car!"

"Calm yourself." Rafe motioned and the doors sailed across the yard and reattached themselves to the automobile. "Behold! The machine is restored to its former state."

"Oh man, oh man, oh man," she moaned.

Staggering over to a plastic beach chair, she sat down and dropped her head in her hands. Everything was spinning and her whole body felt funny and light. As if at any moment, she might float out of the chair into the clouds, weightless as a balloon.

"Bunny?"

"Give me a minute. Please." She took deep breaths. "I need a little time to adjust."

"Adjust to what?"

"You're kidding, right? Like the stunt you just pulled is *normal*?"

"Bunny, you know what I am." Rafe's tone was gentle. "You have seen what I can do."

She lifted her head to glare at him. "Did I say it was your fault? I'm an idiot, that's all. The past few days have been so wonderful that I forgot you're . . . That you're not . . ."

"I cannot change what I am. If you regret marrying me . . ."

"I didn't say that!"

"—then that is too bad, because I am not letting you go."

Hope bloomed. This was it, the moment she'd been waiting for. She loved him so much he *had* to love her a little in return.

"Because you love me?" she asked without thinking.

Way to go, Big Mouth, Bunny thought miserably. Hadn't she promised herself she'd be patient and wait for him to say it? Oh, no. She had to push him into a corner.

Stupid. Stupid. Stupid.

"Love is a human emotion," Rafe said without inflection. "I am Dalvahni."

She *hated* it when he got all cold and detached, like he was made of stone or something. Her chin came up. "Brand loves Addy and he's Dalvahni."

"Brand is an aberration. I enjoy being with you. I want to make you happy and to keep you safe. Is that not enough?"

She dug her fingers into the palms of her hand. She would not cry. She would *not* cry. "No, it's not enough. But I guess it will have to do."

Rafe's steely expression softened. "*Cara.*"

She shook her head. "Don't look at me like that, Rafe. When you look at me I melt into a big puddle of Bunny goo. For goodness sake, leave me a little dignity."

"It was never my intention to hurt you."

His voice was like liquid sex. Deep. Compelling. Mesmerizing. Even when he said things like *Sorry, babe, I don't love you,* it did things to her, made her weak with longing.

He had all the advantages. It was so unfair.

He stepped closer. "*No,*" she said, flinging out her hand.

Rafe's body flew backward, like a puppet pulled by an invisible string. He smashed into one of the house supports and tumbled into the driveway.

"Rafe!" Bunny ran over and knelt on the ground beside him. "Are you all right?"

He groaned and sat up. "My head hurts."

"It ought to hurt. You thunked that post pretty hard." Frowning, Bunny ran her fingers along his scalp. "Oh, my goodness, you've got a goose egg. What on earth made you do such a crazy thing?"

He opened his eyes and looked at her. "I did not do this thing, Bunny. You did."

She recoiled in surprise. "What?"

"You are no longer human."

"I don't believe you."

Rafe stood and pulled her to her feet.

"I told you before, but you would not listen. You are Dalvahni now, ageless, changeless and powerful."

Bunny stared at him in disbelief. This was crazy. This couldn't be true, right? Oh, sure, he'd said something to that effect on their wedding day, but she hadn't believed him. How could she?

Hellooo? Remember what happened with the mayonnaise jar at your mama's house?

Oh God, Smart Bunny was flapping her jaws again.

It was a new jar and she asked you to open it. You gave the top one itsy bitsy turn and the jar exploded in your hands. Your mama's kitchen looked like double coupon day at the sperm bank.

Smart Bunny wasn't just a pain in the butt. She was also gross.

You told your mama the glass must have been cracked, but it wasn't, was it? You cut your hands to pieces and there was blood everywhere. Your mama freaked out and wanted to take you to the hospital. But when you ran your hands under the faucet the cuts were gone.

It was just a paper cut, Dumb Bunny retorted.

Uh-huh. What about the door at the library then, the one you pulled clean off the hinges?

That door was defective, Dumb Bunny protested.

No, it wasn't. And the door to the beach house was locked tight as a drum when you got here. Until you turned the knob. Think about it. You heard the dead bolt turn over. And what about two weeks ago at the library when you had a sudden craving for watermelon and found yourself standing in the produce aisle at the Piggly Wiggly with no memory of how you got there and—

Shut up, shut up, shut up, Bunny screamed inside her head.

Smart Bunny's voice subsided, but it was too late. A floodtide of panic started at Bunny's toes and swept up her body, choking her, making her heart pound and her brain spin.

"No," she whispered. Sweat trickled down her back and between her breasts. The air seemed thick and she found it hard to breathe. "It's not true."

"Why do you refuse to accept what I am telling you?" Rafe asked. "I changed you. I had no choice. You would have *died*."

He reached for her, but she skittered away from him. "There's always a choice, Rafe."

"Do you think I wanted to do it?" His face twisted. "What I did is forbidden by the Great Directive. But I could not let you die." Closing the gap between them, he took her by the shoulders. "I could not do it, do you hear?"

She jerked free. "Why not, Rafe? Why break your precious rules when you don't love me? You're not making sense."

"I do not know. I looked at you and I wanted you. That is all."

"You wanted me? Well you got me, didn't you?" Her voice shook with anger and resentment. "Pathetic little Bunny, in love with a guy who can't love her back because it's not part of his *directive*."

"Bunny, I—"

She slapped him, hard. "You should have let me die, Rafe. It would have been kinder than leaving me here to face forever alone."

There was a red mark on his cheek where she'd slapped him, but he did not seem to notice.

"I am not leaving," he said. "I have decided to request permanent assignment here."

It took a moment for his words to sink in. With a cry of joy, Bunny launched herself at him.

"Rafe, I'm so glad!" Laughing and crying, she rained kisses on his neck and cheek. "I've been out of my mind, thinking about you leaving. Oh, I'm so happy!"

He stood rigid, his body stiff and unyielding. "Do not deceive yourself into thinking that emotion has anything to do with my decision. I am doing my duty."

The brief, bright hope within her fluttered and died. "I

see." She dropped her arms and stepped back. "You're staying because it's your job, is that it?"

"Yes."

"But you don't love me."

"No."

"You're a liar, Rafe Dalvahni." Angry tears filled her eyes. "You love me but you're afraid to admit it."

"A Dalvahni warrior does not know fear. A warrior—"

"Please, no more lectures on the mighty Dal. I've heard enough." She turned her back to him. "I want to go home. Mama and Daddy are expecting us."

Her parents were throwing a welcome home barbeque in their honor that afternoon. It was supposed to be a joyous time, a celebration with family and friends.

Yeah, right.

Bunny walked over to the car and got behind the wheel. A moment later, the passenger door opened and Rafe got in. She backed the Caddy out of the driveway and drove north toward Hannah.

They rode home in silence.

The honeymoon was over.

Chapter Thirteen

By the time Bunny parked the Cadillac in front of her parents' house later that afternoon, her nerves were raw. The silent, tense drive home had seemed endless. She and Rafe were having their first fight, unless you counted the scene in the rose garden at the church, which she didn't. That hadn't been a fight. That had been more like an explosion of surprises culminating in Bunny getting the hell out of Dodge.

Or Hannah, to be more exact.

This was a fight. She was furious with Rafe for a number of reasons.

For one thing, she was pretty pissed off about not being human anymore. Not that she'd rather be human and dead, which is what she'd be if he hadn't saved her. But still, when one person knocked another person clean out of one species and into another without so much as a by your leave that ranked as a major pisser-offer in her book. Especially if she was the one being relocated.

As for the whole Super Friends aspect of the new and improved Bunny, she hadn't wrapped her brain around that one yet. She couldn't pat her head and rub her stomach at the same time, but now she had powers? Puh-leeze.

Still, she was starting to think there might be something to it. She was good at denial, but too many strange things had happened in the past few weeks to continue to ignore the possibility. What if she lost her temper and hurt somebody? The thought horrified her.

As for Rafe's refusal to admit his feelings, that made her insane. He loved her, she was sure of it. It was in his eyes when he looked at her. It was in his touch. She heard it in his voice when he said her name. She read it in his expression when they made love. The big dope loved her, but refused to admit it.

Cooper waved at them from the front porch. "Hey, you two lovebirds, get out of the car. Everybody's out back. We got brisket and butt and ribs on the grill. And Mom's made tater salad and Audrey brought a big old pan of baked beans and we got us a keg. Strap on your feed bag and head for the trough."

Bunny's stomach did a nervous flip-flop. How in the world was she supposed to smile and make nice around her family and friends when she was so unhappy?

"Hope you saved your hungries." Audrey breezed off the porch and onto the sidewalk. She wore a pair of khaki shorts, a white linen top, and brown polka dot flip-flops. Her dark, shiny hair swished around her shoulders as she walked. "We got enough food to feed an army."

It always amazed Bunny that her burly, rough-around-the-edges brother and sweet little Audrey Jones, kindergarten teacher, soprano in the choir at the First Baptist Church, and Mary Kay consultant extraordinaire, ended up together. They were like Jack Sprat and his wife in reverse. But at five foot two and one hundred and five pounds, Audrey ruled the roost and the rooster. And the rooster loved every minute of it. Coop adored Audrey and their two kids and Audrey adored them right back.

Bunny wanted that. That's what she thought she would be getting when she married Rafe. But he claimed he didn't love her, couldn't love her. She didn't believe him, but it still hurt. Oh, man, did it hurt.

A dull ache formed in her chest. Any second now she was going to start bawling like a baby. She had to get out of here. Food, she needed food, massive quantities of it, if she was going to survive this evening.

She jumped out of the car and dashed up the brick sidewalk past Audrey.

"Welcome home," Audrey said as Bunny streaked past.

Bunny mumbled hello and kept going. Behind her, she heard the car door slam and the murmur of voices as Audrey greeted Rafe. He called her name, but she barreled up the sidewalk. Her nose quivered like a hound on the scent. The sweet, smoky smell of barbeque was in the air, tantalizing, mouthwatering. She smelled bacon and the caramelized onions in Audrey's baked beans. Even at a distance, her new and improved super sniffer detected the faint whiff of mustard in the potato salad. And somebody—some wonderful somebody, probably her sweetheart of a mother—had made banana pudding.

She dashed around the side of the house and through the gate. Her parents' backyard was long and narrow and partially shaded by towering oaks. They had a pool and a state-of-the-art outdoor kitchen with a fireplace, a hybrid grill, a pizza oven and refrigerated drawers. Her parents loved to entertain.

And what better excuse to entertain than a welcome home party for their newly married daughter? Their *only* daughter and the baby of the family.

Bunny had tried to talk them out of it. The thought of seeing some of her parents' friends after her disaster of a reception gave her hives. She needn't have worried. Rafe had assured her Brand would take care of everything.

According to him, the Dalvahni were duty bound to

make things right under something called the Directive Against Conspicuousness. Apparently, there was a wheel-barrow load of directives the Dalvahni were supposed to follow. Round up rogue demons. Protect lesser creatures from the djegrali. Clean up after yourself so the locals don't get freaked out.

Don't fall in love.

Brand must have done a good job with the cleanup, be-cause the only memories her parents seemed to have of the reception were glowing ones. Thank goodness.

Mama had called them at the beach all excited because there was a nice write-up in the paper about the wedding. There was no mention in the article of skinny-dipping geezers or a cloud of demon dust hanging over Hannah, or anything else unusual. It was like the weirdness never happened.

Mama had expressed her disappointment that Bunny and Rafe had left the reception early.

"But I do understand," she had said on the phone. "Be-lieve it or not, I remember what it's like to be young and in love."

Brand even planted memories of the wedding cake in everyone's minds.

"I've never seen anything like it," Mama had said be-fore she hung up. "They went through that cake like a horde of locusts! It's a good thing I had the caterer make an extra tier and put it in my freezer. Otherwise, you and Rafe wouldn't have any wedding cake to eat on your first anniversary for good luck."

Her first anniversary? At this rate, she and Rafe wouldn't make it to the end of the week. She was losing him.

Maybe she'd never had him.

Oh God, where was the chow? How was she supposed to deal with a broken heart on an empty stomach? She needed something to eat. She needed it now.

She looked around. Coop's boys were doing cannonballs into the pool. Allison, Cam's teenage daughter, sat in a lounge chair listening to her iPod and pretending to be bored. She kept stealing envious, sidelong glances at her younger cousins frolicking in the water. Over by the grill, Daddy was drinking a beer and talking to some of his friends while he did the manly cook-the-raw-animal-flesh-over-a-fire thing.

Bunny followed her nose. There, under the roofed dining area, was a cloth-covered table loaded with food. Yesss!

She made a beeline for it, only to be drawn up short by the sound of her mother's voice.

"You're home!" Mama hurried over to give her a hug. "My goodness but you look pretty in that dress! Where's Rafe?"

"He's out front talking to Audrey," Bunny said.

Her mother squeezed her arm. "Marriage agrees with you, sweetie. Why, you're practically glowing!"

Great, you're glowing, Smart Bunny said. *Stick a battery up your ass and call you a night-light. Pregnant women glow. People are going to figure it out pretty soon. Your MOTHER'S going to figure it out. Are you going to tell Rafe about this baby or let him read about it in the paper?*

Bunny wanted to scream at Smart Bunny to leave her alone. Instead, she ignored her, mostly because she couldn't think of anything devastatingly clever to say.

And because her mind was on barbeque sauce.

Her daddy made two kinds of sauce, a thick, sweet tomato-based concoction with brown sugar, garlic and black pepper, and a tangy, thin mustard sauce with cider vinegar and chipotle flakes. She liked them both. Should she put the mustard sauce on the ribs and the sweet sauce on the brisket or vice versa? Or maybe she should mix the two?

Her mother's next words brought her thoughts of food to a screeching halt.

Leaning closer, Mama said, "Honey Bun, I can't stop looking at you. It's like you're lit from within. You're pregnant, aren't you?"

Hah! Smart Bunny crowed. *Told ya!*

"What is this?" Rafe materialized at Bunny's side.

"Mercy, Rafe!" Mama swatted him on the arm. "You scared the life out of me. Don't you know better than to sneak up on a person like that?"

"Bunny?" Rafe stared at her with something like panic in his eyes.

He was very pale beneath his tan. He knew. Oh God, he knew. It was all over his face. He looked like somebody had kicked him.

Smart Bunny was making rude noises in the background. Bunny tuned her out. This was not how she wanted to tell him. She didn't know *how* she wanted to tell him, but this wasn't it. Not standing on her parents' lawn at a barbeque. *Oh, by the way, Smoochie Muffin, I'm preggers. Would you pass the coleslaw, please?*

"Mama's right, Rafe," she heard herself say. "I'm pregnant. We're going to have a baby."

Bloop. Rafe disappeared.

Chapter Fourteen

R afe stalked out of the burning bar. Behind him, he
  heard coughing and cursing as the last of the humans
stumbled out of the smoke and flames and into the parking lot. The smart ones took one look at him when he
walked in the door of the seedy tavern and fled. Those
less intelligent or those too drunk to notice him—or both—
stayed. One of these, a beefy, tattooed fellow sitting at the
bar, had foolishly commented on Rafe's warrior garb.

Looking up from his beer, the man eyed Rafe's leather
breeches.

"Look-ee what just walked in," he said, with a dismis-
sive sneer. "Move it on down the road, mister. This ain't
no pansy bar."

Rafe processed the strange term. *Pansy: A hybrid garden plant derived from wild violets. Also a disparaging
slang term used by human males to indicate weakness or
effeteness in another male. Similar terms with same
meaning: Wuss, wimp, candyass.*

Translation: Insult.

Rafe threw the man out the window. The barkeep
charged him and Rafe threw him out the other window—

the squat, tin-roofed structure boasted a grand total of two. The skirmish that followed between Rafe and the remaining patrons was brief and unsatisfactory, ending when the ceiling and walls inexplicably caught fire.

He looked around, itching to continue the fight. The human males who encountered his gaze slunk away into the darkness. He suppressed a surge of annoyance. This was the third alehouse he'd visited tonight in search of a fight. A real fight, not what passed for battle in this dimension. The men of this time were no match for a Dal. Not that they ever were, but human warriors of other eras had some skill in hand-to-hand combat. He'd fought alongside some of the best of them: Persian Immortals, Romans, Vikings, and Crusaders. And against them as well, when they were possessed by the djegrali.

At least a demon-possessed human presented something of a challenge with its superhuman strength, wily intelligence, speed, and ability to shape-shift. An ordinary human, on the other hand, was no match for him, even armed with modern weapons. So far this evening, he'd been shot, stabbed, bludgeoned, axed, and hit over the head with any number of objects, including a chair, several beer bottles and something called a tire tool.

He welcomed the pain. He reveled in it.

It never lasted long enough.

The physical discomfort was fleeting and of no moment. The cuts healed almost as soon as they were inflicted. His body repelled the foreign projectiles the humans fired at him. Their meager blows were no more bothersome to him than a stinging insect. But the momentary distraction helped him forget Bunny's startling pronouncement this afternoon, if only for a heartbeat.

She was with child.

In his eons-long existence he'd been in combat countless times, witnessed firsthand the aftermath of war, famine, death, disease and despair on the innocent. But it was as if he viewed these things from the other side of a curtain, shielded from the pain and sorrow other beings felt.

He had not experienced emotion, other than battle rage and lust . . . until he met Bunny.

She stripped away the curtain, leaving him susceptible to a bewildering onslaught of feelings he was unprepared for and did not understand. He vowed to deal with them. He refused to succumb to the madness that had felled Brand. He would enjoy Bunny's body and the delight of being with her, but he would remain detached and aloof. He would not lose control. He was a Dalvahni warrior, strong and invincible, invulnerable to the weaknesses that plagued lesser creatures. He would conquer this insanity.

He had succeeded for the most part, though it had been vastly harder than anything he'd done before. She was so open and giving, so full of light and love and laughter. He hungered for her as surely as the djegrali, drawn to her goodness like the proverbial moth to the flame. He fought it. Being around her was a constant pleasure-pain as he struggled to maintain his indifference. He told himself he could take what she offered without being affected. He was mistaken. Somehow, she had penetrated his defenses, leaving him weak and vulnerable.

And now this.

A child.

He could not love her. He did not know how. The Dalvahni were not constructed for emotion.

As for being a father, he had no notion of where to start. His earliest memories were of training in the Hall of Warriors. No mother or father, only endless fighting exercises and harsh discipline. The Dalvahni did not love and they certainly did not sire children. Such a thing was unheard of. Under the Great Directive, the Dal spent their lust on thralls, sterile, emotion-drinking sex slaves. They did not couple with human women and they did not have children.

They did not marry, either. But he had married Bunny out of duty, not love.

Hadn't he?

In the distance, he heard the wail of sirens. Something hot and ugly still churned inside him, undiminished by the encounter in the bar. The suffocating rage and frustration boiled to the surface. He flung out his hand and an empty car exploded. He made a fist with his other hand and two unoccupied trucks crumpled like paper. He gestured, and the ruined vehicles flew through the air and smashed into a line of parked cars. The noise of metal bending and glass shattering was terrific, but not loud enough to drown out Bunny's words. *I'm pregnant, Rafe. We're going to have a baby.*

We're going to have a baby. He made a chopping motion with one hand, slicing a car in two. *Baby.* He gestured and a tree at the edge of the parking lot burst into flames. *Baby . . . baby . . . ba . . .*

He raised his arm to strike another blow.

"Enough," a deep voice said out of the darkness.

Rafe lowered his arm. "Well met, brother."

Brand stepped out of the shadows. His face was an expressionless mask, but his green eyes blazed. "I cleaned up the last two messes you made. I will not clean up a third. Take care of it, or else."

"Or else what?"

"Or else I will not fight you. A fight is what you want, is it not?"

Fierce exultation swept through him. "Yes," Rafe said.

"Meet me at the abandoned quarry outside of town." Brand raised his brows. "When you are done with your temper tantrum, of course."

He turned and walked away.

The sirens drew closer. Quickly, Rafe smothered the flames that consumed the beer hall and the blazing tree and restored the tavern to its former state. He did the same with the broken vehicles. One of the trucks was little more than a ragged heap of metal *before* he destroyed it. Now it looked like new. Oh, well, some human would be happy this night.

He made himself invisible and waited. Three black-and-white cars screeched into the parking lot, lights flashing and sirens wailing. The words HANNAH POLICE were written on the side of the vehicles. Uniformed men got out of the cars and looked around.

"Damn if it ain't another false alarm," one of the officers said. "Third frigging one tonight. If I catch the joker doing this, there's gonna be hell to pay."

Men and women trickled out of the darkness in twos and threes. Rafe muddled their memories of the fight and the fire. As an afterthought, he started a small blaze in the kitchen and set off the smoke detectors. The fire would be easily contained and would allay the suspicions of the authorities, a precaution needed in case he overlooked someone who was in the bar. Satisfied he'd set things right, Rafe slipped into the night.

The old quarry was located five miles outside of town. Rafe visited the place once with Bunny when the two of them went for a long drive. Her grandfather had worked at the quarry and Bunny had regaled Rafe with its history. The quarry had operated for several decades, pumping sand out of the Devil River to be used in glass and concrete production, until increasingly stringent environmental restrictions and rising permit costs shut it down. The dredges, front loaders, and crushers were sold off to other companies but the mountains of sand remained, silent white sentinels guarding the bank of the river. In the daytime, Bunny said, it was a popular hangout for bored teenagers, who liked to run the dunes in their pickup trucks. But at night the quarry stayed deserted. Strange things happened at the quarry after dark, and people stayed away.

Brand waited for Rafe just inside the entrance.

He surveyed Rafe with a cold stare. "So, you wearied of bullying humans?"

"They are not much of a challenge, I admit." Rafe saw a ripple of movement out of the corner of one eye. He looked around; nothing there. "But they were willing and accessible. I confess, I did not think of you, afflicted as you are by your peculiar infirmity. The woman Adara has unmanned you."

Brand smiled. It was not a pleasant expression. "We shall see. What is it to be?" He pulled a fireball of energy out of the air and balanced it on his fingertip. In his other hand he held a blazing sword. "Shall we duel with the elements or our weapons?"

"Neither." Eagerness surged through Rafe. He was looking forward to this. He was going to pound Brand to a bloody pulp. Reaching behind him, he removed his battle-ax and tossed it in the sand. "I choose fists."

Brand threw his sword in the sand next to the ax. "I was hoping you would say that."

They circled each other. They had sparred many times throughout the years and were familiar with one another's fighting styles. Sparring was a daily activity in the Hall of Warriors and the Brand of old had been a worthy opponent. But that was before he succumbed to Addy's wiles.

Moving with preternatural speed, Rafe opened the attack with a flurry of punches and a flying sidekick to the head. Brand hit the ground. When he got back up, his mouth and nose were bleeding.

Rafe smiled. This was going to be easy. And enjoyable. Hitting Brand felt good. He didn't have to worry about killing him and it lessened his anger and confusion. It made him forget things.

"Your feelings for the female have made you slow and weak," he said, taunting the other warrior. "Stronger and better than a human opponent—but still weak. You were once a great warrior, but no more. I pity you."

Brand spat a mouthful of blood into the sand. His injuries were already healing. "Save your pity for yourself, brother. You suffer from the same disease. You love your wife."

"You are mistaken." Rafe ground his teeth, some of his enjoyment fading. "I do not love Bunny."

"Liar," Brand said.

He swung his right fist at Rafe's head. Rafe threw up his arm to block the blow. Too late, he realized it was a feint. Brand spun his body in a blur of movement, hooked Rafe's lower legs, and knocked him to the ground. Rafe rolled away and leaped to his feet. He saw a flash of motion and leaned back, narrowly avoiding a head punch. He swung his right arm. His fist connected with Brand's face with a satisfying crunch. Brand's cheek split and his eye swelled.

Rafe followed his first punch with a second and a third to the ribs, ending with a roundhouse kick to the head. Brand grunted and staggered back.

"I do not love Bunny," Rafe snarled.

Brand regained his balance. "Keep saying it, brother. You will not convince either of us. You love her."

The black rage boiled up and overflowed. With a roar of outrage, he lowered his head and charged. At the last second, Brand stepped aside. As Rafe lunged past, Brand stuck his boot out and tripped him. Rafe slid face-first into the sand. Coughing and spitting, he struggled to his knees.

Brand walked up and slammed his fist in Rafe's face, breaking his nose. Blood spurted into the sand. Brand stepped closer and elbow-smashed Rafe in the jaw. Everything went black. Rafe hit the ground and Brand jumped on top of him.

"You love Bunny. Admit it," Brand said, punching him in the chest and stomach.

"No," Rafe mumbled.

His nose hurt and he was fairly certain Brand had cracked several of his ribs. His injuries would quickly heal, but he was in real danger of suffocating under the big warrior's weight.

Brand hit him again. "Say it."

"No."

Brand got up and dragged Rafe to his feet. Rafe had time to catch a quick breath before Brand grabbed him in a headlock and squeezed.

"Say it," Brand growled.

Rafe shook his head. He could do no more, not when Brand was crushing his windpipe.

"Bah, Adara is right. Your head is made of meat," Brand said. "A Dalvahni warrior does not lie, especially to himself. *You* are the weak one, not I. A true warrior faces his fears and his responsibilities. You love Bunny, but you are afraid to admit it. I am done with you."

Brand flung him to the ground. Rafe heard the squeak of Brand's boots in the sand as he walked away.

The boots stopped.

"Arise, brother," Brand said softly. "We have company."

Chapter Fifteen

Rafe struggled to his feet. The sand had come alive. Dozens of sand people surrounded them. Tall and cylindrical, the sand people had long, mournful faces and slack, hollow mouths. They watched the two warriors with empty eyes. Two sand dogs frolicked at their feet. At the edge of the crowd of silent, unmoving figures, a sand kitten washed its face with a gritty paw.

"We have a problem," Brand said in a low voice. "Our weapons are gone. Almost of a certainty our grainy friends have them."

"That is a problem. Perhaps we should leave."

"Not without my sword."

"I thought you might say that." Rafe sighed. Brand's fondness for his sword Uriel was well-known among the Dalvahni. "Very well, we will demand the return of our weapons. If they do not comply, we destroy them."

Brand seemed to consider this. "That might work. Or we could try asking them nicely."

"I did not think of that."

Brand shrugged. "Adara's influence. I have mellowed."

"Since you are feeling so congenial, you ask them."

"As you wish." Brand cleared his throat. "Greetings . . . er . . . quarry people. My brother and I apologize for trespassing upon your domain. I assure you, we did so out of ignorance and without malicious intent, for we knew not of your existence. Return our weapons and we will depart in peace." He paused. "Thwart us, however, and we will unleash the fury of the Dalvahni and scatter you to the four winds."

"Very nice and conciliatory," Rafe murmured. "Except for the last part."

"A warrior only mellows so much."

Rafe rubbed his aching ribs. "So I noticed."

Two of the sand people shuffled forward, the weapons in their upraised hands. Rafe and Brand approached them. The sand creatures stared straight ahead, as unmoving as statues, offering no resistance when the two warriors retrieved their weapons.

"See," Brand said as the two creatures lumbered back into the crowd. "Diplomacy works."

Shoulder to shoulder, Rafe and Brand strode toward the entrance of the quarry escorted by their shambling guard. The company of sand people parted ranks. Rafe and Brand walked between the silent rows and through the gate. They reached the road and looked back. The quarry was empty, except for the sigh of the wind through the dunes.

Night settled around them. Not far away, Rafe heard the rushing sound of the river. An owl hooted in a nearby tree and a chorus of frogs started a new song. A light breeze played through the air. He took a deep breath. His nose had healed. He smelled pine, grass and the earthy scent of the mud along the riverbank. The paved road beneath his feet still held the heat of the day.

"Strange forces are at work in this place," Rafe said,

breaking the silence. "I have been thinking of asking for permanent assignment here."

"Why?"

Rafe gave the other warrior an incredulous stare. "Because it is my duty."

"Ah, we are back to that again. You know, you really are a tedious fellow."

"Meaning?"

"Only that your desire to stay here should have something to do with your wife."

Rafe stiffened. "I consider protecting Bunny part of my duty."

"If that is your primary reason for staying here, tarry no longer." Brand turned and walked down the dark road. "I feel certain Conall will assign another of our rank to protect her."

Once more, Rafe had a vision of Bunny in another man's arms. She was so sweet and beautiful, so giving. How could any red-blooded male resist her? If he left, how long would it be before another warrior lost himself in her embrace as he had?

No, that wasn't right. He hadn't lost himself in Bunny's arms. He'd found himself. With her, he was home at last, after a hundred lifetimes of wandering.

He caught up with Brand in two strides and spun him around.

"Bunny is mine," he snarled. "No one else's, do you hear?"

"Your dog-in-manger attitude is beginning to annoy me." Brand shook his head. "Let her go if you do not love her. It is the honorable thing to do."

The world tilted and dropped away beneath Rafe's feet. He was falling, falling, into nothing. Let Bunny go? And do what? Wander through the dark, lonely reaches of time without her, caught in the endless pursuit of the djegrali?

"No, I cannot," he said.

"Why?"

Rafe stared at him, helpless to put his feelings into words. His *feelings*? Damnation.

"She is with child," he blurted.

"A child?" Brand whistled. "You are sure?"

Rafe sent a rock flying down the road with a vicious kick of his boot. "Yes. She told me tonight."

"This is momentous news indeed. It also explains a multitude of things, including the fire you started in that tavern."

"I did not—" Rafe stopped. He clenched his fists. Had he? He remembered being in the bar and the burning rage that had consumed him. The terrible anger spilled out of him and the walls and ceiling went up in flames. "You are right," he said in dawning self-disgust. "I started that fire. I was filled with a fury greater than any I remember. I could not control it."

"Do not chastise yourself too severely. Certain females can have that effect upon a warrior." Brand's expression grew rueful. "As I know only too well."

"A warrior should always be in control. I was not." The bitter words choked Rafe. With an effort, he continued. "In truth, I do not think I have been in control since I met Bunny." He straightened his shoulders and looked Brand in the eye. "I have violated our creed. My transgressions are unpardonable. You should report me to Conall."

"Tell him yourself if it gives you ease. I will not."

"But duty compels you to—"

Brand held up his hand. "Please, no lectures. I have lived the Dalvahni way as long as you. I am familiar with our code. For years beyond counting I have pursued the djegrali. It was all I knew until I met Adara. But now that I have found her, I will not go back to the half-life of my former existence. I cannot. I have something far better than the emptiness and the endless hunt, something infinitely more precious. I have Adara. And I will fight to protect her and those she loves from any and all danger, including the djegrali, so long as I have an ounce of strength in my warrior's body. I recommend you do the same."

"But . . . but the child. I have no notion how to be a father!"

"You will learn. We Dalvahni are nothing if not resourceful." Brand slapped him on the shoulder. "Congratulations, brother. To my knowledge, you are the first of our kind to sire a child. But do not, for a moment, imagine I will allow you to best me for long." He grinned. "Now, if you will excuse me, I need to find Adara. We have some catching up to do."

Brand vanished, leaving Rafe alone on the road. A moment later, he reappeared.

"Here, it is called chocolate." Brand thrust a small, crinkly package into Rafe's hands. "Consume it wisely and not all at once." He grinned. "As Adara would say, it will rock your world."

He was gone.

Rafe turned the package over in his hands. The narrow box was wrapped in brown, glossy paper. The words *Hershey's Milk Chocolate* were written in silver letters across the front. He tore it open. There were six flat, individually wrapped objects in the pack. Rafe took one out and tore off the covering. A delicious, rich scent wafted up his nose.

He took a large bite of the chocolate and chewed. It was slightly crunchy and sweet but otherwise unremarkable. Then the chocolate melted on his tongue and a strange, warm feeling came over him. He had never felt anything like it. He took another bite. The warm feeling spread.

He liked chocolate. Chocolate was good.

*   *   *

Rafe lounged with his back against the tree, his legs
stretched out on the ground in front of him. His whole
body felt heavy. With an effort, he lifted one booted foot
and crossed it over the other. His feet seemed miles away.
He was singing Coop's favorite song, the one about the
"dawgs" and the man on the table. He wanted to know
why the man was on the table. Coop would know. He
must remember to ask him.

He sang the first verse over and over. It was the only
one he knew.

The fairies did not like it. They buzzed in agitation
around him, beautiful, multicolored blobs of floating light
that chattered without ceasing. He could hear the steady
drone of their high-pitched voices above his singing. A
brilliant green one darted close to hover at the end of his
nose on gossamer wings. He stopped singing and crossed
his eyes. "It" was a she. Her large eyes were dark teardrops
in her pointed face. Long, wispy hair the color of new
leaves swirled around her naked breasts.

"Pretty," he said with a silly grin. He tried to touch the
fairy with the tip of his finger, but she darted away. "Ah,
little one, I mean you no harm."

He held out his hand. She left the swarm of fairies that
drifted around him to settle on his palm. Tilting her
dainty head, she said something to him in a thin voice.

"Sorry," he said. "I cannot understand you."

He reached for a chocolate bar with his free hand. The
package was empty.

"Someone ate all the chocolate." He shifted his bleary
gaze to the fairy. "Was it you?"

The fairy shook her head.

"Next I suppose you will be saying it was me."

The fairy chittered.

"You can say that again," Rafe said. "May I tell you a
secret?"

The fairy's wings slowly opened and closed.

"I will take that as a 'yes.' " He leaned closer. "I love Bunny. There, I said it. It terrifies me, these feelings I have for her, but I can deny them no longer." He glanced to his right and left. "I will tell you something else. I am going to have a baby." He thought about that one. "Well, actually Bunny is going to have a baby, but *I* am the father. That terrifies me, too. I do not know *how* to be a father."

He leaned his head against the tree and burst once more into song. With a tinkling huff of protest, the fairy took to the air. She pointed her finger at him. A cloud of green, sparkly dust smacked him between the eyes. Suddenly, he was very drowsy. He yawned and fell asleep.

Chapter Sixteen

Rafe woke up underneath a tree. He felt awful. His head hurt and there was a bad taste in his mouth. What ailed him? The Dalvahni did not know sickness. He lifted his head and looked around. He instantly regretted it, for the slightest movement made his temples throb. Bits of wadded-up brown paper and silver wrappers lay scattered on the ground.

The chocolate, he had eaten all the chocolate. And, by the sword, it made him drunk!

He picked up an empty wrapper and stared at it. Through the years, he'd seen many different species under the influence of various substances, but the Dal were immune to alcohol and drugs of every kind. Except for chocolate, it seemed.

He had a vague recollection of eating one of the bars and liking the loose, heady feeling it gave him. He'd never felt that way before. He had thought about Bunny and the baby and ate some more chocolate. It had seemed a good idea at the time.

Walking in the woods had seemed like a good idea, too. After a while he got tired of walking and sat under an old oak. He did not recall finishing the pack of chocolate bars, but he must have done so. The evidence was all around him.

He sat up. His stomach roiled and his head ached like the very devil. So this was what a hangover felt like. He could not say he enjoyed the sensation or cared to repeat it.

He ran his tongue across his teeth. A bath was in order. Somewhere nearby, he heard the burble of running water. He followed the sound and found a creek. He stripped off his leathers and waded in.

The water was cold and he made quick work of washing himself. As he dried off in a patch of sunshine, his thoughts drifted back to the night before. He dimly recalled singing. He winced. His singing was painful. He sounded like a lovesick elk. The fairies must have thought so too. Especially the little green one, because she'd—

Rafe went still, remembering the puff of fairy dust and the dream that followed.

More like a vision than a dream, dozens of happy images of the future. His future with Bunny and their child.

A son, the babe Bunny carried was a son, tall and red-haired and strong like Rafe, with Bunny's amazing teal eyes and wide smile and loving nature. They would name him John Bryant, after Bunny's father, and Rafe would teach him to be strong and brave and honorable. And Bunny would teach their child how to love, just as she'd taught him the meaning of that word.

And that was the most important lesson of all.

He needed to see Bunny. He needed to tell her he loved her. Brand was right. He was a coward.

But no longer. It was going to be all right. He could do this. He could.

He needed to tell her.

Bunny checked her appearance in the bathroom mirror. She looked okay. In fact, she looked great. Nothing at all like someone who'd spent the night pacing the floor and crying her eyes out. No puffy eyes or swollen red nose. No sign of fatigue. That Dalvahni DNA was strong stuff.

Too bad it didn't work on her broken heart.

She was afraid this would happen. She'd told herself to be ready for it. But it still hurt like hell when Rafe disappeared. Turned out, nothing could prepare her for having her heart ripped out. She had been so sure he loved her. And maybe he did. But, he was incapable of admitting it. The baby was the final straw. She would never forget the look on his face when she told him or the gut-wrenching pain she felt when he left.

Just like that. No good-bye. No see ya later, chicka, and thanks for the lay.

Gone.

She'd told her parents she didn't feel well and got Coop to drive her home. She stayed up all night waiting for him. He didn't come back. She was an idiot to keep hoping.

She washed and dried her hands and went back into the library. The Fall Art Show was a smashing success. There was a line outside on the sidewalk when she unlocked the doors early that morning. It was midafternoon and the crowd was finally dwindling.

Midafternoon without a word from Rafe. *Pfft,* he was gone and it was over.

She was thankful to have the bustle of the art show to keep her busy. Local artist Amasa Collier sold several of his coat hanger sculptures, including a startlingly realistic likeness of country great Hank Williams. There were dozens of canvases on display and for sale and some wonderful photographs done by the photography class at Hannah High, as well as pottery, handwoven wisteria baskets, blown glass and handmade quilts. Bunny had her eye on a magnificent oil of the Devil River. The river came alive under the artist's brush. He or she—the painting was unsigned except for a small "S" in one corner—had captured the mystery and allure of the water. When she looked at that painting, she felt as though she could walk right in the river and into another world.

Unfortunately, the mystery artist wanted way more for the painting than she could afford on her meager salary, especially with a baby on the way.

Swallowing a lump of sadness at the thought of raising the baby without Rafe, Bunny surveyed the library from behind the reception desk. Twenty or so people still lingered at the tables and easels that lined the library windows, and a few more wandered around in the stacks. In a few minutes, she would shoo everybody out and close the doors. And then she would go home and begin the rest of her life without Rafe.

Oh God, how would she bear it?

The door opened and Audrey came in. She gave Bunny a little wave and hurried up to the front counter.

"Your mama told me and Cooper the good news about the baby," she said, smiling. Audrey always called Coop by his full name. It was *Cooper* this and *Cooper* that. Usually, Bunny thought it was endearing. But for some reason today it got on her nerves. "You left in such a hurry last night. I was worried about you." Audrey's eyes widened. Leaning forward, she whispered, "Your mama said Rafe went AWOL when he found out about the baby. Is everything okay?"

No, everything was not okay. Everything was about as *not* okay as it could get. For one thing, Bunny had a heck of a time last night explaining Rafe's little vanishing act to her mother. She'd finally convinced Mama she might be getting a migraine. Mama saw visual auras right before the onset of a headache. The lie had worked, but it had been a close one. Mama was no dummy.

For another, her husband of less than a week had left

her. She'd gotten a big fat "F" in Marriage 101, and there would be no making it up in another term. School was over. Her marriage had been canceled because her husband had the commitment and intimacy issues of a typical male. Times a squillion.

But she wasn't about to tell Audrey that. Audrey would be devastated for her and she would try and sympathize. And Bunny couldn't take it. Not right now. Not when the pain was so raw.

So, she smiled and lied. Again. "Everything's fine. I want to thank you for letting us borrow the Caddy. Rafe would never have fit into my Mini Cooper."

Audrey giggled. "No, he wouldn't." She looked around. "So, where is Rafe? Is he here?"

Bunny was saved from another lie by the unexpected arrival of Mullet Woman. Nicole came through the front door dressed in black shorts, a white see-through bathing suit cover, and an oh-so-visible black bra. She carried a large, covered canvas in her hands.

"Read about the art show in the *Herald*." She plunked the canvas on the counter. "Just got off my shift. Am I too late?"

"I'm sorry, Nicole, but the art show is over," Bunny said. "I was just about to close the library. But if you give me your name and address, I'll put you on the mailing list for next year. I'm sure your artwork is lovely."

"Huh." Nicole looked crestfallen. "Since I brung it all this way, you wanna see it? I'd kinda like your opinion."

Bunny cut her eyes at Audrey. Her sister-in-law was staring at Nicole's train wreck of a hairdo with thinly veiled horror.

"Uh, sure," Bunny said.

Nicole turned the canvas over and slid her fingernail under the masking tape. What was hidden beneath that butcher paper? A black-velvet Elvis? *The Last Supper* done in elbow macaroni?

Nicole unwrapped the canvas and turned it over. Bunny and Audrey gasped. It was a portrait of Jesus, the most tender, moving likeness of Christ that Bunny had ever seen.

Also the most odiferous.

"Whew!" Audrey waved her hands in the air. "What is that awful smell?"

"Cigarettes," Nicole said. "I made it out of butts I picked up around the gas station. You wouldn't believe how many morons pump gas while smoking a cig." She lifted her thick shoulders. "It seemed like the Earth-friendly thing to do."

"A stinky Jesus." Audrey was frowning. "You made a stinky Jesus. You can't make our Lord and Savior out of cigarette butts. It's not respectful."

"I like it," Bunny announced. "In fact, I *love* it. I want to buy it." She looked at Nicole. "That is, if I can afford it and if it's for sale."

Nicole flushed. "It's yours." She handed the canvas over the counter to Bunny. "Consider it a wedding present."

"Oh, no, I couldn't." Bunny tried to give the picture back. "It's too beautiful. You must let me pay you for it. Better yet, take it to an art gallery in Mobile."

"Nope, I want you to have it. Besides, there's plenty more butts where them came from." Nicole leveled her piggy eyes at Audrey. "That your pink Cadillac out front?"

Audrey gave Nicole a wall-eyed stare. Bunny could tell Mullet Woman made Audrey nervous. "Yes," Audrey said. "Why do you ask?"

"Thought it might be. You sell Mary Kay?"

At once, Audrey morphed into the consummate professional. She straightened her shoulders and pasted a bright smile on her face. "I do."

"Huh," Nicole said. "You got yourself a problem then.

My aunt used to sell Mary Kay and that there car of yours ain't the right color pink."

Audrey looked like somebody had sucked all of the air out of the room. "What are you talking about?"

"Your car is carnation," Nicole told her. "Whereas your Mary Kay is more of a porcelain pink."

"My, would you look at the time?" Bunny said loudly. "I think I'll close up now."

She bustled around the room rounding up people and ushering them out of the library. Out of the corner of her eye, she saw Nicole and Audrey walk out together. They were still talking.

Bunny said good-bye to her library aide, Betsy, and escorted an effusively flirtatious Horace Clement out the door. Good grief, the man was eighty years old if he was a day, and he was coming on to her like crazy. What good was all this sex appeal when the only man she wanted was Rafe?

She checked the library one more time and locked up and dimmed the lights. As she came out of the stacks, she glanced out the bank of windows and saw Nicole and Audrey standing on the curb.

She walked to the front door and looked out. Nicole was pointing to the Mary Kay car. Audrey looked upset. Bunny felt guilty. Audrey loved that stupid car. It was important to her, a symbol of all her hard work. And now it was ruined.

Okay, maybe ruined was a little bit of an exaggeration, but it was definitely the wrong color. And in the world of Mary Kay, the right pink was everything.

Bunny felt responsible. But what could she do, tell Audrey the truth?

Uh, sorry, babe, I got in a throw down with this demon and tore up your car. But my husband—remember him, the supernatural hottie who hung around until after the

*honeymoon?—made it all better. Unfortunately, he only
has one pink in his color palette, and it ain't Mary Kay.*

Oh, yeah, that would fix everything. As if.

Shaking her head, Bunny walked over to the reception
desk and got her purse out of the drawer. The monitor
caught her eye. *Here there be dragons* her screen saver
said. Her computer was still on.

That's right, she thought. *I asked Betsy to delete those
old books from the inventory this morning.*

She reached over to turn off the computer.

That's when the demon attacked.

Chapter Seventeen

The djegrali came out of the drinking fountain near the main entrance. It seeped out of the bubbler, overflowed the basin and oozed onto the floor. Clawed hands reached for Bunny out of the deadly mist.

"*Bun-n-ny*," the demon wraith moaned.

Bunny dropped her purse and ran. She hit the front door and threw her weight against it. It was locked.

Damn. And the keys were in her purse behind the reception desk.

Double damn.

Snick, she heard the dead bolt turn, just like that night at the beach house. Bunny Dalvahni, supernatural locksmith. Maybe not the most impressive of talents, but pretty handy when you were locked inside a building with a spectral psychopath.

A foul wind raised the hair on the nape of her neck. The thing was upon her. She pushed the door open and stopped. Audrey and Nicole were still talking on the sidewalk, oblivious to the danger. If she ran outside the demon would follow her and hurt them. She couldn't let that happen.

She whirled back around. The djegrali loomed over her, a misty, swirling thing out of a nightmare, with twisted limbs and a gaping beak of a mouth. Behind it, three smaller, murky shapes rose out of the drinking fountain.

Great. Papa demon had brought his baby demons to show them how to hunt. And she was Lesson Number One.

"I am angry with you, little rabbit." The horrible, grating voice that Bunny remembered came out of the thing's pointed mouth. The grotesque head lowered. "You have been keeping secrets from me. You are one of them now, and you did not tell me."

Bunny gazed up into the hideous face and nearly fainted from fright. The noxious waves of concentrated evil that emanated from the djegrali were overpowering, not to mention just plain stinky. The demon smelled to high heaven, like old garbage or spoiled meat. Her will and her resistance started to slip away under the combined effects of terror and revulsion. In a flash, her memories of the night of the attack returned. The crack of bone and joint as Mr. Pringle's head distorted into something unrecognizable and his elongated jaws sprouted row upon row of sharp teeth. The mind-numbing fear that robbed her limbs of strength and the terrible, searing pain as the beast ravaged her throat. And then Rafe was there and the pain was gone.

But that was then and this was now. Where was a demon hunter when you needed one?

Her rescue came from an unexpected source.

Hellooo, Smart Bunny said. *Stop mooning about Rafe. You're fixing to die. Move your ass, Cottontail. NOW.*

Smart Bunny was right, of course. Rafe wasn't here. She might not be able to outrun the djegrali. It was smoke and spirit, after all. But she had to try.

Bunny darted into the stacks. To her surprise, she *really* darted. Dalvahni woo woo again. Maybe she had a chance against this thing after all. She streaked like a rocket through adult fiction, large print, and zipped around and around the waist-high display of children's books. *Pfft,* she blurred past nonfiction and the shelves of audiobooks. Newspapers and magazines fluttered like leaves in a windstorm in her wake.

She was fast, but so was the demon. She felt him behind her. His breath was like black frost on her skin.

Too close, too close, Bunny thought, picking up speed.

"Run, little rabbit, as fast as you can," the demon said with a horrible chuckle. The sound of that voice was petrifying, a satanic Tim Curry in *Legend* or Darth Vader on crack. "I will still catch you."

Books flew off the shelves, pelting her like hailstones. Bunny shrieked and covered her head. Artwork and pottery whizzed past. She ducked the missiles and kept running, dodging the bookshelves that crashed around her like dominoes. Her lungs burned and her legs ached. She couldn't keep going at this pace much longer. A rasping cry startled her. The demon's three evil henchmen circled the stacks above her like vultures, watching and waiting, savoring her terror and exhaustion and the kill that was to come.

She heard the harsh rumble of the demon's laughter closing in behind her. The monster was playing with her and enjoying the chase.

"Don't you want to hear my plans for you, little rabbit? I'm going to use your body as my vessel. Humans are so weak and easily broken. But you are Dalvahni and strong. With your powers and mine, I will be invincible. I am going to kill your lover and the other warrior and then this world will belong to the djegrali."

Hear that? Garbage Breath is going to take over the world, Smart Bunny said. *Stop shrieking and running around like a little girl and kick this bastard's ass.*

"And how do you propose I do that?" Bunny said,

gasping for breath. "In case you haven't noticed, I *am* a girl and I don't have any weapons."

What am I, your mother? Do I have to do everything for you? Think of something and make it fast. You're out of time. Garbage Breath is right behind you.

Bunny took a flying leap over a heap of fallen bookcases and landed on the other side. She looked over her shoulder. The demon was right on top of her. It roared in triumph and reached for her with scaly hands. She yelped and did a forward roll. Something hot and razor sharp raked across her back. She rolled behind the front desk and scrambled to her feet beside her desktop computer. The demon stalked to the end of the reception desk on huge, taloned feet. He loomed over her, a roiling nightmare of beak and claw. A flutter of white caught Bunny's eye and drew her gaze downward. Garbage Breath had a tiny piece of paper stuck on his big old demon butt, acquired, no doubt, when he chased her through the stacks.

Suddenly, Bunny knew what to do.

"Stay back." She brandished her Honeywell bar code scanner at the demon with her right hand. With the fingers of her left hand she hit the keyboard. The screen saver disappeared and the open cataloging program popped into view.

The djegrali threw back its hideous, misshapen head and laughed. The three smaller demons fluttered around Garbage Breath like tattered black flags. They were laughing too.

"Foolish rabbit, I am *morkyn,* one of the elders of my kind. Surely you do not think to defeat me with so pitiful a weapon?"

"Surely *you* realize you've got a bar code sticker on your ass and that this—" she waved the gun-shaped object in her hand—"is a bar code scanner?" She pressed the head of the scanner to the strip of white paper that dangled from the demon's filmy carcass.

Are you sure you want to delete this item? the computer asked.

"Oh, yeah," Bunny said.

She pulled the trigger. The scanner beeped and the demon disappeared.

"Ha!" Bunny crowed, jumping up and down. A feeling of power surged through her veins. "That's what I'm talking about!"

With an inhuman howl of fury, the three smaller demons swooped down upon her like avenging black crows.

Bunny heard a hoarse shout and then a high-pitched, metallic whine. To her astonishment, a large double-headed ax spun through the air and chopped the demons to bits. With a high keening cry of agony, the djegrali disintegrated into a thousand peppery particles and vanished.

Rafe materialized in front of her. He lifted his arm and the whirling ax returned to his hand. He looked very pale and there was a stark, haunted expression on his beautiful face. She'd never seen him look like that . . . so open . . . so vulnerable.

He was dressed in some kind of weird, medieval outfit she'd never seen. No . . . wait. She'd seen it once, the night of the attack. She'd opened her eyes and remembered thinking he was an angel, a warrior angel, with his flaming hair, stern features and blazing eyes.

Her gaze traveled from the vest covering his hard chest to the leather breeches that clung to his muscular legs. It was an outlandish getup, something from another age. He should have looked ridiculous, but he didn't. He looked comfortable and at ease in the strange clothes.

And dangerous. Very, very dangerous.

He also looked pissed.

His face went from white to a deep mottled angry red. "Are you insane?" he shouted. "What were you thinking, woman? You could have been killed!"

"Don't you yell at me, Rafe Dalvahni." Bunny's chin quivered. "I've had just about all I can take for one day."

"Bunny, by the gods, Bunny!" He dropped his ax and grabbed her in a crushing embrace. He ran his hands over her body as if he wanted to reassure himself she was all right. "Never do that to me again. I thought you were dead. How could you have been so foolish?"

Suddenly, she was furious. She gave him a hard shove and he released her. She stepped back, her chest heaving.

"Let's see, what were my choices?" She looked around the library. "Nope, nobody here but me. *You* weren't here, were you?" Hot tears spilled down her cheeks. "You left. I didn't think you were coming back. Ever. You *left*."

"I know." He stepped closer. "Look at me, Bunny."

She shook her head. "If I look at you I'll give in and you'll break my heart again. I won't let you do that to me, Rafe. I won't."

He towered over her. She could feel the heat pouring off his big body and smell his warm, spicy scent. God help her, she could talk big all she wanted, but she was a complete and total idiot when it came to this man. She closed her eyes so she couldn't see him, for all the good it did. She didn't have to see him to feel him, to *know* he was there. She tingled all over when he was near. He filled her senses and made her dizzy with longing.

He was a great big Dalvahni roller coaster and she was a thrill junky.

"Do not weep, *cara*," he said. "Please. It breaks my heart."

"You don't h-have a heart."

"Yes, I do, and it is yours." Gently, he placed his fingers beneath her chin, his skin warm against hers. "Look at me, Bunny. I want to see your beautiful eyes when I tell you I love you."

Her eyes flew open. "What did you say?"

"I said I love you." He brushed feathery kisses across her tear-damp cheeks, her eyes and lips. "I love you with every fiber of my being."

"I don't believe you."

He grinned down at her. "I have it on the best of authority that a Dalvahni warrior does not lie, even to himself." He traced her lips with the tip of his finger. "I have been a fool."

"A stubborn fool," Bunny murmured, the fragile beginnings of happiness welling up inside her.

He nodded. "Yes, that too." He tugged her close and wrapped his strong arms around her. "I love you, Bunny Nicole Raines Dalvahni." His lips brushed her hair. "Do not leave me to wander the gray reaches of time alone. I love you. Send me away and I will only come back to stand outside your door and howl like an abandoned cur."

She chuckled against his chest. "The neighbors would complain."

His arms tightened around her. "Then take me in, Bunny, for their sake if not for mine. I need you. I want you. I cannot live without you. And I do not mean to try."

Bunny could not believe this was happening. But it was real. She could see it in his eyes and in his expression. He loved her. She'd never felt so much joy. Her heart was bursting with it.

What's the big deal? Smart Bunny said. *You knew he loved you.*

"Yeah, but now *he* knows it and that makes all the difference," Bunny said.

"What did you say?" Rafe asked.

"Nothing." Bunny stepped out of his arms. "I love you too, Rafe. I think I've loved you from the moment I saw you. But what about the baby? I couldn't take it if you bolted again."

Rafe went to his knees and pressed his face against her

stomach. "I will never leave you again or our baby. You will both be so tired of me you will beg for a reprieve." He lifted his head and looked up at her. "I can do this, Bunny. I can be a good father. I know I can."

She cupped his cheeks in her hands and gave him a misty smile. "I never doubted it for a moment."

"Bunny," he breathed. The next thing she knew he was on his feet and she was in his arms, and he was kissing her as if his life depended on it. And maybe it did, 'cause her life depended on him too.

They heard a noise and broke apart. Nicole stuck her head through the front door.

"Thought I heard something and came back to check on you," Nicole said. "Can't be too careful, you know. There are some real creeps out there. But I see you got your man with you, so no worries." She batted her eyes at Rafe. "Nice outfit. You look good in leather."

Good grief, Nicole was flirting with Rafe. Bunny couldn't blame her. Rafe was irresistible.

Yeah, you'll probably have to carry around a big stick for the rest of your life to beat the women off him, Smart Bunny smirked. *That's what you get for marrying a super sexy, demon-hunting hunk of burning love. But no worries. He loves you and these Dalvahni dudes never do anything half-assed. If he says he loves you, it's the real deal, forever and ever, amen. Sucks to be you, huh, chicka?*

"Yes," Bunny said, smiling. "You are so right."

And she was.

Read on for an excerpt from Lexi George's delightful
DEMON HUNTING WITH A DIXIE DEB, available
now from Lyrical Press!

Deep South legends. Deep fried curses.
Deep dish revenge . . .

THIS DEBUTANTE IS HAVING A BALL!

Way down south in the land of cotton, one belle's plans
are soon forgotten—when Sassy Peterson drives her
Maserati off the road to avoid a deer and lands smack-
dab in the proverbial creek without a paddle. The
Alabama heiress should have known something weird
was going on when she saw the deer's ginormous fangs.
Hello, Predator Bambi! But nothing can prepare her for
the leather-clad, muscle-bound, golden-eyed sex god
who rescues her. *Who wears leather in May?* That's just
the first of many questions Sassy has when her savior
reveals he's a demon hunter named Grim. Also: Why
would a troop of fairies want to give her magical powers
and rainbow hair? Why would a style-challenged beast
called the Howling Hag want to hunt her down? Most
importantly, what's a nice debutante like Sassy doing in
a place like this anyway? Besides feeling Grim . . .

Praise for *Demon Hunting in Dixie*

"A demonically wicked good time."—Angie Fox

"A not-to-be-missed Southern-fried, bawdy,
hilarious romp."—Beverly Barton,
New York Times bestselling author

"A genuinely funny new voice in paranormal
romance."—*Publishers Weekly*

Monday Afternoon

Maseratis don't float.

Sassy's stepfather had given her a list of do's and don'ts as long as her arm before handing her the keys to his gleaming blue convertible. That salient little fact he'd failed to mention.

The front end tilted and the car sank into the creek faster than Sassy could say mani-pedi. Water poured into the open cabin, sweeping her purse and cell phone away and enveloping her in an icy, gasp-inducing wash. It was early May in Alabama and temperatures were in the low eighties, but the water was *freezing*.

The automobile settled to the streambed with a gentle bump. The late afternoon sun was shining, the water clear and full of sparkles. Pebbles swirled in the current on the sandy floor. A school of minnows darted past the submerged vehicle.

Maseratis definitely do not float.

It was a serious design flaw Sassy planned to take up with the manufacturer. The Maserati was a high-end automobile. It *ought* to float. It should come equipped with little wings and flotation devices and toodle across the surface of the water like a Jesus bug, saving its driver a great deal of discomfort and inconvenience.

Not to mention the ruination of a perfectly good silk dress and a pair of laser-cut Sergio Rossi sandals.

A complaint to the manufacturer was definitely in order, as well as a tube of waterproof mascara. Sassy had the horrible suspicion her makeup had run.

First things first. She'd climb out of the creek. Then she'd figure out where she was.

Two hours earlier, she'd sailed out of Fairhope headed for Hannah, a trek of maybe fifty miles. Her GPS had directed her off Highway 31 and down a series of twisting, two-lane roads. By the time she realized the device had malfunctioned, she was lost in the wilds of Behr County.

Sassy hadn't been worried. It was a beautiful day. The gas tank was three-quarters full, and she was behind the wheel of a very expensive Italian sports car. The Maserati handled like a dream. It hugged the curves and hammered up and down the wooded hills, the responsive, aggressive engine under the hood purring like a satiated tiger.

Top down, sound system blaring, Sassy had rounded a curve. A pony truss bridge lay dead ahead, metal railings bleeding rust in the afternoon sunshine.

The narrow, winding road and the bridge set against a verdant backdrop of trees had made a postcard picture. Sassy was admiring the bucolic simplicity of the scene when a deer bounded out of the woods and in front of the car, a big *ugly* deer with gooey black eyes and teeth like knives. Sassy was no Nature Gal, but she knew deer didn't have fangs and claws. Deer are herbivores, for goodness sake. She swerved to avoid Predator Bambi, ran off the road, and that's how she'd landed in the creek.

A broken branch danced across the hood of the submerged car in a flurry of green leaves. Don't panic, Sassy thought, holding her breath. Keep calm. Unfasten your seat belt and climb out. You're charity chair of the Fairhope chapter of the Lala Lavender League. Die and Brandi Chambliss will assume your mantle of leadership.

Energized by the dreadful thought, Sassy fumbled for the seat belt latch. She pushed; nothing happened. The mechanism was jammed. Her heart rate shot into overdrive. She was going to drown. When they pulled her body from the sunken car her sleek golden tresses would be sodden and lank, her makeup smeared. Her flirty little sundress with the pleated skirt would cling to her like Press 'n Seal.

She wasn't wearing a thong.

She would have visible panty lines.

Sassy yanked the shoulder harness over her head. She was trying to wriggle free of the lap belt when a large, masculine hand closed around the restraint. The sturdy fabric snapped like an overcooked spaghetti noodle, and Sassy was lifted, dripping, from the car.

She was slung across a brawny shoulder. The impact knocked the air from her lungs. Wheezing for breath, she shoved her streaming hair out of her face. She caught a glimpse of a broad, muscular back and the best-looking butt she'd ever beheld—right side up or upside down.

The stranger turned and waded for shore. Locomotion did fascinating things for that marvelous rump. His worn leather britches clung to him like a second skin, outlining the ripple and bulge of muscle as he moved.

Leather in May? Goodness, leather was *so* last season. The poor man would get a rash.

Her thoughts scattered as she started to slide. To her shock, a large, masculine hand cupped her rear end. Sassy yelped in surprise at the intimate contact. The back of her dress had ridden up, exposing her bottom. The warmth of his palm through her lacy panties was a red hot brand.

Sassy drummed her fists against his broad back. "Put me down."

He paused a few feet from the embankment. The water swirled around his powerful legs.

"A precipitous notion." His deep voice sent a little *zing* of awareness through her. "Perhaps you should—"

"I said put me down. *Now.*"

The man's massive shoulders lifted in a shrug. "If you insist."

He tossed her into the creek.

The frigid water closed around Sassy once more.

Of all the bad-mannered, ungentlemanly—

Sputtering in outrage, she scrambled to her feet. Her four-inch spike heels sank into the sand. The water hit her below the waist, plastering her dress to her shivering body. The current was strong. She lost her balance and went down on one knee. She struggled upright on the spindly shoes.

He grabbed her arm to steady her. She repaid the act of courtesy with a glare.

"What's the matter with you?" she said. "When I said put me down, I meant on the *road.*"

"Then you should have said so. Humans are woefully inexact."

Ignoring her protests, he lifted her in his arms and carried her up the kudzu-choked embankment. He plunked her down in the middle of the bridge, returning her outraged regard without expression. At five feet two, Sassy was used to looking up at people, but, jeez, he was a big guy, a lean, hard giant of a man. His long hair was a rich reddish brown, the color of cinnamon. He wore some kind of metal-studded leather vest over a muslin shirt. The damp fabric clung to his pectorals and bulging deltoids. The dark swirl of his chest hair was visible through the thin cloth. A necklace of braided silver with an iridescent medallion hung from his muscular neck.

Her gaze moved to his face. She searched for a flaw. There were none. Cheesy Pete, the guy was a looker: eyes like beaten gold, chiseled jaw, and a stern, unsmiling mouth.

Contacts. The thought drifted through Sassy's befuddled brain. *He must wear contacts. No one has eyes that color.*

"Next time you wish to be placed upon the road, say so," he said with more than a hint of disapproval. "Clarity is the heart of useful discourse. Unless you enjoy being difficult?"

"*Me?* Any sensible person—any *gentleman*—would know what I meant."

"I am not a gentleman—"

"No, you're not."

"—I am Dalvahni."

"What's that, some kind of religion?"

"No. We hunt demons."

Books by Bestselling Author
Fern Michaels

___The Jury	0-8217-7878-1	$6.99US/$9.99CAN
___Sweet Revenge	0-8217-7879-X	$6.99US/$9.99CAN
___Lethal Justice	0-8217-7880-3	$6.99US/$9.99CAN
___Free Fall	0-8217-7881-1	$6.99US/$9.99CAN
___Fool Me Once	0-8217-8071-9	$7.99US/$10.99CAN
___Vegas Rich	0-8217-8112-X	$7.99US/$10.99CAN
___Hide and Seek	1-4201-0184-6	$6.99US/$9.99CAN
___Hokus Pokus	1-4201-0185-4	$6.99US/$9.99CAN
___Fast Track	1-4201-0186-2	$6.99US/$9.99CAN
___Collateral Damage	1-4201-0187-0	$6.99US/$9.99CAN
___Final Justice	1-4201-0188-9	$6.99US/$9.99CAN
___Up Close and Personal	0-8217-7956-7	$7.99US/$9.99CAN
___Under the Radar	1-4201-0683-X	$6.99US/$9.99CAN
___Razor Sharp	1-4201-0684-8	$7.99US/$10.99CAN
___Yesterday	1-4201-1494-8	$5.99US/$6.99CAN
___Vanishing Act	1-4201-0685-6	$7.99US/$10.99CAN
___Sara's Song	1-4201-1493-X	$5.99US/$6.99CAN
___Deadly Deals	1-4201-0686-4	$7.99US/$10.99CAN
___Game Over	1-4201-0687-2	$7.99US/$10.99CAN
___Sins of Omission	1-4201-1153-1	$7.99US/$10.99CAN
___Sins of the Flesh	1-4201-1154-X	$7.99US/$10.99CAN
___Cross Roads	1-4201-1192-2	$7.99US/$10.99CAN

Available Wherever Books Are Sold!
Check out our website at **www.kensingtonbooks.com**

More by Bestselling Author
Hannah Howell

Available Wherever Books Are Sold!

Check out our website at
http://www.kensingtonbooks.com